GHOST WATCH

DAVID ROLLINS

CORVUS

First published in Australia in 2010 by Pan Macmillan.

This paperback edition first published in Great Britain in 2011
by Corvus, an imprint of Atlantic Books Ltd.

9 8 7 6 5 4

A CIP catalogue record for this book is available from
the British Library.

ISBN: 978-1-84887-508-1

Printed in Great Britain by Clays Ltd, St Ives plc

Corvus
An imprint of Atlantic Books Ltd
Ormond House
26-27 Boswell Street
London WC1N 3JZ

www.corvus-books.co.uk

For Sam, Jack, Bart and Ruby

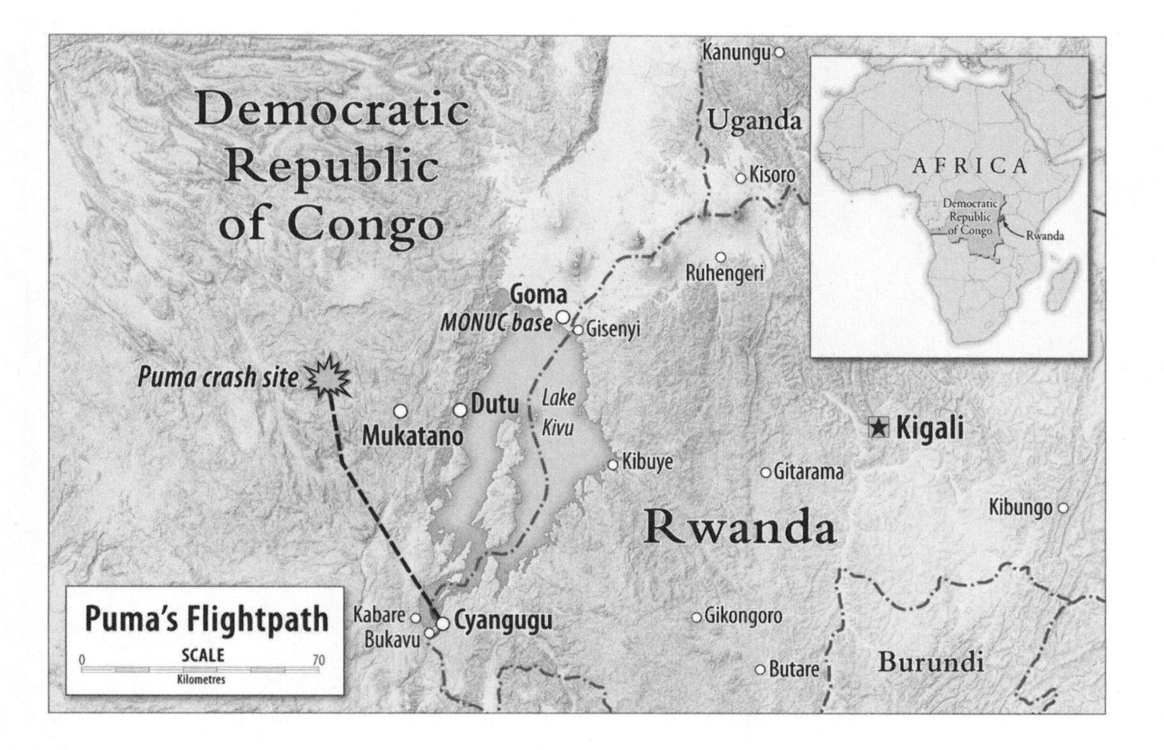
Democratic Republic of Congo
Uganda
Kanungu
Kisoro
Ruhengeri
Goma
MONUC base
Gisenyi
Puma crash site
Mukatano
Dutu
Lake Kivu
Kibuye
Gitarama
Kigali
Kibungo
Rwanda
Kabare
Bukavu
Cyangugu
Gikongoro
Butare
Burundi
AFRICA
Democratic Republic of Congo
Rwanda
Puma's Flightpath
SCALE
0
70
Kilometres

The conquest of the earth, which mostly means the taking it away from those who have a different complexion or slightly flatter noses than ourselves, is not a pretty thing . . .

– Joseph Conrad, *Heart of Darkness*

What's mine is mine. What's yours is mine.

– Unknown

Prelude

Warm sheets of rain fell from clouds piled like towers of shaving foam above the steaming rainforest. Orange mud showed where vehicles and foot traffic had flayed the skin of vegetation from the ground. There was so much mud, it was as if the base had been rubbed raw. The tread in my boots was clogged with it, making my feet feel heavier than a drunk's. The stuff was under my fingernails, grinding between my teeth, in my hair and my groin. The sweat and grease of eight days in the Congo rainforest stung my eyes, and a miasma of flies and mosquitoes trailed behind me, along with the rest of my beaten little troop, as we trudged in the stinking humidity through rust-colored puddles of rainwater.

I was looking for someone among the organized chaos and, when I found him, I was going to spoil the asshole's day.

We looked like the walking dead – a bunch of filthy, haggard, hollow-eyed cadavers lacerated from head to foot by nature's razor wire: the elephant grass that grew everywhere here. Groups of so-called US allies hereabouts, the armed militia known as the National Congress for the Defense of the People, stopped what they were doing and stared at us. The government troops from the Democratic Republic of the Congo, just across the Rwandan border, called these soldiers 'the rebels'. My fellow American advisors, here to train the rebels in the art of waging war against the insurgent Hutu militants hunkered down in the DRC, also stared as we cut a swath of silence through the late-afternoon activities at Camp Come Together – most of which consisted of lounging around, smoking and drinking.

And then I saw him. He was up ahead – supervising while others did the grunt work, loading pallets and crates onto a large flatbed truck. Nothing unusual in other people doing his dirty work. The 'he' I'm referring to was a shithead by the name of Beau Lockhart, from Kornflak & Greene, the guy who had built this base and ran it for the US Department of Defense. He was involved in shit up to his eyeballs. And the motive? Greed – same as always.

By now I was running on autopilot. I hadn't eaten much for several days and been forced to drink river water that was soupy with amoeba. Since then, my bowels had had a mind of their own, evacuating themselves whenever. I walked toward Lockhart, my own shit leaking down my legs.

'Hey, Major!' Sergeant Major Cy Cassidy called out behind me.

'Don't do anything dumb,' said Staff Sergeant Lex Rutherford.

Now, wouldn't that be out of character?

'Cooper! Wait up,' shouted Captain Duke Ryder, further back.

Lockhart was sharing a joke with a group of US Army personnel, who were, no doubt, good men and women for the most part. But I wondered what they were loading. Did they have any idea what was in those pallets? Lockhart didn't see me coming. I pulled the Sig Sauer from my holster. Two rounds left in the mag. A couple of the men, and one woman, doing the grunt work looked up and saw me coming. Saw the intent. Froze.

My weapon was raised, two-handed grip, no mistaking the target. Lockhart had his back to me, oblivious.

'City pussy? It don't rate by comparison,' I heard him say with a *tsk*, like some wine connoisseur unhappy with a vintage. 'You wanna try pussy from the bush, man. Ai, these fuckin' tribal girls rut, know what I'm sayin'? I can't answer for the quality of the local dick, mind. One of you bitches might like to take it from here . . . ha ha . . .'

'You're under arrest,' I said.

He glanced over his shoulder and went instinctively for his pistol. Before his hand got there I smashed the weapon backhand across the side of his skull. Blood burst from a split in the skin on his cheek and spurted from his ear hole as he fell to his knees in the mud.

I had nothing to say to this sack of shit other than the comments posted by my side-arm. The temptation to kick him in the ribs was hard to resist.

Lockhart raised himself on one hand, his head swaying, long strands of spit, sweat and blood draped from his lower lip. Recognition flickered across his face.

'Damn, Cooper. You still alive, motherfucker?' he said.

'Cooper!' Cassidy shouted once more. 'C'mon!'

One of the crates being loaded was half on, half off the truck's tailgate. I leaned on it so that it fell to the ground and I brought the heel of my boot down hard on the green-painted wood packing, splintering it. Shit . . . milk powder. Twenty-four cans of the stuff, not what I was hoping to find.

Lockhart laughed so I struck him again, laying the Sig's barrel across his jaw line. That wiped away the grin. He coughed and spat a clot of blood into the mud between his hands. Splintered teeth dotted the crimson mucus.

'Cooper! Stop! *Now!*'

Cassidy again. I ignored him, pulled back the Sig's slide, chambering a round, one behind it on standby. I fell to my knees behind Lockhart, grabbed hold of his perfumed hair and pulled back his head. He was semiconscious, no fight left in him. He smelled clean, of hair product and a cologne that was ironically called 'Guilty', but there was a stink to this guy that nothing could mask. I placed the business end of the blue-black barrel under his jaw, beneath the joint, and moved my head to the other side, away from the blast of torn flesh, shattered bone, and remaining teeth that would follow the exiting slug.

He again went for the Glock strapped to his thigh. I rapped it sharply with the butt of the Sig to change his mind about pulling it. My purpose hardened. Do it for the dead. For the baby thrown into the bushes; for the women who lost their arms; for all the kids made to grow up mean; for Travis and Shaquand; for Marcus, Francis and Fournier. Do it for what his associates did to Ayesha and for all the men and women mutilated and slaughtered by the people *we* trained. For the weapons, supplied by this fucker working both sides of the river, that made the mess across the border so much more possible. Do it for Anna.

It would be so easy. An excuse to take revenge on all the bad that just seemed to pile up when no one was looking. Kill Lockhart and I win. That's the way I looked at it. Cassidy was wrong about this not being the way to do it. Killing Lockhart was *right*. It would settle so many scores, balance those scales a little. I slipped my finger inside the trigger guard. Three and a half pounds of pressure from my index figure would do it, send one-hundred-and-twenty-four grains of lead up through his brain at twelve hundred feet per second. The slug would be in his head less than a thousandth of a second, enough time to do humankind a big favor.

Muddy water oozed into my pants, mixing with my own funk. My breathing slowed.

'Cooper. C'mon, man. We've come a long way. All of us,' I heard Twenny Fo, my principal, say. 'This is not the way it supposed t' end, you feel me?'

'There *is* no other way,' I told him.

'Hey, *you!*' yelled an unfamiliar voice some distance away, but closing in fast. 'Drop your weapon!'

A swarm of US Army personnel and Rwandan military police were running toward me, drawing pistols, raising M16s.

Cassidy, Rutherford, West and Ryder turned their weapons on the MPs and a horrible feeling of déjà vu came over me. Everyone was shouting at each other to lower their weapons, but I couldn't hear them. I was listening to Anna.

'Vin, no. You'll die here,' she said. 'He's not worth your life.'

But when I looked up, the voice wasn't Anna's. It was Leila's, my other principal.

The security team fanned out on our flank.

A standoff, just like the one at the Oak Ridge Reservation facility in Tennessee that left Anna on the carpet with a hole the size of my fist blown out of her left breast, her heart rolling in the cavity as it struggled to pump.

One wrong move here and I wasn't the only one who would die.

'Put the gun down, Vin,' said Leila. 'Let the law have him.' Her voice wrapped around me like Congo mist.

Lockhart was a sweaty dead weight in my arms, the odor of his cologne clawing at the back of my throat. Maybe Leila was onto something. I threw him to the ground. Seconds later, I sensed Cassidy and Rutherford beside me, felt their hands under my arms, lifting me to my feet.

'You're under arrest,' advised a sergeant MP, a stocky guy with a nose that looked like it had been punched off his face a couple of times. He ripped my arms behind my back and lassoed my wrists together with a pair of flexcuffs. Then he kicked my feet apart and patted down my rags.

'What's the charge?' Ryder demanded to know.

'Assault and battery, Sherlock. Whaddaya think?' the sergeant replied. His buddy, a clone but for the fact he had blond hair, kneed me in the guts. That put me down in the mud.

'Hey!' said Ryder.

Lockhart rolled his head to the side and looked up at me. Grinning with bloody gums, he mumbled, 'Yo' fuckin' dead meat now, man.'

Plea

'All rise,' commanded an Air Force sergeant.

The military judge, Colonel Harry Fink, was squat like a bath plug. He entered the largely empty courtroom from a side door, stepped up to the raised bench and took his seat in front of the seal of the Department of the Air Force displayed on the wall.

My defense team and I resumed ours behind a desk opposite him, as did the trial lawyers.

Colonel Fink got proceedings underway, reading the standard *pro forma* information that ensured there'd be no grounds for appeal down the track. Unlike the many times I'd heard it in the past, where it had brought on a yawning fit, this time the judge's standard intro gave me an unnerving sense of inevitability, like I was caught on a conveyor belt heading for somewhere unpleasant.

When he was done, Fink raised an eyebrow at the trial lawyers and said, 'Proceed . . .'

Major Vaughan Latham buttoned his blouse as he stood. Mid-thirties, lean and sinewy, Latham was the outdoors type. And if he wasn't throwing one into the assistant counsel, a young captain, sitting beside him I'd be questioning his preferences because she was pert, athletic, wore tight pencil skirts and flashed a seductive smile that was as good as a bribe.

Latham took up his part in the script and informed the court that the charges against me were Article 128 Assault with a Deadly Weapon Causing Grievous Bodily Harm, and Article 133 Conduct Unbecoming an Officer and Gentleman.

'And what plea are we entering today?' Colonel Fink asked Major Les Cheung, the Area Defense Council lawyer appointed to my defense. All I knew about Cheung was that he looked Chinese. Like the trial lawyer, Cheung had an assistant. His name was Nelson Macri. And all I knew about him was that he wouldn't look nearly as good as Latham's assistant did in a pencil skirt.

Cheung stood. 'Not guilty, sir,' he said.

'Enter a plea of not guilty for the accused,' Fink informed the court reporter.

'If it please the court,' said Latham, moving through the formalities of pre-trial, 'Major Cooper doesn't own his home. He's divorced, has no children, and no living relatives. The accused has no binding ties, but he does have a valid passport. And –'

'You think he's a flight risk on a 128, Counselor?' Fink asked, cocking an eyebrow at Latham before turning back to Cheung. 'No doubt you disagree with this, Counselor?'

'Vehemently, sir. Pre-trial confinement in the stockade is not necessary here. Major Cooper has been restricted to base by his commander since returning from Africa. He could have absconded at any time should he have chosen to do so. Cooper wishes to clear his name and resume his duties with the Office of Special Investigations, and recognizes that it is not in his best interest to flee. You have before you a recommendation to this effect from his commanding officer.'

Fink read over the letter from my commander, holding it up and inspecting it through a lens of his glasses, like it was a magnifying glass, then sized me up while I kept my eyes fixed forward and did my best impersonation of military bearing.

'Major,' Fink said to me after a moment's consideration, 'we'll go with your commanding officer's recommendation. Consider yourself confined to the base for the duration. Naturally, your suspension from duty will continue pending a verdict.' He shifted position and let his eyes swivel between Cheung and Latham. 'Any further business, gentlemen?'

'No, your Honor,' said Cheung.

'No, your Honor,' Latham echoed.

'Very well. We'll reconvene two weeks from today, at 0900,' Fink said without looking up from his desk. 'This hearing is adjourned.'

The judge got up, slipped behind his door and was gone within a couple of seconds

'What now?' I asked Cheung.

'Go home. We'll see you around seven.'

'Who's bringing the cards?'

'We'll be working, Cooper, to keep you out of Leavenworth.'

'There were twenty witnesses to the 128.'

'Which means we're gonna have to work *extra* hard.'

I CLIMBED INTO MY old Pontiac parked out in the lot and headed to my temporary residence on the base. It had been provided by Billeting, a ranch-style duplex usually reserved for VIPs with kids. Base accommodations were tight at Andrews AFB, nothing small and uncomfortable currently being available, so at least the needle on this one had swung in my favor. The place had four bedrooms, a yard, and a common porch. The previous occupant had hung two Stars and Stripes, one on either side of the front door, for stereo patriotism.

I drove on autopilot, until my cell began ringing and vibrating.

'Arlen,' I said, checking the screen.

'You were supposed to call me after the arraignment,' said Lieutenant Colonel Arlen Wayne, the only person at Andrews AFB Office of Special Investigations – my unit – who gave a damn about my current circumstances.

'Yeah, well, I got a few things on my mind.'

'Vin, snap out of it, buddy. This is *me*. How'd it go? You still have your cell, which means they didn't lock you up. You headed home?'

'No, Cancun.'

'Seriously, can I do anything for you?'

'You could have me moved to Venezuela,' I said. 'We don't have an extradition treaty with them.'

Arlen reset the conversation with a pause.

'Vin . . . I checked on Cheung and Macri. They're good. You're lucky to get 'em.'

'They remind me of a joke I once heard, the one about the Chinaman, the Italian, and the American. Know it?'

'I've heard 'em all, especially all of yours. Look, this is not funny, Vin. You get a guilty verdict on the 128, and you're in a concrete box with razor-wire trim for a very long time.'

'I know; I read the same books, remember?'

The books in question were the *Uniform Code of Military Justice* and the *Manual for Courts-Martial, United States*. One outlined the laws those of us in the armed forces must follow; the other documented the punishments meted out for not doing so. Our system wasn't draconian but it often didn't take into account mitigating circumstances, unless specifically outlined in the Code. If the court-martial found you did the crime, then you did the time stipulated in the manual. In the instance of Article 128, assault – and particularly, in my case, assault with a deadly weapon occasioning grievous bodily harm – the manual said a guilty verdict required confinement in a federal facility, showering without soap while keeping your back to the wall, for a period of eight years, along with a dishonorable discharge and the forfeiture of all pay and allowances. Like Arlen said, this wasn't funny.

'Anything else you need?' he asked.

'Another opportunity to kill Lockhart would be good.'

'C'mon, trust the system, Vin.'

'The system's only as good as the people working it,' I said vaguely, distracted, and the dead air informed Arlen that I wasn't talking about what was really on my mind.

'Let it go, Vin,' he said. 'You're not responsible for Anna's death. We've talked about this. The inquiry exonerated you.'

Yes, it did, but it also found that perhaps the situation at Oak Ridge, where Anna and I had confronted the suspects in the case that ended with her death, might have had a different outcome if I hadn't made an aggressive, badly timed move to end the Mexican standoff that confronted us. I could conjure up the scene at will, as if I were hovering above it, because that's how I dreamed it like it was on a loop. Helping me out with the details was the forensics team that had gone in afterwards and placed line-of-fire rods through the bullet holes in the walls, floor, and ceiling, so that the trajectories of each round could be visualized and the gunfight recreated.

This is how it went down: Anna was being held from behind by a man who also had a gun to her back. A second weapon was leveled at her by another man, sitting in an armchair in front of her, who had relieved me of my Colt .45. I was down on the carpet, an evil dyke bitch pointing a Glock at my head. The guy in the armchair took his eyes off me for a split second just as a fifth person, a bystander, blundered through the door, which, by a stroke of good fortune, took out the evil dyke bitch and her Glock. That's when I went for the fucker in the armchair. But it was a bad move. In all, nine shots were fired in that room, most of them at Anna, or in her general direction. The last of these was the one I fired at the creep holding Anna and then the one he fired at me. Anna was between us. The bullet that took her life came from behind, but the weapon that fired it was never determined beyond any doubt, because she was wrestling with her assailant at the time – spinning, twisting, and grappling with him. I fired a Colt .45. The creep shot a nine-millimeter Glock. Ordinarily, that would have settled the question; however, the ammo we both used was ball. Both types left neat entry and raggedy exit holes, and the actual slug that killed her exited her body and was not recovered from the scene, all of which meant that she could have been shot with either a nine or a .45. Tissue damage didn't resolve the issue either way, but that's the point. It could have been the shot *I* fired. *I* could have been her killer.

Anna died in my arms. She took her last breath lying in a pool of her own blood, the black sucking hole in her chest leaving a bottomless pit in mine.

'Vin . . . you still there? Hello?'

'I'm still here.'

'Hey . . . I miss her, too,' said Arlen.

Arlen and Anna had been pals from the start, when I introduced them after the conclusion of a case she and I had worked in Germany. Both of us were in the hospital at the time. And ever since, whenever things got a little rocky between us, Arlen had been our go-between. I had first met her twenty-four hours after my divorce had gone through. The last thing I wanted was another relationship, but Anna walked into my life and the fireworks were there from the start. Occasionally, they burned us – so much so that along the way we'd had time apart to cool off. Anna even became engaged to a piece-of-shit JAG attorney with questionable morals, to get, as she put it, a little control back into her life. She came to her senses about the engagement just days before walking into the Oak Ridge office and collecting a round from a nine-millimeter. Or a .45. Now she was gone forever. And the guy responsible – me – was still here. That, not my lack of trust in the system or the shower block at Leavenworth, was my problem.

'Are you listening?' Arlen asked.

'What?'

'Stay with me, Vin. I said there's an investigation underway into Lockhart.'

'Did you initiate it?'

'Me? Absolutely not.'

'Then who did?'

'Your court-martial has attracted a lot of press, especially after the Afghanistan thing. You've got plenty of public support. I think maybe the wife of some general up the food chain smelled injustice and leaned on her old man.'

I didn't believe a word of that. An inquiry into Lockhart was a ball only Arlen would have kicked into play. He would have to play it carefully. News of an investigation into the DoD contractor might make it look to Judge Fink that Cheung and Macri were playing dirty pool, hoping to pressure Lockhart into withdrawing his testimony. As the star witness for the prosecution, his withdrawal would destroy the government's case.

'Lockhart has powerful friends,' I said. 'Asswipes like him can't operate without them. Have a look at a guy by the name of Piers Pietersen, from a company called Swedish American Gold. And while you're at it, check out a black guy by the name of Charles White. He's thick with Pietersen.'

'What's their connection to Lockhart?' he asked.

'I'm betting they do his dirty laundry.'

'I'll see what turns up.'

'You should also look into the Congolese and the Rwandans at Cyangugu.'

'Forget about them, Vin. They're beyond our reach.'

I wasn't happy about that, but I understood. Africa swallowed whole populations. It'd be easy for a few connected individuals to disappear. 'What about that M16 with its numbers filed off?' I asked.

'We've got no serial or batch numbers. We know it was made by FN Herstal, but without the numbers the weapon's untraceable.'

Disappointing. I'd carried the weapon all the way through the Congo rainforest believing it would shoot someone important in the foot – hopefully, Lockhart.

'What about the French *Armée de l'Air* pilot André LeDuc?'

'Interpol has a warrant out for him.'

'Can you get access to his records?'

'Paris will cooperate. What are we after?'

'His head on a plate.'

'See what I can do. While we're on the subject of the French, I believe they're going to launch an inquiry into Fournier's death. You'll be called as a witness.'

'Bring it on.'

'Hey, I have to go, Vin. I'll try to drop by soon. Hang in there, buddy.'

'By the neck,' I replied.

I heard the dial tone, put the cell in my jacket pocket and turned into the double driveway that lined up with the double garage attached to the double-fronted house with its two flags waving in the breeze over the landing. Just some of the perks of criminality.

I took a long bath in the master bathroom and watched a little high-def spring baseball on the flat screen TV with the 5.3 surround sound system turned up. I was eyeing the liquor cabinet when the doorbell rang. Cheung and Macri were early.

'You're early,' I said, as I opened the door to a man I didn't recognize.

'Mr Cooper,' he said, holding forth a hand. 'My name is William Rentworthy. I'm a reporter from the *New York Times*. If you've got a few minutes, I'd like to talk to you about the—'

I didn't recognize him, but I knew who he was.

'Speak to my lawyers,' I said and shut the door in his face, wondering who'd let him loose on the base.

Cheung and Macri arrived twenty minutes later.

'We brought some food,' said Macri, as he came through the open door behind Cheung. 'Hope you like vegetarian.'

'I like anything that *eats* grass,' I said. 'Especially if it's medium rare.'

In fact, I don't like vegetarian food at all, though I have dined a few times at Summer Love, a little joint on the ground floor of my apartment block. The only thing I like the look of there, though, is Summer herself, who's hot in a hippy-chick way, with legs so long they could give you a nose bleed just thinking about them.

'You guys want a drink?' I asked as I headed for the kitchen. 'I can offer you single malt or Jacks.'

'Thanks, but I need something solid,' said Cheung.

'I'll put rocks in it,' I suggested.

Cheung smiled and shook his head. 'No thanks. Mind if I set the table?'

'Go right ahead. How about you, Counselor?' I asked Macri, passing Cheung some forks.

'Not for me, either,' he said, as he divested his briefcase of several pounds of notes and forms and dumped them on the dining-room table.

I fixed a Glen Keith with ice and a little soda and left the kitchen with the bottle so that I'd have an ally with me.

Cheung and Macri sat themselves down at the table, the folders they had brought with them now placed on the floor. Food waited for me on a disposable plate.

'What's this?' I asked.

'Asparagus and eggplant lasagne,' said Macri, his mouth already full. 'It's pretty good.'

I gave it a go and was pleasantly surprised, though half a pound of ground beef would've improved it.

'I had a visit from the *New York Times*,' I told them. 'A guy called Rentworthy.'

'What did he want?' Cheung asked.

'Dirt. What else?'

'Twenny Fo and Leila will be called as witnesses, so we can bet on this court-martial getting plenty of media attention, which might hurt or help your case. We'll see how it goes . . . Might be worth lodging a petition for the court to be closed.'

'Won't happen,' said Macri. 'Fink's got a bad case of ASD – attention-seeking disorder. Next time the *Times* approaches you, Vin, hear him out before slamming the door in his face. If he's got something important pertaining to the case, and he's about to report it, he'll come to you first. You can always refuse to comment. But we'd rather have some warning.'

'Who said anything about slamming doors in people's faces?'

'He's a reporter out for a little fame and glory at your expense. What else you gonna do?'

'Let's get started with a little background, shall we?' said Cheung, changing the subject. 'You've got an interesting record, Cooper. I see you've been up on assault charges before.'

I gave no response.

Cheung sat back. 'Cooper, I know this is going to be hard for you, but we're on your side. Here's the deal. We ask you questions and you answer them without holding back. And if you think we're not asking the right ones, then you volunteer the information you think we should be getting. This can't work any other way, all right?'

I shrugged. I didn't have a lot of choice.

'There are twenty witnesses lined up against you, Vin,' Cheung informed me yet again. 'Frankly, it's going to take every trick in the book and a lot of luck to pull this one out of the shitter.'

Macri picked a folder up off the floor. He flicked through it on his lap, eventually pulling out a sheet of paper.

'So you want to tell us about the colonel you, ah, beat up?'

'The government dropped the case. It's not admissible,' I said.

'We know,' Cheung responded. 'But would you mind filling in the background anyway?'

I sighed. There was a time when I would have found this difficult, but now hashing over the facts of my divorce affected me about as much as scratching a rash.

'My ex-wife and I were in marriage counseling. The counselor was an O-6 reservist. Turned out that he was regularly counseling my ex privately. I came home and found them in the shower. He was giving her some therapy around her epiglottis at the time.'

Macri glanced at Cheung.

'As I see it,' I said, 'the colonel got the life sentence.'

They seemed puzzled, so I put it together for them. 'He married her.'

'What about the two drunk and disorderly charges – one substantiated?' asked Macri.

'I went through a bad patch.'

Macri gazed at me. 'You're a difficult case, Cooper. With a record like this, you'll never make lieutenant colonel. Why're you still in the air force?'

I'd thought about that question plenty of times, especially since Anna's death. She'd planned to leave the service, and wanted me to go with her. I remember thinking at the time that I just might. Would I have gone through with it? Now that she was dead, I'd never know.

'You want to hear me say that I probably couldn't cut it anywhere else?' I said.

'That'd be honest, wouldn't it?' Macri replied.

'And here I was thinking this wouldn't be a pleasant evening.'

Cheung gestured at Macri to pass him the folder. 'I note that a significant amount of your record is classified, much more of it than I would have expected,' he said. 'There are big holes.' He put his fork down and flipped through a few pages. 'You studied law at NYU?'

'Know thine enemy,' I said. There was a flicker of a smile from Macri.

'You joined up in time for Kosovo and trained as a combat air controller. You also deployed to Afghanistan as a special tactics officer, and then transferred to the Office of Special Investigations, where you cleared a couple of significant cases.'

'Beginner's luck,' I said.

'Then come those holes.' Cheung flipped a few more pages. 'You've earned quite a few commendations. In fact, there *is* plenty of good here . . . perhaps enough to outweigh the bad.' Macri made a note on a legal pad. 'You've got your jump wings, you're current on High Altitude Low Opening insertion,' Cheung continued. 'I see you've done a lot of work with Special Operations Command. You deploy to Iraq?'

'Not officially,' I said.

'There's the Air Force Cross submission pending . . . Why would you volunteer for personal security ops in Afghanistan? You have some kind of death wish?'

'I lost my partner. We were close. I needed a distraction.'

'Can you tell us the circumstances?'

'Her name was Anna Masters. She died of a gunshot wound to the chest. I was with her at the time.'

They waited for more, but I was reluctant to give it. I freshened my drink.

'Okay, so your third and most recent deployment to the 'Stan. The mission wasn't classified. Why don't you take us through that?'

Cheung sat back and waited for me to begin. I could see what the weeks ahead would be like – every detail that wasn't classified would be picked over by Charlie Chan and Tony Soprano here, then strategized into a fairytale of life achievement that even I wouldn't recognize as my own.

'If I have to,' I said.

'You do,' said Macri.

Kabul

Afghan Interior Minister Abdul al-Eqbal shared the delusion of all politicians who had well and truly reached their use-by date: that his position and power were preordained and that his people would love him no matter what shit he pulled, who he screwed over, or how he behaved.

Al-Eqbal was fat in a country of skin and bone. He was unpopular because he took bribes. And while this was a society where *everyone* took bribes, Abdul al-Eqbal was in a class of his own – he took *bak-sheesh* from one side and put his hand out to the other, then simply made himself scarce and let the parties slug it out or had the next layer of bureaucracy turn up with its hand out for a cut. Intelligence hadn't confirmed it, but the word on the street was that al-Eqbal had stiffed the wrong crowd once too often and was now a high-priority target for the Taliban.

After the mess in Oak Ridge, I wanted the ugliest, most dangerous assignment the Air Force had to offer. I felt I deserved it. That turned out to be personal security operations in Afghanistan. The day I arrived in-country, I learned that volunteers were being sought to make up al-Eqbal's detail. This was the highest risk assignment in the highest risk command. It sounded like the reason I was here, so I took the step forward. And that's how I found myself in charge of a joint PSO unit racing in a three-vehicle convoy down a minor through-road on the outskirts of Kabul. At the time, we were on al-Eqbal's turf. His people lived here; the ones who'd voted for him, supposedly. I could hear the guy wheezing and humming a local ditty as he leaned forward in his seat and watched the dung-colored homes flash by.

'How's it going back there? Anyone cold?' asked Staff Sergeant Chip Meyers, occupying the front passenger seat and throwing the question over his shoulder.

Meyers was a fellow special agent in the Air Force Office of Special Investigations, the OSI. He'd been a male model before joining up, his baby blues and six-pack gut selling underwear for Calvin Klein. I was told that he liked to date married women because dodging their husbands added to the excitement. Maybe one day he'd make a good relationship counselor. Apparently, death threats had chased him into the recruitment office.

It was thirty-nine degrees Fahrenheit outside. Cool by anyone's standards.

'Sir?' He turned around fully and pitched the question to the dignitary once more. 'Cold?'

Al-Eqbal ignored him completely.

Meyers shrugged, turned to face the front, and resumed the eternal scan for roadside IEDs – improvised explosive devices. We were the only two Air Force guys in the bunch. The driver seated beside him was Army, a buck sergeant by the name of Rory Bellows, a skinny guy whose head darted around so much looking for threats that I thought he might have a nervous tic.

The team assembled for this unit was drawn from the OSI and the US Army. Up ahead in the lead vehicle were a couple of Army NCOs named Detmond and Stefanovic. They were both premature. Detmond was prematurely gray, Stefanovic prematurely bald. Stef was also short. He had to sit on a Humvee maintenance manual to see over the dash. Their driver, an Army specialist, was a stand-in I hadn't worked with. The nametag on his battle uniform said 'Mattock'.

Bringing up the rear were Sergeant First Class Reese Fallon, a six-foot-seven black guy who'd played power forward for Notre Dame, and driver Specialist Alicia Rogerson, a small-town librarian in her civilian days. I asked what a nice librarian like her was doing in a shithole like this and she told me that she liked to read thrillers and had decided to join up and write a few chapters of her own. She came across as perky, wide-eyed, and enthusiastic, all of which told me that her boots had been on the ground here maybe a week, tops.

'Stop! Stop the car!' al-Eqbal suddenly shouted. 'I order you to stop.'

I jumped. 'What's the problem, sir?'

'Do as I say and stop the car! I command it!'

We were here to keep the guy alive, and stopping in a place that hadn't been surveyed because maybe the dignitary had to take a shit was not in the rulebook.

Al-Eqbal flicked the lock and opened the door while the vehicle was still moving. 'Now!' he demanded.

Jesus . . . I checked the window. The area consisted of run-down housing and some equally run-down businesses. A few cars were on the road. No one seemed to be paying us any mind.

I asked him again. 'Why do you want to pull over, sir?'

'I have cousin here. Best snuff in all of Kabul. I come here all the time. These are my people. No danger. Stop here, now!'

Clearly, he wasn't going to take no for an answer. I called up the lead vehicle on the radio and asked Stefanovic to pull over. The Land-cruiser's brake lights came on, the tires scratched for traction in the grit and al-Eqbal was out the door. I leapt after him and headed him off, placing the flat of my Nomex-gloved hand on his chest. He looked at it as if it were vermin.

'Sir,' I told him. 'I have a job to do. Please wait.'

He rolled huge brown eyeballs at Allah, while my mind ran through the six basic rules of PSO duty:

1. Under no circumstances leave your principals unaccompanied.
2. The majority of organized attacks are successful.
3. The bodyguards rarely fire their weapons effectively, if at all.

4. The bodyguards almost never affect the outcome of the attack.
5. The bodyguards usually die.
6. The scrotums of bodyguards tighten for a reason – don't ignore it.

Okay, so number six wasn't in the *official* manual, but it was underlined in red in the unofficial one. And mine was now tighter than the skin on a grape.

The detail exited the vehicles, leaving the drivers, Mattock, Bellows and Rogerson, behind. Standard operating procedure was to keep the motors running in case we had to leave in a hurry. Quickly, the rest of us formed the textbook five-man diamond pattern around al-Eqbal: Meyers in front, Stefanovic behind, Detmond and Fallon on each side, and me on the principal's shoulder. Al-Eqbal pointed to where he wanted to go, which was thirty or so meters back down the street in the direction from which we'd just come.

Folks got out of our way, crossed the road, avoided eye contact. Nothing about this behavior was particularly odd. They were used to seeing armed US military personnel on the streets, but there'd been enough situations resulting in civilian deaths to make them nervous about being anywhere near us.

'Where are we going, sir?' I asked the principal.

Al-Eqbal indicated the Kabul version of a general store – a gray two-story structure with several stalls outside displaying newspapers and magazines, various hardware items (from lamps to auto-mechanics' tools), as well as bottled drinks and tinned foods. Wood and Styrofoam boxes on the dirt beneath the stands contained assorted limp vegetables. Two young males loitered out front, just hanging around, smoking. One called out to someone inside the shop when they saw us coming, then both ran off and vanished down an alley a few doors down.

A middle-aged man emerged from the building. The concern on his face brightened into a grin when he saw al-Eqbal. I assumed he was his cousin because no one but family would be happy to see this guy. The two men embraced and kissed and talked rapid-fire Dari, too fast for me to follow, though I managed to catch fragments of the usual string of outrageous compliments. Our dignitary turned to go inside, but I signaled Meyers to perform a site survey and stepped in front of al-Eqbal, blocking his path again.

'Sir, please allow us to search the building first.'

He swore in Dari – something about me being the spawn of a goatherd's tepid urine – but he nevertheless stopped and waited.

I banked the insult to use on someone else one day, while his cousin smiled at me and shrugged, as if to say, 'My cousin's a politician – whadayagonnado?'

We stood on the dirt sidewalk, buffeted by grit, and waited. An icy wind blew the superfine Afghan dust that smelled of human shit and pack animals into our mouths and nostrils.

Meyers came back out as the troublesome fingers in my left hand, which had been broken and shot up on previous missions, stiffened into a cramp from the cold.

'Clear, boss,' he said.

'What's the layout?'

'One main display room full of junk, two smaller ones behind it full of more junk. A back door – locked – looks like it opens onto a dirt alley. No enclosing walls there. Internal staircase leads to a second story. Old woman peeling spuds upstairs, ugly as a big toe. Three other rooms, all bedrooms. On the rooftop is a washing line and a TV satellite dish.'

The place appeared to be free from threat. Any location that's been surveyed and cleared of unauthorized persons is technically secure, says the PSO handbook. But life experience was making me cautious. I moved to the side, allowing al-Eqbal to pass, and our diamond pattern was set to move into the confined space. The overall mission for this and almost every other PSO detail was running through my head: prevent assassination, injury, kidnapping, assignation, and, almost above all, safeguard the principal's schedule. Dual problem right there, I reminded myself. We had us an assignation and it wasn't on the damn schedule.

Al-Eqbal interrupted my thoughts. 'I will go in alone,' he commanded with a wave of his hand as if we were troublesome flies. 'There is not enough room.'

I looked at the shop and he had a point. It was no Wal-Mart. 'You can't go in there without an escort.'

We stared at each other for a few moments before he sighed wearily and said, 'One guard only. Young man, you are worrying too much, I think.'

'We can only spare five minutes here, sir,' I said.

The principal shook his head at me as if to say that I just didn't get it.

'Meyers, accompany our dignitary,' I said.

'Yes, sir,' Meyers replied.

The book inside my head played like a bad song that wouldn't go away:

1. Do not let the principal enter a doorway first.
2. In hallways, keep the principal in the center.
3. Keep the principal away from windows and alcoves and areas limiting escape and evasion.

The cousin put his arm around the principal's shoulders. They walked toward the shop entrance, chatting, laughing. Meyers took up station ahead of them, scoping left and right. A pro.

I scanned the street. A yellow taxi, with a replacement fender and door panels that gave it a patchwork appearance, drove by slowly, blowing smoke. The driver leaned across the bench seat toward us, eternally hopeful for a fare. Fifty meters down the road, several middle-aged men having a conversation crossed from one side to the other. Nearby, the wind had picked up some dust and blew it into a corkscrew that was moving in our direction. More grit flew into my eyes. I opened them in time to see a woman in a dark blue burka that was billowing like a sail – the bottom hem flapping and whipping around her ankles – walk into the middle of the road, stop, turn around, and then retrace her steps. Two young men on pushbikes swerved to avoid her. A couple of blocks further down, a man pushing a wheel-cart pulled over to sell bunches of bananas.

The drivers reversed our vehicles and parked them in front of al-Eqbal's cousin's shop – one of a group of five with common walls. A narrow alley was at either end of the block. The buildings on the other side of the wide street were mostly unpainted gray concrete, two and three storys, with flat roofs, two windows per floor, no balconies. Some were homes; the living rooms of some functioned as shops, like al-Eqbal's cousin's. Over the roofs of these houses rose the imposing mass of TV Mountain. I'd been on its summit years ago when I first came to the 'Stan. The Taliban rocketed our position there, trying to dislodge me and several other special tactics officers while we called in air strikes on their fundamentalist asses. Looking down from the summit, the gray city seemed to wrap itself around the base like a blanket of clothes-dryer lint.

I spoke into the small boom mike, part of the system that allowed our team members to communicate with each other over short distances. 'What's happening?' I asked Meyers.

'Settling in for the long haul, boss. They're brewing tea,' came his reply through my earpiece.

'Tell Mr Big he's got two minutes left.'

Stefanovic, Fallon, and Detmond were all Army. They faced out, looking idly toward the mountain, waiting. Their M16s were pointed at the ground. Detmond lit a cigarette. With the principal out of the picture, so was their focus. Our drivers had the engines running. Gangsta crap thumped from an open window.

To pass the time, I asked Stefanovic, 'So why did you volunteer for this?'

'Who volunteered?' he said. 'I cleaned out my sergeant in a game of hold 'em. It was this or latrine duty. Happens again, I'll take the crappers. You?'

'Brain fart.'

'You *asked* to do this shit?' Fallon said. He glanced at me, seeing but not believing.

Detmond grunted.

'Got a volunteer joke for you,' I said to our little formation. 'A guy walks into a bar with a pet alligator. He puts it up on the bar and says to the freaked-out patrons, "I'll make you all a deal. I'll put my dick in this here 'gator's mouth and keep it there one minute. At the end of that time, the 'gator will open its mouth. If I still have my dick, all of you have to buy me a drink."

'Of course, the crowd agrees, so he drops his pants, puts his pecker in the 'gator's mouth, and the room goes silent. At the end of one minute, he picks up a beer bottle and smacks the 'gator over the head with it. The 'gator opens its mouth and out comes the guy's wang, unharmed. The crowd goes nuts and the free drinks flow. After a while, the guy stands on the bar and says, "I'll make y'all another offer. I'll pay a hundred bucks to anyone else willing to give it a try."

'A hush falls over the crowd.

'"C'mon," says the guy. "Aren't there no damn volunteers out there?"

'A lone hand slowly rises over everyone's heads. It's a young blond woman.

'"I'll do it," she says, "but only if you don't hit me on the head with no beer bottle."'

Fallon's attention wandered off.

Detmond grunted.

'My mother's blond,' said Stefanovic flatly.

I cleared my throat and told them to keep up the good work, then moved away to check the cousin's front door.

No one was coming out. I was getting impatient. Loitering on the streets of Kabul with a Stars and Stripes patch on your shoulder was only slightly less moronic than sticking a fork in a wall socket. Besides, his five minutes were definitely up.

'Meyers . . .' I said into the mike.

'He's telling me he wants *another* five minutes,' came the reply.

'He can't have them,' I said, but I knew this guy would take them whether I agreed or not.

I turned in time to see a girl of no more than fourteen years old, dressed in black and wearing a pink scarf over her head, run into the building adjoining the cousin's. She was bent over with her arms wrapped around her belly as if she were pregnant, and left the front door open behind her.

I was about to say something about this into the mike when a deafening explosion turned the world into a giant dust ball. It punched me backward through the air and I slammed into the house ten feet behind. Dust clogged my nose and eyes and my lungs were clenched, closed tight.

Could.

Not.

Breathe.

I pawed the dirt from my face and saw a massive white, black, and gray cloud boiling into the sky. Below it, two of our Landcruisers were tipped on their sides. My men were down. Something released in my chest, and I sucked down a lungful of powdered building, which brought on a coughing fit. When I pulled out of it, I could see through watering eyes that al-Eqbal's cousin's house was gone, along with the neighbor's, heading skyward in the expanding gray and black mushroom cloud. Jesus . . . Meyers would be in that cloud somewhere. I wanted to move, stand up at least, but everything was in slo-mo. Rogerson's Landcruiser was parked outside the spot where the neighbor's house used to be. I could see her profile. Something about it was wrong. Oh, shit . . . her face . . . she didn't have one.

My body didn't want to work. I managed somehow to pull myself up on one knee, and thanked the K-pot on my head and the ceramic plate in the back of my body armor for taking most of the wall's impact. I could see that Stefanovic, Fallon, and Detmond were flat on the ground, with only sluggish movement from all three. They were closer to the blast than I had been, and harder hit. Detmond was wounded, a red stain advancing down the gray-green pixels of his Army battle uniform toward his elbow. He managed to sit up but was almost immediately hit square in the chest by an invisible force that knocked him down onto his back. Shit, we were being fired on! Fallon and Stefanovic struggled to their feet and dragged Detmond behind the second of the scuttled Landcruisers – my Landcruiser, the one Bellows was driving. Where was Bellows? I couldn't see him; Mattock either. All three drivers – dead?

The situation would head from fucked up to fucking fucked up if someone didn't do something fucking quick. Static burst into my earpiece.

'Who's this?' I asked.

Static.

I was about to tear out the earpiece when I heard a voice croak, 'Cooper . . .'

The voice was familiar, but my hearing wasn't so good. 'Meyers?' I asked.

'Legs . . . broken.'

Yeah, it was Meyers. Definitely someone who wasn't able to do something fucking quick or any other way. But, shit, he was alive.

'I'll come to you. Don't move.'

I heard him cackle. 'Move . . .?'

Bullet holes appeared in the bodywork of the Landcruisers. It occurred to me that while Fallon, Detmond and Stefanovic were getting pounded, I wasn't attracting any inbound fire, which meant that whoever had us pinned down was not aware of my position. There was no planned kill zone, where the fire was coming in from all angles, cutting off our escape. So, either the attack was impromptu or we were up against the remedial arm of the Taliban.

I was in the only blind spot for the shooters – directly below them. I looked up. Sure enough, rifle barrels poked out from both second-story windows above me, as well as one from a window on the third floor. I counted a total of five protruding barrels.

'Stefanovic,' I shouted into the mike. 'How's Detmond? Check on Mattock and Bellows.'

I heard a voice in my ear, but it was muffled, woolen.

'Get on the radio, and get us some air support!' I yelled. A response came back, but I couldn't make it out.

Stefanovic had crawled out of sight behind the second Landcruiser, presumably on the hunt for a working radio. I went through a weapons and ammo check to steady my nerves and get some perspective: one Colt M4 carbine; four mags – one hundred and twenty rounds; one Sig Sauer P228 with two mags, one round up the spout; one Ka-bar. No grenades – *shit*!

The front door beside me was closed and probably locked. My back close to the wall, I moved over to an alley on the left. At the corner of the building I momentarily put down my rifle, pulled the Sig and took it off safety. I popped my head and the Sig around the corner simultaneously. Movement. Two rounds later, a Taliban fighter with an AK-47 found himself haggling with all the other dead martyrs over whose turn it was to get with the virgins.

I holstered the Sig, picked up the M4, shouldered it, and made my way down the alley. I put my fingertips against the brickwork and felt the vibrations. The AK-47s inside the house were spraying away with such exuberance that the percussion was vibrating through the wall. My hearing cleared with a 'pop', and what I heard was Stef and Fallon returning fire, the M16 making an altogether different sound than the AK's.

I followed the Sig around the next corner and came into another alley out back, overlooked by a row of tightly packed dwellings. Men and boys were peering around corners for several blocks up and down the narrow road, eager to catch the action; a good gunfight in these parts being the equivalent of a game of football. One of the boys waved at me from an alcove. I waved back and he flipped me the bird – rooting for the home team, obviously. Maybe he had a big blow-up hand somewhere with 'Osama' printed on it.

Pushbikes were scattered behind the rear entrance. The gunmen had cycled to work. The Sig went back in its holster. The M4's thirty-round mag and short barrel made it the ideal weapon for cleaning house. I flicked the selector to three-shot burst to conserve ammo, took it off safety, and crept inside. It was dark. I stopped against the wall, tried to get my breathing under control and gave my eyes a few seconds to adapt to the available light. There was a room both to the left and right off the short hallway. I checked them and they were clear, so I moved forward into the main room on the ground floor. Also clear. Retracing my steps, I closed the back door – there was no lock – then found the stairs against the wall and crept up the single steep flight to the first floor. It ended on a small landing; the rest of the floor was divided into two rooms, gunfire banging away from my left and right. I cased both rooms quickly. Room on the left had one shooter. Room on the right had two. The floors in both were littered with spent casings and magazines.

The Taliban fighter in the left-hand room was old – mid-fifties – and dressed in black. Pops was making so much noise that he didn't realize I was behind him until the Ka-bar took out his windpipe and partially severed his spinal cord. Blood went everywhere. I gently laid him down among all his brass trash as he gurgled and shook, then I took his AK and replaced the mag with a fresh one from a satchel sitting on a broken chair. There was no food in the bag, suggesting that this gig was unplanned – good to know. Propped against the wall behind the door were an M16A2 and a bag full of mags. I picked up the rifle. It was brand new, still with that showroom shine. The serial numbers on its receiver had been ground off. Where does a Taliban fighter get one of these? I hooked the weapon over my shoulder and took the satchel with the mags.

Had I killed Pops with the M4, everyone would know that Uncle Sam was making home deliveries. To head off any concern, I fired a couple of bursts from the guy's AK out the window to reassure his buddies that the old man was still on the job. Then I dropped the weapon and walked across the landing into the room on the right. The door was wide open. Both targets, also dressed in Taliban black, were in their late teens or early twenties. They had their backs to me, firing on full auto on the crippled Landcruisers, wasting ammo, washing my buddies in lead. From the sound of it, one of the targets was firing an M16.

Then a couple of rounds tore into the ceiling above my head. Gray powder drifted down, dusting my shoulders. My guys across the street were zeroing in.

'Yo, fellas,' I called out, raising my voice above the din. 'S'up?'

The shooters glanced over their shoulders, eyes wide. The fighter with the M16 had an orange beard and large blue-green eyes, maybe a throwback to when Alexander the Great arrived here with his army to subdue the local population and get in a little R&R. I didn't have to think about what to do. Both men got three rounds in the chest. The force of it pushed Ginger out the window, ass first. He fell in silence, already dead.

The shooter on the floor above me stopped firing. He knew something was up, probably when he saw his Islamic brother take the big step backward into the street below. He started calling to his friends. When no answer came, he began firing down through the floor. I made myself small against the wall and changed mags. Plaster, wood splinters, and lead rained down, which gave me some idea of his position. I fired upwards – single shots – emptied the mag, then waited for an answer. I stood on the spot for ten seconds or so, changed mags, listening, looking up. No one was walking around up there, and the shooting had stopped. Blood clogged the bullet holes in the ceiling and began dripping down onto the floor.

I climbed up to the second floor to confirm that only one fighter occupied it, and that he was now dead. I searched him quickly for the benefit of folks back at intelligence but found nothing of interest. I picked up his AK, released the mag, emptied the chamber, and swung it against the wall a couple of times, splintering the stock. Then I went back down to the other rooms, collected the M16, and put those AKs out of action for a while also.

Moving over to the window, I gave my people a whistle. Movement up the road attracted my attention. Shit, half a dozen armed, bearded men were running toward us, black robes flapping in the breeze. Three of them ducked into one of the houses thirty meters away. I lost sight of their friends. Time to go. I searched the corpses and their satchels but came up empty-handed. Sporadic firing was beginning again. Exactly how many more Taliban were in the area? It wouldn't have been a good idea to hang around and conduct a census.

I took the steps down to the ground floor and contemplated my next decision – leave by the back door or by the front? I figured that my guys would put holes in any enemy fighters who were in full view; and maybe in me, too, if I wasn't careful. The back door was still closed the way I'd left it, but I wasn't confident about what might be waiting on the other side. So I moved to the front door and slipped the bolt. It was jammed. The wood was ancient and dried out. I took three steps back, and charged it with my shoulder just as the back door opened a few inches and three grenades rolled in. I hit the door and it splintered into matchsticks. Tangled up in rifle straps, I stumbled and planted my face in the road. And then, behind me, the building exploded in a howl of mudbrick chunks. A torrent of grenade fragments and glass shards warbled as they flew close overhead and landed with a musical tinkle between the Landcruisers and me. Gunfire came next as Taliban fighters charged through the suspect back door and reoccupied the remains of the house that their buddies had just died in.

I got to my feet, dove for the Landcruisers and scrambled behind them. I was relieved to see Mattock and Bellows hunkered down with Stefanovic, Fallon, and Detmond. They'd taken up firing positions behind the Landcruiser on its side, the one I'd occupied with al-Eqbal. Unfortunately, though, we were now being outflanked by enemy reinforcements and gunfire was coming in on us from a number of directions. It was only a matter of time before the Taliban closed all the angles and started picking us off. Now the assholes were firing on the fuel tanks, too. I smelled diesel. At least it wasn't gasoline.

'Radio?' I yelled at Stefanovic.

He shook his head. 'According to ops, nothing on the ground this sector.' He checked his watch. 'We've got Apaches inbound, ETA fifteen minutes.'

We didn't have fifteen minutes.

I took a few seconds to assess Detmond. He was lying on the ground behind the others, going into shock, and not entirely with us. His eyes were closed, but he was moving.

'Wounded in the neck and just below his armpit – he's lost a lot of blood,' Fallon informed me, shouting into my ear.

In fact, the sergeant was lying in a pool of it. We had to get him out of there. He also looked dazed. The blast had deafened him.

Stefanovic's hand and M4 were also sticky with blood. He was pale, the color having leached from his face.

'Where'd you get hit?' I yelled at him.

He turned slightly. I could see a large chunk of flesh had been chewed out of the back of his arm.

'Need a compression bandage here!' I shouted at Fallon.

We had two dead: Rogerson and al-Eqbal. Including myself, Stef, Fallon, Detmond, Mattock and Bellows, there were six of us left. Hang on, someone was missing. Oh, yeah . . .

'Meyers is alive,' I said. 'Fallon, you're with me. We're going back in there to get him.'

The look on his face said, *You're shitting me . . .!*

'Stand by. I'm gonna check Rogerson's vehicle first.'

Mattock and Bellows threw some rounds downrange at the enemy.

AK rounds buzzed around my head. I could almost see them. I was in the groove, juiced up on adrenalin. It wasn't that I believed I couldn't be killed; I just didn't give a damn if I were.

The third vehicle was badly mauled, but at least it was still on its tires. I ditched the M16, crawled back to the vehicle and, staying low, opened the door. Specialist Rogerson was belted into the front seat, her hands clasped around the steering wheel at the ten-two position. I saw that she had beautiful nails; manicured, painted red. She wore a wedding ring. I reached in and released her belt and she slumped sideways across the bench seat. I tried not to think too much about her. The red lights burning on the instrument panel told me that the ignition was on – a good sign – but the motor had stalled. I hoped there was no disabling damage. If this thing wouldn't start, we were screwed. Leaning in below the steering column, I twisted the ignition key off, and then twisted it on. Nothing. It was dead. Shit. Then I noticed the transmission was in drive. I banged it into park, pressed on the brake with my free hand, gave the key another twist and the motor hummed to life.

I backed out of the vehicle, sprinted to the others, and tapped Detmond on the shoulder.

'Three minutes!' I yelled, 'Then you go!'

I motioned at Fallon to follow me and we ran at a crouch into the smoking dustbowl behind us. Meyers was in here somewhere, lying in the rubble. We found the old woman, her arm protruding from beneath a ton of broken masonry, then encountered a pile of bloody rags that looked like al-Eqbal's – but no cousin, no girl, and no Meyers.

Fallon smelled burning American tobacco through the dust haze and followed the scent. The trail led us to Meyers, propped up against a wall beside a bicycle. The guy was pulling hard on a Marlboro, his boots turned at impossible angles on the ends of his shattered legs. The blast had happened minutes ago; he still had some time before his nerve endings started screaming. I hunkered down beside him and hunted through my medical pack for a shot of morphine to see him through.

'I took a second quick scan out the back and al-Eqbal locked me out,' he said drowsily. 'What happened?'

I pictured the girl pregnant with C4 explosives running into the building next door. 'No birth control in this place,' I said. She'd probably run into al-Eqbal's cousin's building through an adjoining door that Meyers had missed.

He nodded, finding the crack about birth control perfectly reasonable, which told me he was also in shock. I found the morphine, administered it to his upper thigh, and then checked his limbs. Both femurs had compound fractures, and the wounds were messy. He would need a good surgeon to save them. I used his blood to paint an 'M' on his forehead. Fallon took the defensive position and swept the area while I did what I could to control the bleeding. Carrying him between us with those legs in such bad shape was not an option, and one of us would need to provide covering fire if required.

I handed his weapon to Fallon. Meyers was no lightweight; this was not going to be easy. I took one of his arms and pulled his torso over my shoulder.

'Help me up,' I grunted at Fallon.

I could hear the gun battle behind me in the street intensifying.

I managed to stand with Fallon's assistance, squatting Meyers' two-hundred-plus pounds in a fireman's carry. I remembered doing this very exercise at Fort Benning, running a mile with some guy across my back who was pretending to be a wounded pilot. But that was a long time ago, when I was younger, fitter and stronger, and before several bullets fired at my ass over the years had torn me a new one.

'Jesus,' I groaned, 'what the fuck do you weigh?'

Meyers was singing a Miller Lite commercial.

'Gone to his happy place,' suggested Fallon.

'Bastard could'a taken us with him,' I gasped, sucking oxygen and dust.

I staggered forward then centered the weight. Meyers grunted. The dust was settling. We had to get back to the Landcruiser before we were fully exposed to the Taliban's fire. I managed to get through the rubble and come up behind the vehicle without tripping or breaking an ankle, and without being fired upon. I laid Meyers on the ground beside Stefanovic, who was up on one knee in the firing position. His condition was deteriorating fast as his blood leaked away, the bandage saturated. His eyelids were heavy, every blink a microsleep; he was having trouble keeping his weapon aimed anywhere but at the ground. Enemy fire was coming in hot and heavy. We couldn't hold our position much longer. One Landcruiser, eight passengers, one of them dead.

'Give me your smoke,' I said to Stef, seeing the canisters hanging from his webbing. His wounded arm wouldn't allow him the movement required to unhitch them. His eyes moved around, unable to focus. An incoming round whined off the road beside my hand, fragments of stone chips ripping through the fabric of the battle uniform around my wrist.

'You're a ghost,' Stefanovic murmured, and he dragged his bloody fingers down my face, across my mouth.

I spat the copper taste of his blood out of my mouth and took his canisters.

'Smoke,' I said to Fallon.

He handed his over and I collected more from Detmond and Meyers.

'Get everyone in the vehicle,' I yelled.

I popped two canisters and threw them upwind. Ribbons of green and red smoke swirled and drifted down the road toward us. I ran to open the driver's door of the third Landcruiser and verified that the engine was still running. Then I sprinted around to the back and opened the rear hatch. The enemy figured something was up and concentrated their fire on the upright vehicle, but the smoke was making their aim uncertain. A volley of AK rounds, sounding like a heavy-metal drum solo, punched new holes all over the roof of the Landcruiser shielding us.

I dashed back and hoisted Meyers across my shoulders once more. With Fallon shooting over us, we made it to the open rear hatch. I laid Meyers sideways across the width of the floor and hooked one of his arms around a rear seatbelt anchored to the car's bodywork above his head. Detmond helped Stefanovic into the back seat; Bellows and Mattock provided covering fire. I ran back to the driver's door. Fallon had climbed in and was struggling to prop Rogerson against the passenger door. There wasn't enough room; at least, not for me.

I popped smoke, tossed it, then slammed the doors shut.

'C'mon, Cooper!' Fallon shouted. 'Get in!'

'Go!' I said, smacking the roof with the flat of my hand.

The incoming fire was getting more accurate. Holes were gouged in the hood; the windscreen shattered. Fallon was about to argue but changed his mind. He jumped back behind the wheel, jammed it into drive, and stomped on the gas. The Toyota took off, wheels spinning in the packed dirt, the vehicle fishtailing into the smoke, drawing some of the fire and leaving a vortex of red and green swirls in its wake. Within seconds, my unit was out of range and out of danger.

I once more took up a position behind the second Landcruiser, the ground crimson with coagulating blood. I had my M4 and the captured M16s. I put a couple of them on single shot and fired them from the hip at the buildings occupied by the enemy. Changing mags, I did the same again. When those mags were spent, I threw more smoke and emptied another couple of mags, changing to three shot bursts, hoping the opposition might think there was more than one idiot left down here.

I put down the M16 with the others, crawled to the rear bumper, popped two canisters, the last of them, and threw them short. Bright red smoke swirled over my position, but mostly over the wrecked building behind me. A barrage of lead poured in, cutting me off from those

M16s. I had to leave them, and crept through the smoke and the rubble of the destroyed building, back to where we'd found Meyers.

Still no sign of those damn Apaches. Time to boogie.

The choking, cloying dust and smoke stung my eyes as I ran crouched over. I came out into the open and movement stopped me. Two kids with AKs were creeping in my direction. I saw them before they saw me. The way they were moving, it was obvious that they were hoping to come up behind my position. I recognized them. They were the boys outside al-Eqbal's cousin's place when we rolled up. Maybe they were the ones who blew the whistle on our arrival to the Taliban. One of them looked right at me and his eyes widened. Terror filled his face. He pointed at me and screamed. His buddy did likewise, and they both turned around and ran, which was a relief. Killing kids, even ones that would happily plant me in the ground, was not something I wanted to have to answer to myself for.

I wondered what had spooked them.

With still no sign of the choppers, I followed through with my plan, hopped on the pushbike I had seen beside Meyers and pedaled back to the base.

Photograph

'We sure as shit don't need this kind of crap.' Lieutenant Colonel Charles Mertins tossed a copy of the *New York Times* on the desk in front of me. 'You want to explain what got into you here?'

Mertins's nose was white with anger. It was a big nose and didn't go with the shape of his long, thin head, or the size of his ears, which reminded me of Dumbo's. In fact, I wondered if Mertins had been assembled from spare parts. My commander wasn't my kind of guy, or anyone else's as far as I knew. A guardsman from Montana, he'd left the OSI in the mid-nineties and joined the Helena PD. He was a detail hound, not very popular, and within a year they'd packed him off to Siberia – running the evidence lockup in the basement of a secondary building at the bottom of a long stairwell. His unit's call-up to Afghanistan was like giving him parole.

'I wouldn't know, sir,' I said.

'You don't know? That's not good enough, Cooper. You usually go out on a mission looking like this?'

'No, sir,' I said. The photo was printed in full color beneath the headline 'Harrowing escape in Afghanistan – Hero up for Air Force Cross'. I was familiar with the picture, of course, as was everyone here at Camp

Eggers. Fallon had snapped it with his iPhone when I rode into camp on the pushbike. That it had reached the media was news to me. Even more surprising was this business about the decoration. Aside from the fact that I was being considered for it, the consideration for a thing like that was supposed to be a closely held secret. Someone must have leaked it.

I took another glance at the photo. The powdered masonry dust gave my head the color of bone. The overhead position of the sun caused black shadows to gather in my eye sockets. I looked like a skull, an extra macabre touch being the crimson stripes of Stefanovic's blood that he'd finger-painted down across my mouth. I recalled the terror on the faces of those Afghan kids when they looked up and got a load of me. Thank God the fight had gone right out of them – I owed Allah one for that.

'US Forces don't slip into costume when they're out on patrol, goddamn it,' he said.

'No, sir.'

'Cooper, shit like this makes us look like cowboys – on top of the fact you lost the principal *and* Specialist Rogerson. Al-Eqbal might have been a jackass, but he was an *elected* jackass. Democracy's fragile here. Losing him to the Taliban chalks up major points on their scoreboard. To the local populace we look weak as camel spit.'

I could have added that al-Eqbal was an elected crook who got even more crooked when he believed he was beyond reach, largely because US Forces rode shotgun on his wagon. But the flames were doing fine by themselves; I didn't need to throw gasoline on them.

Mertins stood and walked to a vase of wildflowers on top of a cupboard. He topped up the vase with water from an old bottle. I wondered if he knew that the flowers were plastic. Maybe being kept down that stairwell in the evidence dungeon all those years had rewired his reality.

'I've read your report,' he said, taking his seat again. 'I spoke with the people on your team. Fortunately for you, they supported your story. Meyers said the principal was jumping out of the moving vehicle.'

'That's how it was, sir.'

I was going to mention those M16s, but decided to let it pass. I'd brought it up with intelligence, but the anonymous weapons didn't seem to arouse anyone's curiosity. Perhaps it would've been a different story if I'd managed to bring a couple home. There were plenty of US-made weapons AWOL in the 'Stan – apparently, too many to worry about the ones I'd turned up. Personally, I'd have been less interested in the guns if their numbers had been intact, but their removal suggested that they were significant. Otherwise, why go to all the trouble of grinding them off?

'What happened out there was a total fuck up. You know it, I know it, but I suppose giving you a decoration diverts attention from that fact as far as the folks higher up the food chain are concerned. Command must be down on its hero quota this month.'

Mertins leaned forward, lifted the newspaper for another look, and shook his head in disappointment. 'Well, at least a silver lining arrived this morning.'

'Sir?' I said, a little confused.

'A lite colonel from OSI HQ is here to see you. Seems you're leaving us, Cooper, thank God. He's waiting for you in the briefing room. Dismissed.'

LIEUTENANT COLONEL ARLEN WAYNE reclined along a row of chairs with a *Time* splayed across his face. He was snoring. I picked up the magazine. Inside was an old *Playboy,* camouflaged to avoid the ban on porn. Arlen's mouth was open, and Miss July had a wet patch on one of her jugs. He stretched his arms above his head and pointed his toes.

With his eyes still closed, he said, 'I hate damn C-17 red-eye flights. The loadmasters on those fuckers have no concept of service.'

'Hey, Arlen,' I said. 'S'up?'

He opened his eyes. 'In a word, me. I've spent the past week at thirty thousand feet, flying between Washington, Stuttgart, and LA. And now Bagram. I'm a wreck.'

He sat up, swung his legs off the chairs, and said, 'How about you,

Vin? Been pissing anyone off lately?' He stood and we shook hands.

'It's what I do best.'

'At least it's the enemy for a change, according to what I've read. I wonder who leaked the AFC to the press? I can't find anyone who'll confirm it – but it sounds like you deserve it. So,' he said, examining my eyes, his gaze shifting from one to the other, 'you doing okay?'

I knew Arlen. He was referring to how I was doing without Anna. 'I'm fine,' I said.

'As in fucked up, insecure, neurotic, and emotional?'

'As in I'm fine until some bozo reminds me about it all over again.'

'Sorry,' he said, giving my shoulder a squeeze. 'I'll take off my clown nose.' He turned away and stood at a desk with his old leather briefcase. 'So why am I here?' he said with a flourish.

'Good question. You're an oh-five. You could have dispatched underlings.'

Arlen was several years older than me and a couple of inches shorter. He was a good agent in a stickler-for-protocol kind of way. So they made him a lieutenant colonel, and these days he was virtually running OSI HQ while our fearless leader was either sucking or blowing some overlord, depending on what was required. And yet, standing here, I noticed for the first time that the desk job seemed to be taking its pound of flesh. Those brown eyes of his weren't as bright as they used to be, his dark hair lightening to gray at the temples, a small Japanese car tire-sized roll around his waist. The price of command.

He took a laptop from his briefcase, opened it, and tapped on a few keys. A copy of the *New York Times* materialized, which at least hinted at a context for his visit. 'So anyway, along with me, the rest of the world has been reading about your exploits,' he said. 'Your buddy Sergeant Fallon has made you famous. Do you know about his blog?'

'Nope,' I said, as a picture of Fallon in his army combat uniform slam-dunking a basket appeared on screen. The blog was titled *Fallon's Folly – What the hell am I doing here?*

'Apparently he's been blogging since he arrived in Afghanistan.' Arlen's fingertips rattled across the keyboard as he spoke. 'It's become a hit with some folks at the Pentagon who see it as a way of gauging the morale of our boots on the ground. Turns out some newshound named Rentworthy at the *New York Times* got wind of the blog's popularity with the brass, checked it out, and became a daily viewer.'

Up came Sergeant Fallon's iPhone shot of me looking like something that had crawled out of the ground in a Hollywood horror movie.

'The press saw your photo on the blog, read Fallon's account, and made a few calls confirming the event. This photo has since been around the world several times. You're right in the middle of your fifteen minutes, buddy. And that's kinda why I'm here.'

'You want my autograph?'

'Funny.' He opened another window on the browser, dropped his 'favorites' folder down and stabbed a key. 'No, strange as it may seem, this is not all about you. Park your trailer for a moment while I bring up Part B – the website for a rap artist by the name of Twenny Fo. You know this guy?'

'Not personally,' I said. Twenny Fo was up there with Snoop Dogg and Fiddy. I didn't like the guy's music, but it was impossible to escape his publicity machine.

'Well, you're gonna,' said Arlen. 'He read the article in the paper and wants you on his PSO team.'

'What PSO team?'

'The one escorting him to Africa.'

'Africa?'

'Yeah, You know, lions, zebras, hyenas.'

'And he asked for me?'

'The guy thinks you have mojo.'

I gave a snort. Twenny Fo lived his life in the gossip columns and, from what I recalled, it was a train wreck – a former gang member who promoted his tough guy roots by being pro-automatic weapons, pro-drugs, pro-misogyny and anti-everything that wasn't antisocial. 'Wasn't he the guy who got arrested at an after-party for donging his girlfriend with a Grammy?'

'You remember that, huh?' said Arlen.

'I never forget a great moment in assholery. Why's he going to Africa? And why are we offering to chew his bullets?'

'We've got a training base in Rwanda, at a place called Cyangugu – Camp Come Together.'

'Camp Come Together. A worthy goal,' I said. 'I usually get there too early.'

'Vin, the Pentagon wants to put on a show for our people there. Twenny Fo released a single called "Fighter", a tribute to US Forces. It went to number one and a recruitment surge followed.'

'So getting a bunch of tone-deaf morons to shoulder M16s wipes the slate clean.'

'The job is to entertain our training forces – who, as it happens, are all African-American.'

'Are you telling me that we've got a training outfit based on something other than aptitude? And that Twenny Fo got the gig because he passed the color test?'

Arlen shifted uncomfortably in his seat. 'I said, "As it happens" – pure coincidence. And Twenny Fo's girlfriend is coming along, too.'

'You mean, his *bitch*.'

Arlen looked pained.

'Hey, *you* let the anti-PC cat out of the bag, pal.'

The look didn't waver.

'So who's the lucky girl this week?' I continued.

'Leila.'

'*The* Leila?'

'The one and only.'

Leila was the star of the moment. You couldn't turn on the TV without seeing her, the radio without hearing her, or go to a newsstand without her pouting back at you from half a dozen magazine covers. I gathered she was originally from Cuba and of mixed parentage – a black Cuban father and Argentine mother. Or maybe it was the other way round. She was the color of honey and very tall and, unless it was all done with retouching, had eyes that burned like fire opals under lights. I'd read somewhere that Twenny Fo and Leila had met in the singles bar for celebrities – rehab. I caught a few of her music videos from time to time, and they seemed to focus on the fact that her ass was double-jointed.

I wanted to ask what she was doing with a deadhead like Twenny Fo, aside from the usual reason: that he had money. He also had a cabinet full of awards and one of them was bloodstained. Instead I asked, 'So what's the mission? And who's heading it up?

'The officer in charge will be a lieutenant colonel by the name of Blair Travis, from Africa Command out of Stuttgart, Germany. His background is Air Force public relations. He's on the AFRICOM Major Command team. His role will purely be liaison – shake hands, smooth the way, remove the red M&Ms. Security issues will be deferred to you. Those issues will, of course, take priority over all others. As for the mission profile, it's perfectly straightforward. You'll meet everyone in Kigali, brief them on the security arrangements at the airport and—'

'And what are the security arrangements?' I asked, interrupting him.

'I was getting to those. By security arrangements, I mean the way *you* like to do things. There'll be helicopter transport at Kigali provided by the UN. It'll take you to Cyangugu, which is on the Rwandan side of the border with the Democratic Republic of Congo. Everything's arranged. The entertainers will entertain, and then you'll fly back home the following morning. Easy.'

'Long way to go for a single concert.'

Arlen shrugged. 'Ours is not to reason why . . .'

'Cyana-what-what? Never heard of it,' I said.

'Cyangugu. It's an AFRICOM base. One of those nice Kornflak & Greene communities we love so much.'

K&G was a preferred DoD contractor. They didn't ask questions and charged extra for it. K&G mostly built stuff where a lot of killing took place, or very soon would. Mercenary ops with deniability were another specialty.

'Who are we training there?' I asked.

'Remnants of the CNDP, otherwise known as the National Congress for the Defense of the People.'

'With a name like that, I bet the only thing they defend is their own interests.'

'They're our allies.'

'I rest my case.'

'A lot of the fighters in the CNDP are renegades from the Democratic Republic of Congo's armed forces – the DRC is Rwanda's neighbor. We're doing what we can to stop the violence and reintegrate members of the CNDP back into the Congo's army.'

'Who's on the team?' I asked. 'Anyone I know?'

'Special Agent Ryder and—'

'Lieutenant *Duke* Ryder?'

'Captain. Just pinned on his bars.'

'Captain Ryder, eh? Nice to see you're putting our best people on this.'

I knew Ryder and what I knew about him was that Mr and Mrs Glutt, his parents, named him Duane Junior, and that on his twenty-first birthday he went down to city hall and changed his name to Duke Ryder ''cause it sounded like a po-leece show'. His words. Next stop was a desk at the USAF recruitment center. I had nothing against Ryder personally but the word on the street wasn't exactly glowing.

Arlen sighed wearily. 'Don't give me any grief. Duke went to college with Leila's makeup artist.'

'And here I was thinking the guy was just ballast.'

'You're being difficult,' Arlen yawned, reaching for another look at Miss July.

'You're making difficult easy.'

'I promise you this'll be a milk run.'

I gave an internal shrug. I could think of worse things to do, and most of them were in Afghanistan, which I seemed to be leaving behind for a while at least.

'Two experienced US Army PSOs from SOCOM will be joining you. They'll be on the aircraft with the principals.' Arlen leaned forward and flicked through some paperwork. 'Their names are Cy Cassidy, a sergeant major, and Sergeant First Class Michael West. You're also getting a Brit Special Air Service sergeant by the name of Lex Rutherford who has been working with SOCOM. Those names ring any bells?'

I shook my head. I didn't know them personally though I'd had some prior contact with the British Special Air Service and I'd worked with SOCOM – Special Operations Command – serving in Kosovo and Afghanistan with their people. Both were tough, well-trained outfits. I wondered how they'd feel about taking orders from an 'Air Force puke'.

Arlen must have seen something of this in my face. 'Don't worry, Duke will keep 'em in line.'

'I'm sure he will,' I said drily. 'Who else is in the party besides the principals?'

'Well, Leila apparently doesn't travel without her makeup artist.'

'Who does?'

'She's also bringing her stylist and fitness trainer. Twenny Fo has his three "bloods" – his words. Apparently they can handle themselves.'

'Let's hope in private.'

'Both stars want to bring their personal assistants, and Twenny Fo has hired a film crew to capture the event for his fans. There are also four dancers and half a dozen sound and light technicians, who stage the show.'

'Who's bringing the kitchen sink?'

'Yeah. We've asked both stars to keep it to the bare essentials. The principal doesn't know it yet, but the movie has bitten the dust; the people at AFRICOM don't want cameras rolling down there. And, as we speak, the PAs are having their visas denied by the Rwandan government. We've also had them cut back on the number of dancers and technicians.'

'That's still a lot of folks to protect for four PSOs and one Duke Ryder.'

'More resources will be made available to you at Cyangugu.'

'What's the security situation like in Rwanda? Weren't they all killing each other not so long ago?'

'That was back in the mid-nineties, when the Hutu majority decided the world would be a better place without the Tutsis, their traditional enemy. The Tutsis convinced the Hutus otherwise and today Rwanda is in reasonable shape. There are echoes of this conflict across the border in the DRC – the Congo's the problem child these days. Too much wealth there for its own good.'

I yawned.

'I'm not feeling the love, Vin. You've got to admit this beats the crap out of getting shot up by the Taliban.'

'Okay, I'll admit it, but it sounds thrown together.'

'The concerts have been in development for a while. The call to have you lead the PSO team is the only thrown-together detail. You can thank your snap-happy pal Fallon for that.'

'So I'm meeting everyone in Kigali,' I said, going with the flow.

'Kigali airport.'

'And when does this happen?'

'You're taking the C-17 I came in on. Go get your toothbrush. It's leaving in about . . .' Arlen checked his wristwatch and gave himself a surprise. 'Shit! You need to hurry – forty-five minutes from now. A car is waiting for you outside.'

'That's mighty considerate of you, Arlen. But I'm still not solid on what I'm supposed to be doing.'

'Just make sure no one gets killed. Lieutenant Colonel Travis will do the rest. Like I said – milk run.'

Kigali

Thirty-two hours later – after transiting through Incirlik, Turkey, and overnighting at Ramstein, Germany – another C-17 deposited me at Kigali airport. Packed into the long sausage-shaped bag at my feet were the bare essentials: body armor and Ka-bar knife, a metal case containing an M4 carbine and a Sig Sauer side-arm, a couple of changes of combat uniform, clean underwear, socks, disposable razor, and toothbrush.

The airport consisted of a single runway, a couple of crumbling taxiways, and one terminal that looked like some kind of traditional African grass hut built in concrete and steel. I stood on the square of paved ramp, sweat blooming on my scalp from the high temperature and choking humidity, my airman battle uniform sticking to all the wrong places. The clouds suspended above the airfield were spectacular – a thousand puffy white sails set on top of each other against a royal blue sky. Looked like rain and plenty of it.

I went into the terminal and found an old lady holding the insects at bay with a flyswatter. She stamped my passport, glanced at my papers and the firearms authorizations on my orders. Then I wandered around the deserted building, looking for a soda, but there were no vending machines and the one shop was closed. I had no local currency anyway.

The arrivals board was equally busy here in Sleepy Hollow, so I went back outside.

Of Kigali itself, there wasn't much to see, at least from where I was standing. Low hills flanked the airfield, and the closest one behind the terminal was dotted with small, nondescript shanty-style homes, nothing over two storys and only a few of those. On the opposite side of the apron I could see a faded old Soviet Mi-24 Hind gunship that was missing two of its five main rotor blades. Thinking about it, the presence of the relic was the only indication that this was an airport.

It was airless. Only the insects broke the silence. I brushed the flies off my face so many times that it looked like I was waving goodbye to an invisible plane. A large insect flew an orbit around my head, reconnoitering a place to land, before touching down on my neck. I slapped at it, and the thing flew off sounding like a door buzzer with too much voltage. It was ten-forty am. If everything was running to schedule, the principals would be here in twenty minutes.

Ten minutes short of the aircraft's scheduled arrival time, a black limousine drove onto the far side of the apron, followed by five others, plus a khaki-colored truck bringing up the rear. When the convoy got close enough, I could see little flags flapping from atop their front fenders. The line of vehicles scribed a wide arc around the ramp, eventually stopping opposite me, fifty meters away. Soldiers jumped down from the back of the truck, some of them wearing Vietnam-era fatigues but many more outfitted in what appeared to be Rwandan Army Class As. The men in the fancy uniforms were also holding shiny nickel-plated AK-47s, and they formed up in an orderly straight line to one side of the lead vehicle, then stood at ease. The guys in the greens carried more businesslike H&K MP-5 submachine guns with the blue anodizing worn off, and they fanned out around the cars. Aside from the fact that the folks in the limos were obviously important, I had no idea who they were. No doubt Travis would, but he was on the inbound plane. The front passenger door of the fourth vehicle opened and out stepped a man wearing a blue suit, blue business shirt open at the collar, and wraparound sunglasses. He walked casually toward me. When he came within ten meters, I could also see that he was wearing an earpiece, which tagged him as security.

'*Bonjour*,' he said, smiling without any kind of warmth.

I nodded. 'Hey.'

He followed with some French I couldn't follow, then summed it up by holding out his hand, palm up, wiggling his fingers, and saying, 'Documents.'

I handed him my paperwork and diplomatic passport.

'US Air Force,' he said, reading the words off my shirt. He turned his attention to the forms, and raised his eyebrows at the firearms authorizations. Then he toed the bag at my feet and said, 'I see this.'

I knelt, unzipped the bag, and let him take a peek. 'This,' he said, motioning at the locked case. Despite the Status of Forces Agreement between the US and Rwanda that okayed the weapons I was bringing in, he was clearly nervous about it. He wanted the case opened, so I opened it. There was a moment's indecision on his face, and I knew he was considering one option that had me face down while his buddies with the submachine guns stomped me into the pavement. But he checked the documents again, looked me up and down once more, and decided that maybe I was who and what my documents said I was – friendly, legal, and not to be messed with. I could feel the sweat on my back forming rivulets.

'Hot, isn't it?' I said, flicking the droplets off my forehead with a finger.

He nodded, pinched his shirt away from his body, and said, '*Oui, monsieur. Il fait chaud ici.*' All of which I took to mean, 'Yeah, hotter than fuck.'

He handed back my papers and said, 'Twenny Fo *et* Leila,' and with his hand mimed a plane landing.

'Yeah,' I repeated. 'Twenny Fo and Leila.'

He gestured over his shoulder and said, '*Le président*.'

'The president,' I repeated and made a face that conveyed wonder, respect, and surprise all at once.

We stood there looking at each other.

'*Alors*,' he said finally, then turned and walked back to the car. He got in and shut the door.

An hour later, I was sitting on my bag, the engines burbling in the black cars opposite me, their air-con units putting in overtime. I burned some minutes wondering why the presidential party was hanging around waiting. I stood and scoped the airport's open expanse. I couldn't see any spinning radar antennae. Maybe they didn't have phones here, either. Maybe Monsieur President was relying on the same worthless schedule I was.

The air was growing thicker, along with the humidity. The underbellies of the clouds were now dark gray and about to break open. My ABUs were sweat-logged. I should have mugged the woman with the flyswatter and stolen it when I had the chance. I'd capitulated to the insects, which were now the owners of whatever piece of me they could carry off. Where the hell were these people I had come to meet? Impatient, I walked to where I could see the end of the runway in both directions. I stood there for another ten minutes and was finally rewarded by the sight of landing lights shimmering to the west, the plane a couple of miles away on final approach.

'At *fucking* last,' I said aloud to the insects.

Five minutes later, a United Airlines 767 kissed the runway and its engines screamed in reverse. It came to a stop at the eastern end of the strip, slowly turned one-hundred-and-eighty degrees, and taxied back.

In response to its arrival, the doors of the two limos at the rear of the convoy flew open. Secret service types jumped out, then moved to the front two cars and held open the rear passenger doors. Apparently, the security was traveling in a separate vehicle from the principals'. In a PSO sense, I didn't like what I was seeing, but I had noticed that, as a general rule, foreigners do pretty much everything wrong.

First to exit were a perfectly groomed man and a woman, the president and first lady. The protection detail bowed. Two more men climbed out of the vehicle. The heads of the security detail were on a swivel, either looking for non-existent threats or trying to make it difficult for the flies to land. The president was in his mid-forties and wore an expensive navy blue suit, white shirt, and red tie. His wife was about the same age he was, but taller. She was wearing some kind of African dress in bright reds, yellows, and greens, and a matching scarf. The two overweight men who'd been sitting with them in the lead car were also in their mid-forties. I pegged them as high-ranking bureaucrats – fat cats who looked the same no matter which government they served. Out of the fourth limo spilled four kids – two boys and two girls – ranging in age from around five to ten, dressed in what I'd call their Sunday best. A young woman in loose white and gray clothing – a nanny presumably – chased them around the car. It must have been hell for her, cooped up with those kids all this time. I waved. The kids waved back.

A man holding a wand in each hand marched out of the arrivals hut and walked onto the ramp to a spot roughly midway between me and the presidential welcoming committee. The 767 turned onto the ramp and taxied in the direction of the man with the wands, who directed it to veer a little toward the limos over the last twenty meters. Then he crossed the wands over his head. The pilots hit the brakes; the plane dipped on its nose wheel, and then sprang back. An instant later, the engines died, and the man with the wands became the man who drove the pickup with stairs mounted on the back that would go to the aircraft's front door. One of the president's men ran to the trunk of the third limo, pulled out a bolt of red carpet, and unrolled it from the base of the stairs.

I looped around to the front of the plane, as the action would be happening on the side facing the president and his people, then stood out of the way. With the stairs and red carpet in place, and the honor guard now standing at attention with their gleaming rifles over their shoulders, the aircraft's front door cracked open and swung inwards. A US Army lieutenant colonel appeared in the doorway, stooping slightly, and stepped out on the landing of the mobile stairs. A split second later, a woman barged past him as if the doors had just opened to a fifty-percent-off sale. I recognized her instantly – Leila was dressed in tight jeans, tan boots, and a pale green jacket. A pair of Ray-Ban aviator sunglasses sat on her face, and her long jet-black hair was pulled back in a tight ponytail. She stormed down the stairs, gesticulating with her hands above her head, followed by two black women who were having a hard time keeping up with her. The one immediately behind her had buzz-cut blond hair and wore jeans and boots, and a photographer's shirt with lots of pockets. The third woman was tall, black, and wore a tailored safari suit and pith helmet. They looked as if they'd been dressed by *Vogue* for a photo shoot with Tarzan.

Leila's rant became audible.

'Shaquand, I don't see why – this concert being so damn important – we couldn't have been given a private plane so that I could have brought all my people,' she said to the taller of the two. 'I am *completely* exhausted. *Look* at me! I'm a mess! The paparazzi will have a field day with this.'

'I don't see any of them around,' Shaquand said, a hand above her eyebrows as she scanned the ramp. 'Maybe they hiding. Using those long lenses, y'know.'

'Uh-huh,' Leila said. She stopped to examine the ends of her hair. 'Lord, I *hate* this *humidity*. We need to get inside before it rains. Is this what it's going to be like the entire time? My hair will turn into frizz.' Over her shoulder, she said, 'Ayesha, I hope you brought plenty of moisturizing treatments.'

The buzz-cut blonde nodded emphatically, as all three women stopped abruptly when they reached the bottom of the stairs, all forward movement blocked by the official welcome.

Finally the lieutenant colonel, who I figured was Travis, came rushing down the stairs and squeezed past the women.

'Mr President,' he said. 'We are all so thrilled to meet you and your wife, Margaret, who is well known the world over for her style, elegance and graciousness. I am pleased to introduce Leila, our international star, her stylist, Shaquand, and makeup artist, Ayesha.'

The first lady was no Miss Universe, or even Miss Trenton, but after several tours of the Middle East, I was used to hearing extravagant compliments.

'On behalf of my people,' the president said with a heavy French accent, 'I bid you welcome to Rwanda, the most beautiful country in all of Africa.'

'I kindly thank you, your wife, and your people,' said Leila, now with a beam that I was sure could be turned on and off like a flashlight. 'I love your dress,' she said to the first lady. 'Those colors . . . they are gorgeous! Please accept these gifts as a token of my appreciation of your hospitality.'

Shaquand placed a number of CDs in Leila's hand, which the star then distributed among the Rwandan VIPs. 'They're all personally signed,' she let them know.

Meanwhile, Ayesha handed out posters to the kids. One of them unrolled and I saw a head-and-bust shot of Leila, hair tousled, her bulging cleavage slick with perspiration. The hunger on her face suggested a long period of sexual thirst about to be quenched. The four-year-old boy squashed it under his arm and went back to sucking his thumb.

Now emerging from the plane were two men in army combat uniforms, one black and one white, both NCOs, with eyes hidden behind dark sunglasses. From Arlen's briefing notes, I knew that the black guy was Cy Cassidy, a massive human being two pick handles across the chest with arms as black and thick as a couple of truck tires. His buddy, Mike West, was white and more reasonably proportioned – maybe two hundred and ten pounds, a shade under six feet tall, with dark hair and serious acne scars.

Behind them was a black man who towered over everyone. He was at least six foot six and fast-food-addict soft, the International House of Pancakes written all over his three-hundred-plus pounds. He wore loose basketball gear, several layers of t-shirts from a number of eastern conference teams, a fat gold chain around his neck, a bowler hat on his head, and a sneer on his lips. He was followed by Twenny Fo, rodent thin and of medium height, wearing a blue Adidas training suit, sunglasses with small, round red-tinted lenses, and a white Nike baseball cap with gold pinstripes. He spat the toothpick he was chewing over the stair railing. Behind the rapper was a medium-sized version of the behemoth with the bowler hat, all round shoulders and girth, and a big fan of the Denver Nuggets if the logos plastering his clothing were any indication. The guys waved at the gathering in a way that reminded me of the Queen of England.

Twenny Fo's third and final 'blood' had a goatee on his chin and looked part black and part Hispanic, his hair tightly braided into roughly parallel rows across his head. He wore a combination of green and gray Everlast gear and a tattoo of a pit bull was on his neck. His body was compact and hard, and he walked like a street fighter, a threat in every step. He came down the stairs, lighting a cigarette.

Bringing up the rear was Captain Duke Ryder, short, slightly stooped and a little overweight, and Lex Rutherford, the blond Brit on loan from the SAS, who reminded me of a baby-faced choirboy.

Ryder caught my eye and tipped a finger to his brow in greeting, which I returned. Then he gestured behind him with a tilt of his head and gave me the thumbs-up sign. I took that to mean that the staging personnel and all the dancers mentioned in Arlen's briefing notes were still on the plane and doing okay. The PSOs would have given them the standard operating procedure – wait on board until the principals were secured inside the terminal, after which they too would be escorted to the safety zone.

A traffic jam was forming at the base of the stairs. Travis steered Leila and her people away to make room for Twenny Fo's crowd.

'Ah, Mr Twenny Fo,' said the president. 'How wonderful it is to meet you.'

'Is good to be here, you know,' said the rapper. The two men shook hands.

'Allow me to present my wife, Margaret.'

'All right,' said Twenny, leaning forward to take her hand.

The muscles of the first lady's face were locked in a smile that mimicked a bout of tetanus. She probably didn't speak English, not that it would've helped her much if she did, Twenny's Baltimore patois being tricky to grasp even for English speakers.

'These my associates, yo,' Twenny continued economically. 'Boink – head security.'

Mr IHOP gave them a nod.

'This here's Snatch, my bidness manager. An' Peanut, who just is. Not his fault – you feel me?'

More nods.

Boink, Peanut, Snatch – Larry, Mo, Curly.

Travis appeared at my shoulder, tall and gangly, with sharp features and the type of pale freckly skin that sprouts melanomas at age forty.

'Special Agent Cooper,' he said. 'It is Major Cooper, isn't it?' He leaned forward and read my name tape.

'Yes, sir,' I said, standing vaguely at attention.

'Oh, don't do that. Too much formality for a rock concert. I'm pleased you could join us. I thought our wires would get crossed and they'd send you to the wrong place or something.'

He obviously worked for the same outfit I did. 'How was the flight over, sir?'

'Call me Blair. The word "interesting" just about covers it. You'll find out why soon enough. As I'm sure you're aware, we're running a little behind schedule. Apologies for that. A certain party arrived late and delayed our departure.'

I didn't have to work hard to figure out who that party might have been.

'The UN helicopters will be here in about twenty minutes. We need to clear the ramp so they can land, and you should introduce yourself to everyone. Is there a place we can do that?'

'The hut,' I said, motioning toward the terminal.

'Excellent.'

'How many personnel are still on the plane?' I asked.

'Twenty-two.'

Just then, Leila stomped over, storm clouds on her face as dark as the ones above us. Despite her mood, I decided that all those magazine covers hadn't done her justice. Her olive skin was almost poreless; her eyes the color of emeralds under polished glass; the proportions of her lips and nose, flawless. The only problem I could see was that she knew it.

She ignored me and said to Travis, 'I didn't come here to get drenched and catch a cold. My people and I are going inside.'

'This is Major Cooper,' said Travis. 'He'll be—'

Leila walked off before he finished his sentence.

'Interesting,' I said.

Travis nodded. 'You got it.'

A few heavy droplets of rain broke up the party. An umbrella appeared over the first lady's head, and she made for the limo. With a final wave, the president followed in her footsteps, motioning at the nanny to saddle up his children. As soon as his car door shut, the honor guard beat a retreat for the truck, along with their submachine gun-carrying buddies. The man who delivered the red carpet rolled it back up and threw it in the trunk. Moments later, the convoy was heading to the far corner of the field.

I walked over to Cassidy and West and exchanged the usual pleasantries. We all shook hands.

'Let's get everyone in the terminal,' I said. 'Have you briefed them on how we do things?'

'No, sir,' said Cassidy. 'We thought we'd leave that up to you. You know, save on the confusion.'

'Okay. Once we get our dignitaries secured, we can come back for the personnel still on board.'

Cassidy and West nodded.

'Send Duke to eyeball the terminal. There's not much to it, and no one's home. I've already had a look around.' I glanced over their shoulders and saw that Leila and her troop were already halfway across the ramp. 'I'd hurry if I were you.'

'Roger that,' said West, summing up the situation.

I went up the stairs into the 767 and was met by a dried-out, petite blonde flight attendant.

'Mind if I use your PA system?' I asked her.

'Everything okay?'

'Yep. Just keeping everyone informed.'

She pulled the handset off its cradle and showed me which button to press.

I thumbed it and said into the mouthpiece, 'Thank you for your patience, folks. You'll be disembarked from this aircraft in about five minutes and escorted by your security team to the terminal building. Please collect your belongings and be ready to move.'

I went back onto the stair's landing. It had stopped spitting. The clouds were teasing us, though the far side of the airfield was covered in a heavy gray mist of rain. A small jolt moved the aircraft. I looked down and saw that a tug had attached itself to the nose wheel.

Cassidy and Rutherford had left the terminal and were jogging across the apron toward the aircraft. Perhaps I was being overly cautious with all this escorting, but I didn't know this place and losing al-Eqbal was a good lesson, especially for al-Eqbal.

I went back inside the aircraft. 'Do you mind?' I asked the attendant again, motioning at the handset.

'Please,' she replied.

I told the passengers to make their way to the forward exit and stood back on the landing. They filed past as I did a head count. Almost all of the staging crew were male, and even the ones who weren't, looked male. Black jeans and old t-shirts predominated, as did dreadlocks, tattoos, and piercings. The dancers among them were easy to pick out, being the ones wearing deodorant. I totaled twenty-three persons, the right number. Then I went through the cabin checking seats, galleys, and lavatories. All clear.

Cassidy, Rutherford, and I escorted this second group into the terminal, getting them inside just as the clouds above us burst open with a flash of lightning and a crash of thunder. Blinding rain came down like buckets of six-inch nails. Inside the hut, the downpour was deafening. As the Boeing was towed to a far corner of the parking area, a tractor pulled up outside the front door with the luggage in a covered trailer.

There was plenty of tension in the room. Twenny and his buddies occupied one side of the terminal, while Leila and her girls took the other. Were we about to have a dance-off?

'If I could have everyone's attention,' I called out. The room settled down. 'My name's Vin Cooper. I'll be managing the security arrangements. We don't think there'll be any need for special precautions, but the Pentagon does a lot of unnecessary things, right?'

I grinned at a sea of blank faces that remained blank.

'Yo, Mister Army. Head of security for Mister Fo is me,' said Boink, folding his arms, head on a tilt. 'I say who does what, dig?'

I blinked a couple of times.

'Don't think for a moment I'm getting on no helicopter with that,' Leila said.

By 'that', she meant Twenny Fo, because she was pointing at him.

Ayesha and Shaquand stood behind her defiantly, chins jutting.

'Well, you know, the feeling is mutual, bitch,' said Boink.

'You wanna piece a this?' said Shaquand, flicking Twenny and his cohorts the bird.

'I wouldn't touch you bitches with rubbers on my fingers, yo,' said Snatch.

I glanced at Travis, who again mouthed the word 'interesting'.

Weren't Twenny Fo and Leila supposed to be slurping each other's juices? The room was suddenly full of shouting. I found Cassidy in the crowd, and he shrugged at me. I whistled hard, the piercing note cutting through the squabbling like an oxy torch through ice.

'Okay, then we'll go with plan B,' I said in the sullen silence and with a hand gesture drew an invisible line down the middle of the room. 'We've got two choppers inbound. Everyone on this half goes in one, the rest of you go in the other. Twenny Fo and Leila – either myself or one of my team will be accompanying you at all times. Apologies if that inconveniences you at all, but we have our rules.'

Boink shook his head and turned away, either not happy with the arrangements or displeased that I hadn't consulted him. Twenny Fo sidled up to him and had a quiet word, a hand reaching up and resting on the big man's shoulder.

'Can we just go and get this shit over with?' said Leila, addressing me, a hand on her hip.

I went across to her. She avoided eye contact. 'Ma'am, we'll be lifting off as soon as we can,' I said. 'We haven't had an opportunity for personal introductions – Vin Cooper.' Still no eye contact from the woman. I held out my hand to shake and she left it in midair. I let my hand drop. 'It's a pleasure to be working with you.'

‘I’m sure it is,’ she said as she walked off.

Twenny Fo sauntered over. ‘I was right ’bout choo, man. Choo one bad motherfucker,’ he grinned. ‘That’s why y’all here – keep that bitch an’ her bitches in line, you feel me?’

I missed the Taliban. I could shoot them.

Cyangugu

Changed into full battle rattle, I rejoined Travis watching two United Nations SA 330 Pumas hovering a dozen feet off the ground on pillows of water thrown up by their main rotors' downwash. They were maneuvering into the space vacated by the Boeing. The lieutenant colonel glanced at a sheaf of paperwork in his hand and said, 'Our contact is a French *Armée de l'Air capitaine* by the name of André LeDuc.'

Cassidy, West, Rutherford and Ryder joined us.

'Bloody frogs,' said Rutherford.

'Cy, you're with me in one chopper with Twenny and his people,' I said. 'Lex, Mike, Duke – you got the women in the other.'

The guy with the wands was back out there again, now in a bright yellow spray jacket. He brought the choppers in quite close to the terminal, then directed them to kick sideways so that their side doors were facing us. The blue Pumas settled on their wheels with a couple of light bounces and blasted the hut's windows with a fine mist of water. 'MONUC' was painted on their sides in large white letters, which I knew from Arlen's briefing notes was the acronym for *Mission de l'Organisation des Nations Unies en République Démocratique du Congo* – a mouthful for the French-led United Nation's effort in these parts. The side door of the nearest chopper slid open, and two men in dark gray flight suits made a dash for the door of the hut, which Travis opened for them.

'*Alors, il pleut à verse, non?*' the man who won the race said, running his hands through black unkempt hair.

'What'd he say?' I asked Travis.

'He said it's raining hard.'

'*Oui*,' the Frenchman agreed. He wiped his hand down the side of his flight suit and held it out to shake.

'*Capitaine* André LeDuc,' he said, the name confirmed by a patch on his suit. 'And this is Lieutenant Henri Fournier, my co-pilot.'

We all shook.

Being somewhere between a midget and merely short, LeDuc was the right height for a pilot, and swarthy in that southern European way. He was either growing a beard or had forgotten to shave, I wasn't sure which. His black hooded eyes were the same color as his hair, their whites red. He also smelled like the shower he just got jogging from his aircraft to the hut had been his first in a while. Fournier was similarly groomed, but taller and coffee-colored. If I had to guess, I'd say one of his parents was white.

'Do you speak English?' I asked them.

'We have to. You fly, it is the law,' said LeDuc. '*Parlez-vous Français?*' he asked me in return.

'No,' I said.

'Fucking Americans. You are as bad as the English.'

'Worse,' I said. 'And proud of it.'

The *capitaine* laughed, as did his co-pilot.

LeDuc asked me. 'You are security?'

'No, I always dress like this,' I said.

The smile stayed on his lips as he reviewed Travis's paperwork. 'So, 'ow many passenger do we 'ave?'

'Thirty-five in total,' said Travis, 'as originally planned.'

LeDuc surveyed the crowd in the room. '*Bon*.'

'Seventeen in one chopper, eighteen in the other,' the colonel suggested.

'They 'ave *les bagages?*' LeDuc asked.

'There.' With a nod, Travis indicated the covered trailer on the apron.

'*Alors,*' he said. 'We will get it on the aircraft first, *non?*'

Fournier ran out into the rain to make it happen and whistled to his crew. A man appeared in the side door of the Puma. The lieutenant shouted instructions at him and he shouted at the wand guy. Chain of command in action.

The wand guy disappeared around the corner and an elderly black man arrived soon after, wearing a green reflective vest over a dark blue cardigan, dusty gray pants and an old peaked cap. He walked over, under the eaves of the hut, and then slowly pulled himself into the tractor's driver's seat. The vehicle belched smoke as he fired it up and drove the luggage out to the Pumas.

Soon after, with the loading complete, Rutherford, Ryder, and West accompanied Leila's people to the furthest aircraft. Cassidy and I herded Twenny Fo's entourage and the balance of the support crew into LeDuc's machine.

We were airborne within twenty minutes, heading generally west. With some elevation I could see that Kigali, the Rwandan capital, was only a large village with few substantial buildings and almost no paved roads; at least, not where the airport was situated.

We flew low, not more than two thousand feet above the ground. The Rwandan countryside was a monotony of treetops, scrub, and rust-colored earth punctuated here and there with flimsy huts.

'Flying time is under an hour,' came LeDuc's voice in my headset. 'We cannot go as flies the crow today, and I cannot provide you with a precise flight time – there is much of the weather over the mountains to the east of your base.'

I made no comment and sucked some water from my camelback.

'You have not been to Africa before?' he asked.

'No,' I said. 'Where do they keep all the lions and tigers?'

'There are no tigers in Africa, except at the zoos. But there are plenty of lions. Your people will be entertaining at Cyangugu?' he asked.

'Yeah. The skinny guy back there in the white baseball cap can rhyme "motherfucker" with almost anything. And Leila, who's traveling in your other chopper, has a pretty good routine, too.' Here I was referring specifically to those things she could do with her ass.

'Yes, those two are big news in France also. I mean, no concerts other than the one at Cyangugu? It is a long way to come for one performance.'

'Yes, it is, unless the schedule has changed. Travis, has the schedule changed?'

'No, no. Not as far as I know,' he said.

I examined his face. All those 'no's suggested a yes but he gave nothing away, so I turned to see how my principal was getting on. The rapper was asleep. On the seat across the aisle, Cassidy's head was at an angle and I couldn't see his eyes behind his glasses. 'How's it going, Cy?' I asked.

'Good,' he said. 'How's it going with you, sir?'

'Good,' I said. Glad we'd settled that, although Cassidy's manner, tone and body language hinted at his true feelings about Air Force guys – that we were a life form elevated only slightly above bugs.

I did my best to ignore Boink, who'd been giving me a disapproving glare from the moment we boarded, daring me to contest his authority as Twenny Fo's chief protector. Beside him, Peanut was staring out the window, his knees knocking together while he pointed excitedly at something of interest below, his eyes wide with wonder.

In the row behind them, Snatch was sitting forward in his seat, wringing his hands, body twitching as if he had Tourette's. Any second now he was going to shout 'fucknuts' or something. Either that or he had a phobia about flying. If so, I could relate, having had one of those once.

I looked back through the front windshield over LeDuc's shoulder. 'Hey, ever crash in one of these things?' I asked him.

'French helicopters never go down,' he replied.

'Unlike French women, right?'

No response from LeDuc.

One thing I know how to do is get along with foreigners.

*

LeDUC GUIDED THE PUMA into a descending arc. Out the front window, steady rain was falling from a solid horizontal wall of black cloud cover. Camp Come Together was laid out ahead of us like any temporary base I'd ever seen on the front lines – everything prefab in neat rows set among heaps of boxes, drums, broken concrete, and rusting machine parts, all safely tucked behind a perimeter fence of coiled razor wire. This one, though, appeared to be sinking in a sea of orange mud.

The welcoming committee, standing next to the chopper pad, turned their backs on the Puma's downwash as the aircraft bounced and then settled on the steel matting. Snatch lunged for the exit door, which earned him a palm in the face from the French loadmaster who commanded him to sit.

'Yo, Snatch. Be cool, man,' Boink called out, stepping into his hall monitor role.

As soon as the aircraft was shut down, the loadmaster slid the door open. The air rushed in. It smelled foreign, laced with hot aviation fuel, the tang of rainwater, sodden earth, wet cooking fires and trash. Beyond the pad, I could see men ambling around in jungle-pattern fatigues I didn't recognize. Their pants were soaked black by the rain and streaked with orange mud.

A man with a large bald head, rusty-gray mustache and heavy black-rimmed glasses shouted through the open door. 'I'm Colonel Firestone. Welcome to Camp Come Together, Cyangugu,' he said. 'Where's Lieutenant Colonel Travis?'

Travis removed his headset, fired up a smile, ripped off a salute and led with a handshake as he made his way toward the door. 'Colonel,' he said, jumping down onto the matting. 'Have we got a show for you, sir.'

'Excellent, excellent. Good flight?'

'First class all the way,' Travis said, full of baloney.

I thanked LeDuc for the transport and then followed Travis, Cassidy instructing the principals to stay put.

Firestone was accompanied by his own entourage, a mix of civilians and US Army and local officers who'd come to ogle the celebrities.

I approached the colonel and said, 'Special Agent Vin Cooper, sir – Security Team Leader.'

'Ah, yes. Now, are you the same Vin Cooper we've been reading about in the news lately?' Firestone asked, shaking my hand.

'I think so, sir.'

'You think so. You're not sure? Is there another Vin Cooper up for the Air Force Cross? How many of you could there be?'

'I couldn't say, sir,' I said, giving him the smile he was after. Full colonels are allowed to have a lame sense of humor – comes with the bird. I turned to Cassidy and signaled at him to disembark the principals from the Puma.

Twenny Fo hopped down from the chopper, followed by Boink, who made the maneuver look difficult. Peanut came next, staring open-mouthed at the new surroundings, as if he'd been catapulted into a fantasy. Snatch followed, looking pale, with Cassidy right behind him. Travis herded them away from the chopper toward Colonel Firestone.

The humidity had frosted up the colonel's lenses like they were beer glasses. 'Have to apologize for the weather,' the colonel said to Travis. 'Wet season came later than usual this year, and it's still hanging around.'

'Colonel, allow me to introduce Twenny Fo, our headliner,' Travis said, bringing him forward, his arm around, but not quite touching, the star's shoulders.

'Mr Twenny Fo. Well, I'm a big fan,' said Firestone.

Somehow I doubted it.

'Dis be the land of my forebears, you feel me? Dis be my dream. You want any special songs, Gen'ral, just tell my people, yo.'

Colonel Firestone cleared whatever it was that had stuck in his throat and said, 'Well thank you, thank you very much. That's very gracious of you. You can call me Colonel.'

Standing behind Twenny were his bloods, definitely fish out of water, or, in Boink's case, beached whale.

'Twenny, why don't you introduce your assistants?' Travis said.

'Yeah,' said the star, 'I was gonna. The big man here is Boink. He be my security man. Snatch – he take care of my bidness. An dis here is

Peanut. I take care of Peanut, 'cause Peanut ain't so good at takin' care o' hisself, you feel me?'

Boink and Snatch were standing side by side. Boink had his arms folded, detached and above it all. Peanut smiled and tore off a thumbnail.

'Wonderful, wonderful. Well, I'm pleased to meet y'all, too,' said Firestone, hurriedly shaking each of their hands. 'Y'know, we're doing some great work here to help freedom take root in Africa.'

The noise from the arrival of the second Puma, carrying Leila's troop, obliterated all conversation. I turned to watch its arrival just as a burst of rain fell as hard as marbles from the low black sky.

'Let's get you folks out of the weather,' Firestone shouted over the roar of the chopper's turbine and rotor noise.

Firestone led the way, trotting over to a hangar at the edge of the helipad. I scoped it as a matter of course and saw that it was mostly empty. The only activity going on inside was the servicing of an old Mi-8 Soviet helicopter, one of its engines lying in pieces on the floor. A couple of mechanics were standing over the oily puzzle, scratching their heads as if they didn't know where to start. No threat here, except perhaps to that aircraft's next payload.

Colonel Firestone brought his VIPs over to meet my principal.

'If you don't mind, Mr Twenny, I have some introductions of my own,' he said.

'Meet your people be my pleasure,' the rapper said, with a lopsided smile.

'This is Colonel Olivier Biruta of the National Congress for the Defense of the People, and his second in command, Major Jean Claude Ntahobali. Colonel Biruta commands the CNDP brigade currently in training here.'

'Please t' meet choo, brother,' Twenny Fo said, unsure about what he should do next – bow or shake hands. He settled on both. The rapper seemed genuinely overwhelmed by the occasion.

'Yeah,' said Boink, joining in, giving the colonel and his offsider some kind of homie salute, sliding his hand diagonally across his chest with thumb, forefinger, and pinky prominent. 'Real pleased.'

Biruta smiled broadly, showing receding gums and very large teeth. He was tall and slim, with skin the color and luster of liquorice, his face almost perfectly divided in half by a scar that ran nearly as straight as a desert road from his forehead to his chin, leaving a grooved trench down the middle of his nose. Biruta's XO, Commandant Ntahobali, was equally thin and black, though not as tall as his boss. A three-inch chunk of flesh was missing from the muscles of his right forearm, where a badly applied skin graft had created an ugly pink raised keloid scar. Both men had the detachment of soldiers who'd seen far too much.

Peanut, disengaged from proceedings, gazed in wonder at the dismantled Soviet aircraft.

Firestone stuck to his game plan. 'I'd also like you to meet Beau Lockhart. Beau's from Kornflak & Greene, the contractor that built this camp. He's ex-Army Special Forces, so he knew from personal experience what we needed, didn't you, Beau?'

Lockhart nodded and stepped forward into the space between the rapper and Colonel Firestone, and more handshaking ensued. He wore a diamond stud in his left ear and his nearly shoulder-length hair had been coiffed into glistening black ringlets. The guy was swimming in a pool of cologne. He didn't seem the Special Forces type to me, retired or otherwise.

'Can't wait to hear the concert,' he said.

'Pleasure to entertain y'all,' Twenny Fo replied.

Pulling Travis aside, I said, 'I need to speak with someone about security.'

'Yes of course,' he said. 'They gave me his name already – Holt. I'll see if I can track him down.'

Just then, the people from the second French helicopter ran into the hangar, with a squad of enlisted soldiers holding ponchos over their heads. Biruta, Firestone, and the other officials seemed to forget about Twenny Fo completely and craned their necks to get a better view of the new arrivals.

'Colonel,' said Travis, smiling broadly, 'come and meet America's hottest female performer.'

'Love to,' the colonel replied, licking his lips.

'Look at us,' Leila said to Ayesha and Shaquand, as she brushed a few drops of water off her thigh with the flat of her hand. 'I mean, just *look* at us!'

She didn't need to say it twice because that's what every male in the hangar was doing. Biruta was acting as though he'd just been given a shot of morphine; he was staring at probably the most beautiful creature he'd ever seen in his life. Drooling was a real possibility.

Ayesha held up a small mirror so that Leila could examine her makeup disaster zone.

'Leila,' said Travis, approaching her, 'how was your flight?'

'Appalling. The plane leaked.'

'Oh, I'm sorry.' Realizing that it wasn't a particularly good idea to continue down this path, Travis changed the subject. 'The commander of the camp would like to meet you.'

'Can't it wait? Is there a dressing room I can use?'

'I'm sure there is, but you look amazing. A couple of quick introductions, and then you can start rehearsing.'

The star sighed heavily, then turned away from Travis and said, 'Shaq, honey, see if you can't find me a bottle of Evian?'

Shaquand scoped the hangar, I guessed for a vending machine. I didn't like her chances.

Colonel Firestone was standing to one side, waiting patiently beside Biruta, Ntahobali, Lockhart, and their assistants.

When Leila turned back, it was as if a new personality had invaded her being. A warm smile suffused her features, and she radiated light.

'Gentlemen,' she said, holding out her hand, which Firestone eagerly took. 'I can't tell you how excited I am to have been given the honor to come here and do my patriotic duty.'

I had to smile. Leila played the room like a hit single.

Firestone more or less repeated the introductions I'd already heard, although with considerably more fawning.

Travis extracted himself from the center of the male vortex swirling around her and brought me one of Firestone's junior officers.

'This is Alex,' said the colonel. 'Holt' was stamped on his nametag. He was US Army and black, with the build of a quarterback and sharp, intelligent eyes.

'Name's Vin,' I said, completing the introductions. 'Tell me about the natives. Any chance that a suicide bomber might run into the accommodations and rearrange the furniture with C4?'

He read my name, saw the OSI unit badges, and something clicked. 'Oh, *now* I know who you are. You're *that* Vin Cooper. Kabul, right? The whole skull thing. What you did was pretty awesome.'

I didn't know where to look.

'Don't worry, you're among friends here – on *both* sides of the wire. And I've put a ten-man security detail at your disposal. Oversee them personally if you like, but if I were you, I'd relax and enjoy some down time.'

'Can I please have everyone's attention?' said Travis, raising his voice over the crowd. 'I need to see the stage managers, get you people orientated. Colonel Firestone has given us the mess hall, a place for you to rehearse. Leila, Twenny Fo – whenever you're ready, I'll take you over there.'

'So what's she really like?' Holt asked, his eyes feasting on the celebrity.

'Interesting.'

Holt continued staring at her for another moment and then snapped out of it. 'I'll get the team to rendezvous with you over at the mess,' he said.

'Thanks.' I scanned the area, checking on everyone's whereabouts. All except one present and accounted for.

'You see Peanut anywhere?' I asked Rutherford.

He gestured over his shoulder. The guy was covered in grease and kerosene, holding up parts of the Mi-8 as if he'd struck gold.

THE CAMP HAD ALREADY set up its own sound system in the mess hall – a big prefab box built to feed two thousand men at a time, with movable seating and a cafeteria at one end – and now Twenny Fo's recorded backing tracks were rattling the windows. The room was huge and plain, beige tiles on the floor and the walls unadorned but for awards extolling the military's equivalent of employee-of-the-month – photos of smiling personnel who'd served the most meals or washed the most pots.

Major Holt's security detail arrived as Leila and Twenny Fo were rehearsing, ten armed men to guard the only two doors in and out. That was a lot of security. Nevertheless, one of us still had to chaperone the principals – rules.

Cassidy, Rutherford, West, and Ryder stood just outside the mess. Over on the other side of the open quadrangle, we could see some US Army engineers putting the finishing touches on a stage constructed from scaffolding.

'Duke, I nominate you to babysit our principals,' I said. 'You okay with that?' I was doing him a favor. The guy hadn't been able to take his eyes off Ayesha.

'Sure can do,' he said. 'Where're you fellas gonna be at?'

'Taking in the sights.'

'Okay – later,' he said, almost skipping back inside.

Cassidy, West, Rutherford and I went off to nose around. None of us was even aware that the US had a military base down here, and we wanted to see what mischief the Pentagon was up to.

'So which ones are the advisors?' West motioned toward half a dozen soldiers cutting across our path. Beyond them, three platoon-sized squares of men were out double-timing it between truck convoys crawling down a muddy access road.

'Have you noticed that, aside from Firestone, all of our people here are black?' observed Cassidy.

'Hiding in plain sight,' I said.

'How do you know which ones are the Americans?' asked Rutherford, the Brit.

'Look for the roll,' West said.

'What roll?' inquired Cassidy. Then he stopped, annoyed. 'Do I have a roll, motherfucker?'

'Yeah, you do,' Rutherford insisted. 'You know, the stylish, fluid movement that suggests a certain level of cool. The slight push off your left foot, followed by the telltale thrust of your right shoulder. I'm an Anglo. If I tried to do something like that, I'd look like I was having some kind of spasm.'

A couple of guys strolled past with rhythm in their step.

West nodded at them. 'The roll. For damn sure, made in the USA.'

Cassidy grunted. 'How many advisors are we supposed to have here, anyway?'

'I was told a thousand,' I said.

The base was big enough to house maybe five thousand men, though I couldn't say for sure how many of them were actually on post. The place felt like a busy frontier fort gearing up for a mid-level conflict just over the horizon.

A truck stopped at one of the large pre-fab boxes with two forklifts parked outside suggesting that it might be Supply. The Kornflak & Greene guy, Beau Lockhart, hopped out of the truck's passenger side and stood at the open door, discussing something with the driver.

'Why don't we ask The Man?' I suggested, and then called out in Lockhart's direction, 'Hey, nice place you have here!'

Lockhart turned. He was preoccupied with the driver; it took him a moment to place us. 'Why thank you,' he said. 'And that's a nice piece of ass you've brought with you.' He leered at us. 'She could *Leila* with me anytime, you know what I'm sayin'?'

Lame joke. Maybe this guy was a colonel when he was in Special Forces.

'The boys and I were just wondering what goes on here,' I said, throwing out a line.

'You mean, what *we're* doing down here, ol' Uncle Supply and Demand?' he asked.

'Uh-huh.'

'The usual,' he said. 'We train our side to go out and teach the other side where and how to smarten up so that they can kill our side right back.'

'And who *is* our side killing, generally speaking?'

'Generally speaking, the enemy,' he said with an easy smile.
'And who's that?'
'Nosy for a PSO, aren't you?'
'This is just my day job,' I said.
His eyes flittered over the words 'Special Agent' above my nametag.
'You're a cop. So you'll understand me when I say – move along, nothing to see here.'
And that often means there's something you really should see and it's mostly dead, but I didn't press it.
Lockhart's smile went someplace else. 'Well, looking forward to tonight's concert. If you'll excuse me . . .'
Cassidy stood aside. Lockhart squeezed past him and trotted toward the supply building.
'Make friends easily, skipper?' Rutherford asked as we watched the man's back.
Lockhart opened a door and disappeared behind it. My natural curiosity was getting the better of me, probably because Arlen had provided next-to-no detail on this place. But asking questions wasn't my gig here, as Lockhart had pointed out.
A couple of Americans rolled past, wearing jeans and t-shirts and smoking cigars.
'They don't look like regular military,' said West.
'Contractors,' said Cassidy.
'Kornflak & Greene turf,' I reminded them. 'They're mercenaries.'
'Speaking of turf, they should rip all of it the fuck up.' Rutherford pulled his Ka-bar, leaned on West, and prized away the orange mud accumulated on the soles of his boots. 'This shite is like wet concrete.'
'Smacks of deniability,' said West, looking around. 'If things go wrong – it weren't us, no sir.'
Possibly, but there were enough people at the command level here parading around in US Army battle uniforms – Firestone, Holt, and the rest – to make plausible deniability difficult to pull off. The truth, whatever it was, would still escape. Truth had a habit of doing that.
We walked for another twenty minutes and saw nothing that we

hadn't seen at countless other camps and bases. It began raining again; not hard, just a steady, sapping drizzle. We made our way over to the stage, which had been built adjacent to the camp's HQ, a two-story structure with a couple of flagpoles out front: a blue, yellow, and green-striped flag – I guessed the national flag of Rwanda – hanging limp on one of them, the Stars and Stripes on the other. A luxury Mercedes 4×4 followed by a Toyota Kluger pulled up outside the HQ. Fancy vehicles for a place like this, I thought. Two men got out of the Mercedes, one white, one black. Five large black men with nervous eyes exited the Toyota and formed a loose diamond around the two from the Mercedes – PSOs. Then Lockhart came out of the HQ, armed with a couple of umbrellas. This guy got around. The Mercedes combo took refuge beneath them and they all made a dash for the building.

'Vin, wait up,' a voice called behind me. It was Ryder. He was out of breath, something urgent on it.

'What's up?' I asked him.

'Twenny Fo wants a word.'

'What about?'

'No idea,' he said.

'He still rehearsing?' I asked.

Ryder nodded.

'I'll catch up with you later,' I said to Cassidy and the others.

Ryder and I walked back to the mess. 'How's it going?' I asked him.

'Gonna be a great show,' he said.

'How're the principals getting along?'

'Great.'

'As long as they're not breathing the same air,' I said.

'Yeah.'

So far, the only danger I could see on this detail was getting caught in the crossfire between those two.

When I walked into the mess, Leila had the floor. She was singing a song I was familiar with about a guy with a big gun – I figured not of the Smith & Wesson variety. It was slow and sexual, as though the tune itself were riding on its own lubricant. A bunch of US Army folks, including Firestone, Holt, and his security team, were somehow managing to watch without panting.

'Over here,' said Ryder.

I followed him to a far corner, where Twenny Fo, wearing white Nike sweatbands on his head and wrists, was trying on a US Army combat uniform, a tailor pinning it here and there in an attempt to wring what he could from the performer's scrawny, free-range street physique.

'Yo, Tee – that look the biz on you, man,' Boink complimented him.

'You be The Man's secret jungle weapon,' said Snatch, massaging his goatee and holding his tightly braided head at an angle. He saw me coming and said, 'Heads up, Tee. Ghost Man in da house.'

Fo looked across and acknowledged me with a lift of his chin, then walked away from the tailor as if the guy didn't exist.

'Wanna ask you sommin', man,' he said, his brow furrowed as if he were weighing the answer to an important question.

'Yes, sir,' I replied.

'You know my tunes?'

'One or two.'

'What about "Fighter"? Choo know that one, homes, right?'

'I'm familiar with it, sir,' I said.

'Yo,' he called to Boink. 'You got it on you?'

'Ai.' The big man reached into his shirt pocket and pulled out a white rectangular piece of paper. He lumbered over to Fo, sweat rolling down his forehead, and handed it to the celebrity.

'I want choo to picture this, you feel me?' He put one hand in the air and then looked up at it as though a vista of the future were about to project from his fingertips. 'This is what I thinkin', man. At the end of the song, we gonna have a lot'a smoke, yo. It be pouring out, man, drifting across the stage while I do what I do. Then, we gonna turn on the back lights – big white searchlight motherfuckers. That's when people gonna see the silhouette of a man standing on stage with his weapon in the crook of his arm like so,' he said, striking the pose he was after, his arm the weapon. 'This man be you. And then we're gonna put a front light on you, you know, so everyone can see yo' bad-ass motherfucker ghost face.'

He flipped over the rectangle of white paper that Boink had given him. It was Fallon's cell phone photo, the one taken of me in Kabul. Christ, Arlen was right, the goddamn thing was following me around the world.

'We gonna make you up,' Fo said, 'just like this.'

'I spoke with Ayesha,' said Ryder, chipping in behind me. 'She says she can do a great job: white powder on your face, a little black around your eyes, crimson lipstick for the lines of blood across your mouth. Easy.'

'No, thanks,' I said, without hesitation.

'Choo not sure, right? Well, think on this,' Twenny Fo said, gesturing at Snatch. 'Yo, give the man three.'

Snatch reached into his pants pocket, extracted a roll of cash, and began peeling off notes, his fingers translating 'three' into three thousand dollars. He held the moist wad toward me.

The photo brought back memories of the action in Kabul, one of them being of Specialist Rogerson with no face at all, sitting in the Landcruiser with her perfectly manicured nails still resting on the rim of the steering wheel.

'No. And I'm sure,' I said, handing the photo back to Boink.

One of the security guys whistled softly. I glanced up and saw the reason why – Leila had just broken into a dance routine that I'd loosely describe as X-rated. I felt her eyes on me as I made for the exit.

'Change your mind,' Twenny Fo called after me, 'the offer stands, yo . . .'

CASSIDY, WEST, RUTHERFORD, RYDER, and I watched the performance from the wings. The audience was on its feet the whole time. I estimated the assemblage at close to two thousand. The numbers were less than I'd thought they would be. Maybe part of the brigade was somewhere else. Half a company of Firestone's men was handling crowd control. Better them than us. Things were getting ragged out there. Leila had been on stage for over an hour, and her set was coming to a climax along with, I suspected, half the men, including me.

The song was called 'Peep Show'. Two of Leila's dancers had lathered moisturizer all over her, and then all over each other, and now the three of them were moving in and out of each other's legs and arms while Leila sang a rhythmic song, the beat pulsing, the lyrics on the verge of pornographic. A roar of testosterone rose from the men and rolled over the oiled-up performers. I saw Leila flip the bird at Twenny Fo waiting in the wings. She was stealing the show and letting him know it.

I turned back to scope the audience. A commotion was going on in the front row. The overhead lighting flashed on a blade of steel. Suddenly, two men vaulted onto the stage and raced for Leila and the dancers. Holt's security men were too thinly spread out to be effective. Rutherford and I moved at the same time. I went low, taking out their legs. The SAS sergeant went high, and all four of us slid on a slick of moisturizer. The two men were Rwandan, dressed in battle uniforms. Using a thumb lock, I immobilized the guy who I thought had the knife and dragged him offstage. I patted him down, but the knife was gone. Maybe he dropped it before he jumped on stage. Maybe he left it in one of his countrymen. I frog-marched him out the back and handed him over to a couple of Rwandan MPs with a quick report. Rutherford released his captive back into the wilds of the mosh pit, and I resumed my place in the wings. The crowd was going nuts as 'Peep Show' came to its conclusion, Leila lying exhausted and prostrate on the floor, her heavy, sated breathing booming through the sound system.

Then Twenny Fo jumped into the picture, pulled Leila to her feet, and the two sang an upbeat number followed by a saccharine duet that made me want to reach for a bag. Leila waved to the audience and blew everyone kisses as she walked offstage, the crowd applauding, wolf-whistling, and calling out lewd propositions.

The rapper diverted their attention with a change of pace, a song recalling neighborhoods in the Bronx, wrapped in a beat that made as much sense to my ears as French. But the black audience responded, moving and swaying, hands in the air, lost in the music. Twenny Fo performed about fifteen or so songs and the crowd was functioning as one organism, the music its lifeblood, its oxygen. And then Fo was gone. Initially stunned, the crowd refused to believe that the concert was over and demanded more, chanting and stomping and clapping. Something was missing. He hadn't performed his signature tune. The audience knew it and wouldn't let him go.

I scanned the crowd for more threats but couldn't see any. It was a sea of expectant, enthusiastic black faces out there. I continued scoping the area and saw that Colonel Firestone was enjoying the concert from the second-story balcony of the base HQ overlooking the stage. Five men were with him – Biruta, Ntahobali, Lockhart, and the two men I had seen getting out of the Mercedes. There was no room up there for the bodyguards.

'You were slow getting to those guys,' said a voice behind me as I caught the scent of mountain flowers on a warm spring day. It was Leila. She was toweling off her wet hair, having just come from taking a shower. Without makeup, her beauty was almost freakish, the type that could launch a thousand ships. Unfortunately, the personality that went along with it would happily see them all dashed onto the rocks, the passengers and crew drowned. But maybe I was doing her an injustice.

'Do you like your job, soldier?'

What was I supposed to say?

'Well?' she asked.

'I'm in the Air Force, ma'am, which makes me an airman,' I said.

'Well, whether you like it or not, *airman*, one word from me, and you won't be doing it no longer.'

Her attack took me by surprise as much as the guy with the knife had. If I'd been expecting anything from her – and I wasn't – maybe it was just a plain, ordinary thank you.

She turned and walked off, still toweling her hair. I signaled West to stay with her while I imagined how she'd react to being thrown over my knee. I glanced at my watch. In another thirteen hours or so, we'd be back at Kigali airport, and this detail would slip from the uncomfortable present into the happily forgotten past.

Then a familiar tune brought my attention back to the stage. It was

'Fighter', Twenny Fo's mega hit. He had re-appeared and the audience began singing along with the familiar lyrics from the chorus: *There ain't got no force righter than a US Army fighter.* I wondered what the Marines and the Navy had to say about that.

'Hey,' said Travis, appearing beside me. 'Great concert.'

'Great,' I echoed.

'Nice take down, by the way. And good of Leila to come over and thank you,' he said.

'That's just what I was thinking,' I said.

Smoke machines swamped the stage with a white mist. Twenny Fo was two-thirds of the way through his big number. The song was building, getting louder, harder. Then some familiar sounds made me flinch involuntarily: small arms fire, helicopters, rocket-propelled grenades. Explosions boomed through the speakers, seemingly getting closer. Brutal searchlights kicked in with a blazing light that backlit the smoke and reminded me of blinding white phosphorus. Suddenly, a powerful downlight illuminated the scene from overhead and the crowd went berserk. I shook my head in disbelief because there I was – on stage. The figure took two steps forward as the smoke curled in and around it, and I saw my face, the one in the photo taken by Fallon: bleached white skin, black eye sockets and grinning jaws defined by vertical red lines. Finally, a real explosion boomed out like a powerful grenade detonating in an enclosed space. A ball of orange light and a giant white smoke ring rolled up into the overhead lighting and brightened the night sky.

'Jesus,' said Rutherford, joining Travis and me. 'Is that fuckin' Ryder?'

'Uh-huh,' I said. It was either Ryder or a dead man. Come to think of it, perhaps it was both.

The audience was whooping and hollering as the music died down. The figure remained on stage, looking even more ominous in the growing silence. Then the lights were turned off and the stage went dark. Only when the crowd went completely manic did a single spotlight snap on. Ryder was gone. In his place stood Twenny Fo, and waves of adulation poured forth.

Whatever I thought of Fo and Leila as people – and so far I didn't think much of either – they burned hot in front of a crowd.

The rapper told them he thought they were one of the best crowds ever, if not the best. He said they were doing a great and worthy job of representing their country's values. Then he gave them a last wave, punched the air, and ran off into the wings.

The audience wouldn't stop chanting until the stagehands appeared and started packing up the equipment. Only then did the crowd begin to disperse.

Rutherford and I met up with Cassidy and West backstage, where our principals were having their egos stroked by Colonel Firestone and Colonel Biruta.

'Excuse me, ma'am,' I said, stopping Ayesha as she wandered past. I looked into her almond eyes for the first time. She wore tinted contact lenses to make them a bright blue, a striking contrast to her coal-black skin and white close-cropped hair. 'Have you seen Captain Ryder anywhere?'

'Calling me "ma'am" makes me sound like my grandmother,' she said with a smile. '*You* can call me Ayesha.' She touched my body armor with her finger. 'As for Duke, yes, he'll be out in a minute. Hey, I saw what you did out there – quick off the mark.'

'That's 'cause I gave him a shove,' Rutherford told her.

She smiled at us flirtatiously, then walked over to Leila. I noticed that Firestone had pulled Travis to one side, and the two were involved in a heated conversation. Firestone waved some papers at him.

'Man, what a rush!' said Ryder, who came up behind us.

His eyes were the size of dinner plates. One of them was still edged with black makeup and beneath his left ear was a patch of white he'd missed. I wanted to be mad at the guy, but he'd come here straight from a seat behind a battery-operated pencil sharpener at Andrews and probably didn't know any better.

'They pay you?' I asked.

'I did it for free. Why?'

'I was going to ask for my cut.'

'Can I have everyone's attention, please?' It was Travis, and he was standing on a box backstage. Everyone stopped what they were doing to listen. 'I know it's late and everyone wants to hit the hay, but Colonel Firestone has asked us all to assemble at the mess hall in ten minutes.'

'You know what this is about?' Rutherford asked me.

'Nope,' I said, but I had a suspicion that when I did find out, I wouldn't like it.

'So, if you could all make your way over there now . . .' Travis said.

Cassidy, West, Rutherford, Ryder, and I formed the standard loose diamond around the principals and their companions and headed over to the mess.

'You care to give us a preview?' I asked Travis when we caught up with him.

'There might be a change of plan,' he said.

'There *might*?'

'Okay, there *will*.'

'Surprise, surprise,' I said. 'Give it to me.'

'Sorry, Vin, but you'll have to hear it from the colonel – orders.'

Firestone was waiting with Biruta, Lockhart, and the two men from the Mercedes and their bodyguards. The tour arrived pretty much en masse, and then split into either Camp Leila or Camp Fo.

'The civilians with Firestone and Lockhart,' I said to Travis under my breath. 'What's their story?'

Before I could get an answer, Firestone held up his hands and said, 'People . . . can I please have everyone's attention?' He waited until the room had quietened down. 'A couple of items. First of all, congratulations to everyone for putting on such a wonderful show. It was a huge morale booster for the men, knowing that people of your caliber were prepared to come all the way to Africa just to entertain them. So, again, on behalf of the whole camp, thank you.'

A short round of self-congratulatory applause followed. I noticed that neither Twenny Fo nor Leila was clapping.

'Second, we've had a request from the French. Now the French – the folks who brought you in on their choppers – provide the lion's share of the UN peacekeeping force across the border in the Democratic

Republic of Congo. They've formally asked if you would be prepared, on your way home, to delay your trip by just one evening,' and he held up an index finger to underscore the point, 'to give a performance to their peacekeepers in Goma.'

Everyone looked at each other for a reaction.

'This has been on the cards from the beginning, hasn't it?' I whispered to Travis.

'Not as far as I knew,' he replied.

I stared at him.

'Okay, I apologize.'

'Not accepted.'

All I could do was shake my head. Arlen had assured me that PSO security issues would transcend all others. In this instance, a higher-up who spent most of his time with his lips on the rim of a cocktail glass had made a promise or repaid a favor and, if Fo and Leila agreed to the diversion, there was nothing I could say to stop it.

'The request has come through proper channels,' Firestone continued. 'And it's been given the green light by Washington and your respective management, but the decision is up to y'all, of course. Unfortunately, though, we must have your answer within the hour so we can pave the way with the French MONUC forces.'

The stagehands and dancers were mostly shrugging or nodding as they discussed it, their body language saying, 'What the hell . . . Why not?' I glanced at Leila. Her arms were folded, and there was a frown on her face. Seemed, for once, we were on the same page.

'Well, I'll leave y'all to talk it over,' Firestone said. 'And once again, thank you so much for the fantastic show.'

'What do you think?' Travis asked me.

'You know what I think.' Then I turned to Cassidy, West, Rutherford, and Ryder and said, 'Feel free to agree or disagree, but I say no.'

No one said yes.

'What's the problem?' asked Travis.

'There are only five PSOs providing protection for thirty people,' I answered.

'That's a big consideration, obviously.'

'Though not big enough, obviously. Leaving the numbers aside, we have no appreciation of what the situation is like in the DRC.'

'True,' he said.

But I knew he didn't care what I had to say. The only people he wanted to hear from were Leila and Twenny Fo. I was sure about Leila's position. Twenny Fo was the variable. My take on him was that he actually *wanted* to be here for reasons I didn't fully understand. Question was, did he want to be here *longer*?

The rapper turned and faced Leila, and once again their courtiers and hangers-on lined up against each other for a showdown.

'I have scripts to read, an album to cut. I'm leaving,' said Leila, loud enough to be heard throughout the room.

Twenny Fo walked over to her. 'C'mon, Leila. One day extra,' he said, 'That's all they askin'.'

'No,' she said, her weight on one leg, arms folded tightly across her chest.

'When we was together, we promised ourselves we would give somethin' back to our fighting boys,' Twenny pleaded. 'Come to Africa, make a contribution, and see where we come from. We were gonna tour, remember? And then our managements got involved, and it got whittled back and whittled back again, and then it was down to one concert. Now we got t' opportunity to do one more. It's jus' one more. The people here are makin' a sacrifice. What sacrifice we makin'?'

I was starting to wonder about Twenny Fo. Just maybe all the bad boy crap was record company marketing and there was more to Fo than he was prepared to admit in public. And then there was Peanut – the guy standing behind Twenny, chewing on a Mars Bar, barely engaged with the situation. The kid was plainly a float short of a raft, yet the rapper had taken him in and was looking after him.

Leila eyed her ex-boyfriend. 'Maybe if you hadn't got with that bitch from Electric Skank, or whatever they called, we'd have had us a different story here,' she said.

Shaquand said, 'Uh-huh.'

Ayesha said, 'You know it.'

'I didn't get with no one,' Twenny said, palms face up. 'You're talkin' about photos in a motherfuckin' magazine. They made somethin' innocent into somethin' else, you feel me? You know what they like.'

'I think you're lyin' to me like you always do.'

The rapper shook his head. 'C'mon, Leila. We're in Africa, baby. You ever gonna come back here?'

'I don' know why I came here in the first place.'

'We wuz asked. And we wanted to do some good. Just one more day.'

Leila shifted her weight to the other leg and placed a hand on her hip. 'No.'

'C'mon . . .'

'No.'

'Leila . . .'

The singer sighed heavily and looked up at the ceiling.

'It's only one more night,' he reminded her.

Something about her stance suggested that she might be wavering. 'One show. That's it. But you *owe* me.'

'All right!' Twenny exclaimed and stepped forward to embrace her. Leila held up a hand to palm him off.

'Don't think this changes anything 'tween us,' she warned him. 'And you can be sure I *will* collect.'

I pictured a couple of pounds of flesh.

'Sure, okay. But dis is *right*.' Twenny stepped back and went into a huddle with Boink and Snatch.

I could smell something coming, the scent building in strength the way a siren increases in volume the closer it gets.

'Excuse me, Colonel,' said Lockhart to Travis. 'There are some people I'd like you to meet. This is Piers Pietersen from Swedish American Gold. And this is Charles White.'

Pietersen was the tall guy with blond hair and blue eyes. White was black with a stocky Neanderthal physique and a heavy jaw that reminded me of Magilla Gorilla. Who were these guys? And who were their goons, a small posse of heavy-set knuckle-draggers of mixed genealogy who looked vaguely African but were probably from someplace else?

'Gentlemen,' Lockhart said, introducing the players and ignoring the hired help. 'This is Lieutenant Colonel Travis. The colonel was responsible for organizing the show you saw this evening.'

Handshakes ensued.

Then Lockhart noticed me standing next to Travis. 'Oh, and this is . . .' his eyes dropped to the name tape on my pocket, '. . . Cooper, rank unknown.' I saw his eyes snag briefly on my OSI patches before turning away. I didn't rate a handshake. He turned to Travis. 'If possible, Mr Pietersen and Mr White would like a word with Leila.'

'Leila would be delighted,' Travis said.

I wasn't so sure. Delight was not something I'd seen her do. But the special agent side of me was intrigued. Why was a guy from Swedish American Gold hanging around a US Army training base? Who was Mr White? And why were they buddies with Mr Kornflak & Greene? I followed them over to where Leila was standing, and Travis handled the introductions. The meeting was short. Leila claimed fatigue and a headache, delight eluding her, and Travis had a second concert to organize before he hit the sack. Tomorrow was going to be a big, bad day in a country I knew nothing about, except for the one comment Arlen had made about the Democratic Republic of Congo across the border being the problem child these days.

‘Merde’

'Aren't we supposed to be heading north-east?' I said into the microphone, looking over LeDuc's shoulder and checking our heading on the compass among the flight instruments.

The French pilot's now-familiar voice came through my headset over the cacophony of the Puma's whirling parts.

'There is a front all the way from Lake Kivu to Kigali, but a narrow band of clear weather is on the DRC side of the border. This is the best choice,' he said.

I'd been briefed that Goma was only a hundred klicks away and just inside the DRC, as Cyangugu was just inside Rwanda. The plan I agreed to was to fly parallel to the border heading generally nor' north east, keeping the aircraft within the relative safety of Rwandan territory and ducking across into the DRC only when we were adjacent to the MONUC encampment. Instead we were flying northwest across the border with the vast expanse of Lake Kivu away on our right when it should have been stretched out beneath us. A thick band of black cloud sat low over the lake and, to the east of its shoreline, gray wisps of rain hung from the underside of the cloud base like veils of a spider web. Flashes of lightning rippled through mighty thunderheads. Above us, however, the sky was a friendly late afternoon blue, the color mothers dress baby boys in. I conceded defeat. The flight path was the Frenchman's call, just as the security arrangements were mine. Supposedly.

'We won't arrive in twenty minutes' flying time. It will be closer to fifty,' said LeDuc.

At least Travis had listened to my request to cut the show down – an unplugged version of the one given at Cyangugu. So on this trip, there'd be no stagehands, no dancers, no pyrotechnics, and no Ryder stand-in. At first, Leila had put up a fight, but then Ryder had a word with Ayesha, who then fed it to Leila that she was the only entertainer the men really cared about seeing. Of course, the diva found this argument utterly convincing.

The retinue accompanying each star to Goma was now the problem. The person who seemed best able to handle Leila was Ayesha, which meant, as far as I was concerned, she got a golden ticket. Twenny Fo then insisted it was only fair that one of his entourage accompany him. He chose Boink, who, according to Leila, was really worth two people, given his size, which meant she could have Shaquand. The rapper then lobbied hard to bring Peanut; my take was that Fo wasn't too keen on leaving Peanut with Snatch unsupervised. Maybe he was concerned that his hair would get all braided up. Whatever, I agreed to the settlement on the condition that everyone got along, because we were all flying together in the one chopper. I amused myself with the thought that I could always throw the troublemakers out if I had to.

I watched the rainforest slide by under the Puma's front windshield, the mid-morning sun beating down through the break in the clouds. Below, the thick triple canopy reminded me of a lawn with lumps in it. I glanced at Travis, and he gave me a nod. Arlen had implied that Travis was the keeper of all information on this trip; in other words, he knew everything I didn't. Given that I knew dick, that made him a regular Einstein by comparison. I flicked a switch on the comm panel to have a private word with him.

'So, be honest, Colonel. When did you know about this Goma gig?' I asked him.

'It wasn't a firm arrangement. I was only told that it *might* happen.'

'And why were you told to say nothing about it?'

'Because it looked like Leila might say no to the whole trip if she got wind of it.'

'Which reminds me, the base at Cyangugu – that's supposed to be a secret, right? Why were she and Twenny Fo permitted into the inner circle?'

'They were approached by the Pentagon. I think the concert at Goma is what this gig was all about from the beginning. Promises had been made.'

'To the French?' I asked.

'Yeah, a peace offering.'

'I didn't know we were at war with them.'

'We're not – at least not at the moment. But we weren't on good terms here in Africa a little while back. Our Army shot at theirs during the Rwandan civil war and the French shot back.'

That was a new one on me. 'What do you know about Cyangugu and the army we're schooling there?' I asked.

'Not a lot. I'm PR, not foreign relations.'

'You'll know more than I do.'

'They told you. They're CNDP – National Congress for the Defense of the People.'

'Yeah, but *who* are they?'

'Ethnic Tutsi. Mostly drawn from tribesmen across the border in the Congo.'

'We're training Congolese soldiers in Rwanda who then go back across the border to fight in the DRC?'

'Their enemy is the Democratic Forces for the Liberation of Rwanda, otherwise known as the FDLR, the ones who fled Rwanda after the civil war. They're Hutus.'

'Sounds messy.'

'You don't know the half of it.'

'What about the civilians back there? Lockhart's friends. The Swedish guy from the gold company and his simian buddy – White, I think his name was.'

'Expat businessmen. Maybe they helped Lockhart get his job done down there.'

'What can you tell me about Goma?'

'The UN has twenty thousand peacekeepers in the DRC – it's their biggest peacekeeping force anywhere in the world, but they're largely ineffectual. The DRC's as big as Western Europe, and the UN would need four times that number to do the job. Goma was besieged several years back by the CNDP and things got ugly. I'm told that there are several big refugee camps there.'

'Besieged by the people we're training?'

'We weren't training them back then.'

A clusterfuck if ever there was one.

'Sorry about the obfuscation,' he added.

'Was OSI in on it?' I asked.

'No, not as far as I know. AFRICOM likes to keep everyone bumping into each other. They don't call this the "dark continent" for nothing.'

At least Arlen was off the hook.

'Well, if you don't mind,' he said, 'I'm going to try to get some shut-eye. It has been a long night.'

'Sleep tight,' I told him. I reached up and switched the intercom back.

Travis closed his eyes and rested his head against the quilted vinyl that lined the aircraft's insides.

'So, *Capitaine*. What's your base like?' I leaned forward and asked LeDuc, fighting a yawn. 'The facilities and so forth.'

'Goma – she is the Paris of small, muddy African bases,' he said, turning to grin at me.

'How does it compare with Cyangugu?'

'There is no comparison. Your camp is uncivilized. Where is the fresh bread? Where are the croissants? In the bakery department, I tell you, Americans do not know *merde* from clay.'

I twisted around and checked on the payload. Ayesha, Leila, and Shaquand were sitting shoulder to shoulder behind Travis. The singer and her girls were more sensibly dressed now, wearing US Army wet weather jackets and ball caps. Leila was asleep between Ayesha and

Shaquand, her head resting against her make-up artist's, wearing a Chanel eye mask and with yellow plugs in her ears. Across the aisle, Twenny Fo and Peanut were seated in one row with Boink behind them in a row to himself, lots of brand names and gold chains between them. Lined up across the back of the aircraft was the loadmaster whose name I couldn't pronounce, Cassidy, Rutherford, West and Ryder. Including myself, our party numbered twelve. Almost everyone behind me was either asleep or dozing. The POS-to-principal ratio wasn't ideal, but it was better than it might have been.

I took a deep breath, put my head back and closed my eyes.

'WHAT WAS THAT?' SAID a voice in my headset. The statement woke me up. Almost immediately after I opened my eyes, I felt g-forces load up, pushing me down into the seat. The aircraft was in a tight turn. I opened my eyes and saw that LeDuc and Fournier were talking heatedly to each other. I checked my watch. The mood on the flight deck had done a one-eighty from relaxed and cheery sometime in the last ten minutes. I leaned into the space between the pilots and flicked the comms switch. 'So how are we doing?' I asked them.

LeDuc ignored the question and snapped at the co-pilot. Then both of them began attacking a multitude of switches on the central and overhead consoles. And was that a warning bell I was hearing? I wasn't sure about the specifics, but a warning bell accompanied by a sea of red lights was a problem in any language, especially when it happened in a chopper at seven thousand feet.

The pilots worked fast, reading dials and throwing switches, trying to get on top of whatever the situation was. They got a massive hint when one of the engines suddenly flamed out.

Shit! 'Harnesses!' I shouted behind me. 'Check your harnesses!'

Through the headset and over the engine and rotor noise, I heard screams and shouting.

The aircraft lurched to one side; then the second engine coughed and backfired. The Puma was dropping into a spiral. LeDuc and Fournier were now shouting at each other – swearing or running checklists, I couldn't tell. The chopper tipped down into a spiral dive. Then the second turbine stopped completely. Now it was the loadmaster's turn to yell. My rough translation was that we were all going to die.

'Mayday Mayday Mayday,' yelled one of the pilots. 'MONUC flight zero six, MONUC flight zero six for Goma . . .'

Everyone in the chopper was screaming, but I switched off at that point and closed my eyes. Two chopper crashes I'd experienced in Afghanistan had prepared me for what would come next. At least I was strapped in this time. My head was pushed violently from side to side by the forces acting on the aircraft. The airflow shrieked. Correction – that was the girls.

I was suddenly jammed down into my seat. That meant the pilots had lift from the airflow rushing through the spinning main rotor; they still had some control. That was good news. We were slowing, the nose coming up. We were going to be okay.

And then we hit.

My head slammed forward into my chest. The harness compressed my ribcage in an instant and air blasted from my lungs. Through it all I heard crumpling sounds like a car in a compactor. All went quiet as the chopper dipped forward and back, rocking. Then something snapped and the helo plunged forward, nose down. A weight came crashing through the centre of the cabin – a person. Whoever it was smashed through the Perspex windscreen and vanished into the blackness below. The air filled with the smell of garden clippings as all manner of metal debris from the back of the aircraft hurtled past me. And then something—

I REGAINED CONSCIOUSNESS FACING downhill. The air in the cabin was filled with the smell of shredded leaves and the sound of warning bells. A headache thumped behind my eyes. I could hear people groaning. And then our world lurched again and dropped several feet with a tortured, gouging, scraping whine of metal under intense strain.

An object slapped me hard in the side of my face. I turned as far as the harness would allow and saw that the branch of a tree had speared through the observation window behind me.

I was coming to the conclusion that the ride hadn't quite finished when something else broke with a loud crack, and the Puma plunged, smashing through more branches, which obliterated most of what was left of the windshield. The nose of the aircraft hit something solid and immovable at an angle and the instant deceleration snapped my head forward again, the harness winding me a second time. And then, rolling slowly, the aircraft tipped lazily onto its side and came to rest like a large dead animal.

All motion ceased.

After a brief silence, people started groaning again.

I just sat, taking a moment to come to grips with what had happened. But then the smell of hot jet fuel permeated the shock and gave my brain a kick-start. *Get out get out get out* . . . I ripped off the headset and patted myself down, first mentally, then physically. All I found were bruises. Blood dripping on my shoulder caused me to look upward. I jumped up unsteadily. It was Travis, hanging out of the seat by his harness. A deep, ragged slice ran from his shoulder up the side of his head. Jesus . . . his skull was cracked open. I didn't need to check his pulse, but I did anyway, confirming that I hadn't needed to check his pulse.

Shaquand, Leila, and Ayesha were behind him, hanging down, also suspended by their harnesses. Ayesha and Leila had their hands over their mouths, screaming as the numbing effects of the wild ride they'd just survived wore off. I counted twelve PAX. The right number. So who'd gone through the windshield? I did a recount. Shit, of all people, it was the loadmaster. Either his harness hadn't been fastened properly, or it had failed. If anyone was a candidate for a broken harness, I figured it would have been Boink, but the big man was still buckled in, slowly shaking his head from side to side with his eyes closed, no doubt hoping this was all a bad dream.

In the back of the cabin, Cassidy dropped out of his seat onto Rutherford below him.

'Fuck,' I heard Rutherford say.

'Shaquand! Someone help her!' Leila screamed.

Ayesha was sobbing hysterically. Shaquand, seated beside Leila, wasn't moving. I stepped over to her, careful not to fall. The tree branch that had gone through the side of the Puma had impaled the woman through the collarbone and continued through the skin of the aircraft. Her eyes were open and placid. I closed them.

Blood had spattered over Leila's jacket. I checked the singer; she was all in one piece. I hit the harness release and supported her weight, then helped her down and out of the seat and sat her on the floor.

I checked Ayesha next. She was shaking but nothing was punctured or broken. I hit the release and lifted her down, her body racked with sobs.

'You're okay,' I told her. 'You hear me?' I rubbed her arms up and down. Her eyes looked into mine, and the sobbing ebbed. 'You need to focus so that we can get you and Leila out of here. She's going to depend on you, okay?'

Ayesha nodded.

I crouched in front of Leila.

'You all right?' I asked.

She gazed at me unresponsive, in shock.

LeDuc and Fournier fell out of the cockpit behind me. I turned briefly and saw LeDuc's face smeared with blood from injuries to his nose and mouth. The aircrew was damn lucky to be alive as the Puma's nose was flatter than a wristwatch, squashed from its impact with the ground.

'Get them out – hurry,' LeDuc gasped, breathless, coming up on all fours.

The smell of jet fuel was heavy in the air, overpowering. I scoped the situation. Getting out was easier said than done. At first glance, the Puma appeared to be a sealed coffin.

'*Le panneau,*' said LeDuc. 'The hatch.' He pointed at what was now the ceiling.

I left Leila with Ayesha, climbed up the floor, now a wall, then reached across and threw back the hatch's locking mechanism. Swinging out, I kicked the handle, hoping the door would slide open, but the rails it was mounted on were bent out of alignment. The hatch was jammed shut.

'Cassidy,' I called out. He stood, shaky on his feet.

I made a gesture that could loosely be interpreted as get your shit together. He nodded, gave Rutherford a hand out of his seat, then checked West and Ryder before coming forward to see how Twenny Fo, Boink, and Peanut were doing.

The rapper and Boink were moving their heads and arms slowly, their movements oddly disconnected from the situation, as if they were in zero gravity. Peanut appeared to be unconscious. West gave him a shake and he opened his eyes.

'C'mon,' I yelled at my team. 'Move it!'

The only exit possible was through the cockpit's smashed front windshield.

'There!' I pointed forward.

Rutherford scrambled past me, climbed into the cockpit over the center floor console and kicked out the remaining Perspex.

'Duke, you get the principals clear once they're outside,' I said, sending him through.

There was a lot of hot metal in those turbines. We didn't have a lot of time before this crate blew.

Cassidy lifted Leila in his arms and passed her through the limited space into Rutherford's waiting hands. Next was Ayesha. Twenny Fo pushed Peanut ahead and then jumped out after him. Boink climbed through the space on his hands and knees, but his gut became wedged between the pilot and co-pilot's chairs. Cassidy and I put a shoulder to each butt cheek and shunted him free.

'LeDuc, got a medical kit on board?' I asked the Frenchman.

'Down the back. I get it. You go. It is my ship. Henri and I are last off.'

Fournier agreed, grim-faced.

This was one argument I was happy to lose. I tapped Cassidy on the shoulder.

'Go!'

The big sergeant didn't need to be told twice. I had a last look at Shaquand and Travis. There was nothing we could do for them. I snatched off the colonel's dog tags and leaped after Cassidy. Stumbling over the windshield frame, I came down heavily onto the ground, which was covered by torn tree branches and shredded leaf litter. Lying beside me was the loadmaster who'd shot out of the Puma to his death. I got to my feet and looked down at him. The man's body was crumpled, his legs and arms splayed out at impossible angles. His eyes were open, and he'd bitten off the end of his tongue. I pulled his tags and stuffed them into my pocket.

Whump. Heat warmed the side of my face. A fire had burst into life on the far side of the chopper. Flames illuminated the metal around the main rotor housing. Hot kerosene fumes flooded my nostrils. The flames built quickly, searching for more fuel. Pretty soon they were going to find it.

'LeDuc,' I yelled into the chopper. 'Get out!'

I saw two desperate shadows tangling together as they scrambled into the cockpit. LeDuc shouted something at Fournier.

A small explosion shuddered the Puma's airframe and a cover blew off part of the fuselage. It spun through the air and smacked with a crumpling sound into a tree. A hand reached out of the cockpit. I grabbed hold of it and pulled, and Fournier tumbled clear, rolling some way down the hill.

The flames were rising ten feet into the air on the far side of the fuselage. The heat was now searing my skin. The tanks were going to blow any second.

'LeDuc!' I screamed into the chopper.

A white plastic case with a red cross on it flew through the opening, followed by a man. LeDuc. I grabbed him, took hold of his clothing and heaved him down the hill after Fournier. I took a running leap away from the wreckage at the instant the ground beneath my feet shifted. An explosion rent the air and a shockwave followed that lifted and hurled me down the hill into a screen of dense wet bush. Burning fuel fell around us along with chunks of metal. I covered my head beneath my arm and lay where I landed, waiting for the shower of metal and flaming jet fuel to bury me. Then my nose picked up something other than kerosene burning. I lifted my head. It was LeDuc. He was only a handful of feet away and his legs were on fire.

LeDuc jack-knifed when he realized that he'd become a Roman candle. He rolled and slapped at the flames while I jumped up and doused them with handfuls of wet leaf litter and earth.

When the flames were extinguished, we both lay there in the bush, exhausted, the fire-retardant flight suit protecting the French pilot's legs steaming and smoking along with my Nomex gloves. We caught our breath watching the chopper burn twenty meters up the hill, the heat from the inferno only just bearable.

I got to my feet eventually and held out a smoking hand to LeDuc.

'*Merci, mon ami*,' he said, hoisting himself up.

I handed him the tags taken from the dead loadmaster. LeDuc accepted them, unzipped a small backpack hanging off one shoulder and dropped them into it.

'Claude was a good man,' the Frenchman said. 'Married to a local woman in Goma. One child.'

The hill we found ourselves on was reasonably steep, about a forty-degree incline. Here and there were outcrops of wet black volcanic rock. The ground was a tangle of tree roots, mud and flint.

I heard a whistle and scoped around for its source. It was Ryder. He waved at us from thirty meters up the hill. I could just make him out through a tossed salad of palm fronds and snaking vines. I could also see Cassidy and West, but not Boink or Leila. Aside from the dense greenery, the fact it was dusk wasn't helping with the visibility. I looked up and a burnished sky twinkled like pale blue stars through the holes in the tree canopy. Technically, at least, it was still daytime up there. We'd come down on the side of a heavily wooded valley, more rainforest than jungle. Wet black tree trunks patched with lime-green moss mingled with various species of palms, or shrubs with broad, fleshy, boat-shaped leaves. Liana vines, the type Tarzan swung on, hung down everywhere, some with no apparent anchor point overhead. I took another look at the canopy. It was mostly a solid roof, except where a fallen tree had left an opening and the plant life had burst forth on the forest floor below it as if with a steroidal fury, each bush and shrub competing in a life and death struggle with its neighbor to claim the precious extra sunlight.

From the looks of all the broken tree limbs and shredded foliage lying around, the trees, many well over a hundred feet, had cushioned our fall and saved our lives, gloving the Puma like a big green catcher's mitt.

'French helicopters never go down, huh?' I said to LeDuc as I hoisted Fournier to his feet. Both pilots' faces were black with burned kerosene. Mine was probably the same.

'I think perhaps we took on dirty fuel,' he replied and then, with a shrug, added, 'Nothing we could do.'

'You could've checked it.'

'We did, of course.'

'Injured?' I asked Fournier, who was wincing.

'*Mon épaule,*' said the co-pilot. 'My shoulder. *C'est disloquée.*'

'Dislocated?'

'*Oui,*' said Fournier.

I checked the lieutenant's arm. It wasn't broken, but I could feel that the joint had sprung.

'I can put it back in,' I told him.

'Do it,' said Fournier with a nod, turning away.

I took hold of the forearm and put my thumb on the joint so that I could feel what was happening under the skin. He let out an extended grunt as I rotated his arm back and forth slowly and popped it back in.

'Rest it,' I told him. 'Nothing's broken. You should be able to use it again in a day or so.'

'*Merci, monsieur,*' he said, forcing a smile.

Picking our way up the hill, we came across the plastic medical case. The heat from the fire had distorted it on one side, but its contents were intact.

Further up the hill, Rutherford, Cassidy, and Ryder had gathered our principals together behind an ancient fallen moss-and-fungi-covered tree.

'How're we doing?' I called out as we approached.

Ryder was about to provide an answer when I heard Leila scream, 'I hate you!' Then I saw her pummeling Twenny Fo in the chest with her fists. 'This is your fault! Your fault! Shaquand would still be alive. I hate you!'

'I'm sorry. I'm sorry,' the rapper responded, 'She was good. I loved her like family. I'm sorry, yo.' He wrapped his former lover in his arms, and Leila stopped hitting him and merely sobbed, her shoulders heaving, but then she wrenched herself free and slapped him across the face as hard as she could.

'Ouch,' said Rutherford.

'I hate you,' she repeated in case he hadn't caught it the first two times, and then burst into tears and allowed herself to be embraced by Ayesha.

A little away from them, Peanut was standing and staring at the tree canopy. Beside him, Boink was rocking from side to side as if he'd lost his marbles. When I was a kid, I'd seen an elephant doing the same thing at the circus. The animal eventually broke its chain and sat on its handler, killing him. I hoped the big guy wasn't planning on sitting on anyone.

I could see that Ayesha had a cut on her forearm and that Peanut had a minor cut and Boink a more serious one. I handed the medical kit to Ryder and said, 'See what you can do with this, Duke.'

A couple of fat drops of rain landed on my face from above, the advance guard of a major assault from that quarter.

Great.

A peal of thunder rolled through the trees, and a downpour began to slant through the hole that our arrival had punched through the canopy. I heard a squeal from either Leila or Ayesha as they took cover in the lee of a tree trunk. This wasn't rain. These were half cups of ice-cold water dropped from a thousand feet. It was an attack.

Cassidy, down at the far end of the log, beckoned me with a signal.

'Listen,' he said.

It took a few seconds for my hearing to adjust so that the familiar sound of small arms fire could be heard within the fusillade of rain. The gunfire was coming from somewhere in front of us, beyond the burning chopper, and it was coming closer. My gut felt like an eel had been released into it.

A sudden flash of lightning lit up the trees and, a split second later, thunder burst over us with the boom of an artillery shell.

'LeDuc,' I called out, motioning for him to come down.

The Frenchman trotted toward us with his co-pilot following, the man's arm now in a sling.

'Who the hell's shooting at who?' I asked him.

'I don't know,' he said, his voice full of concern. 'There are at least six armies fighting each other in the DRC.'

'How many of them are friendly toward the UN?'

'Sometimes one, sometimes none.'

'You got a map?' I asked him. 'I'd like to know where shit creek is relative to Cyangugu.

'*Oui*,' he said, opening his pack. He pulled out a tactical pilotage chart and rested it on the log. 'We are here,' he said, pointing to a spot on the chart along a line drawn with a grease pencil. Rainwater pooled in the map's creases, and then ran off its plastic-coated surface.

'You get a response from the Mayday call?'

'*Non*,' he said.

Conventional wisdom said to stay with the downed aircraft, but it appeared that we'd had the extra bad luck of coming down in the middle of an argument that was being settled with cordite and lead. Conventional wisdom didn't take that fairly major detail into account.

LeDuc produced an emergency locator beacon, or ELB, from his pack.

That was good news.

Just then a sudden *whoosh* of a shell arced overhead, fired from somewhere behind us. Mortar fire. The round burst out of sight further down the hill.

And just like that, the good news ended.

'Jesus, where the hell have you put us down?' Rutherford shouted at LeDuc over the thunder, just so the Frenchman knew who was to blame.

Then a rocket-propelled grenade came out of nowhere, ripped through the air and exploded inside the Puma, sending a fireball into the treetops.

'Shit,' West exclaimed. 'Where did that come from?'

Behind us, Leila and Ayesha were shrieking, their hands over their ears.

'Quiet!' I shouted at them. They ignored me.

I signaled Ryder and pulled my finger across my throat, telling him to silence them any way he had to. He pulled the women to the ground and put his arms around them. Twenny Fo, Boink, and Peanut dropped to their knees where they stood. Cassidy, Rutherford, and West had taken up firing positions, sighting their M4s on the forest downhill, covering any approach from that direction.

Men's voices were calling out from the forest below the burning Puma. They were whooping and hollering. I couldn't understand the language, but it was full of bloodlust.

'Ammunition?' I asked Cassidy.

'Standard loadout,' he said. 'Same as the others. I already checked.'

That meant four magazines each for the M4s, two spares for the side-arms, Sigs for Ryder and me, Berettas for the Army guys. No frag, no smoke. *Shit*.

Our position was roughly forty feet up the hill from the blazing helicopter.

'There's a lot of lead being passed around. Could even be company strength down there – a hundred or so men,' said Cassidy, assessing. 'Assault rifles, light machine guns. RPGs we know about, grenades we don't, but only because, so far, no one's tossed one. At least, not at us.'

Men surged through the trees, firing wildly into the aircraft wreckage.

'Who else flies Pumas in this part of the world?' I asked LeDuc.

'Only MONUC – the UN force.'

'Looks like you've really built some bridges in these parts,' I said.

More mortar rounds began dropping into the trees downrange, beyond the Puma's remains.

'And where's that coming from?' West wondered aloud.

'The ridgeline, I'd say,' Cassidy reasoned. Several rounds hit the trees and airburst over their position. A whirling thrash of metal fragments stripped off the leaves and caused men to go down screaming.

'Let's go,' I said.

'Where to?' Cassidy gave me a look that said he needed an answer before he'd do anything.

'We can't go down the hill and heading up's probably not an option till we know who's there. So do we slide left or right? We've got three right-handed shooters and one lefty – you. I say we head right so that the majority of us can shoot downhill across our bodies, if we have to, without having to turn before firing. We traverse till we make the ridge-line on our flank and rely on LeDuc's ELB to get us a dust off.'

'What if the threat comes from the high side?' Cassidy said.

'You're the lefty,' I said, keeping things light. 'I'm counting on you.' I nodded at his M4. 'You *can* use that thing, right?'

'Done much field work in your time, Major?' he retaliated.

'Some,' I said.

'The mission's changed. No one's gonna think any less of you if you hand off responsibility in this situation.'

'You mean hand it off to you?' I asked him.

He shrugged.

So here it comes, the macho SOCOM bullshit. And where was Ryder to keep him in line like Arlen had said he would?

'We've got a couple of principals to deliver in one piece,' I said. 'I can't see what's changed.'

He shrugged again. 'Okay, sir, your way. Just trying to help out.'

'You think there's a problem with the plan?'

'I got no mind to change it.'

The small arms fire had tapered off somewhat, as had the mortar shelling. The thunderstorm, however, had only been warming up. There was lightning every second or less, and the rain had gone from heavy to blinding. I signaled Ryder to gather the principals and bring them down to us.

Thirty seconds later, we were huddled in a circle behind the log, Rutherford and West keeping watch.

'Anyone got a cell phone?' I asked. Mine was now a liquid somewhere inside the Puma.

Leila pulled out a personalized rose-gold iPhone from her jacket pocket. Ayesha, Boink, Ryder, Cassidy and Rutherford also produced cells.

'Anyone raising a signal?' I asked.

Six heads shook.

I moved on. 'Who has serious injuries that need further attention?'

No one piped up. I saw that the gash on Ayesha's arm now wore a bandage, as did a cut on Boink's hairline. Both cuts seeped blood.

'Your arm. You doin' okay?' I asked Fournier.

He nodded.

Ayesha's chin quivered and Leila's makeup needed emergency treatment. Boink seemed a little more present than he had been, but Peanut was still off on some other planet beyond our solar system. I envied him.

I came straight to the point. 'We're vacating this area immediately, walking in that direction,' I said, indicating with a hand signal, 'keeping the low side of the hill on our left. We appear to have landed in the middle of a disagreement. We have no intelligence on the forces below us or further up the hill. We have no radio either, so we can't identify ourselves as friends or neutrals to the folks doing the shooting. But we have a map, and we know our position. Now all we have to do is get to a clearing where the electronic homing beacon can tell the MONUC rescue choppers where to find us. And I'm confident that by this time tomorrow we'll be turning our noses up at snails in the French compound. Everyone clear?'

Leila and Ayesha looked at me, their eyes wide with terror. Twenny Fo had his arm around Peanut. Boink stared at me, frowning. I noticed for the first time that he'd somehow managed to hang onto that bowler hat of his, pulling it down so that it covered his bandage. Barely perceptible nods from all but Peanut made me think that maybe the principals had actually taken in what I'd said. I demonstrated a few simple hand signals and got everyone up on their feet. And that's when I froze. Nervous young soldiers with full automatic weapons had surrounded us. The raging storm and small arms fire had concealed the sound of their encirclement, and their line of approach had been outside Rutherford and West's line of sight. Leila and Ayesha started screaming. The Africans closed in, yelling. One of them slapped Leila backhand across the face, which stopped her screaming and also silenced Ayesha. I counted ten men.

LeDuc began plying them with French. I heard the word 'MONUC' mentioned several times, along with the word 'allies'. He was telling them that we were supposed to be pals.

One of the Africans responded by giving him a friendly jab in the ribs with the stock of his AK-47, which doubled the Frenchman over in pain. Fournier went to help his *capitaine* and took a rifle butt to the head, which put him on his knees.

Cassidy took his hands off his M4 and raised them behind his head.

It wasn't one of the signals I'd demonstrated to our civilians, but they got the message anyway and followed suit.

A soldier a little older in years than his comrades barked an order and our weapons were stripped from us. One of the others went around and checked that our fingers were interlocked behind our necks.

The soldier giving orders walked over to Cassidy, flicked with a broken fingernail at the Stars and Stripes patch on his shoulder, and said, 'American.' He said it with interest, as if Cassidy was from an intriguing species that would look good stuffed and mounted over a fireplace.

'You speak English?' I asked him.

'*Tais-toi!*' the African shouted.

'That's a no then,' I said.

'He wants you to shut up,' LeDuc whispered.

The officer – at least, I assumed that's what he was – hit LeDuc in the side of the head, knocking him down. The ELB fell out of his hand. The officer bent over and picked it up. He examined it, then threw it back on the ground and stomped on it a couple of times till the plastic casing disintegrated, revealing a smashed circuit board.

One of the soldiers pushed me in the back to get my feet going, then shoved me a second time. They were marching us down the hill in a loose column. At the head of the column I saw West lower one of his hands, testing the rules. A soldier kicked him hard in the leg. The African then aimed his weapon at West's head, which had the effect of making the sergeant duck into a half crouch as if he were expecting a bullet.

The Africans laughed at him.

Yeah, hilarious.

A bolt of lightning lit up the area for the briefest instant, freezing the moment like a snapshot. Thunder rolled right on top of it, another bursting artillery round. The rain pelted the ground and broke into a mist that rose as if the earth itself were exhaling.

Sporadic fire was still coming from the area below the wreckage. I doubted the ELB would have been able to get its signal through the electrical storm anyway, which meant the MONUC air traffic controllers at Goma International Airport only had an approximation of our last position, the one the pilots would have given in the Mayday call, assuming we were high enough for them to have had it received.

I drank the kerosene-tasting water streaming down my face and wondered what would happen to us once this unit met up with the people who'd popped a rocket into the chopper. I was prepared to bet that at the bottom of the list would be a Napoleon brandy, a croissant and a ride back to Cyangugu. As I saw it, we didn't have much of a window here. We had to act before too many more soldiers became involved, and the odds went from bad to zip-me-in. And, while I knew this with absolute certainty, I hesitated. *The majority of organized attacks are successful; the bodyguards usually die; the bodyguards rarely fire their weapons effectively, if at all; the bodyguards almost never affect the outcome of the attack.*

As I was thinking this, I saw the briefest flutter of something black flying through the air. It alighted on the back of the head of one of the Africans accompanying the column. Was it a bat? I peered at it hard. No, Jesus, it was a black throwing knife, barely visible against the victim's black hair. The blade was embedded in the man's skull just above the juncture of the spinal column and the base of his brain. There was nothing accidental about the target area. Whoever threw it knew exactly where to put it. The man began stumbling like he was drunk. Then he collapsed right in front of me, tripping me up so that I fell forward, out of control. As I went down, I grabbed the first thing I saw – the barrel of a rifle beside my face and pulled it down. The stock at the other end swung around and smacked into the mouth of the soldier holding it. His finger, caught inside the trigger guard, caused the weapon to fire off a three-round burst, which shot the kneecap clean off the soldier walking ahead of me, and he went down with a scream.

The next four seconds were a blur.

Cassidy swung his arm into the head of the distracted soldier closest to him, crashing the point of his elbow with ruinous force into the soft temple area. The man crumpled to the ground like an old suit slipped off its hanger. West turned to the guard beside him and buried his forehead in the guy's face, smashing his cheekbone with a crack that reminded me of the sound the Puma made when it hit the tree. Then Rutherford took on his guard with a shoulder charge, propelling him into a tree trunk. And when he bounced off it, the SAS sergeant completed the move with a palm thrust to the throat that crushed the man's windpipe.

I turned around in time to watch Leila using her fingernails to rake the face of the African struggling to hold her. The man howled and let go of her and covered his face with his hands as he ran – unfortunately for him, straight into Boink. The man mountain lifted him into the air, one hand on the African's back and the other on his head. He then twisted his head, instantly breaking the man's neck, and threw the body aside like a bag of trash. It landed beside LeDuc, who was face down in the mud – either dead or out for the count, I couldn't tell which – but the soldier accompanying him was nowhere to be seen.

'Ayesha! No!' Leila cried out and started running down the hill. A shadow picked itself up off the ground and tackled her before she'd taken more than half a dozen steps. It was Ryder. The two thrashed around, a tangle of arms and legs, Leila going for the agent's eyes with those nails of hers until she understood who it was.

Movement down the hill caught my attention. I realized that the gun I'd grabbed was in my hands, and the Africans were running away. We couldn't allow them to regroup, inform on us and bring reinforcements. So I found targets, fired once, twice, and two men dropped to the ground as if their shoelaces were suddenly tied together. Sighting the rifle left and right, I counted four more soldiers, including the officer – all of them backing away toward the exploded Puma. But these guys weren't running, they were taking it slow. And I couldn't shoot them, on account of they were holding Twenny Fo, Peanut, Fournier, and Ayesha in front of them, using them as human shields.

Hostage

'We have to get them back!' Leila demanded. 'Twenny Fo, Ayesha, Peanut, the other pilot . . . You can't leave them!'

'We have to get out of here *now* is what we have to do,' I told her.

'That's bullshit, man,' said Boink, his fat forefinger stabbing the front of my body armor. 'Give *me* a gun and I'll go down there and fuck their shit up.'

'Ryder!' I called over my shoulder.

'Here,' he said, right behind me.

I turned three-quarters and saw him rubbing a bloody wound on his head.

'You okay?' He'd received a rifle butt from the departing Africans that had knocked him out cold.

'Yeah.'

'Get the principals secured further up the hill, then sit down for a while,' I told him.

'What about Ayesha?' Ryder asked, his voice cracking.

I faced him and said quietly, an inch from his face, 'Duke, head 'em up the hill to that tree.' I indicated the one I meant, a tree with a vast splay of roots, like a cage that seemed to drop from branches high above the forest floor.

'People everywhere are gonna know what kind of man you are, Cooper,' Leila hissed, her face disintegrating as she began to cry, the hopelessness of the situation getting its hooks into her. 'Coward,' she spat, and it was like the word itself landed in the mud at my feet.

Ryder hesitated and looked into my face before deciding further conversation probably wasn't a good idea, and then herded Leila and Boink up the hill. Coward. I wasn't going to let it get under my skin. Our survival chances were diminishing moment by moment. There was only unavoidable unpleasantness ahead.

'LeDuc!' The Frenchman materialized at my shoulder as I walked to the African whose kneecap had been shot off. 'They speak French here, right?'

'*Oui*,' he said.

We walked several paces and I waited for the plea to rescue his co-pilot.

'Do not worry about Fournier, he is a survivor,' LeDuc said, surprising me.

'I need you to translate,' I told him.

Sergeant Cassidy was patting down one of the dead Africans. He was wearing the man's green beret and held up my Ka-bar as we walked by.

'Yours, I think,' he said.

I took it and sheathed it.

'And we've got our M4s back,' he said as he turned the man's head to one side. The metal haft of the anodized black throwing knife was sticking out of the corpse's skull, covered in mud and streaked with blood and brains. Cassidy pulled his Ka-bar and gave the embedded blade a few taps left and right to loosen it before attempting to pull it out. He'd done this before, obviously. Jerking the blade free, he wiped it clean on his leg and then scraped the goop off his pants and flicked it onto the ground. He replaced the knife in a scabbard hidden in the top of his body armor, right where he'd submissively clasped his fingers before being asked to do so by our captors.

'Insurance policy,' he said, adjusting its position.

'We move out in three minutes,' I told him. 'Pass it on.'

Rutherford and West were also checking the dead and wounded and stripping the corpses of anything useful.

LeDuc and I approached the African writhing slowly in the mud, making noises like a wounded animal, his bloody, mangled leg cramped rigid in front of him. The guy was small, in his late teens with a youthful beard, a front tooth missing and its partner brown with rot.

'You told me there were six armies fighting in the Congo,' I said to LeDuc. 'Ask him which one's his.'

'I don't need to ask him this. The blue patch on the shoulder of his uniform tells me that he is FARDC – *Forces Armées de la République Démocratique du Congo*. These are DRC government troops.'

'I thought you said the DRC army was on your side?' I asked him.

'Generally speaking, yes.'

'When you told them that you were MONUC, what was their reaction, apart from encouraging you with a rifle butt to shut your mouth?'

'They said they knew this.'

'That you were allies?'

'*Oui*.'

'Funny way to treat a friend.'

'The FARDC is not an army like we have in France. It is corrupt. There are many factions and agendas. You want me to ask him why they are not friendly toward us?'

'First ask him what his unit strength is.'

LeDuc kneeled and spoke to the man in French. The soldier ignored the question. LeDuc persisted and still got no response. The man was either so deeply in pain that he'd lost touch with the real world, or he was using it as an excuse to play dumb. There was no time for games.

'Sir, I think this is yours,' said West behind me. He handed me my Sig. 'A full mag, nothing up the spout,' he informed me before walking back to see to the dead.

I dropped out the magazine and then pulled back the slide. As he said, the chamber was empty, the mag full. I reinserted the mag, racked a round into the spout and put the safety on.

The man on the ground cried out. He was shaking, his eyes locked on the Sig. And then he started talking like his life depended on it. Maybe that's exactly what he thought, that I was going to bust a cap in his ass. I holstered the weapon.

LeDuc repeated the question. Now the guy wouldn't shut up. He shouted, his voice competing with the noise of the thunder and torrential rain.

'They are company strength,' LeDuc said. 'He is not exactly sure how many, but more than one hundred and twenty men.'

'Ask him who occupies the ridgeline. Who are they fighting up there and why?'

A handful of seconds later, LeDuc had the answers.

'It is the CNDP. The numbers are similar, though the rebels have mortars, causing his unit much harm. He says they chased the CNDP out of a village a day's march away. They were killing civilians. He says they are bad men.'

'Do you believe him?' I asked.

LeDuc gave me the Gallic shrug. 'This man is a private soldier. What would he know?'

'Ask him why they blew up your chopper.'

The Frenchman asked the question, and the African pleaded with LeDuc in a way that I knew meant he didn't have an answer, despite his private fear that I was going to whack him if he didn't.

'He says he doesn't know,' LeDuc confirmed. 'He thinks it was fired on for target practice.'

'There's lot of rainforest out there, but his patrol found us quickly. Ask him if they were looking for us.'

'*Oui, oui,*' the man said immediately, adding a barrage of French to go with it.

'He says their orders were to find us and take us prisoner.'

'How did they know there was anyone on board to take prisoner in the first place?'

LeDuc asked the question and the man on the ground shook his head and mumbled a reply.

'He does not know,' said the Frenchman. 'They were just doing what they were ordered to do.'

Hmm . . . maybe it was just expected that an aircraft the size of the Puma would be carrying passengers, more than they found dead in the wreckage. I had one more question. 'How long is FARDC going to occupy the valley?'

After a brief discussion the Frenchman said, 'Once they have chased the enemy from the heights.'

I didn't like their chances of that. Armed as they were with mortars, the folks occupying the high ground would take some dislodging.

I stood and LeDuc stood.

Two shots blasted away behind me, making me jump back and twist around and reach for my own pistol.

Boink lowered a Beretta.

'*Merde!*' LeDuc exclaimed.

'You're finished with him, yo?' my principal said.

I looked back at the captured FARDC soldier. Smoke curled from two black entry holes in the man's forehead, blood starting to well from both; one eye was open and sightless, the other half hidden by a heavy lid. I tried not to think that the kid had a mother – we'd gone way past that now.

Further up the hill, I saw Leila lower her iPhone from her face. Her other hand covered her mouth, horrified by what she'd just witnessed, her eyes locked on me like somehow it was my doing.

'What the fuck?' I shouted at Boink. 'Give me the gun!'

He stood there, unmoving, the pistol pointed at the ground. He was considering holding onto it, or maybe even using it again . . .

'We killed their people already,' he said. 'There won't be no peace accord, yo.'

'Give me the damn gun!' I repeated, taking a step toward him, hand out.

He brought the pistol up. I didn't know this guy, but I'd seen what he was capable of doing. Was it my turn next?

'Careful,' I told him.

'Easy, soldier man,' he said, reading the danger.

He flicked his hand and the weapon spun in midair and landed in his palm, handle out toward me. I snatched it away from him.

'What the hell do you think you're doing?' I asked him, pointing at the dead man with the pistol.

'Doin' my job.'

'Your job?'

'His people took Twenny. I took him.'

'Do that again and there'll be consequences.'

He shrugged and turned away.

When their people came back and saw the man's head resting on a pillow of his own gray matter, they'd know he'd been killed in cold blood. This would come back on us. I leant over the body, patted him down. Two magazines were stuffed into the webbing on his chest. I took them and checked his pockets. Empty. His green battle uniform was baggy, from the Vietnam War era and several sizes too big for him. And there was the unusual blue patch on his left shoulder that LeDuc said marked him as FARDC. I stood up.

Rutherford and Cassidy were checking the other downed Africans.

'Any wounded?' I called out.

Cassidy shook his head.

'We're gonna have to watch him,' said West motioning at Boink's back.

'Yeah,' said West. He stood and nodded at the rifle slung over my shoulder.

I looked at it properly for the first time, wiped the blood and saliva off the stock with my sleeve. The weapon was a Nazarian Type 97, the export version of the standard assault weapon issued to infantry units of the Chinese People's Liberation Army: 5.56mm NATO rounds, M16 mag, single shot, three-shot burst, and full auto options at the flick of a lever on the receiver. A good and capable rifle. It might have been the export version, but I still wondered where someone would come across a weapon of this sort in the Congo.

'Found this on the ground,' said Cassidy, interrupting my thoughts.

Twenny Fo's diamond ring was between his thumb and forefinger. 'What you want to do with it?'

'Hold onto it for the moment.' I turned to Rutherford. 'Souvenir a few of those uniforms with the blue shoulder patches. The berets too. They might come in handy.'

'Got it, skipper,' said Rutherford.

Although barely ten minutes had passed since Twenny Fo, Ayesha, Peanut and Fournier had been taken prisoner, I expected another, larger patrol would be along soon to finish the job, assuming the FARDC was organized.

West, Cassidy and I trotted up the hill toward Ryder, Leila and Boink.

'I'm going to make sure you're all kicked out of the Army,' said Leila when we were close enough. 'Your job was to protect us and you failed.'

I wasn't *in* the Army but maybe now wasn't the time to tell her.

'You still alive, ain't you?' said Cassidy.

'I'm going to sue you to the poor house,' Leila said, her eyes boring into Cassidy and then me.

It wasn't the right time to tell her I was already in it. 'We didn't cause that to happen,' I told her, slipping into debrief mode. 'The soldiers that took our people are government troops of the Democratic Republic of the Congo, supposedly friendly to MONUC. But for some reason they've decided to be *un*friendly. What we do know is that we've come down in a war zone where there doesn't seem to be a lot of rules. Bottom line, we're no longer protecting you against possible attack. There's nothing *possible* about it. So you can stop behaving like a child who isn't getting her way and do what we tell you to do, when we tell you to do it. Because, otherwise, you're not getting out of here alive.'

'I ain't listenin' to this bullshit,' said Leila, turning away and holding her hand palm out at me as if to deflect my words.

I wondered what to do next – our options were limited and diplomacy wasn't my strong suit. We needed our principals' cooperation to have a chance of bringing them out in anything other than body bags.

I glanced at Cassidy. 'You got that ring?'

He fished around in his webbing and put it in my hand.

'Recognize this?' I asked the diva. 'We found it on the ground.'

'It's Deryck's.'

'Who's he?'

'That's Twenny Fo's name. I gave it him when we were . . .' Her chin dented, and she looked skywards briefly in an effort to get control of herself.

I put the ring in the side pocket of her Army jacket. 'You hold onto this for . . . Deryck. Give it back to him when you see him next. Now, let's go.'

'If we leave now, I'll never see him, or Ayesha, or Peanut, ever again.' Leila's emerald eyes were glossy with tears. She sat down on the wet earth and wrapped her arms around her legs. 'Say what you like, but I ain't leavin' here without them.'

'Jesus Christ,' I muttered, scraping the bottom of the options barrel. 'LeDuc. Do we have sedatives in that medical kit that we can administer with a hypodermic?'

'*Oui*.'

'Then rack it up.' I looked down at the woman. 'Ma'am, we're gonna have to carry you out.'

'Not unless you gonna carry my ass too, yo,' said Boink. He moved to stand beside the singer and crossed his massive arms in a further symbol of defiance.

That was it. I had no more cards to play. The rulebook had nothing on this. I took a deep breath and let it out. 'Okay, you win. We stay. But, just so you have all the facts, there are about a hundred and twenty soldiers down there, who seem intent on taking us captive for purposes unknown. Their people were killed on their first attempt at this, and you can be sure we won't get a pat on the back for that. So, fortunately, with the additional weapons we've secured, we have enough guns to arm everyone. But our ammunition is limited. If the bad guys attack in strength we can probably hold out for ten minutes, maybe less, depending on how many of us get killed or wounded in the initial exchange, and how bad the wounds are. There's going to be a lot of lead flying around, so perhaps ten minutes is optimistic. The electronic beacon we had is smashed, so our people in Cyangugu and LeDuc's in Goma don't know for sure where we've come down. What I'm saying is, there'll be no last-minute rescue. Our bodies may never be found. Leila, if you happen to survive and they capture you, my suggestion is that you tell them you're a rich and famous star who'll pay millions for your release. Assuming they go for that, rather than using you for some other purpose – and I think you know which one I mean, which they may do anyway – when you finally get in front of those TV cameras, you can tell the world that your security team fought bravely and died so that you could keep making music videos.'

I was rambling because I was angry. In truth, I was on the verge of defaulting to my duty as the officer in charge and doing what was best for the men I was commanding, which, at the very least, was to vacate the area as soon as possible. If it meant leaving the civilians behind to accept whatever fate they were determined to meet, I didn't see that I had much choice but to let them do exactly that.

Leila stood up. 'I want you to know that this is not about making music, this is about *not* giving up on the people you love.' She brushed the wet leaves off her butt and pulled the Army ball cap down low over her face. 'Now, which way are we going?'

'That way,' I said, stunned by the sudden change of heart. Maybe my little speech had gotten through to her. I pointed in the opposite direction to the one we'd initially decided to take before we were surrounded. 'Any movement?' I asked West.

'*Nada,*' he replied.

'Rutherford?'

'Clear.'

'Let's do it,' I said.

There was very little light left. Walking in this terrain in the pitch dark was also a big risk. We could stumble into an ambush or walk off a cliff. Lex Rutherford took point, with Cassidy behind him and the rest of us lined up behind them. I brought up the rear. We learned that the hill the Puma came down on was actually part of a valley that curved horseshoe-like around to the northwest on one side and southwest on the other. The walk was taking us away from Lake Kivu and Cyangugu. We picked our way through the rainforest for half an hour, by which time the thunder and lightning were only sporadic, and the small arms fire was far enough away that it sounded like corn popping in a pot with the lid on. I called a halt between a couple of vast trees that gave us cover on two sides, then kicked off the discussion we had to have. Cassidy and Ryder took the watch this time, but the space between the trees was tight, so they weren't left out of the conversation.

'A hundred and twenty of them. Five of us,' I said.

'I ain't running,' Boink said.

'Who said anything about running?' I responded.

Leila, looking at me as if she were witnessing a spectacular sunrise, said 'So you're *not* running out on Deryck and Ayesha and Peanut and the pilot?'

'Let's be clear. A hundred and twenty-odd to five are big odds,' I said.

'That all? Those fuckers are in a shitload of trouble,' said West over his shoulder.

I'd wondered which of the SOCOM boys would turn into John Wayne.

'I ain't never lost a principal before,' said Cassidy. 'Don't want to start now.'

John Wayne had a brother.

Ryder chewed his bottom lip.

'On the basis of the enemy of my enemy is my friend,' said Rutherford, 'what about the other side – the opposition up the hill? Might they be inclined to lend us a little assistance?'

Cassidy's eyes were black caves and his face had the luster of polished wet granite. 'The hostages are alive . . . for now. But we wait, they die.'

'LeDuc, what do you think?' I asked.

'Up there, on top of the hill, according to the FARDC soldier, they are Laurent Nkunda's rebels – your allies, the CNDP. But these men are also often no better than murderers and rapists. Our source was just a private soldier. What would he know? It *could* be the FDLR up there – the Democratic Forces for the Liberation of Rwanda. Or even the Lord's Resistance Army, from Uganda, that kills in the name of Christ. They could also be Mai-Mai militia. Or they could be just another unit of FARDC settling an old score,' he said, using two fingers across his blackened forehead like they were windshield wipers to flick away the water and sweat.

I had the picture of a lunatic walking up to half a dozen large bears and kicking all of them in the shins. 'Back it up a second,' I said. 'Who's this Nkunda guy? I thought our allies were part of some National Congress.'

'Yes, the *Congrès National Pour la Défénse du Peuple*. Or as you English say, the National Congress for the Defense of the People. CNDP for us. NCDP *pour vous* – the soldiers you are training across the border in Rwanda. Laurent Nkunda was a general in FARDC, the army of the DRC, but he rebelled, took his best units, and continued to fight the remnants of his enemies, the Rwandan Hutus, who fled the 1994 Rwandan genocide and set up camp in the east of the DRC. That is what the CNDP claims, but the wider truth is that the CNDP is in the Congo to protect Rwanda's interests here, which are also America's interests. That is why the CNDP are your country's allies – at least for the moment. Those were the soldiers you met at the base in Cyangugu, the ones commanded by Colonel Olivier Biruta and his second in command, Commandant Jean Claude Ntahobali.'

'So where is this Nkunda?' I asked.

'Under arrest. Held in Rwanda on charges of murder and other crimes. But he will never come to trial.'

'Because?'

'Because he is an embarrassment to the DRC, Kigali and Washington.'

'Okay, well . . . are any of these armies, rebels or otherwise, likely to help us?' I asked, getting us back on track.

'In the DRC, especially here in Nord-Kivu province where there is so much wealth, it is impossible to say.'

The complication of who was who in this fucked-up zoo was exasperating. 'But, in your experience, is it worth taking the risk to find out?'

He shrugged; something, it seemed to me, this Frenchman did almost as often as breathing. 'Perhaps *oui*, perhaps *non*. They might also kill you just for the fun of it.'

'They'd be jumping the queue,' I said.

'What kind of wealth are we talking about?' asked Rutherford.

'There is Coltan.'

'Doesn't he fight Batman, or someone?' I said.

'Columbite-tantalite – "Coltan" for short. It is a rare mineral used to make electronic printed circuit boards. You cannot make a computer without it. This part of the Congo has the world's largest deposits. Gold – there is very much of that here, also.'

'So we've established that everyone is killing everyone in this little enchanted forest. And that it's probably over Apple Macs and bullion. Back to our principals. What are we going to do about them? Any suggestions?'

'We need to recon the enemy's position,' said Cassidy, checking his weapon. 'What's their morale like? Are they vulnerable to a night attack? How do they have our principals guarded?'

The sergeant was on the money. Once we had a better feel for the situation, we could take action or not.

'Agreed,' I said. 'Volunteers?'

'I'm in,' said Ryder.

'I'm coming,' said Boink.

'*Moi aussi,*' said LeDuc, raising his hand.

Cassidy, West and Rutherford all nodded.

'Duke, I need you to stay and guard Leila.'

'I want to be there for Ayesha, Vin,' said Ryder, his chin jutting forward.

'I need you here, Duke,' I repeated, making it an order. The truth of it was that I didn't want Ryder anywhere near a mission like the one on the table. Wanting to go, no matter how desperate the desire, didn't cut it. The guy didn't have the required combat skills, simple as that. His lack of experience could get himself and the people with him killed. Still, Ryder was far from happy about this.

'You're not coming either, big guy,' I told Boink.

'You gonna stop me?' he said, taking a step toward me.

I stood my ground. 'If I have to.'

He stood his.

I tried a different approach, risky though it was, and handed him the Type 97 I was holding. 'Look, Boink, I need you here with Ryder. So, I'm going to give you one of these. I'm assuming you know your way around a carbine.' This was tricky but there simply weren't enough PSOs. If we could trust Boink, arming him would be an asset. Given what I knew he was capable of, though, it was a big if. He pointed the weapon in my general direction; not the reaction I'd been hoping for. I didn't move, held my breath.

'Bin around guns all my life, yo,' he said, his finger slipping inside the trigger guard. There was nothing in his face that I could read. Not so smart after all, Cooper, I told myself. No one moved. This could go badly for me. I wondered if my body armor would stop a round fired from a rifle at point blank range. I tensed. But then Boink raised the weapon to give it a closer inspection and the world started breathing again, or perhaps it was just me.

'So who's got recent jungle experience?' I asked, moving on. 'Anyone?'

West gave me a nod. 'Sir, post before last I was instructing at the Jungle Warfare School at Fort Sherman down in Panama,' he said, keeping one eye on Boink as he moved the selector on his M4 to safety. A tragedy had been averted. 'That count?'

'It'll have to do,' I said, giving him a grin.

'What experience *you* got, Major?' Cassidy asked.

He had the right to ask. 'STO stuff – jumping out of planes with your people, mostly.'

'Where?'

'Kosovo, Afghanistan.'

Cassidy lost interest, turning away. In effect, I'd just told him that I'd spent time behind enemy lines, causing havoc, so apparently I'd passed the test; at least till the next test came along. I turned to LeDuc. 'André, I'm going to need you to come along, in case we need a translator.'

'*D'accord*,' he said, glancing around uncertainly, his earlier bravado fading.

Maybe he was aware that if we needed to call on his language skills, it would be because things had fallen into the meat grinder. I sincerely hoped I would be bringing the Frenchman along unnecessarily.

Ryder, not a happy camper, picked up a stick at his feet and threw it down. I took him aside. 'Duke, you'll be the officer in charge if I don't make it back. If that happens, rely on Cassidy to get everyone out. We clear?'

The reply wasn't exactly snappy.

'Yes, sir,' he said eventually.

We rejoined the others.

'So, Cassidy and I are also staying back,' said Rutherford.

'Looks like,' I told him.

They knew the score. The rulebook required a solid protection detail for Leila and Boink. We had no choice but to split our strength down the middle.

'But you'll need more than just the two of you, won't you?' Leila told me. 'You said there was a hundred and twenty of them.' Her face somehow managed to convey confusion, concern, and surprise and stay unlined. Finally, it dawned on her. 'You're not going back to rescue them, are you?'

'We have to go look at the enemy's positions. Only then will we know what we can and can't do.' I turned to West. 'The company's HQ – that's where they'll be held.'

'Yep,' said West, agreeing.

'I think you're making excuses,' Leila said, standing up like she was going someplace. 'Why don't you just go and demand our peoples' release?'

Yeah, just like demanding a better suite at the Ritz. I didn't want to talk about it any longer. 'Lex, you got those FARDC uniforms handy?'

Rutherford gestured at LeDuc, who reached for his backpack and pulled them out.

'They're big sizes,' I said, hoping they'd fit over our gear.

I tried on a shirt but the fit was tight – too tight with body armor on – so I took the armor off. That sky blue patch on the shoulder interested me the most. If we were spotted, that identifying flash of color might confuse the issue of our identity long enough for us to fool the enemy for an important couple of seconds.

We had no food; nothing to carry except for our weapons and ammo. I chose an M4 over the Nazarian Type 97 because I knew it like an old buddy.

'I have no combat experience,' LeDuc informed me, checking his pistol. I handed him one of the spare Nazarians and a couple of spare mags.

'Just do what I'm gonna do – follow Mike's lead.' I turned to Cassidy. 'Cy, give us four hours to recon the Congolese positions. If we don't make it back within twelve hours, head due east. According to the map there's a road around the shores of Lake Kivu. Once you hit it, take a ride south to Cyangugu.'

'Good luck,' he said.

We'd need it.

I glanced back over my shoulder at Leila as we left the trees. She was sitting with her back to me, her head in her hands.

West led the way, followed by LeDuc, followed by me. We walked toward the sound of corn popping. Along the way, West blackened his face and arms with charcoal from a tree long ago struck by lightning. Neither LeDuc nor I needed it; our faces and arms were still black from the burned jet fuel. We pulled the green berets down low over our foreheads so that they threw shadows over our eyes.

The blackness under the canopy was soon complete and the going was slow because of it. But at least the rain had mostly been reduced to occasional showers mixed with fat droplets running off the overhead leaves and branches. West stopped us every few minutes to listen. Aside from the sound of distant gunfire, which quickly died away with the last vestiges of light, running water and a howling frenzy of a million mosquitoes were the sounds that accompanied our careful footsteps.

'Malaria. It's a problem here,' West whispered as he came past.

He was searching the floor of the rainforest like he'd lost his keys.

'What are you doing?' LeDuc asked.

'Looking for an ant's nest,' he said. 'Like this one.' A mound of smooth gray dirt rose out of the leaf litter to about knee height.

'*Pourquoi?*'

West kicked the top off it with the heel of his boot, grabbed a handful of the dirt mixed with crushed ant and wiped it over the exposed skin on his arms.

'Formic acid,' he said. 'Nature's insect repellent. These driver ants are full of it. It'll stop the mosquitoes cold.' He took a couple more handfuls of dirt, squeezed it in his hands to kill the ants and then rubbed it over his face and the back of his neck.

LeDuc and I followed his lead.

We walked stealthily for a little more than an hour, taking a course that would bring us lower down into the valley, away from the forward picket lines that were no doubt occupied by jumpy soldiers with itchy trigger fingers.

West stopped abruptly beneath a spread of palm fronds and signaled that a target lay dead ahead, ten meters away. I couldn't see a damn thing. And then the shadow he was pointing at turned and moved slowly away from us. The barrel of a rifle caught some starlight coming through a rent in the canopy. We needed to find out how far apart the pickets were before trying to penetrate the FARDC positions.

We slid to the right, moving the way chameleons do, keeping our boots in midair before placing them carefully on the ground. Finding another picket fifty meters along, we retraced our steps twenty meters or so, then pushed forward between them. The sound of men's voices soon reached us, a low hum with occasional shouts. Somewhere close by was a company of riflemen doing what men do after battle – eat, talk, dress wounds, die, clean weapons, shit, gamble, urinate, complain, doze, argue.

A sudden, violent thrash in the bushes ahead, lasting no more than a few seconds, cause LeDuc and I to drop to a crouch. I waited till I saw West's hand signal before moving forward. I took half a dozen steps and saw a FARDC soldier flat on his back, staring up with pinpricks of light in his open eyes. There was not a mark on him that I could see. I cut a couple of palm fronds and laid them over him.

'Walked into him,' West whispered in my ear. 'Had no choice.' He put a finger to his lips and pointed.

Ahead, through a screen of palms, was a clearing of maybe five meters in diameter. In the center of the clearing, a solider was kneeling on the ground with a small flashlight producing a flickering yellow beam. The man had his pants down and was beating the meat over a deck of cards that I guessed featured naked women. Job done, he picked up one of the cards, wiped it with a wet leaf and put it in his top pocket. We left him to it and worked our way around the edge of the clearing. I spotted a satchel hanging from a tangle of vines and a rifle leaning up against a tree beside it. I stopped West and LeDuc and signaled my intentions. The guy who carried his girlfriend in his pocket was too busy getting his pants back on to notice me. I reached in and took the satchel. The rifle looked familiar. It was an M16. I took it, too, and retreated into the shadows. Checking the satchel, I saw I'd hit the jackpot. Inside were tins of food and a couple of spare mags for the rifle. I gave the weapon the once-over. It was brand-new and its serial numbers had been ground off the receiver, just like those M16s I'd found in Kabul. The same question struck me: why would the numbers be removed if they weren't somehow significant? A tap on the shoulder refocused my attention. West wanted to keep moving.

Soon the murmur of many voices and the smell of jet fuel caused us to get down on our bellies and inch forward. Through the dense foliage at the edge of a larger clearing, we saw more than thirty men bivouacked under ponchos, screens of umbrella palms, cardboard packaging, blankets – whatever could be used to provide shelter. Tents were non-existent. Here and there, soldiers were cooking their dinners on small portable stoves, the type that utilized bricks of compressed kerosene, which accounted for that smell of jet fuel. A group of half a dozen kids wearing grossly oversized uniforms huddled together under a couple of ponchos with their rifles. Back in my world, kids just a few years younger than these hugged their teddy bears and watched *Barney* reruns.

West took us on a detour around the clearing. The HQ, our target, would be further in the rear. We found it eventually, ringed by trees with massive trunks and spreading root systems. The roar of fast-moving water told us that a ravine was close. The HQ itself was a collection of four large five-man tents and several smaller ones. Gas lanterns smoldered blue-green within the larger tents. The silhouettes of men moving around inside them played on the tent walls. A number of trestle tables had been set up. Several fires burned and smoked beneath small shelters thatched with wet umbrella palm fronds. More than a dozen soldiers armed with submachine guns patrolled the perimeter. I was worried that the tins in the satchel would clank together, so I left it, along with the M16, behind a tree and shaved a little bark off the trunk so that I could identify the hiding place on our way out. Slithering on our bellies, we kept to the shadows and worked our way around the edge of the clearing to reconnoiter it.

Then West motioned that he saw something up ahead. I came forward. It was Twenny Fo, his head beneath a black hood and his hands tied behind his back with a rope that looped over a tree branch above him. The rope was tight so that his arms were raised. He was leaning forward, balancing on his toes to take the pressure off his shoulders. I could see that if he lost his balance and fell, his weight would rip his clavicles clean out of their sockets. Peanut had been strung up to another tree; same deal. I could hear him sobbing beneath his hood. Fournier and Ayesha were nowhere to be seen. Around them, half a dozen armed men stood smoking and spitting on the ground.

Just then, a short Asian guy, an athletic type with pale skin and dressed in civilian clothes, strolled out of one of the bigger tents. He walked to a slit trench, scratched his ass, urinated, then went back undercover.

'What's a Chinese guy doing here?' I whispered.

'An advisor,' LeDuc replied under his breath.

Suddenly, a movement in my peripheral vision distracted me. It was a man on his knees, in a begging position. I was as certain as I could be that it was the same DRC officer who'd captured us earlier. Standing over him were two soldiers, both young and gangly, wearing uniforms that were a size or two too small, as if they'd taken delivery of someone else's laundry. One of them secured the officer's forearms on top of a tree stump. The officer was wailing and speaking rapidly in a language I didn't understand and that wasn't French. Then the other man swung down several times with a machete, and the officer's arms came up, without hands on the end of them, blood spurting from the stumps.

The officer screamed long and hard and the hair on my head stood on end.

'Jesus . . .?' West whispered.

The Asian guy came out of his tent again briefly to investigate the noise and then went back inside, uninterested.

The officer howled as he bent double, curled over his spurting stumps. The guard and his pal who had done the machete work reappeared with a metal poker, its end steaming. They pulled the officer back on his haunches and smoke rose as each wound was cauterized while the victim shrieked.

I tapped West on the shoulder, and we wriggled backward. The tents, including the one occupied by the Asian guy, obscured a third of the clearing. Though we'd seen enough in one sense, our reconnoiter wasn't complete. I led the way on my stomach and forearms around the clearing's circumference, moving slowly, trying to get the picture of the officer having his hands chopped off out of my mind.

The position of the underbush on the other side of the clearing allowed us to crawl to within ten meters of Twenny Fo and Peanut, close enough, perhaps, to let them know that help was near, though of course it wasn't. Giving our position away to the armed guards wouldn't help our principals or us, or the folks depending on us to return. Twenny stumbled a little, and his arms pulled upward behind his back against their natural range of motion. He cried out in pain as he regained his footing. A couple of the guards wandered over to check on him, but then lost interest when they saw that the prisoner's bonds were working as intended. Dickfucks. They had to know Twenny was an American, but did they know what he was worth? Maybe they did. Maybe, as I'd suggested to Leila, the possibility of a ransom with a big payday was keeping Twenny Fo and Peanut in possession of all their appendages, at least until . . . until what, exactly? Did this theory also account for Fournier and Ayesha's absence? Had they killed them because they couldn't cough up bags of loot?

I heard a roar above the sound of the ravine. Rain. It moved across the HQ like an attacking formation.

West motioned with a tilt of his head to take a look at the Asian's tent.

Ayesha was being led away from it by two guards. She was naked, cowed and terrified, some kind of fruit jammed in her mouth, her hands tied behind her back. The guards took her to a trestle table barely discernible in the night shadows and tied her to it face down, securing her wrists to the table legs. One of the men, joking with his buddy, undid his fly buttons, pulled out his dick and jerked it around a few times until he was happy with its condition, then rammed his way into her from behind while she struggled, twisting away from him, grunting in terror. His pants fell around his ankles, and the man pulled back to speak with his pals. He wasn't happy about something. That something was resolved for me when I saw them each take one of Ayesha's legs, force them wide apart and bind them to the legs of the table.

I backed away, my face hot, muscles twitching with anger.

'Stay here,' I whispered to LeDuc, then signaled West to follow.

I was back on my stomach, pushing through the mud, keeping to the shadows, slithering fast through the bushes. On this side of the HQ, the rain together with the water rushing through the nearby ravine was making a hell of a racket. I lost visual contact with the compound for a brief period while I skirted around some bushes armored with thorns. When I regained it, the tactical situation was in danger of becoming Defcon Fucked Up. Number one rapist had blown his load, number two was undoing his fly, and now a third guard had joined them. West and I were outnumbered, and it was only a matter of time – moments, perhaps – before more of these fuckwits got the scent and wandered over for their turns.

The front of the trestle table was hard up against a massive tree trunk. I came up behind the tree, with West at my shoulder. I could hear Ayesha whimpering, making the sounds of the utterly terrified and powerless. I turned to West and signaled what I wanted him to do. He shook his head vehemently. I repeated the signal and mouthed that it was a *direct fucking order*. I unsheathed my Ka-bar and waited while he pulled his. I gave him no choice. The plan was only going to work if we did it quickly, and together. I got down low and had one last look at the angles, because the first few steps coming around the tree would be blind. Then I moved around behind the trunk to the opposite side and, using my fingers, gave West a count of three.

Three.

Two.

One.

Walking around the tree, nice and casual, I resisted the desire to run past the front edge of the table, keeping my mind on the job by counting steps. The asshole bending over Ayesha glanced up helpfully, presenting his throat. I slid the Ka-bar across it, making sure the steel found his jugular before I finished the slice and he had the pleasure of watching his own blood mingle with the sweat and rain on Ayesha's ass before slumping over her, dead. I took another step past him, angling the knife so that it would slip unhindered between the fourth and fifth rib of the number two party guy. I buried the blade almost to its hilt, venting the fucker's heart, his mouth open in a big silent 'O' of surprise. He was a corpse before the surprise left his lips. I lay him down in the mud for the first few moments of his eternal rest, stood on his chest, and pulled the knife free. West took out number three guy, giving him a smile from ear-to-ear with his Ka-bar that made him gurgle softly. Apart from that, there was no sound. We gave them no warning and made no mistakes. Neat and professional. None of the other guards even looked our way. I gathered the dead soldier's weapons, a submachine gun and two M16s, and patted down the bodies for extra mags.

The deceased were tall but not heavily muscled. I pulled the body off Ayesha, laid him beside his limp buddy, then grabbed both their lapels and dragged them behind the tree. Twenty meters beyond it was a screen of bush, then a drop into the ravine. I reconnoitered it quickly. Satisfied that the area was clear, I dragged the bodies behind the bushes and rolled them into the roaring darkness but didn't hear a discernible splash over the sound of the churning waters. I prayed that they were gone, washed downstream by the torrent, and not jagged on a rock or hung up on driftwood where they would be easily found come morning. West dragged the other corpse to the edge.

'Strip him first,' I said, before going back to Ayesha.

I cleared her mouth, cut her bonds and stuffed them in a pocket, and then helped her off the table. She whimpered and cringed away from me.

'It's Cooper,' I whispered.

But Ayesha was still afraid, unable to see past the DRC uniform. I grabbed her by the shoulders and gave her a quick shake.

'Ayesha, it's me, Cooper.'

She swallowed and blinked and grabbed my forearms, her nails digging into my skin.

'Cooper,' she whispered, as if pulling herself out of a nightmare.

West put the dead man's shirt over her shoulders and handed her a pair of pants. I scouted the ground quickly for signs of a struggle. There was plenty of blood, but the rain would take care of that. Leaving no indication of what had happened here would be a big help. West put a finger to his lips so that Ayesha knew the drill. We still had to get around the other guards and make our way out. We led her behind the back of the tree and crawled into the bush on our bellies. We picked up LeDuc where we'd left him, then found the tree I'd put in charge of the satchel and the M16.

There were four additional weapons to pull through the mud in silence, making the outbound journey slower. We kept heading for the rear, toward the flatter ground behind the HQ, where there was less chance of crawling into someone. We encountered no pickets and quickly found ourselves in unoccupied rainforest. But as the adrenalin wore off, exhaustion set in.

I watched Ayesha walking ahead, silently pushing aside the foliage with the barrel of one of the captured M16s. She was a combat veteran now and, like me, she'd have the nightmares to prove it.

Enemies

Approaching Cassidy, Rutherford and Ryder in complete darkness and dressed in enemy uniforms was probably more dangerous than infiltrating the FARDC's lines. Three of us had gone out two hours earlier, so it made sense that only three of us should come back; only, now there were four of us. LeDuc and I came forward with Ayesha – she didn't want to be left on her own – with our hands raised high. I made the prearranged signal: a short, low whistle.

A whistle came back.

I relaxed. We lowered our arms and walked toward our encampment, West not far behind.

'Ayesha,' Leila cried out when she saw her makeup artist's silhouette in the dark. She ran down and threw her arms around her friend. Ayesha wept and buried her face in Leila's neck, and the two women stood there sobbing in each other's arms, their shoulders quaking.

Eventually I heard Leila say, 'You're safe now, honey. Safe,' as she stroked the back of Ayesha's neck.

Boink and Ryder gathered around the two women.

'Ayesha – you okay?' I heard Ryder ask his old school chum. She nodded. The nightmare was hers and she didn't want it shared around. I knew that feeling. If she kept it to herself, then maybe it never happened.

Cassidy and Rutherford pulled West and me aside, leaving LeDuc with the principals. 'What about Twenny and Peanut?' Cassidy wanted to know.

'They were alive when we left them,' I said. 'And all of them still had their hands.'

'What?' said Rutherford.

'Tell you in a minute,' West replied, gesturing at the civilians. They were still within earshot and what we had to report was not for general consumption.

'Hey, Cisco, where'd the ponchos come from?' I asked. Several of them had been strung up to provide shelter from the rain.

'They walked here. A FARDC patrol – three men. They're over there, getting cold and wet,' Cassidy said, nodding uphill, 'though I don't think any of them will mind. At first we thought you were another patrol out looking for their lost buddies.'

'What changed your mind?' I asked.

'You weren't singing and smoking like they were,' said Rutherford.

'They were carrying these.' Cassidy showed me a submachine gun.

I pulled mine out from behind my back and said, 'I think they grow on trees here.'

'The QCW-05,' Rutherford said. 'Made in China.'

'Ain't everything?' I replied.

The QCW was a handy weapon. I'd tested one on the firing range back at Andrews – a rate of fire up around four hundred rounds per minute, a fifty-round magazine, a reasonably accurate sight, and less weight than the M16. Best of all, it was silenced.

'There was a Chinese guy back at the FARDC HQ,' I said.

'Chink weaponry, Chink advisor,' said West. 'Gotta be related.'

I took several more steps away from our civilians and West, and debriefed Cassidy and Rutherford on what we saw: numbers, layout, weaponry, conditions, pickets, naked babes on playing cards, and so forth. I also told them about the officer and what had happened to him.

'As punishments go, makes latrine duty seem rather tame,' Rutherford observed.

'What about Ayesha?' Cassidy asked. 'How'd you pull that off?'

'There was a window. We took it,' I said.

'And no window for the others?'

'If there was, we'd have taken it,' West said.

'Ayesha was kept a little apart from the rest and the isolation worked for us. We could take out the men guarding her without alerting their buddies, but that wasn't an option with Twenny and Peanut.'

'How many were on her?' asked Rutherford.

'Three.'

'Three guards for one prisoner?'

'Maybe they thought she was dangerous,' I said, not wanting to go into details. Ayesha had made West and me promise to keep the rape a secret and neither of us was prepared to break that trust. I changed the subject. 'Fournier is MIA. No sign of him.'

'You think he's still alive?'

'I wouldn't put money on it. They rocketed the chopper. Maybe they've got a special dislike for the UN.'

'Guard numbers overall?'

'Twelve that we saw,' I said.

'Can they be rescued?' Cassidy asked.

'The guards seem happy where they are,' I replied.

Rutherford grinned. 'You lifted one of their prisoners. Surely alarm bells must be going off down there now?'

I glanced over at our principals, who were now having a group hug with Ryder and LeDuc.

'We fixed it so they might not know what happened to Ayesha and the men guarding her,' I said.

'So there *is* a chance we *could* get the others?' said Cassidy.

'My honest opinion? No,' I said. 'It's a suicide run. They aren't good soldiers by our standards but they have modern weapons and plenty of them, and you can't ignore the numbers. And leaving all that aside, lifting them from the HQ isn't the problem, it's getting away. How do we vacate the area? There's no handy Chinook on a hilltop with Apache gunships flying air support. We don't have the tools for the job.'

I put my hands on my hips and the cans in the satchel I was carrying clanked together. Food – I'd forgotten about it. I dropped the bag on the ground and tins spilled out of it, to which I added the ones stuffed down my shirt.

'What's on the menu?' asked Rutherford

'Your guess is as good as mine,' I said.

'Lucky dip. Every army's favorite.' He leaned down and picked up one of the cans, and then examined it in the darkness before giving it a shake. Liquid slopped around inside.

I hadn't eaten in six hours. My endocrine glands had been keeping me going and, now that I thought about it, I was hungry enough to eat bark. Prior experience told me that the first twenty-four hours without sustenance were the worst. Get past them, and the next few days aren't nearly so bad. Go without food for longer than four or five days and the body starts to go out on strike. Water was more critical, but there was plenty of that around. We just had to make sure that what we drank was clean. I glanced at our civilians, who were still huddled together. Maybe I could sell the rationing to Leila as a miracle military diet. All I had to do was figure out how to work astrology or Kabala into the program and she'd swallow it, no problem. Boink, I wasn't so sure about.

'We need to move further away from the FARDC's lines,' said Cassidy. 'If they sent one patrol out here, they're gonna send another, even if it's just to go looking for their missing buddies.'

He was right about that. Cassidy, Rutherford and I rejoined the principals while West assumed the watch.

'Thank you for giving Ayesha back to us,' said Leila, her voice thick with emotion.

'Yeah, thanks, Vin,' said Ryder. 'And Mike,' he said a little louder. West gave him a quick wave without looking back over his shoulder.

'We were lucky,' I told them. 'Right now, we have to move.'

'But it's night,' said Leila.

'The best time to do it. We're too close to the enemy here.'

'What 'bout Twenny and 'Nut?' asked Boink, slapping the mosquitoes on his neck.

'Strategic withdrawal,' Rutherford said. 'You know, we pull back, make a plan . . .'

The big man didn't buy it. 'You leavin' him behind, yo,' he said, shifting his weight from one foot to the other, angry, disappointed, and helpless.

'No one's getting left behind,' I told him and waited for lightning to strike me dead because, as things stood, we really didn't have very much choice but to leave Deryck and the others to whatever fate held in store for them.

'Bull fucking shit, motherfuckers,' said Boink, seething, seeing through the lie.

'You *can't* leave them behind,' said Leila. 'No sir, I won't allow it.'

Ryder opened his mouth to speak but I cut him off with a look before he said something he'd regret.

'We need to move because the danger is still too close.' I didn't wait for consensus. They got the drop on us once; next time we might not be so lucky. 'Get your personal items and let's go. Leave nothing behind.'

None of the principals moved.

'Now,' I said.

Still no movement.

'*Hello?*'

Ayesha began to walk and resistance from the others crumbled. Our principals seemed to give a collective shrug and put one foot in front of the other. I wasn't going to complain. We stopped by the nearest anthill. West kicked the top off the mound, and wiped his face and neck with the foul-smelling dirt while he explained why.

'I'm not doing that!' Leila exclaimed.

'Malaria is not something you want, ma'am,' said West. 'It's a bitch to get rid of. You get chills, fevers, enlarged spleen and liver. Get it bad enough and it'll kill you. The mosquitoes carry it, along with Dengue Fever, Philariasis and River Blindness. The dirt mixed with dead ant will keep them at bay.'

'No.'

Ayesha rubbed the dirt on her neck, face and hands. Boink did likewise.

'There's no paparazzi here,' I reminded the celebrity.

'You're enjoying this, aren't you?' she said as she resigned herself to what she considered ignominy and smeared a handful of dirt on her cheeks.

'Whatever gives you that idea, ma'am?'

'You're smiling.'

I looked away and took Cassidy forward to scout the path ahead. The volume of water coming down the hill was mind-boggling, the ground criss-crossed by rivulets gurgling, splashing and dribbling. We picked our way silently in the dark through the dense foliage, heading for the deep, rumbling sound of a massive volume of water tumbling and boiling in a confined space; a waterfall, perhaps. It turned out to be a ravine like the others we'd encountered. I reconnoitered upstream a hundred meters while Cassidy headed down and found us a fallen tree to use as a bridge. Fifty metres further on, another ravine. We crossed this one by wading through a waist-deep pool of icy water where the current wasn't as strong. With luck, the ravines were natural barriers that discouraged patrols. Not far beyond this second ravine, we came across three trees in a clump, surrounding a small room-sized clearing. Thick liana vines hung down from branches hidden somewhere in the total blackness of the canopy. This was as good a place as any to hole up and get some rest. It was two thirty-five in the morning and we were all dead on our feet.

I split the watches between Cassidy, Rutherford and me – I took the first – and everyone else did their best to sleep until dawn, the women, wrapped in a poncho, spooning each other. LeDuc, Cassidy, West, Rutherford and Boink shared two more ponchos between them.

Shivering in the light drizzle, I sat with my feet and ass in a puddle with a Nazarian and M4 for company, and counted frogs jumping through the water that ran down the hill, some of them chased by large black snakes. To keep myself awake and the exhaustion at bay, I thought about the Chinese guy and what he might have been doing in the FARDC camp. I agreed with West that he probably had a connection to the weapons, but was that where it ended? I thought about

Twenny Fo and the assurance I'd given Boink about us leaving no one behind and his reaction to it. I thought about Fournier and what might have happened to him; about Peanut; about the officer on his knees with his hands lying twitching in the mud in front of his eyes. I thought about the FARDC troops shooting RPGs into the Puma. I thought about the patrol ambushing us, and about the flutter of Cassidy's black throwing knife as it flew like an attack butterfly, burying itself in the back of the African soldier's head. I thought it was luck of the most fucked-up kind that, given the size of the DRC, we should come down in the middle of a firefight. I mean, what were the odds? And something about all this congealed into a vague pattern that left me with a feeling of unease, which led to thoughts of Anna and the office at the Oak Ridge facility and the black hole in her chest; her heart pumping furiously while her life leaked onto the carpet through the ragged wound in her back.

Half an hour into my one-hour watch, footsteps on the leaf litter behind caused me to squeeze the Nazarian tighter, but it was Leila. I wondered what she wanted.

'You should be asleep, ma'am,' I told her as she walked in front of me.

'I couldn't. Too many ants. And I . . . I wanted to thank you for bringing Ayesha back for me.'

I hadn't done it for her, but I let it slide. 'There's no need to thank me.'

'Just doing your job, right?'

'It's going to be a long day tomorrow,' I reminded her. 'You need to get your rest.'

'Do you find me attractive, Vin?'

I wasn't sure which part of that surprised me the most, and then decided it was the fact that she knew my name. 'I'm not sure I know what you mean, ma'am,' I said, stalling.

'Call me Leila, okay?'

'Sure.' I said, nearly putting 'ma'am' after it.

'Well? Do you?'

'Do I what?'

'Find me attractive?'

Hmm . . . one of the more unexpected questions I could have had to answer, given that it was three in the morning, we were in the middle of the rainforest, and she'd given me the impression that she thought my station in the universe was a rung above dirt. I thought about the answer. Yeah, she was beautiful, as well as sultry, and even sexy, in a put-you-over-my-knee kind of way, but attractive? No, she was way too selfish, too spoilt, too needy and too narcissistic for my tastes. I liked women who were happy to concentrate on *me*, not on themselves – even if they were faking it.

She sighed impatiently. I was taking far too long to answer, obviously. 'What I want to know is whether you want to fuck me?'

'What?' I said, the question making me gawp.

She kneeled in front of me, threw her hair back and slid down the zipper on her jacket.

'Stop right there, ma'am,' I told her. Going to sleep on guard duty was a punishable offense, and, though I wasn't sure of the statute, getting laid while on it was probably in the same ballpark. And besides, being completely sober, I had enough control to realize that the offer was going to come with strings attached – make that steel cables. I knew enough about Leila by now to understand that she was used to having her way, even if she had to work a little to get it.

'If you call me "ma'am" one more time, I'll slap you,' she warned me.

'What are you doing?'

'I'm a woman, you're a man . . .'

'You're a woman who wants something and you think I'm the man who can make it happen. And none of it has anything to do with sex.'

'Fuck . . .' Leila sat on her haunches and pulled the zip back up to her neck.

'So what's going on?' I asked her.

'I don't like you, Cooper.'

'You don't like me so much, you want to get jiggy with me.'

Silence.

'What is this about, aside from me being irresistible?' She glared at me. 'Leila, I'm gonna have to ask you to go back with the others and—'

'Not long ago, Deryck and I had something special,' she blurted. 'I was hoping that we'd find a way back to each other on this trip. That's the real reason I went through with it – this concert. Losing him has taught me that. And now you're gonna leave him to die.'

'And you think a little hubba-hubba with me will get you what you want?'

Leila stared at me. Even though I couldn't see her eyes in the darkness, I knew that they were projecting waves of anger. There was a time not too long ago when I would have given the consequences a careless shrug and put this woman on her back anyway, but that was before Oak Ridge. I considered the best way to handle this and decided that subtlety wasn't my friend.

'Do you want to die here, too?' I asked her.

'No.'

'Leila, there's a better-than-even chance that none of us will get out of here alive. We're surrounded by hostiles in a foreign environment and we're on the run. We have no radio, next to no food, zero intel and limited ammunition. The odds of a successful rescue are massively weighted against us. If we try to do what you want, go to the FARDC camp and demand the release of our principals, *our* survival chances will reduce to somewhere around zero. Said another way, and you're forcing me to be blunt, your ex has ceased to be a priority. Like it or not, keeping you, Ayesha and Boink breathing is top of our hit parade right now.'

Leila stood up and looked down at me. 'You ever been in love, Cooper?'

'What's that got to do with anything?'

'Everything,' she said.

'Look, I can't – *won't* – risk everyone's life because you believe your needs are more important.'

Leila turned and walked off, after she'd taken a few steps pausing to say, 'One day, Cooper, you're going regret that we ever met.'

I watched her walk up the hill and the old Cooper shook his head at the missed opportunity. If I'd let her have her way with me and then said no to the quid pro quo, would I have been any worse off than I was now?

The new post-Anna Cooper, however, knew what she meant about love giving everything meaning, and he congratulated me for realizing that actions had consequences and that, for once, the old Cooper had considered what they might be before letting his dick out to play.

Leila's poster came to mind, the one showing the star all steamed up, her sexual appetite looking for a solid three-course meal. And the old Cooper wished the new Cooper would go get lost in the forest.

At three forty-five, I got another tap on the shoulder. It was Cassidy.

'You're early,' I told him.

'Couldn't sleep. The ants in this place are gonna be a problem. Anything out there I should know about?'

What I want to know is whether you want to fuck me? 'Yeah, I've seen a thousand sets of frogs legs hopping past. Should make LeDuc happy.'

I left the sergeant to the watch, walked over to the trees and found some steaming rancid warmth under the poncho with the men. Despite the ants, sleep took me away almost immediately. It started out peaceful enough, but then I found myself alone with my usual nightmares – on top of a cold brown mountain with the remains of my unit as sword-wielding half Taliban–half scorpion creatures arrived to cut up my men. And then I was falling backward from a great height as a human wave of fanatics charged while I froze in the snow beside a dead man whose machine gun fired bullets that had no effect on the advancing horde. After which, pink froth bubbled from the crimson hole in a ribcage while I reached in and tried to find the bullet. And then I was on a wind-blown hill, strangers blaming me for Anna's death while scorpions poured out of the earth that had been freshly dug for a coffin.

Lying in the semi-conscious zone between sleep and wakefulness, I had the feeling that there were other twisted memories on the way, or that maybe I'd replay these ones and twist them still further, so I opened my eyes. It was five-forty and my muscles were cramped in the fetal position. Somewhere above the canopy, the sky was sliding to gray and mist was floating through the trees. The rain had stopped. I untangled myself from various arms and legs, brushed ants from my neck and forearms, and walked stiffly a dozen meters from our bivouac to take a leak. Rutherford was on duty. I walked across and down to him and said, 'Morn—'

He cut me short and informed me with a couple of hand movements that a five-man enemy patrol had crossed the second ravine and was coming our way.

I stood absolutely still rather than taking cover, movement being what the human eye is most sensitive to. It was difficult to see the men and I eventually picked them up thirty meters below us and to our right.

As Rutherford indicated, it was a six-man patrol, and they looked to be on the job, moving slowly and carefully through the mist, no one talking or smoking. Our position was relatively well hidden among scrubby bush. In this low light we were black on black to them. Confirming this, one of their number looked our way but didn't see us. The men kept walking, heading right to left across our front. I wondered what the purpose of the patrol might be. Were they out looking for us?

Three of them carried QCWs, three had assault rifles, and one of them had another type weapon slung over his shoulder, a telescopic sight slipped into its top rail: a sniper rifle. All six carried packs.

When we were well behind in their six o'clock, I went to wake the rest of our band while Rutherford kept watch. The SOCOM boys woke quietly when I squeezed their shoulders, their eyes opening wide – alert. Ryder needed heavy prodding. LeDuc was already awake. With a bunch of hand signals I gave them all the story. As I saw it, there was no doubt about our course of action. We couldn't have an enemy patrol operating in our area. Also, the Africans had guns, which meant they had ammo and we needed that. The brief council having concluded, each of us took a civilian to wake, covering their mouths with our hands so that no one made any noise.

'Enemy patrol nearby,' I explained in a low whisper to cold, shivering bodies. 'No noise, stay here.' I gave Ryder my Nazarian and two extra magazines. LeDuc had his own service pistol. 'They're yours,' I told them, tilting my head at the principals. Ryder seemed happy to be left behind. 'If we're not back in half an hour, head for the top of the ridge and hope the folks up there are friendlier than the ones down there.'

LeDuc nodded and whispered, '*Bonne chance.*'

'You really think taking them on is a good idea, sir?' asked Ryder, frowning.

'If we get their weapons and ammo, yes,' I said. 'If they shoot us all dead, no.'

'Okay,' he muttered, shaking his head. My logic was messing with his mind. I happened to glance at Leila. Her arms were folded and she was glaring at me hard.

WE STAYED BEHIND THE enemy patrol, dropping down into the mist, which was becoming genuine fog as the air warmed slightly in the pre-dawn light and convection currents got into it, thickening the mixture. The waterlogged air deadened noise transmission. When we found suitable terrain, Cassidy, Rutherford and West hunkered down while I went forward, maintaining contact with the patrol's last man. They kept on the move for another ten minutes, walking slowly across the hill, maintaining a generally easterly heading. And then they stopped, paused for a few minutes, relaxing, and passed around a pack of cigarettes. The sun was higher, and although the fog was reasonably heavy, color was now discernible and I could see the blue patches on the shoulders of their FARDC uniforms. I dropped behind an old fallen tree and put my chin in some sticky rotting goop. I could hear the patrol talking, laughing; sharing a quiet joke, perhaps. I wondered what Congolese soldiers found funny, what the joke – if that's what it was – was all about.

The patrol then stopped following the script. Instead of simply retracing their footsteps and going back out the way they came in, they started walking up the hill diagonally, coming toward me. If they kept to their current course, they'd walk right into our bivouac. I heard them coming closer. They'd stopped chatting like friends off to see a game, and were again stalking quietly up the hill. I slipped back the machine gun's bolt and took a couple of deep breaths to steady my nerves. Something moved in the leaf litter. I glanced across and froze. Less than a foot from my eyeball sat a black scorpion the size of a small Maine lobster. This close, the thing looked like a Suburban with a tail. Its copper-colored stinger, curved like a scimitar, was poised over the top of its back, quivering, tensing for the strike. I swallowed hard. That goop under my chin – maybe it was the damn thing's breakfast. It wanted to fight me for it and was scuttling back and forth, dancing like a boxer, its claws raised and ready for a one-two combination. The sight of it took me back to the hill in Afghanistan, superior numbers of Taliban fighters swarming over our mauled, exhausted unit, hacking left and right with their swords, taking off heads. Scorpions, almost a plague in Afghanistan, populated my nightmares, marshaling them forward, leading them over the trenches. I'd just spent two hours of harried, grueling sleep with a few thousand of them. I fucking *hate* scorpions. Despite the cold, I was sweating, immobilized. And then it struck, whipping forward and stabbing my cheek with that stinger. I yelled and jumped up, the side of my face on fire.

The FARDC patrol stopped and stared up at me.

I looked down at them.

There was a moment of indecision, but then they visibly relaxed. One of them raised a hand. While I seemed to have come from nowhere, there were those distinctive blue patches on my shoulders. They waved at me and the patrol leader took a few steps in my direction. The mistaken identity was only going to last a few seconds. A couple of them hesitated. One raised his weapon. I swung the QCW forward and fired the first burst from the hip. The weapon made a sound like a fart in a cushion. The rounds caught the lead soldier in the shoulder and stitched him across his neck, which exploded like a can of Coke that had been punctured and shaken. He fell back against the second man as I dropped to my knee and used the sight. The distance between us was no more than sixty meters – fish in a barrel distance. I pumped rounds into the chests of the remaining men, who were fumbling with their weapons, firing wildly and mostly straight into the ground. It was over in seconds.

No movement animated any of them, but I knew one was still alive. He was lying under the man who'd been shot first. I walked up to the fallen, trying not to think about what had just happened. I toed the body of the man playing possum, keeping the muzzle of the QCW on his face. His eyes were shut but his lips were trembling, tears running down his cheeks. He was maybe twenty years of age.

'You!' I gave his leg a prod. 'Hey,' I said again.

His eyes opened and he looked into the barrel of the QCW, smoke curling from it.

'*Non, non . . . ne me tuer pas . . . ne me tuer pas . . . ne me tuer pas . . .*' he said, his chest convulsing.

I wasn't exactly sure what he was saying, but I figured he was begging for his life. The heat of battle was past and this guy hadn't caught a scratch. I don't do cold blood. I heard the noise of people running up behind me. My people.

'Cooper!' Cassidy called out in a harsh whisper.

I raised a hand to acknowledge them in the dissipating fog, just so that they could be sure it was me and didn't start shooting. They got to me twenty seconds after that, breathing heavily, as I pulled the corpse off the lone survivor.

'What happened?' West asked, slightly annoyed, the plan to ambush the FARDC patrol in an orderly fashion fucked up.

'*Ne me tuer pas . . . ne me tuer pas . . .*' interrupted the Congolese soldier, who was blubbering and shaking violently.

'Got a live one, eh?' said Rutherford.

'What's he saying?' West asked.

'"Don't kill me" I believe would be the direct translation.'

'I didn't know you spoke French,' I said to Rutherford.

'Schoolboy French,' he said. 'I can swear like a proper Frog.'

'Keep him away from Boink. He can fill us in on his buddies down there in the valley. He might also know a thing or two about the force occupying the ridge.'

I grabbed the African's weapon, another of those M16s with its numbers removed, then dragged the man by the back of the collar away from the carnage and turned him face down in the leaf litter.

'Search him,' I told Rutherford. 'If he gives you trouble, inspect your side-arm. Seems to work.'

Rutherford patted the guy down, removing a flick knife and several full mags, Chinese-made and interchangeable with the Type 97.

West and Cassidy stripped the bodies of valuables – weapons, backpacks.

'Nice little windfall,' said Cassidy.

'Lookee here,' said West. He opened up one of the backpacks. There was a poncho, cigarette lighter, packets of South African beef jerky and more tins of food. We also had their QCWs and Nazarians, the M16, spare mags, two sets of high-powered Chinese-made binoculars, plus the extra-special prize – a serious-looking Chinese-made 7.62mm sniper rifle, with eight spare magazines.

The haul suggested that this patrol had a longer-term mission.

'How'd you get the drop on them?' West asked me.

'Mistaken identity. The blue patches. My face still blacked out?'

'Yeah. And now that you mention it, you look funny,' Rutherford said.

And now that he mentioned it, one whole side of my face was itchy, pulsing, throbbing and hot. I touched my cheek. It was puffed up like a soufflé, a teardrop of semi-crusted blood running from a puncture wound. I couldn't see the humor in it.

'I am not an animal,' said Rutherford, enjoying himself.

'You been bit by something,' said West, stating the obvious.

I walked up to the fallen log, drawing my Ka-bar, and came back down with the struggling monster arachnid skewered on the end of it.

'Shee-it, Cooper,' said West, horrified by the size of the thing. Him and me both. My nightmares had themselves a new gatekeeper.

'What about the bodies?' said Cassidy, all business.

'We could just leave 'em,' Rutherford suggested. 'They could've been slotted by anyone in this place.'

He was right. And it was time to vacate the vicinity. I shook the bug off my knife, toed some leaf litter over it, and dug the blade into the soil to remove a smear of yellow and green pus. I grabbed a handful of the prisoner's shirt and hoisted him to his feet. Cassidy gave him a nudge to get him moving up the hill. The side of my bloated face wobbled like a plate of Jell-O with every step. I tried not to think about it. The fog was burning off fast now and there were wide patches of blue between the layers of cloud overhead. The day was trying to make up its mind about what kind of day it was going to be. Personally, I hoped it would come down in favor of putting on a little sunshine. The cold and wet were beginning to wear a little thin.

Fifteen minutes later we were back at our base camp. Boink was keeping watch. He stood up when we came closer, uncertainty in his face. Four went out, five were coming back. How was that happening?

'What's for breakfast?' I asked the big man as I walked past.

'Radishes,' he said, looking at me strangely, not quite connecting the face with the voice.

I returned the strange look with interest – radishes?

LeDuc and Ryder came down to meet us. Leila and Ayesha stayed beside the ponchos now strung between the trees.

LeDuc checked the man up and down.

Rutherford said, 'Feel free to start the interrogation – name, rank, et cetera?'

The African smiled at LeDuc, much of his fear appearing to dissipate.

'Looks like you remind him of someone,' I said. Maybe the fact that the Frenchman was MONUC put him at ease.

LeDuc snapped at the African and the man's smile faltered. A rapid-fire exchange then ensued between them. When they'd finished, LeDuc said, 'His name is Marcel Nbendo and he is twenty-one years old. He comes from a village twenty miles from here, and was recruited forcibly. His chief was paid money to vote for the local government man, plus an extra bounty for contributions made to the army. Marcel was one of those contributions. That was three years ago. He says he wants to desert, but has nowhere to go if he does because he can't go back to his village. The chief wouldn't allow it – too risky.'

'Where was his patrol going and what was its mission?' I asked.

LeDuc asked the man and then said, 'Their orders were to kill the commander of the force holding the heights. His name is Colonel Makenga. Marcel did not want to do this mission, believing his patrol would not come back.'

'Got that right,' Rutherford observed with a grin as he walked within earshot.

'Ask him if our principals are still alive down there,' I said to LeDuc.

The pilot translated, and then said, 'He and the others in his unit were briefed at the HQ. He saw two prisoners held out in the open.'

'Both black men?' I asked.

A moment later, LeDuc said, '*Oui.*'

'Still no Fournier,' West commented.

'He says that when their patrol was briefed, he saw them tied up and under guard.'

'Are patrols out looking for us?'

LeDuc and the prisoner had a brief exchange. 'He says no.'

'How would he know?' I thought about the question and qualified it with another. 'Did breaking Ayesha out set off the alarm bells?'

The French pilot considered the questions before putting them to the African.

The man gave a stuttering reply, his eyes wide with fear.

'He says that the commander of the FARDC force is a proud man. He would tear the hillside down in order to kill us if he knew we had dishonored him by stealing into the encampment, murdering his people and taking back a hostage.'

West yawned. 'Bring it on,' he said.

'What are they going to do with the prisoners?' I asked.

After another exchange, LeDuc said, 'He does not know. Marcel is, how you say, "a grunt".'

The sun burst through the trees, flooding our campsite with warmth.

Almost instantly, wisps of steam began to rise from the shoulders of our rain-and-sweat-soaked shirts and body armor.

'If this colonel knew his captives were wealthy, would he be interested in ransoming them?' I asked.

LeDuc and the African batted this around.

'Marcel says his colonel is already a rich man, but that riches make a man greedy for more.'

'We've captured a bloody philosopher,' observed Rutherford. 'What about numbers? How many have they really got down there?'

'Around a hundred and eighty,' said LeDuc after a quick consultation.

'One-eighty – shit,' said Rutherford. 'More than we thought.'

'Morale?' I asked.

'*Comme si comme ça,*' the African volunteered, without the need for translation.

On the right ride of my face, my lips were swelling, and I noticed that it was getting more difficult to talk and swallow without dribbling.

'Ask him if he knows anything about the big scorpions around here – how poisonous they are?' I said, just as preoccupied with my own situation.

'Can you say that without spitting, skipper?' Rutherford asked, wiping his forehead, grinning.

'Is that what happened to you? *Le scorpion?*' LeDuc inquired, looking at my face like it was something in a specimen bottle.

'Ask the damn question,' I said, losing patience.

LeDuc got back to me. 'Marcel wants to know – how big or small was the animal that stung you?'

I held my hands apart; no need to exaggerate.

The African seemed impressed and said something to LeDuc.

'No, these ones are not so poisonous,' the Frenchman translated. 'There are smaller ones.' He held his thumb and forefinger an inch and a half apart. 'These ones are much worse. Some of the men keep the big ones as pets. They have fights, make bets – like cockfights.'

'I think you lost your bout, Cooper,' said Rutherford, enjoying himself.

My cheek was sagging so much under the weight of whatever was making it so puffed up that I felt like I needed to support it with my hand.

'There's an Asian guy down there in the FARDC HQ,' I said, wanting to sit down. 'Ask him if he knows who the man is and what he's doing there.'

'I don't need to ask this to know the answer,' said LeDuc. 'The Chinese are helping the DRC. They get weapons, money and loans from China, because from the West – America – all they get is a lecture from the International Monetary Fund.'

'Jesus . . .' I said, patience gone.

The Frenchman gave me one of his shrugs and then had a brief conversation with the African.

'*Oui*,' LeDuc said when they were finished. 'The man is Chinese – PLA. He is giving instruction.'

'Instruction?' I said.

'Training,' said LeDuc, correcting himself.

'He's PLA?'

'*Oui*. Central Africa has become, how you say, a two horses race between your country and the Chinese.'

'We need to secure Marcel here, somehow,' I said.

A pair of black flexcuffs bobbed in front of my eyes, Ryder's fingers holding them. 'I packed a few pairs,' he said. 'Thought they might come in handy.'

This being Ryder's first positive contribution to the mission – at least as far as I could see – I felt I should say something team-building to the guy, but what I in fact wanted more than that was just to sit. My face throbbed, I was producing more saliva than I could swallow and I could feel my heart galloping in my chest like one of LeDuc's plural horses. And then, before I knew what I was doing, I was down on one knee, throwing up and seeing double, which is pretty much all I remember about that.

Friends

'How long have I been out?' I asked Ayesha, who was sitting beside me. The sun was higher in the sky than I remembered it. A gentle breeze moved the tops of the trees in small circles. I was actually warm and mostly dry.

'Less than an hour,' she said.

I pushed myself up into a sitting position and felt my cheek. It wasn't nearly as swollen or hot, and there was a plaster strip covering the puncture. I also had a sense that my face had been cleaned and, with the exception of several minor cuts, my hands and forearms had also regained their former coloring.

'The stinger broke off under your skin. Did you know that?' she said.

I didn't.

'You had an anaphylactic reaction to the poison. It could have been worse. You seen what nuts can do to some people?'

I had the feeling that both of us were drifting along, floating in a semi-reality, like maybe we'd pulled off the river onto the bank and were having a nice picnic on a blanket. She was still in shock. I wondered what I was in.

'I cleaned you up, in case you were wondering,' she said.

I thanked her and looked into her face. Those blue contact lenses were gone, but she was still striking.

'Can you see without them?' I asked.

'I only wear them for effect.'

I was surprised that she knew what I was talking about, but that was the bubble we were floating in.

'There's quite a bit of useful medicine in the captain's first aid kit,' she informed me. 'I did two years of nursing school before I went into makeup.'

'Why'd you quit?'

'There are only certain bodily fluids I want anything to do with. A nurse can't be choosey.'

'I guess not,' I said.

'Like blood. I see it, I pass out. Well, I did when I was younger.'

I could see how that might be a problem for a nurse.

Neither of us spoke.

Eventually I asked, 'They hurt you?'

She looked up at the sky and then down the hill and said, 'I don't remember.'

I watched the treetops scribing the circles against the blue far overhead.

Eventually, breaking what I can only describe as an ethereal silence, Ayesha said, 'Thank you, Vin.' She gave my hand a brief squeeze, which seemed to transfer a lot that had been left unspoken, then stood and walked off before I could spoil it by opening my mouth.

I became aware of the staccato snap, crackle and pop of distant small arms fire, which brought me back to a damp hillside in the middle of a battlefield in a country I knew absolutely nothing about.

'They're at it again,' Cassidy said as he came over, glancing off in the direction of the fighting. 'We're packed and ready to move out,' he said.

'Where to?' I stood up, making the sounds old men make when they stand. My head felt light, my joints creaked and my muscles ached like they were pumping the stuff that runs through refrigerators.

'To wherever you say,' he replied.

'Now there's an interesting development,' I said, forcing a grin.

He shrugged. 'So far so good, Mr Air Force.'

I glanced around to get my bearings. Ayesha, Leila and Boink were seated on a log, LeDuc chatting to them about something. West and Ryder were keeping watch, one up the hill, one down. Our prisoner was seated by himself, flexcuffed to a branch, staring at the ground. Nearby, keeping an eye on him, Rutherford was checking over the spare, newly captured Nazarians and QCWs.

'Saved you some breakfast,' Cassidy said, handing me a tin and his Leatherman to open it with.

'Lemme guess,' I said, 'radishes?'

Cassidy gave me a smile – a first – showing more gum than the Wrigley display at a 7-Eleven. I could see why he might not want to make a habit of it.

'Red Cross.' Cassidy replied as if that explained everything, and handed me a packet with a couple of strips of beef jerky in it.

'We don't know how much time Twenny Fo and Peanut have got,' I said, opening the can. 'We need to make a few hasty decisions.'

Cassidy agreed.

I drank the juice out of the tin and then ate the contents. The taste was hot and also bland.

Standing wearily, I made the 'on me' hand signal. Our band huddled up as I walked to Leila, Ayesha and Boink. Rutherford kept one eye on the African secured to the tree, while West and Ryder abandoned their watch.

Keeping it brief, I said, 'After yesterday's skirmish, both sides will try to outflank each other today. We'll get caught in a pincer.' *Pincer.* I shuddered, the word making me think of the scorpion.

There were nods from the other SOCOM guys.

'Man, this is bullshit,' said Boink. 'What 'bout Twenny Fo and Peanut? What's gonna happen to them?'

I turned to Cassidy, West, Rutherford. 'What do you guys think?' I asked them

'We got more weapons and ammo,' said West. 'Maybe we can cause a diversion, you know . . .'

I knew where he was going because I'd wrestled with the same thought. 'Aside from our M4s, we've got some 97s, a few submachine guns and the sniper rifle,' I said. 'Do we really think that launching ourselves into what's down there in the valley would achieve anything other than getting all of us killed?'

'We'd need a plan,' West said.

'I'm listening if anyone's got one,' I told them.

Silence.

'Cassidy?'

The big man said nothing.

'Look, we can handle a patrol or two, possibly even a platoon,' I said, 'but a whole reinforced rifle company? Maybe our best chance of getting them back alive is up there, sitting on the ridgeline. The rebels are supposedly our friends and allies . . .' I looked directly at LeDuc, who reminded me with a hand motion that maybe they were and maybe they weren't. 'So then let's go hang out with our friends,' I said, ignoring the equivocation. I didn't see that we had much choice but to throw ourselves on the benevolence of the folks who held the high ground. 'If nothing else, perhaps up there we can get access to communications, and organize evacuation for Leila, Ayesha and Boink while we negotiate the safe return of the others. Has anyone talked with our prisoner to see if he knows what we can expect up there?'

'*Oui*,' said LeDuc. 'He expects death.'

'Aside from the general dying thing, are there any specifics – numbers, for example?'

'No, he does not know.'

'Whoever's up there sure is throwing down a lot of iron,' said West.

'We'll need a white flag, Cooper,' said Cassidy. 'Coming from the valley, we might be mistaken for targets.'

Good point. 'Anyone got anything white?'

No one stepped forward.

'Nothing?' I asked.

Everyone looked at each other.

'Not even a hanky?'

Boink got up and lumbered up to where our possessions were packed and disappeared from view behind a tree. As the discussion had moved on from his buddy's rescue, I guessed he'd had enough.

'Okay, let's get ready to move,' I said. We'd have to take our chances without a flag of truce.

'You can't take Marcel into the rebel positions wearing a FARDC uniform,' said LeDuc. 'They will kill him. You should also change.'

Those blue slashes on my shoulders. The Frenchman was right, but it presented a problem. I had my battle dress uniform, but what was our prisoner going to slip into? 'Anyone got any spare clothes?' I asked.

Ryder reached into a small daypack he'd scrounged from the MONUC chopper before it blew and pulled out a clean, pressed ACU, complete with Office of Special Investigations badges and 'Special Agent Ryder' nametag. 'This do?'

'Yeah,' I said, playing down the surprise. I mean, a clean uniform? I took the clothes, dropped them on the round and stomped on them half a dozen times so that it wouldn't seem like Marcus had walked straight out of the Clothing Sales.

West shook his head. 'I dunno. Two Ryders? Could be too much of a good thing, Duke.'

'You should give him Ryder's dog tags as well,' said Rutherford, 'in case he gets checked a little more thoroughly.'

Made sense to me.

Louder booms of exploding mortar shells peppered the sound of distant small arms fire. Boink reappeared from behind the tree, carrying a white flag, and a couple of minutes later, loaded up with our gear, we were heading slowly up the hill, picking through the thick foliage, walking behind a stick on which the biggest pair of white undershorts I'd ever seen hung like a wet sail. West took point. Ryder had the rear. As we walked, LeDuc and I schooled OSI's newest special agent and briefed him with an overview of our intentions. The guy listened, sweating bullets.

The first indication that we were getting close to the rebels' forward positions came after we'd walked for about an hour, and was a fragment of conversation carried on the breeze down the hill. The second was the crack of a rifle shot that carved a large splinter off a tree inches from Boink's face, showering him with moss and wood dust and making him jump. If he'd still been wearing that white flag we were following, there'd have been a big brown smudge in the bottom of it.

We stopped and LeDuc called out a phrase in French that we'd agreed on previously to use in this eventuality: '*Nous sommes Américains. Nous sommes avec vous. Nous portons le drapeau blanc*', which, loosely translated, meant, 'We're Americans – white flag. We surrender.'

Cassidy cut the flexcuffs off and handed Marcel one of the Nazarians with an empty magazine. He then showed him that the safety on his own weapon was in the off position, in case the African should decide to make a run for it. Marcel nodded understanding, his forehead slick with sweat and dark, wet patches under his armpits.

At that moment, a four-man squad – or, more correctly, three men and a baby of no more than ten years of age – raced down the hill toward us. They were nervous as hell and carrying semi-automatic rifles. Those of us with weapons put them slowly on the ground in front of us and we all put our hands up.

'*Nous sommes Américains, Américains.*' LeDuc and I took turns saying it. I noticed that the Africans had their fingers resting on triggers, and had no doubt that their safeties were off. I hoped none of them was prone to sneezing. Two more soldiers strode down between the trees, one of them with his hand resting on the side-arm belted to his hip. He snapped orders at the detail, which then stepped back but kept their weapons trained on us.

'*Nous sommes Américains. Nous sommes avec vous. Nous portons le drapeau blanc,*' LeDuc repeated.

'*Mais vous êtês Français?*' the man asked LeDuc.

'*Oui, je suis Français,*' LeDuc answered. 'MONUC.'

An exchange between the two men followed as the African inspected Leila and Ayesha. He seemed to like what he saw. He then moved up and down the line, not so happy to see the US Army and the USAF.

The kid from the squad, accompanied by someone probably not much older than him, stepped forward, picked up our weapons and ejected the magazines before placing them back on the ground. Junior snatched the backpack from Ryder and stuffed the mags into it.

'He accepts that we are not their enemy,' LeDuc told us, 'but he is still nervous. He is only a junior lieutenant and I think he is not sure what he should do.'

The officer nodded as LeDuc spoke, as if he understood English, but he plainly didn't. He approached me and said, '*Vous êtes Américain, hein? Ou en êtes-vous en Amérique?*'

'What did he say?' I asked LeDuc.

'He asked whereabouts in America you come from.'

'Tell him Shitsville, New Jersey.'

Whether the lieutenant understood or not, he nodded, moved up the line and stopped at Marcel. '*Parlez-vous Français?*' he asked, looking the man up and down.

Sweat leaked from every pore on Marcel's body. He shook his head, maybe a little too vehemently. 'N-no, no speak French,' he managed to get past his lips.

The lieutenant nodded and something caught his attention on the ground, sticking out from under Cassidy's boot. He bent down, tapped Cassidy's leg to get him to shift his weight, then picked the object up. Jesus – the flexcuffs removed from Marcel's wrists. He twirled them in front of his eyes and looked at Cassidy and then at Marcel. Did he understand their significance? The lieutenant's squad passed a couple of quiet, nervous comments between themselves.

The officer didn't say anything, but kept looking at the cuffs and then back at us.

'*Nous sommes amis,*' LeDuc reassured him – we're friends.

'*Oui . . . oui,*' the officer said, puzzled by something. But then he seemed to come to some agreement with himself and said, '*Amis.*' Friends. He motioned to the kid to pass him the pack containing the magazines. He opened it, pulled one of them out, inspected it briefly and then tossed it back in. From the hollow sound it made, I knew it was the empty one, the mag from Marcel's weapon. He extracted another mag from the bag and gave it the once-over, dropped it back in, frowned and zipped up the bag. I didn't like any of this.

'*Les armes de Chine,*' he said, motioning at the guns at our feet.

He'd observed that we had some Chinese weapons – that much French I could take a stab at understanding.

'*Oui,*' LeDuc spoke up. '*Nous avons pris vos adversaires.*'

'*Avez-vous les tuer?*'

'*Oui.*'

'What was that about?' I asked LeDuc, his exchange with the officer having lost me pretty much out of the starting gate.

'I told him that we killed his enemies and took their weapons.'

The lieutenant and his unit seemed to have relaxed somewhat, their beaming smiles being a big clue. Apparently, we'd done the right thing here at least.

'Tell him that we are survivors from a helicopter crash and that several of our party have been captured by his enemies,' I said.

LeDuc told him and the man nodded, taking it in.

He walked past Leila and Ayesha and grinned like an idiot as he looked them up and down. I had no doubt about what was on his mind. Two minutes alone with Leila and I knew he'd change it.

'Can you tell this clown to stop leering at me?' said Leila, flicking her eyes at me.

'LeDuc, tell the officer the women in our company have HIV,' I told him.

'What?' Leila spat.

'I'm just giving him a good reason to stop thinking about what he's thinking about.'

LeDuc passed on the news about the unfortunate condition of our women and the officer shook his head, saddened, and took a couple of paces back, as if Leila and Ayesha were contagious.

'See?' I said. 'Worked.'

Leila's eyes flashed dangerously, like some kind of poisonous sea creature changing color.

The lieutenant moved on to Boink, and looked him over like he couldn't quite believe humans grew that big. And, mostly, he was right.

'Wass this motherfucker want?' Twenny's lieutenant asked.

'Don't know,' said West calmly. 'Just smile and be cool, Gigantor.'

The African said something to Boink.

'Wad he say?' Boink asked.

LeDuc informed him. 'He said you must be very rich to be as big as you are.'

'Motherfuck,' Boink muttered.

The officer said something in rapid-fire French to his patrol, and then addressed LeDuc.

'He wants us to follow him,' said the Frenchman.

'Do we know for sure which outfit these men belong to?' I asked.

'*Oui*. They are NCDP – your allies.'

'All right!' said Ryder. 'Friends and allies.'

'The jury's still out on both points,' I reminded him, doing an impression of a smile, my face still a little swollen.

The unit part-led, part-escorted us diagonally up the hill, toward the extremity of their lines, LeDuc chatting to the officer as we climbed. Once on the crest, we turned roughly northwest and followed the ridgeline, the sound of small arms fire getting closer and crackling like squeezed bubble wrap. Eventually, we came across soldiers guarding the flanks of the rebel's line. The men stopped what they were doing and stared at us, many standing as we walked by. Some gave Leila and Ayesha predatorial grins.

'So what's the verdict?' Rutherford asked. 'Are they friendly?'

'Have they shot us?' LeDuc answered. 'We are lucky they are not Mai-Mai or Ugandan renegades.'

'If you say so,' I told him, not convinced.

In attitude, age, numbers and disposition, these men seemed identical to the FARDC force opposing them. The only differences I could see were in the uniforms they wore – superseded US Army jungle pattern BDUs. They carried mostly M16s and some AK-47s. I saw a couple of M16s propped against a log and went close enough to see that both had their numbers intact, which told me that they were meant to have them. *Friends and allies.*

We came out of the rainforest on the crest of the ridgeline, and an unobstructed view across to the eastern horizon opened out. The trail took us close to the edge of empty space. I looked over a precipice and the rock face quickly fell away to a sheer cliff – a drop of close to a hundred and fifty feet. At the base of the cliff was a lake of milky blue water. I'd been wondering why the FARDC company hadn't just retreated to another, more tactically favorable, position, which suggested that maybe it was the rebels who were pinned down up here on this hill, forced into a corner of sorts with the cliff at their backs and nowhere to retreat to. But even if that were the situation, it was a hell of a position to have to assault. A little down the hill, in the dappled light streaming through the treetops, I could see a mortar crew working up a sweat, the explosions hammering the FARDC positions in the valley below, the sound muffled by eight hundred meters or so of rainforest.

This HQ was roughly the same size as the FARDC's one that West and I had scoped, though the rebel HQ was better appointed, with half a dozen US Army tents similar to the ones our forces used in Iraq and Afghanistan. Several uniformed men were standing behind a trestle table, in discussion over a map, surrounded by a cohort of men armed with newish MP-5 machine guns. West nudged my elbow and motioned off to the opposite side of the area, where four corpses with black, swollen tongues and broken necks were hanging motionless from the bough of a tree, entertaining a black swarm of flies. A bird perched on one of the heads, leaned over and nonchalantly pecked at an eye socket. A blue patch on the corpse's shoulder told me that these were DRC men. I glanced at Marcel, who appeared to be shaking, on the edge either of falling to the ground in a blubbering heap or breaking into a run, neither of which would be healthy for him, or us, right at the moment.

Even though the men at the trestle tables were maybe only in their late twenties, or early thirties, they were obviously the commanders. The lieutenant escorting us waited till one of the men looked up and motioned him over, which happened eventually. The lieutenant marched to the desk and saluted a short, fat guy in his early thirties, who wore a thick leopard-skin headband, Ray-Ban 'Aviator' sunglasses and held a black walking stick with gold handle. A brief conversation ensued between them and then Tubby with the fancy headdress came over to us, accompanied by the lieutenant and three of the men with the Heckler & Koch rattles.

'Good morning,' he said in a deep French-accented voice. 'We are Colonel Makenga.'

Given the use of the plural 'we' here, I wondered whether one of the folks accompanying him shared his name and rank. Or maybe English was not his first language and he'd simply gotten it wrong. Or – third option – the guy was an asshole, prone to using the royal 'we' on account of his ego was selling tickets on itself.

'Which one of you is in command?' he continued.

'Me,' I said. 'Major Cooper, United States Air Force Office of Special Investigations.'

'We are pleased to meet you, Major.'

Hmm . . . option three.

'And what are you and your people doing in our quiet little corner of the world?' He glanced at Leila and Ayesha and gave them the slightest of bows, creating another couple of chins that butted up against all the others and pushed out beads of greasy sweat along the crease lines.

The colonel's lieutenant hadn't had the opportunity to pass on our story in any detail, so I gave him the headlines about us being on our way to the MONUC compound at Goma, where two of our party were to give a concert for the UN contingent, before our French-made helicopter decided to fall out of the sky.

He stroked his chins while I talked, appearing to be in thinking mode.

'We came down close to your enemy's line,' I continued, 'and several of our party were captured and taken prisoner.'

'Hmm, that is not good news,' he said. 'So . . . how can we possibly be of assistance?'

'We need to contact our people at Cyangugu, let them know what's happened. So, if you've got a satellite phone . . .'

He gave a big sigh and then shook his head like he was deeply sorry. 'We agree that this could be a course of action; however, your country has seen fit not to provide us with such luxuries as satellite phones. Our communications here are extremely limited.'

'Is there any way we can get word out?'

'We could send a runner, perhaps, but not in our current predicament. We're afraid you will have to stay with us.'

He admired the handle on his walking stick – a solid gold rooster. Chunky gold-link bracelets manacled his wrists, and a nugget of gold the size of a pork knuckle swung from his thick neck on a gold chain. Even aside from the fact that he wore more bling than a Reno pimp, there was something off-putting about this guy. Maybe it was the affected speech patterns together with the disconcerting fact that, snake-like, he didn't appear to blink. Or perhaps it was the violence that seemed to sit, suppressed, just below the civility. I could imagine this guy petting a puppy one minute and then dashing its brains out with that cane of his the next. And, of course, the four hanging ornaments looking at their toes on the edge of the compound helped this allusion along nicely. The bird perched on one of those ornaments squawked and flew off.

'Oh,' Makenga said, raising a finger as if he'd just had an afterthought. 'Your Chinese weapons. Our lieutenant informs us that you claim to have taken them from our enemies down in the valley.'

Claim? 'That's correct,' I said.

'Along with the weapons you were captured with, there was a sniper rifle and high-power binoculars.'

I saw that all our weapons, backpacks and camelbacks were collected on one of the trestle tables.

Captured? 'Yeah,' I said, wondering where this was going.

'How do we know you weren't sent to kill us?'

What?! Even though the use of the words 'claim' and 'captured' were ringing alarm bells, the question was so left of field that I found myself wondering whether this guy's ham and cheese on rye was missing something important, like the ham and cheese. I noticed again that there were a lot of guys standing around with MP-5s. I also noticed that they were now glaring at us and, from the expressions on their faces, all of them appeared to have eaten something that hadn't agreed with them.

'Pardon me?' I said, trying to think fast. I felt a little like I was back in LeDuc's chopper when things were spinning out of control.

'How can we be sure that you and your party are not mercenaries?'

I blinked. Jesus . . . This was a possibility none of us had considered, but with Kornflak & Greene's fingers in the pie around here, I could see how someone who spent their life dodging bullets at every turn might jump to that conclusion. Moreover, if this guy believed it was possible that American contract killers might go on a mission in the African rainforest with two women and a shoe-in for *The Biggest Loser* along for the ride, then he probably wouldn't accept their presence as proof of our innocence. Nevertheless, I didn't have much else to work with.

'We are a joint US Army and United States Air Force personal security detail,' I said, hardening my tone. 'These are three of our principals.' I motioned at Leila, Ayesha and Boink. 'If you had a satellite phone, you could verify it.'

'And here we are, back at the start without one,' Colonel Makenga said with his hands apart. He gestured at the lieutenant holding one of our backpacks – it was Ryder's. The lieutenant handed over the pack and the two men held a quick conference while they rifled through its contents.

Makenga produced one of the magazines – the empty one. 'When you were intercepted on your way here trying to infiltrate our flanks, you were disarmed. One of your people carried a weapon with an empty magazine. If you are all together, why would one of you be carrying an unloaded weapon? Why would that be?'

He then pulled out Ryder's nylon bracelets. 'Wrist restraints were also found. Would you care to explain these inconsistencies to us?'

I couldn't – not without ending Marcus's life as surely as putting a gun to his head and pulling the trigger. This was a bad situation. I avoided specifics and reached for straws. 'The American people are allies with the CNDP,' I said. 'I'm not a mercenary and nor are any of my men here. I told you that we departed the CNDP training camp at Cyangugu two days ago, after our principals put on a concert for your soldiers and the US advisors there. If you have any doubts, contact your own Colonel Biruta, who's in camp there.'

A nerve in Makenga's face twitched, indenting the skin and muscle of his cheek. 'Perhaps there is enough in your assertion to prevent the immediate summary execution of you and your people.' The colonel pushed out his lips and rolled his tongue across his front teeth. 'You will remain here as our guests until your claims can be verified, or until we decide what to do with you.'

I could feel Cassidy and the others tensing for a fight. I said, 'We have other principals who are being held, captured by the FARDC below. We need to do something about negotiating their release.'

A sly grin slid across his face. 'We were of the belief that you Americans never negotiate with hostage takers.'

'We don't negotiate with terrorists – the rules get rubbery for straight criminals.'

'I see. Interesting. Nevertheless . . .' he said, opening out his hands again to show me that there was nothing, such as options, in them.

The daylight suddenly faded as if the sun had blown a fuse. I looked up. Gangrenous thunderheads were boiling into the sky overhead, their undersides gray-green and tending to black in places. The storms in this place lined up like barges in a busy canal.

'Well,' Makenga continued, 'we would be delighted to extend our hospitality to you and your party.'

There was a spike in the noise level of the battle still going on down the hill, indicating a wind shift. A breeze arrived and freshened quickly into wind, heralding the arrival of the storm front.

The colonel raised his gold cock several inches, an apparent signal to those unhappy guards with their machine guns, who stepped in, surrounded us, and marshaled us out of the HQ and off toward a little hospitality, CNDP style. Somehow I didn't see us getting any Napoleon brandy from these folks, either.

'Gee, LeDuc,' I heard Rutherford say, as we were led away at gunpoint, 'lucky for us they're not Mai-Mai or Ugandan renegades. Then we'd really be in the shitter.'

The armed escort herded us through the encampment until we arrived at one of two circular corrals made from saplings sunk in the ground and lashed together. One of the guards shouted at us.

'They want us to empty our pockets,' said LeDuc, translating.

We were surrounded and heavily outnumbered by people armed with frowns and submachine guns. Like the man once said, resistance was futile. I turned my pockets out on the ground. The rebel soldiers moved through our group, cleaning us out of anything useful. Cassidy, LeDuc, West, Rutherford and Marcel and I were individually searched. Ayesha was individually groped, which seemed to improve the disposition of the gropers. Then it was Leila's turn.

'Hey. What the hell do you think you're doing?' she shouted at the man with his hand between her legs. She spun around and slapped him, and he slapped her right back hard so that she went down into the mud. Cassidy and I took a step forward and machine gun muzzles were jammed into our faces.

The rain began to fall. The corral stank of animal feces and urine. The soldiers disengaged, backing out through the door of our open prison, the door to which was then closed and bound shut. Cassidy and Ayesha helped Leila up and we all just stood and shivered for a time, with nowhere to go and battered by raindrops the size of hens' eggs impregnated with ice chips. Thunder arrived simultaneously with the lightning as the storm front passed overhead.

'That business about the US negotiating with criminals,' said Cassidy, his teeth chattering. 'It'll never happen. We're on our own.'

'The colonel doesn't know that.'

'What are they going to do to us?' Leila asked.

Ayesha could give her a couple of clues.

Marcel moaned and shook his head. He didn't need to ask, either.

'We shouldn't have brought *him*,' said Leila, pointing at Marcel. 'That man has put all of us at risk. Those questions about the handcuffs and the empty magazine – the man with the cane knew what was up.'

I doubted it, but I let it go and no one else said anything. If Leila was determined to be a superbitch right to the end, who was I to stop her?

The star burst into tears and hugged Ayesha to her. I felt sorry for Ayesha.

Within half an hour, the thunder and lightning had ended, but the torrent was still coming down hard, falling, at times, more like an avalanche than like rain. The noise it made completely drowned out the sounds of battle drifting up from the valley below. West, Cassidy and I went on an inspection of our cage, a circular area maybe fifty feet across. We all very quickly came to the conclusion that we couldn't go over, under or through it – not easily and not before we were spotted. The bars were green saplings over twelve feet in height, the ends of which were buried two to three feet in the mud, and the whole structure was lashed together with some kind of green vine. The rain only seemed to make it all bind together tighter. Sets of eyes peered at us through the gaps.

LeDuc came over. 'These pens are common,' he said. 'I've seen bulls charge at walls such as these.'

'They ever make it through?' I asked, half an eye on Boink.

He shook his head. '*Non*.'

I pulled and pushed the wall here and there, testing its strength. Cassidy, West and Rutherford joined in. A pole suddenly speared through a gap between the saplings and slammed into the side of my head, knocking me down.

'Hey!' Rutherford yelled out, kicking the wall.

I was down on all fours, the ringing between my ears like that of a church belfry on Sunday morning. Hands under my arms lifted me onto my feet.

'You okay, Cooper?' Cassidy asked.

I opened and closed my jaw in an attempt to stop the clanging. 'Now I know how a cue ball feels,' I said.

'They're going to do us, skipper,' said Rutherford. 'No question.'

'Yeah,' agreed West.

There was a lump on my skull. Blood seeped from ruptured skin.

I didn't believe the bullshit about verifying our claims, either. Yeah, Makenga was going to have us whacked for sure. And if the asshole was anything like the psychos down in the valley, he wouldn't be whacking us clean.

'So what we gonna do about it?' asked West.

'They will come for the women first,' said LeDuc.

I rubbed my face. We were completely on our own, locked in an empty enclosure with no hope of any outside assistance. The four men were looking at me, apparently waiting for me to reach behind and pull a rabbit out of my butt, given that I didn't have a hat. 'Well, I once saw this movie where some prisoners built an airplane and flew it out of the attic,' I said. 'We could do something like that.'

They kept looking at me.

'They're gonna come for us,' I said, repeating LeDuc's take on the situation.

'Yeah, that much we know,' West said.

'Then let's work with that.'

WAITING FOR THE NIGHT, we sat in the mud on the high side of the enclosure and glommed together to conserve warmth. No one talked. Someone grabbed my hand and held on tight. It was Ayesha. I could only imagine what was going through her mind. No one said a word, not even Leila. When the darkness was complete, I put our one and only chance into action and slid away from the group, working through the mud on my belly to the far side of the enclosure. LeDuc believed word would get around about Ayesha and Leila. I was hoping order might be a little on the lax side among the CNDP rank and file and that some of the boys might drop in for a little Intercourse & Inebriation.

OUR WRISTWATCHES HAD BEEN confiscated, but it would have been after 22:00 when the door to our pen was forced ajar. I could make out four – or maybe five – shapes coming through the gap, creeping quietly. Moments later, I heard a woman's muffled scream. Dropping to the ground and keeping low, I moved in the night shadow that lived at the base of our prison wall, making my way around the circumference of the enclosure. Cassidy, West, Rutherford, LeDuc and Ryder were making things difficult for the Africans, but not too difficult. The soldiers had to think that we were soft targets.

Going down on my belly for the last twenty meters, I snaked through the mud, coming up behind the intruders. From the sound of the gruff commands and muffled shouts, the Africans – five of them – were fast realizing that they'd bitten off more than they could chew. One of them had had enough. He backed away from the entangled shadows on the ground and I heard him hoarsely whisper in French. He leveled his rifle, serious about taking what they wanted. Two of his buddies went forward and dragged a struggling body away from the others.

'No! No! Help me!' I recognized the voice – Leila's.

Then a second body got hauled out by her foot: Ayesha.

I was getting closer, close enough to smell the intruders – a pungent, stale, unwashed animal funk mixed with cheap, coarse tobacco. The intruders hadn't seen me, or conducted a head count to see if someone were missing. They didn't know it but, rather than being their friend, the night worked against them. I came up behind the man holding the rifle. He sensed rather than heard my presence, but not before I kicked him between the legs hard enough to put his nuts over a goal post. He began to sink to his knees but I broke his neck with an elbow strike before he reached them. Attacked by a shadow, the Africans were momentarily disoriented and stood rooted to the spot while they processed what they thought they'd just seen happen to their buddy. A few seconds of uncertainty was all we needed. I took out a second African, sweeping his legs out from under him so that he landed on his back, the air rushing out of his lungs. I snapped his head to one side and the vertebrae in his neck cracked like dry walnuts. A flurry of intense violence broke out. Cassidy leaped up and strangled the man standing over him. West and Ryder tackled their man, Ryder pounding in his skull with a rock the size of his fist. Rutherford got Mr Lucky Last, sending him off to the land of nod with a sweet right cross to a glass jaw. I kept watch for more intruders, while the Brit sat on the man's back and pushed his face in the mud, holding it there until he drowned, gurgling and shaking to the end.

Run

They died peacefully, if not in peace, alerting no one. Dragging the bodies to one side, we stripped them of their weapons, collecting knives, three H&K MP-5s and two M16s with spare mags for both.

'Question is, were they Makenga's messengers?' I wondered aloud as we cleaned up. 'Or were they out on their own initiative?'

Hard answers would've been handy. If the guards we just killed were on orders from Makenga, it meant we probably had more time to play with. If, however, they were just out for a little opportunistic gang rape, then the real hit squad could turn up at any minute. Assuming it was the latter, we couldn't hang around.

'Now what?' Rutherford whispered as he checked a captured MP-5, making sure it would work as H&K intended, and that its magazine was full.

'I've got half of an idea,' I said, following the SAS sergeant's lead, giving my weapon the once-over.

'You beat me,' said West.

'Ditto,' said Rutherford.

We hurried back to the civilians.

Leila was hyperventilating, Ayesha beside her. I could hear their teeth chattering.

'Man, that was some evil shit, yo!' said Boink in an excited whisper. 'You fucked those motherfuckers in the *ass*.'

I hoped not, but I knew where he was coming from. I breathed hard. Adrenalin levels were high. We'd had the fight. Now came the flight.

'Stick close to us,' I told our civilians. 'Be as quiet as you can and keep to the shadows.'

Leila let out a sob. If this was diva crap, it had to end. I considered slapping her but decided this was not the right time to make myself feel better, so instead I sat beside her. Convulsions racked her body. She was in shock, the realization of what she'd just managed to avoid knocking the Rodeo Drive out of her attitude. All that was left was a scared young woman struggling to deal with her current reality.

I put my arm around her. 'You can do this, Leila,' I said quietly, giving her a squeeze.

She shook her head. 'N . . . no . . .'

'Yes, you can.' I took a deep breath and let it out, which always helps when you're about to lie through your teeth. 'We are going to walk right out of this place, one step at a time. You'll see.'

'They were going to r . . . rape us.'

'That's not going to happen.'

'I'm sc . . . scared,' she said.

'We're all scared, but it's time to go.'

'Yeah, Leila; c'mon, girl,' Boink whispered.

'I don't want to d . . . die here.'

'That's not going to happen,' I repeated. 'They'd fire my ass for sure.'

Ryder crouched beside her and hooked a lock of her wet, muddy hair behind an ear.

'You'll be back in the recording studio next week and all this will just seem like a bad day in rehab,' I said.

It took a moment for my words to penetrate. She half cried, half laughed.

'Duke's going to stay right beside you all the way, aren't you, Duke?'

'Right beside you,' he repeated.

'But you have to be as quiet as you can. I want you to breathe.'

She breathed.

'Deeper.'

She breathed in and out several times and her shoulders gave a final shudder.

'Better?' I asked her.

She nodded.

'Things get hard to handle, that's what you do – breathe deep.'

Leila sucked in another breath.

'One step at a time, okay?'

She nodded again.

'Ayesha? How about you?'

'I'm oh . . . okay.'

'Good. Got your bags packed?'

'Yes.'

'Then I'll send someone up to collect them,' I said, standing. 'LeDuc – Marcel's your buddy. He misbehaves, let me know. Better still, let Boink know.'

The African got the drift, if not the specifics, and his eyes were wide with fear, the whites showing in the almost complete darkness.

'*Oui*,' he said.

Rutherford and West rearranged the corpses so that they appeared to be sitting with their backs against the enclosure, mimicking our positions. We all then moved to the enclosure gate, pausing there to make sure the guys who had paid us a visit had no one keeping watch. Nothing moved. The loudest noise was my own heartbeat. I followed the advice I gave Leila and Ayesha, and dragged a couple of breaths down to my toes to get the nerves under control.

The downpour had become a misting of light rain, which neither helped nor hindered us. There was no moon, however, which sat on the asset side of the balance sheet. The rebel force had long since retired for the night and this being the very rear of their encampment, I was hoping for fewer rather than more guards on duty. Nevertheless, we took it slow and careful. Cassidy and I scouted forward, keeping to the foliage, which was patchier up on the ridgeline than it was down in the valley.

It made moving around easier, but reduced the cover. West, Rutherford, Ryder, and LeDuc brought the principals forward only when we were sure that the coast was clear.

It wasn't that late, maybe a little after ten thirty, but the place was quiet, the exhaustion of the day's battle weighing heavily on the men. As hoped, security proved to be light. Cassidy and I found several large groups of men huddled under ponchos, tentless like their enemies, and we skirted around them easily. Along the way, we encountered three guards, all of whom were asleep at their posts, wrapped in ponchos and seated at the bases of trees, their weapons cradled in their laps.

We arrived at the HQ without incident, and stopped behind a rock outcrop to survey it. All lights were out. Frogs were everywhere, making a sound that reminded me of someone knocking on a door. There were hundreds of them. The overall effect was like a large team of salesmen let loose inside an apartment building. In the HQ spread out before us, the landscape was black on black, which made detail difficult to make out, but the layout of the area was in my head from our earlier welcome by Colonel Fucknuts, which helped. I let my eyes get used to the shapes and then waited for any movement to highlight potential threats.

Ryder nudged my arm and indicated something going on off to my left. I saw nothing, and then a red dot in the darkness expanded and briefly illuminated a face. A smoker. His weapon was slung on his shoulder, which suggested he wasn't expecting any trouble. As we watched, another guard revealed himself, smoking, wandering around apparently randomly among the tents. So, two guards. We kept watching.

Correction, three guards.

Correction, five guards, including another smoker.

Shit. Our chances of success were diminishing.

We waited another few minutes, but the count stopped at five.

'One of those suppressed QCWs would come in handy right about now,' Rutherford whispered in my ear. After a few moments, he added, 'With a night scope.'

I put my finger against my lips then drew it across my throat.

He nodded, and produced a US-made Ka-bar taken from the soldiers we killed back at the pen. The knife's razor-sharp blade was a non-reflective dull black and perfect for the job at hand, as was the SAS sergeant wielding it.

I indicated that he should take West with him, and leave the smokers till last so that we could see when the threat was negated. Rutherford confirmed that he understood the orders, backed away from the rock in company with West, similarly armed, and I lost them just seconds later, their black silhouettes becoming one with the night shadows.

I waited, watching the smokers who were by now at opposite ends of the HQ. One of them dropped his butt and didn't pick it up. Scratch one. At almost the same instant, on the opposite side of the HQ, the other smoker put the cigarette in his mouth but didn't get to inhale. Scratch two. Smoker number three took a few seconds longer for his habit to get him killed. I heard nothing. As the smokers were the last to go, I knew that the HQ was now clear and that we could move. I signaled Cassidy and Ryder to follow with the principals and we all rendezvoused with Rutherford and West, meeting up with them in front of the trestle tables.

I was surprised to see what appeared to be a large rifle cradled in West's arms. I ran my hand down the long barrel. Yep, that's what it was. He pulled back a canvas cover on one of the tables to show me where he'd found it and I saw the familiar black shapes of body armor and submachine guns – our guns – the ones the lieutenant and his unit had confiscated. Shit, it seemed that our gear had simply been left here and forgotten about. We recovered what we needed: the backpacks containing the spare mags, tinned radishes and beef jerky, a couple of the QCWs, most of the Nazarians and M16s and, of course, the sniper rifle. The binoculars were missing, dammit.

This was where the half an idea I said I had was really going to get interesting. I led the way to the far corner of the HQ area, and picked up the trail that we'd followed in, frogs jumping out of our way. A couple of minutes later, we were standing at the spot I'd seen when we arrived here, the one that provided the view across to the east. Now, however, it was just a very large black void.

'You're fucking kidding me?' said Cassidy, my half-a-plan suddenly becoming clear to him. From the way he said it, I was thinking maybe he thought I had half a brain.

'No I'm not,' I said. 'This is the way out.'

Boink leaned forward for a closer look at the nothingness that yawned a few inches in front of his Adidas.

Marcel spoke rapidly and fearfully to LeDuc.

'Cooper, he cannot swim,' the pilot translated.

'Me, neither,' said Ayesha.

'I got a problem with heights,' I said. I didn't, but I told everyone that to make them feel better. It didn't appear to.

'Swimming's not the immediate problem,' said Rutherford. 'How exactly we gonna get the big man down there?'

'And how do we know the water's deep enough for us to jump into?' asked Ryder.

My answers weren't nearly as good as the questions, but I gave them anyway. 'I had a look when we came in. A couple of ravines empty into it, but the pool down there is pretty still, which means it's probably got some depth.' No one appeared particularly convinced. 'Look,' I whispered, failing to keep a lid on my impatience, 'if anyone's got an alternative, now's a good time to put it on the table. But we've left a trail of dead people behind us, like Hansel and Gretel left bread crumbs, so whatever we do we'll have to do it quick.'

'A jump gets bad for your health at six storys,' Rutherford said.

I could have told them about the time I fell out of a plane without a parachute and survived a fall of around twenty thousand feet. But I knew no one would believe it – hell, I still didn't believe it – so I kept that to myself.

'A hundred feet is about the limit,' said Cassidy. 'Land the right way and you should be okay.'

'What's the wrong way?' Ryder asked.

'On your head,' the master sergeant replied.

'Get me the hell down to where I have to jump an' I'll do the rest, yo,' said Boink, sucking it up.

I realized that, being as large as he was, Boink probably hadn't seen his feet in quite a while. We'd have to rope him down to the jump point. We had no rope, but I knew where to get some. To Cassidy, I said, 'Find some cover. If we're not back inside ten minutes, get everyone down as best you can. Mike, follow me.'

Keeping to the shadows, West and I skulked back to the HQ, where everything was as quiet as any mortuary invaded by frogs would be. I tripped on a dead smoker.

'Watch your feet, boss,' West whispered in my ear.

'Next time, clean up your mess,' I told him.

The DRC men hanging in the trees hadn't gone anywhere.

'What are your climbing skills like?' I asked.

'Average,' he replied.

'Then they're better than mine. Up you go and cut three of them down. Wait till you feel me take the weight of the body before you cut. Don't drop the rope ends. Bring 'em all down with you.'

'Roger that,' he said.

We moved one of the trestle tables, positioning it under the bodies. West chose one of the dead guys on the end of the row, jumped and grabbed the rope above his head, and then shinnied up. The rope was tied around a bough maybe twenty feet off the ground. Three lengths of it would give us enough to do the job. When I felt West had stopped climbing, I took the weight of the corpse, and lifted it. A disgusting ooze with a putrid, unspeakable stench leaked out of its nostrils, trickled onto my ear and ran down my neck. A second later, I felt the rope cut. I lowered the body onto the table, then onto the ground. We repeated this a couple of times while I concentrated on stopping the gag reflex. West brought down the ends of the cords and we slipped the nooses off the cold, broken necks.

A movement on the other side of the HQ distracted West. He pointed at two men walking slowly along the path. Perhaps the watch was about to change, in which case our time here was up. We gathered the ropes together and retreated, putting the hangman's tree between us and the newcomers. Our people were off the track behind a screen of bushes. Cassidy, Rutherford and Ryder were busy transferring the spare weapons to the backpacks that contained drysacks, which would make them buoyant and easier to handle in the water.

'Jesus, Vin,' Rutherford whispered. 'Is that you? What stinks?'

'Been a while since I flossed,' I said. Moving on quickly, if only to distract myself from the ghastly smell, I added, 'We've got around sixty feet of rope.' I looked Cassidy up and down. He had maybe twenty pounds on me, and in other circumstances would have been the natural choice to help someone like Boink rope down, but as this was my plan – and, as plans went, it wasn't one of my better ones – I felt I should be the one who anchored the big lug.

West had almost finished tying the rope ends together. When he was done, I took an end of the rope, wound it around my thigh and then looped it around one shoulder. I got the other end and looped it twice around Boink's midriff and tied it off.

'I'll go first and scout a path down,' said Rutherford.

'Okay,' I said, 'but keep one eye on us.' If Boink lost his footing and I couldn't hold him, I didn't want the guy's subsequent roll down the hill cleaning up the Brit. 'Who's going after us?'

'I'll take care of everyone else,' said Cassidy. 'You've got enough on your plate.'

A distant cry of alarm silenced the frogs, and the night stillness came alive with urgent distant voices. I doubted Colonel Makenga's men would look for us where we were temporarily hunkered down; not straight away, at least. But time was running out.

I looked at each of our civilians and Ryder in turn. 'All right, people, we can do this. The way down's going to be tricky. Make sure of your footing before you put your weight on it. When the going gets steep, you might find it more comfortable going down backward. If you need help, don't be afraid to ask.'

Leila, Ayesha and Ryder all nodded gravely.

LeDuc translated for our prisoner.

'Let's go,' I said when he'd finished.

Rutherford led the way. He criss-crossed the edge of the dropaway, going back and forth a couple of times, before making a decision on the best way down. Nimbly, he slid down onto a ledge five feet below, turned and motioned for Boink to follow.

'Take your time,' I told him. We both knew I meant hurry the fuck up.

Without protest, Boink got down on his hands and knees and wriggled further out as I took the weight on the rope.

'Easy,' I cautioned as he disappeared over the edge a little faster than I had anticipated. Two seconds later, the rope snapped taut. And suddenly the world became a rolling, tumbling spin cycle as I was yanked over the edge and pulled down the steepening incline, my fall interrupted by impacts with bushes, rocks and mud outcrops. I went into a ball and rolled faster, out of control and tangled in the rope, smashing into solid objects. And suddenly the collisions stopped and I was falling upside down through clear air. I was going to fall to my death unless something—

A powerful force grabbed my ankle, gave me a vicious flick and almost pulled my leg out of my hip socket as I came to a near-instant stop, hanging upside down. I bounced and swung pendulum-like, the rope wound around my lower leg and ankle, and the blood rushing to my head. The arc I was dangling on carried me into the sheer rock wall, and I bashed my right shoulder against it as small rocks and gravel pulled down from the fall rained over me, filling my mouth and nostrils and hitting my neck and chin. I closed my eyes and did my best to shield my head. Once the worst of this had passed, I relaxed a little and wondered what to do next. At least nothing felt broken.

Somewhere above, Boink had obviously come to a stop while I'd continued falling and now I was hanging in space over the water, joined to him by the hangman's rope. I looked down but couldn't see anything below. There was no moon and no stars. The only color was black and there was nothing discernible in this inverted shapeless world of darkness.

No vibration or movement was coming down the rope. That told me Boink wasn't moving. At my end, things weren't much better. The rope wrapped around my ankle presented its own problem. I checked the scabbard on my thigh. I'd lost the Ka-bar somewhere on the way down, which meant I had nothing with which to cut the rope. I had to get my foot untangled somehow, but to achieve that, I had to take the pressure off that knot. Swinging upward, I grabbed the rope just above my ankle, and tried to heave myself up. I got nowhere. Who the hell was I kidding? There was no way I could pull off a Cirque du Soleil stunt like that.

A gray shape flew past, falling fast, falling silent. Another followed, screaming. I knew that scream: Leila. A line of sparkles crackled up in the sky. Muzzle flashes. Shit, the rebels had us pegged. Another shape dropped through the air not far away. An instant later, the rock face above me exploded into flying chips as the soldiers fired at the next jumper, leading its descent, trying to hit it. The line of semi-automatic fire raced down the wall toward me. Jesus, I was a sitting duck. Worse – I was a hanging one. Stone chips flew and fizzed past me, some ripping through the fabric of my battle uniform and cutting up my skin. From the downward march of the sparks against the rock wall, I could see that the rain of lead was coming toward me. It was going to saw off my foot. Something punched into the rope, viciously shaking my leg. And then I was free-falling, accelerating into the black void, upside down, head first – the wrong way.

Animals

I smashed into something hard, which gave way beneath me. Sudden cold made me want to gag for breath, and my nose and throat filled with water as the back of my neck ploughed into the rock bottom of the lake floor. I fought the panic brought on by cold and disorientation and stopped moving until natural buoyancy told me which way was up. Turning, my feet found the rocks and I pushed off, lungs burning as two torpedoes shot into the water beside me, dragging me down again.

Thrusting off the bottom a second time, I came to the surface choking and coughing, and Cassidy bobbed up beside me with Boink's head cradled in the crook of his arm, rescue-style. I reached down to my ankle, untangled the rope. I coughed and snorted the cold water out of my nostrils. 'You need help?' I asked Cassidy as he struck out for the bank, shimmering a ghostly white in the moonlight.

'I got this,' he said. 'Look for the others.'

I scoped the surface of the lake. Lucky random shots fired from the ridge speared into the water here and there, pulling up small gray geysers edged with phosphorescence. I hoped Uncle Sugar hadn't sweetened the deal with Makenga by handing out night vision scopes to his people.

My feet felt the gently sloping bottom. Pebbles gave way to a soft ooze. I waded in as close to the water's edge as I could, then pulled myself up onto the bank, the mud sucking and gurgling at my hands, knees and feet. On the shore, several meters beyond the mud, I could dimly make out tall elephant grass. All except Cassidy and Boink had dragged themselves out of the water and onto the bank and were lying there, exhausted. I let myself fall beside the backpacks, the rifles and submachine guns still lashed to them.

'What have we got?' I asked no one in particular.

'So far, bruised ribs, one mild ankle sprain,' said West close by, lying on his back. 'Could've been worse. You?'

I was sore all over but then, who wasn't? 'Fine,' I said.

'The place went nuts when they found our handiwork in the HQ,' said Rutherford behind me, also lying on his back. 'A couple of guys stumbled onto us. One of them got away and we had to leave in a hurry.'

'Marcel,' said LeDuc, standing unsteadily, his feet sinking in the ooze. 'He is gone.'

'You jump with him?' I asked.

'*Oui*. He landed badly. Hit his head on a rock. He drowned.'

I felt a pang of guilt, but there was not much we could do about a dead guy and there were other priorities. I scoped the bank. Leila and Ayesha were flat on their backs, covered in mud, chests heaving with exhaustion and fright, but they seemed okay. Ryder was sitting between them, head between his knees.

'Duke. All right?' I asked him.

He managed a nod.

'Who's got the ankle sprain?' I asked Rutherford.

'Me. More of a rolled ankle. No big deal.' There was a shrug in his tone.

The CNDP above us had given up firing blind into the blackness.

I heard splashing in the water. Cassidy was dragging Boink through the shallow water.

'Need help here,' the sergeant gasped.

Cassidy was a big man, but Boink was in a whole other league. West and I waded back in and hauled him up onto the bank while Rutherford and Duke went to Cassidy's aid.

'What happened up there?' I asked.

'I think that first ledge gave way under him,' said West. 'After that, I'm not sure, but dragging you along behind slowed him down. A tree growing out of the top of the cliff finally stopped him. You missed it and went over.'

'How's he doing?' I could hear Boink's teeth clacking together. He was shivering with cold.

'He was conscious when the rest of us jumped,' said Cassidy. 'I think he went into the water in reasonable shape. Might have hit his head somewhere along the way.'

'Thanks for cutting the rope,' I said. 'Perfect timing.'

'Wasn't cut, not by me anyway.'

I thought back to the moment. There'd been a lot of lead flying about. If a bullet had done the job, I'd been luckier than I thought.

'Everyone make it?' Cassidy asked.

'We lost the prisoner,' I told him.

'Solves a problem then, doesn't it?'

It did.

Boink, lying face up, looked like a beached Manitou in basketball gear. He groaned, his head moving from one side to the other. His eyes opened.

'Yo,' said Rutherford leaning over him. 'Wasssuuup?'

Boink's eyes moved between all of us, roving uncertainly.

They came into focus. 'Fuck,' he said. And then again, with meaning, '*Fuck!*'

Cassidy patted down Boink's legs and arms. 'No breaks,' he reported.

'What about his neck and spine?' asked Rutherford.

'Move your fingers,' Cassidy told him.

Boink wiggled them.

'Now your toes.' Cassidy grabbed the end of his mud-encrusted Nikes. After a few uncertain seconds, he said, 'Yep, got movement.'

'Let's get everyone to dry ground.' I tapped Boink on the leg. 'Can you get up?'

He gave it a go, groaning as he rolled onto his stomach before coming up on all fours. Cassidy and I took an arm each and helped him stand. Boink took a step and the mud sucked hard at his shoes, gurgling loudly. The guy faltered, and then regained his balance.

'I'm over this shit, you know what I'm sayin'?' he said, shaking his head.

Yeah, I knew. We wrestled him up the greasy bank and then onto the flatter ground up beyond the erosion. The elephant grass was thick and each blade of it had a sharp edge, but when flattened it provided a reasonably dry bed. We sat the big man down and went back for the others.

Five minutes later, everyone was higher and a little drier. Unless the troops up on the ridge cared to take the jump into the unknown like we did, which none of them seemed prepared to do, we were beyond their reach. Rutherford and West unpacked the gear, pulling out the packets of beef jerky. There wasn't a lot to go around, but something was better than nothing.

'We need sleep,' said Cassidy. 'I'll take the first watch, and split the remaining time between West and Ryder. You get some sleep, Cooper. You look like shit.'

'But at least you don't smell like it anymore,' said Rutherford.

'Anyone got a watch?' I asked.

West handed me my Seiko. 'Found it in one of the rucksack pockets,' he said.

It was just after eleven. 'We'll have to move before dawn. We don't want anyone up there on the ridge getting lucky with a 97.'

Cassidy agreed, and then said quietly, 'Done good, sir. We live to fight another day.'

Too tired to think of anything snappy, I just nodded and took one of the available ponchos. I lay down under it and sleep hit me like an angry circus animal.

In what seemed like a handful of seconds, I heard Rutherford's sing-song voice in my ear saying, 'Wakey, wakey.'

Would he go away if I told him to? No. I opened an eyelid, seemingly the only muscle not bruised black and blue and cramped in place. I moved my tongue around my teeth, got a hint of my morning breath. The awful smell of the nose ooze from the hanging guy had taken up residence in my mouth. I needed a hot shower that lasted till the water ran out, two black coffees – extra strong – and maybe four toasted ham and cheese sandwiches. No, make that five. My bladder ached like it was full of cold acid. I opened the other eye and realized that I was spooning Boink, and that a body behind was spooning me, an arm over my waist, a hand on my chest. Leila's. It was steamy under the poncho, and stank of river mud, wet body odor and stale farts.

I removed Leila's hand and propped myself on one hand, disturbing the others still trying to sleep. Somehow I got to my feet and managed to step over bodies without leaving boot prints on anyone, and the dark masses wriggled together, closing the gap my departure had created.

I stopped to allow the contents of my bladder to kill a bush before following Rutherford over to where Cassidy, West and Ryder were quietly talking. It was four thirty-five.

'Sleeping Beauty has riz,' Rutherford said as I made my way over to them.

'How's your ankle?' I asked him.

'Better.'

'Boss, found this in the mud,' said West. 'Yours, I think.' He held the knife toward me, handle first. I told him thanks and sheathed it.

While I'd been catching somewhat less than forty winks, the crescent moon had climbed a little higher and was mooching around behind a thin screen of high cloud, providing enough light to see that all our weapons and other stores were laid out on a poncho over a flattened square of elephant grass. If all this stuff worked as the PLA intended, we really could give a platoon-sized force a good mauling. There was a change in the mood. Preparation was in the air. West was reassembling one of the QCWs after having cleaned and dried it, getting ready for something. I didn't need an itinerary to know what, but I said, 'We going somewhere?'

'That's up to you,' said Cassidy.

'Do we believe they're still alive?' I asked, sinking onto my haunches.

No one had spoken out for some time on the possible state of our captured principals' health, but the subject on my mind was obviously also on theirs.

'We have to find out one way or the other, right?' said West.

Twenny and Peanut had endured two nights in hell. And perhaps Fournier, too, assuming he was still alive. On the other side of the coin, they could all be dead. Staying was a big risk, but now we had additional weapons and ammo, I felt a little more confident about getting some answers. 'Yeah, we do,' I said finally.

West handed me the sniper rifle. 'This one's headed for recycling,' he said.

'What happened?'

He broke it down quickly and handed me the barrel.

'It's bent. Hit a rock on the way down.'

I held it up to catch the meager moonlight and sighted down the rifling. Sure enough, there was the slightest of bends, which turned it into scrap metal.

I handed the barrel back and he swung it underarm toward the lake and waited till I heard the splash.

'Vin,' Ryder called out in a hoarse whisper. 'Jesus, sir – guys . . . come here.'

I managed to haul myself up to the standing position, every muscle in my body threatening to desert. I could dimly make out Ryder's outline. He was motioning us over with some urgency.

'Look,' he said, when I got close enough, pointing at something on the ground. It was Leila. Ayesha was kneeling beside her and holding her hand, which was shaking. And then something lying across one of her legs shifted, a completely unnatural movement. I thought perhaps it was a fold of the poncho. It moved again. Shit, this was hardcore. My mind had trouble coming to grips with the picture sent from my eyes. A big motherfucker of a snake had eaten Leila's boot with her foot still inside it, and had thrown its coils up around her calf and thigh and was trying to squeeze the living shit out of it. One of the coils slid inside another, tightening, causing Leila to gasp.

'What up, yo?' asked Boink with a groan, waking, rolling onto his back beside Leila and slapping at something on his arm.

LeDuc was still asleep.

'What are we gonna do?' Ryder asked.

'Get it off me,' Leila shouted suddenly, providing a suggestion. 'Get it off!'

LeDuc woke with a start.

Of all people, why Leila? Why couldn't this have happened to – well, yeah, Ryder, for example?

'An African Rock Python,' said West, crouching beside me as I examined it, not overly concerned. 'I remember these guys from jungle training school. Adults grow to thirty feet. This one's a teenager, probably only around ten feet.'

'Only,' I said.

'Just get it fucking off!' said Leila, hysterical.

'This is going to make a nice handbag,' he told her as he pulled his Ka-bar and chopped the blade down on the snake's spine just behind its head with precisely enough force to sever it. The coils loosened immediately. The sergeant ran his knife blade around the snake's head in one fluid motion, then, using both hands, pulled its thick body back, and the star's boot was disgorged from the reptile's gullet with a sucking sound. Next, the sergeant slit its mouth at the hinges of its jaw and peeled the head away from her calf, her skin and muscle shielded from the needle-sharp teeth by the leather of her high-cut boot. West passed the bloody head to me. It was heavy, meaty, and bigger than my hand.

'Might need some help here,' he told me.

I tossed the head over my shoulder into the elephant grass as West uncoiled its body from around Leila's leg, and heaved the coils into my arms. The thing weighed a ton and its skin was dry and gave off a musky, gamey smell.

When the last coil was pulled free of her leg, Leila scrambled backward on her hands and feet into the unflattened elephant grass. Something big slithered in the grass behind her, which caused her to cry out and clamber forward onto one of the ponchos. She stopped there on her hands and knees, breathing heavily, and whispered, 'Holy Mother of God . . .'

'You're okay, honey,' said Ayesha, kneeling in front of her and cradling her face between her hands. 'Everything's all right.'

'Can you feel your leg, ma'am?' West asked.

'It . . . it was numb,' Leila said. 'N . . . now I got pins and needles.'

'Good. No permanent damage.' West turned to me and said, 'Let's straighten this sucker out.'

The python turned out to be around thirteen feet in length.

'She's lucky we caught this thing when we did, before it got her all coiled up with its full length,' West said as he slit its underside. 'Gotta do this fast to stop the meat going off. There'll be worms and bacteria in its gut,' he explained as he cut. 'So, you know what snake tastes like?'

'Like ham and cheese, I heard,' I said.

'Since when?' Cassidy asked.

'Don't spoil it for me.'

After he'd pulled out the viscera, West skinned the reptile before trimming a dozen large steaks off its flanks and throwing the remains of the carcass in the lake.

'We can't eat this raw,' he said. 'We'll have to make us a fire.'

'Risky,' I said. A fire would telegraph our whereabouts to anyone within a quarter-mile radius.

'Not here.' West reassured me. 'Later.'

'How we gonna do that? Rub sticks together?' asked Boink, who'd been standing behind West and observing him as he worked.

'The easy way.' West pulled a disposable cigarette lighter out of his pocket, cupped it, rolled his thumb over the wheel and sparked up a small flame. 'Found this in one of the African's packs. We're gonna need fire to boil water, fill up the camelbacks.'

'Cooper!'

It was Rutherford.

'Look what just washed up.'

I went down to the water's edge in time to see the Englishman dragging a body up onto the mud. It was Marcel's. Rutherford flipped the corpse onto its back. The eyelids were half closed. As LeDuc suggested, he might have drowned, though the more likely cause of death was the hole bashed in the top of his skull through which his brains were falling out.

LEILA, AYESHA AND BOINK kept to themselves and said little as we moved away from the lake in the thin pre-dawn light, a surly lethargy in the way they dragged their feet, heads down.

The main source feeding into the lake appeared to be an angry tumble of water hugging the base of the cliff. Keeping to its flank, we picked our way over smooth black and gray granite rocks, the forest occasionally overhanging in places.

We pulled up after half an hour's walk when a bend in the watercourse took us out of the shadows and into sunlight. Overwatch was delegated to Ryder and Rutherford, who went to find good vantage points. The principals sat on rocks on the edge of the forest and passed around the last of the jerky while West worked on a fire. We were going to be leaning heavily on the sergeant's survival skills here. Like most everyone, I'd done a jungle course once upon a time, but it was basic and general in nature. Almost all of my combat and survival experience had been gained in higher latitudes. From what I remembered of the files on my team, it was the same for Rutherford. Cassidy was a counter-insurgency expert. And Ryder's instincts were restricted to surviving concrete jungles.

Having a cigarette lighter was a piece of luck, as there weren't any dry sticks around, let alone Boy Scouts to rub them together. West overcame the problem of wet fuel by locating a variety of palm that had a high concentration of oil in its pith that caught fire easily and burned with a strong flame. Over this, he placed kindling shaved from the frond stems of another variety of palm. More substantial dry fuel was sourced from inside rotted trees that had recently toppled. Within forty minutes we had a fire going, python steaks grilling, the sun on our backs, and Ayesha and Leila taking their clothes off to bathe. The day was looking up.

While the steaks cooked, I pulled LeDuc aside and got a few things off my chest. 'The guy we had a chat with back at the ambush after we came down.'

'The boy your principal killed?'

'That's the one. He told us that his patrol was looking for us, right?'

'*Oui* . . .'

'How did they know there was an "us" to look for?'

LeDuc frowned and then an answer appeared to dawn on him.

'You are police, yes?'

'So?'

'Maybe you are looking for something that isn't there, yes?'

'Captain, coincidences are like little green men from Planet Nine – I don't believe in either. You said the DRC was the size of Western Europe, right? So, coming down where we did, right in the middle of a battle . . . I'm thinking the chances of that would be like hitting a hole-in-one, blindfolded.'

'You are saying that you believe our flight was sabotaged?' said LeDuc, horrified. 'That we crashed here because of some plan?'

Putting it together like that without any window dressing did make the notion sound implausible but, yeah, that's what I was saying. 'Yeah, maybe.'

He gave me a blank stare.

I wanted to go back over things. 'You said there was a problem with the fuel. You also said that you checked it before we took off.'

'*Oui*. It was checked.'

'By you personally?'

'*Non*. By Henri.'

'Fournier.'

'*Oui*. It was also his job to monitor our fuel load during flight. He switched the fuel from the exterior sponsons so that our main tanks were full and he did this just before the engine failures. Henri also made the Mayday call.'

'The Mayday call that you got no response from?'

'*Oui*.'

The Frenchman's face under the dirt and blackened kerosene was suddenly haggard.

'*Baise-moi* . . .' he said under his breath.

'Meaning?'

'Fuck me.'

'You're not my type.'

'I do not want to incriminate anyone without evidence.'

'And I want to know why we're up to our necks in elephant grass rather than heading home with a bunch of crumby posters autographed by our celebrities.'

'It is possible that Fournier did not make the transmission at all,' said LeDuc.

Shit. My bad feeling was baking into a real who, what and how scenario. 'I heard something while I was half snoozing, just before the chopper's engines failed. It woke me up. Someone said, "What was that?" '

'I am sorry?' said LeDuc, puzzled.

'"What was that?" I heard someone say that just before your engines failed.'

'Perhaps it was said just at that moment.'

'I'm pretty sure I heard it a handful of seconds *before* everything went into the toilet bowl. I think the voice I heard was Colonel Travis's.'

'I do not know why this is important.'

'And I'd like to know why he said it. If everything was okay, why say, "What was that?" What made him say it?'

LeDuc peeled off one of his shrugs.

This was leading nowhere, so I let it go. Maybe I just had my timings mixed up. What it looked like, though, was that Fournier wanted us on the ground, and that the spot he'd chosen was pre-planned. He'd caused the Puma to crash, switching to tanks with contaminated fuel that would bring us down. The FARDC patrol had specifically come looking for us. How did they know there was an 'us' to look for? Had some arrangement been made with the DRC force before we took off from Cyangugu to capture us? And if I needed a motive for all this, one was close by. I glanced around until I saw it – Leila. She and Ayesha were now down to bras and panties – Leila's, red lace; Ayesha's, pink cotton. Ayesha was washing their clothes in the ravine while Leila stretched out on a boulder, the droplets of water on her honey-colored skin sparkling in the morning light. Her head was back as she drank in the warmth of the sun. She looked a million bucks – or, rather, many millions of bucks – and perhaps Fournier wanted a few of them channeled into his bank account. Add Twenny Fo's net worth to the picture and there was plenty of motive – kidnapping and ransom. Crash landing a chopper was a hell of a risky strategy. Perhaps the lieutenant put in some extra hours of practice on the simulator before this mission to get it right.

'Where are the fuel tanks in a Puma?' I asked.

'Why do you wish to know?' LeDuc asked.

'In case it comes up in Trivial Pursuit. Humor me.'

'There are four main tanks. They are under the cargo floor. The sponsons are exterior, located on the sides of the fuselage.'

I sucked some water from my camelback tube.

'What do you want to do?' LeDuc inquired. 'Will you tell the others about this?'

'I think so.'

'When?'

'After I've had a toasted ham and cheese sandwich,' I said.

Right on cue, West called out in a hoarse whisper, 'Come and get it!'

There was enough python to feed twice our number. Leila ate without complaint, which threw me a little. Ayesha and Boink likewise tucked into it as if they hadn't eaten anything substantial for a couple of days, which, of course, they hadn't.

I took a seat on a rock beside Boink.

'You okay?' I asked him.

He glanced at me sideways. 'You hep me down the cliff. Thanks, man.'

'All part of the service.'

He stuffed half a pound of snake in his mouth.

'Where'd you get a name like Boink?' I asked him.

'From my folks. They look at me when I come into the world and said, "Fuck", but they couldn't put that on the birth certificate, yo.'

He looked at me angrily. But then he grinned. 'Messin' wit choo, man. Got the name 'cause I bin known to fuck people so bad they don' get up, you know what I'm saying?'

I'd seen the guy kill twice – with a pistol and with his bare hands, breaking a man's neck, giving his head a twist like he was taking the lid off a jar of peanut butter. Yeah, I knew what he was saying. 'Where'd you and Twenny meet?'

'We wuz neighbors. His ol' man worked corners selling drugs wit my ol' man. But we didn' like each other back then. Deryck, he wuz small and sick all the time with a real smart mout', you know what I'm sayin'? So, his ol' man pay me to protect him.'

'You were his bodyguard when you were kids?'

'That's right.'

'How'd he get to be . . .' I wasn't sure what Twenny was – icon, rock star, rapper, idealist, jerk. 'How'd he get to be who he is?'

'He won a competition at the mall when he wuz fifteen. A music exec was a judge. He gave Deryck a contract, and Deryck called hisself Twenny Fo, 'cause he love all the ghetto chic bullshit. Me, I stayed in the projects. Then, one day, Twenny, he got some death threats from a punk rival and a Hummer wit' driver and half a dozen bitches turned up at my home. The driver, he tol' me that the car and the girls were mine if I cared to sign on as Twenny's head security man. I was nineteen, workin' as some psycho drug boss's lieutenant. Now I'm thirty. I own a block of apartments in Chicago, a cleaning bidness in San Francisco and a couple of bars in Miami.' He turned to look at me again. 'So, workin' for Th' Man like you do – what choo got?'

'Job satisfaction,' I said.

Boink shook his head with pity, put a snake rib in his mouth and sucked the meat off the bone.

'There's a story about Twenny braining his girlfriend with a Grammy,' I said. 'That true?'

The big man snorted. 'The only thing I ever seen the boss hit is the bottle once or twice. That was some bitch who wanted her own music career. And Deryck's manager and record company went along wit it 'cause they wanted him to be badass. The bitch got a record and Twenny got his reputation. Everyone got what they wanted.'

'You didn't approve.'

'Don't matter what I think. Is wad it is, yo. Suppose you wanna know 'bout the 'fair Leila said he had?'

I didn't, but what the hell. 'So what about it?'

'Of course he did what she said he did, man. Choo seen that woman from Electric Girlfriend? Damn!'

I sure wasn't in any position to throw stones.

'It's a law of nature.'

'What is?' I asked.

'Like I say, behind every fine-looking woman is a man wanna get with some other piece o' ass, you dig?'

'I think it was Isaac Newton came up with that one.'

Boink grinned.

'What about Peanut?' I asked. 'How does he fit into the picture?'

'Peanut lived near Deryck in the projects, a couple doors down. Had no father, momma left him on his tenth birthday. Folks said she didn't want no retard gettin' in the way of things. He was living in the park, sleeping rough. Deryck took him in, like a brotha, you know what I'm sayin'? He takes care of him. Peanut, he's autistic or somethin'. Goes to a special school 'n' all.'

The more I knew about Twenny Fo, the more I felt I had him figured wrong.

'Now, if y'all 'scuse me.' Boink stood and went to the river to dispose of the bones while I stayed where I was, finished my ration and contemplated the halo Boink had just placed over Twenny Fo's head. Just maybe the guy deserved better than he was going to get, strung up in a tree, waiting to die. And, of course, there was Peanut. He deserved the death coming his way even less.

Rutherford took breakfast to Cassidy and Ryder while West wrapped the leftovers in what looked like banana leaves and placed them in one of the packs. Job done, he walked over to the ravine to wash various items and came back a couple of minutes later.

''Scuse me, ma'am,' he said, standing over Leila as she sat on a rock in her underwear. 'Got something here for you, something to remember the Congo by when you get home.' He rolled out a three-meter length of brown and green snakeskin on the rock beside her. 'You'll gonna get more than a handbag out of it. Maybe a skirt with matching shoes. I'll keep it for you.'

The star wasn't so sure, prodding the skin and wrinkling up her nose, but said thank you anyway. 'You *really* think we'll make it home?'

'Yes, ma'am. No doubt in my mind.' He rolled up the skin, tucked it under an arm and went off to douse the fire's embers.

West sounded so convinced he almost convinced me. 'So, feeling better now you've eaten the thing that ate you?' I asked her.

'Excuse me?'

'Y'know, revenge is a dish best eaten grilled.' I gestured at the steak on the leaf beside her.

She threw her head back either to get the sun on her face or to strike a pose, I wasn't sure which, but I took a good long look anyway. Her red lace underwear was fashionably cut and expensive. Not too brief, but brief enough. There was a diamond in her belly button, and a couple of bars of music with notes and lyrics tattooed down her left side. 'Give it to me.' That was the song's title. I knew that one. It was her breakout hit. Her breasts pushed into the cups with a perfection that suggested a surgeon's handiwork. A pair of knee-high leather boots completed the package.

Ayesha arrived with a pile of clothes, all of which were wet. Leila gestured that she should just lay them on the rock beside her. Then, to me, she said, 'We gonna be here long? Have I got time to dry these?'

'They'll dry quicker if you put them on,' I said, barely able to believe what I was hearing myself say. I was sure no one else could believe it either. I could almost hear the booing from Rutherford and company.

She pushed her arms in the shirtsleeves. 'I . . . I owe you an apology, don't I? I've been a bitch from the get go, haven't I?'

'Nooo . . .'

'Yes, I have. I know I have. Look, I want to thank you for what you did back there in the camp, when those men came for us. They were going to . . . you know.'

She examined her hands. They were badly cut all over from the elephant grass. One of them shook a little.

'All part of the service,' I said, repeating what I'd told Boink, not knowing what else to say. 'Ask Ryder to put something on those cuts.'

She flicked her hair to one side. 'I've been looking back on everything that's happened since we came down here and I know that if it wasn't for you, I'd be dead. Or worse.'

I felt a blush coming on.

'I also want to thank you for not taking me up on my . . . my offer the other night, when you brought Ayesha back.' She rolled up the shirt-sleeves. 'On top of everything else, you're also a gentleman.'

She might have taken the compliment back if she knew that I could recall at will the picture of her on her knees in front of me, pulling down the zipper on her jacket, the thrust of her breasts visible. As memories went, it was a good one, worth filing away for later retrieval, along with the one of her all wet and leaning back on this rock in her lace bra and panties and boots, stretched out like a poster on a teenager's bedroom wall.

'I wasn't always like this,' she continued.

I wondered what kind of 'this' she was referring to.

'Life has become a little unreal for me over the last few years. People want a piece of me so bad they'll do anything for me to get it. When you realize that you can manipulate people easily – that they *want* to be manipulated by you – it changes you. It changed me.' She adjusted one of her bra straps. 'I just wanted to say sorry for the way I been. I'm putting my faith in you, Cooper, to get us all out of here alive. I know you can do it.'

The dependent, trusting female. Was I getting softened up for something? She leaned forward and I felt the warmth of her lips on my cheek. Then she bent down to take her boots off so that she could put on her pants and, inside her open shirt, she threw a few glimpses of dark nipple my way. Lo and behold they were large, hard and erect. And before I knew it, there was a rush of blood to my own personal snake in the grass.

'You're not going to ask me about Twenny Fo, Peanut and Fournier?' I asked, fighting back Little Coop's desire to dive in headfirst.

She stood and put a hand on my shoulder to steady herself as she slipped a foot into the leg of her jeans.

'I was talking to Duke. He said you lost someone close. That right?'

Hmm . . . Duke and I really were gonna have to share a few words.

'When he told me, I felt I understood you.'

'Uh-huh.'

'You were lost long before we came down here in this place. That's true, isn't it?'

And, just like that, the mood evaporated. I wanted to move, but I was trapped – hemmed in on one side by the forest, by the ravine on the other, and by her honey-colored, semi-undressed, lingeried-up body blocking the remaining escape road.

'I'll pay you one million dollars to lead us out of here right now,' she said.

'What?' I asked her. I shouldn't have been surprised. And at least we were back to more familiar ground, the one I'd already charted with her: the land of the selfish and self-obsessed star.

'One million dollars,' she repeated.

I put my pinky against the corner of my lips. 'That much?'

'Then give me a figure. Those men back there, they were going to rape Ayesha and me.'

The way she said it suggested that Ayesha hadn't brought her employer in on her experiences at the FARDC HQ. 'And what about your former boyfriend and his buddy? Is that all they're worth to you? A measly million bucks?'

She smiled. 'I said give me a figure. I'm open to negotiation.'

I just looked at her.

A note of uncertainly crept in when I didn't jump at the offer. 'I've thought about this. We don't know what's happened to Deryck and Peanut, do we? They could be dead.'

'They could be alive.'

The note went up an octave and a hand went to the hip.

'You're going to put us all at risk, aren't you?'

Well, well, back to the Leila I knew. The only risk she was concerned about was the one to herself. I folded my arms.

'You were right, Cooper. I can see that now. Like you said, we're all gonna die if we stay here,' she continued.

I said nothing. She tried a different angle.

'You've lost someone because you made bad decisions. Don't make the same mistakes again and get us all killed. This place is . . .' She looked around, hunting for the right word but couldn't find it. She clenched her fists in frustration and made a sound through gritted teeth.

'Get ready to leave,' I said. In fact, I wanted to leave her behind, staked out on the forest floor for the ants. I pictured doing exactly that, and it helped.

'What's there to smile about?' she asked.

'You don't want to know.'

'And my offer?'

The woman was a case. I turned my back on her, giving her my answer, and went to the ravine. I bent down, took off my gloves, and splashed water on my face. I could have used a long hot shower with a scrubbing brush. Standing up, I caught first Ryder's eye and then Cassidy's. I signaled 'on me', and walked over to West, who was doing what he could to eradicate the signs of our presence. I put the conversation with Leila out of my mind, and decided not to say anything for the moment about the chat I'd had with LeDuc about Fournier. While I had a set of circumstances and a theory that seemed to fit, I had no hard evidence. Among our group there was a belief that bad luck had brought us all to our present circumstances. It would be counterproductive to exchange the fickle finger of fate for suspicion and the mistrust that would come with it.

I made a beeline for Rutherford, who was parked on a boulder, sharpening one of our acquired machetes with a river stone.

'So what are we doing?' Cassidy asked as he approached with Ryder. 'Cyangugu's that way,' he said with a nod up the hill, 'and Goma's in the opposite direction.'

'And unfinished business lies somewhere in between,' West said.

'Damn straight,' said Cassidy.

'We've picked up a few more guns since we last put this on the table, but otherwise not a lot has changed,' I said. 'To even out the odds, we'd need something that makes plenty of noise and causes a lot of fright.'

'The mortar operated by the rebels was a US infantry M224 lightweight company mortar system,' said West. 'And they were firing M49A4 high-explosive rounds – a good all-round anti-personnel, anti-material shell. You meaning something like that?'

'That'd do it,' I said, 'but I think we've stirred the rebels up a little too much to get anywhere near their armory.'

'Interesting bit of kit to have,' Rutherford commented. 'Wonder where they got it?'

I'd wondered as much myself, and filed it away with the questions I had about those M16s with their ground-off numbers.

'If you're a buyer, you'll find a seller,' observed Rutherford.

'FARDC had RPGs – not a bad alternative,' said Ryder.

They were, and it was a nice to see the guy paying attention to something other than Ayesha.

'We penetrated their flanks once,' said West. 'Who's to say we couldn't do it again?'

'Around a hundred and eighty guys with guns,' I said. 'We were lucky. And there's still the problem of getting everyone out once we go loud. That's where something that made big holes in the ground would come in handy.'

Rutherford absently popped the mag in his M4 and checked it. 'Sounds like one of your half plans is in the wind.'

'Let's move it,' Cassidy suggested. 'Our intel gets staler with every passing minute.'

Frankly, after two days it was growing mushrooms, but it seemed like we were emotionally committed at least to reconnoitering the FARDC positions to see whether there was anything left to rescue. For all we knew, by now it might all chopped up into handy-to-dispose-of lengths.

Retreat

We followed the ravine, successive floods having washed away some of the undergrowth along its flank, making it easier going than cutting a path through the forest, which was mostly impenetrable. The space between the trees was occupied by a malicious variety of elephant grass battling with entanglements of vegetation hung with brightly colored banded snakes that screamed 'hazardous'. Occasionally, the forest swallowed the ravine and we had no choice but to hack our way through the tangles of liana and elephant grass. Overhead, birds screeched at each other like inmates in an asylum and animals darted away, unseen, through the compacted undergrowth nearby. None of these were going to be fluffy white rabbits, so I was fine with the darting-away thing.

And, just as I was thinking that, a nearby wall of bush trembled with something very big that departed in a hurry. We all froze.

'LeDuc, didn't you say we'd be lucky to see any wildlife?' I asked him quietly.

'*Oui*,' he whispered, looking around. 'Perhaps this valley is too remote for the bush meat hunters.'

'What other predators live here besides lions?'

'Every one you can think of, and many you cannot.'

There were no stragglers in our line after that. We stayed close and watched each other's backs, and brushed away the spiders and insects that dropped or alighted on us, before stingers, jaws or fangs could get to work.

Up ahead, Ayesha screamed and broke into a kind of dance, jumping around, her hands whipping through her hair, jerking forward and backward. Leila began slapping at her, like they do at NASCAR races when someone in the pits gets engulfed in those invisible methanol flames. Rutherford called this 'the spider dance'. We'd all done it; all of us except Cassidy, that is, who moved like a leopard through his surroundings – flowing from one space to another, disturbing nothing. Ryder caught up with Leila and Ayesha, to lend a hand. The guy was sure putting in some heavy spadework.

I watched Boink's meaty shoulders roll from side to side as he walked. The guy had lost a dozen pounds at least. A week in this place and he'd need a new wardrobe. I was about to point this out to him when something wet landed on my shoulder. The stuff reeked. More of it smacked against the side of my head and, suddenly, the trees above us came alive with yelling, shrieking and chattering, and black shapes charged out of the bushes at us, running and scampering down our line, feinting in and out, teeth bared.

'Hey! Aggro little hairy guys,' said Rutherford, amused, shouldering his weapon.

'*Ne tirez pas!* Don't shoot, don't shoot. *Les chimpanzés, chimpanzés.*' LeDuc rushed forward and pulled down on the gun's barrel.

'Who's going to shoot?' Rutherford protested, offended.

I watched as one of the chimps crapped into his buddy's hands and then threw it at Rutherford. The Brit ducked. I was too slow and the stuff slapped into my face.

'Thanks,' I said as I wiped away the warm, stinking mass.

'Do not look at them in the eyes,' LeDuc warned. 'They will think you are challenging them.'

'Poo at twenty paces?' I asked.

'Keep moving!' Cassidy called out and we lifted the pace to clear the area.

We stuck to the ravine for the best part of two hours, taking advantage of the clean water and the sunlight and the relatively easy going. Eventually the forest closed in overhead again. We were back to slashing into the bush for every yard of forward movement, dodging reptiles and arachnids, and the elephant grass with its razor's edge, all of which seemed intent on attacking exposed skin. But with every step bringing us nearer to the territory occupied by FARDC, taking to the cover of the forest was going to be a healthier option than being out in the open and easy targets for snipers, pickets and patrols.

A cluster of moss and liana-covered rocks pushed up through the leaf litter and away from the ants that seemed to cover every square inch of the forest floor no matter where we were; red fuckers with jaws like interlocking fish hooks that latched on and wouldn't let go.

'Can we rest for a while?' I heard Leila ask Ryder.

Cassidy heard it too and called a halt. Both women collapsed against a boulder. Boink leaned against the face of the rock, sucking in oxygen, his sweaty face lined with exertion.

'How much further, yo?' he puffed.

Further till what? If he meant Cyangugu, he was looking at days. If he meant till we made contact with his buddies, Twenny and Peanut, his guess was as good as mine. So I told him what I thought he might want to hear. 'Not far now, big guy.'

'Good, 'cause I wanna shoot some motherfucker dead,' he muttered.

'Map,' I said to Cassidy.

The sergeant extracted it from his webbing and flattened it against the rock.

'We're somewhere around here,' he said, using his Ka-bar as a pointer.

The ridges and the lake at the bottom of the cliff tallied. It looked about right. We'd come further than I'd though.

West passed around some barbecued snake and everyone took the opportunity to rehydrate.

'What now?' Ryder asked, wiping snake grease off his mouth with his shoulder.

'You and I are gonna scout forward,' I said.

'Oh . . . all right,' he said with no enthusiasm for the idea.

'And you might like to muddy yourself up a little,' I suggested. Apart from a light growth on his cheeks, he looked like he was ready for Sunday school, his face and arms all scrubbed nice and pink. His 97 was propped against a rock beside LeDuc. I picked it up and handed it to him. 'Get a couple of spare mags, a machete, and make sure of your water supply.'

'What, now?' he asked.

'Got something else to do?'

No response.

'Leila, Ayesha,' I called up. They'd climbed the rocks and their heads appeared over the top ledge. 'Where's Boink . . .?'

'Yo,' said Twenny's buddy, walking around from behind the wall, cupping some water from a bottle and splashing it on the back of his neck.

I made a general announcement. 'Duke and I are going on ahead. We need to know how far the FARDC lines extend.'

'Why?' asked Boink.

'So that we don't just walk into them,' said Cassidy.

'Can I ask a question?' said Leila.

Asking for anything was a pleasant change where she was concerned.

'What's on your mind?'

'I can't hear any shooting. How do you know we're close to the enemy?'

'This hill we're on plateaus not far from here, ma'am,' said Cassidy. 'According to the map, the valley the FARDC occupied is down the other side, and around a mile and a half to the east. We've got a lot of rock between us and any gunshots. But you're right, we should be able to hear *something*. Maybe when we get onto the ridge.'

'And what if something happens to you?' Leila asked me.

I figured that she included Ryder in that.

'We'll be back.'

'But what if, yo?' Boink said.

'You'll head due east to Lake Kivu.'

Neither he nor Ayesha seemed overly happy about this, but for different reasons. I was starting to think that maybe Leila looked on me as some kind of lucky charm – her own personal rabbit's foot. And Boink wasn't going anywhere without his boss, whether I was dead or alive. The big man cocked his head on an angle, a crevasse between his eyebrows – not happy.

To avoid a raft of unnecessary questions, I didn't tell them that I intended to go back to the FARDC encampment to check on whether Twenny Fo and Peanut were still alive. 'If we don't make it back,' I said, 'the best hope Twenny, Peanut and Fournier have got rests on you getting word back to Colonel Firestone as quickly as possible.'

The silence was thick. No one liked the idea that more of us might get left behind. I had expected an argument from Leila because one seemed to follow every decision, but everyone knew the score – even her, for once.

'Be careful, Vince,' Leila said.

Her concern for my health took me by surprise. Her getting my name wrong didn't. I checked over the M4 and wriggled the additional mags jammed into my webbing to make sure that they were secure.

'Take this,' said Rutherford, putting the telescopic sight from the sniper rifle into my pack. 'Might come in handy.'

'You'd better have this, too,' said Cassidy, handing me the map.

'No, keep it. I know where I'm going. If we don't make it back, you'll need it.'

'You've got five hours of daylight left,' said Cassidy. 'Less under the canopy. You'll want to be back well before that or you'll walk right past us.'

'Give us till the morning. If we're not back by noon tomorrow, your next stop is Lake Kivu.'

Ryder glanced my way. *Overnight?*

Cassidy motioned at the rocks. 'This is as good a place as any to hunker down for a while.'

'We miss the deadline, you're gone,' I said.

'My dad used to say, "He who was not there is wrong."'

'Cy, getting these folks back to Rwanda is not a suggestion.'

'So it's an order?'

'It's an order.'

The subtext of this was that if Ryder and I didn't make it back and Cassidy left us behind, there'd be an inquiry into our disappearance. The sergeant just wanted my position as the team leader stated in front of witnesses. I'd officially told him the lives of the people around him were now in his hands.

'Good luck,' said Rutherford. He and West lifted their weapons in a gesture of 'see you later'.

'*A bientôt*,' LeDuc said with a slight bow.

Ayesha waved. Leila and Boink glared. I noted the departure time as Ryder and I walked into the forest, heading a little west of south, according to the compass on my Seiko. A dozen paces beyond the rocks, and the forest behind closed in and cut us off from the main party. The machete was sharp and perfectly weighted. Letting it fall on the greenery in front was mostly all that was needed to slice a little more headway, as long as we stayed clear of the elephant grass and clumps of bamboo. We made good time and kept the angle of the incline steady underfoot so that we tracked a straight line, more or less.

'What happened to Ayesha?' Ryder asked after a while.

'When?' I answered, bunting the question away. I knew exactly what he was getting at.

'When she was held captive. Something happened down there.'

'She saw a man's hands get cut off,' I reminded him, sticking to the facts. The closest she'd come to something like that in her civilian life was maybe a broken nail. With the flat of the machete blade, I turned away the head of a mustard-colored viper dangling from an overhanging palm frond.

Ryder stepped beyond its reach. 'You're not giving me a straight answer.'

'Look, Duke, I know you and Ayesha are friends, but if it's any more than that, you're not helping her – not in this place.'

'What does that mean?'

'You're in uniform, buddy, cowboy-up.'

'I resent that,' he said. 'I *volunteered* to go on the mission that brought her back, remember?'

For some reason I thought of the blond in my alligator joke. Was I being unkind? 'Look, this isn't a challenge on some reality dating show, and Ayesha is not the only principal whose life is in danger. You want to be effective, then join the team and stop behaving like you're her gimp.'

'That's offensive.'

I didn't care what he thought it was. I hooked the machete into a wall of fronds. Ayesha mesmerized the guy. It was time he did his job and avoided the emotional involvement. Maybe then he wouldn't end up feeling personally responsible for her safety; avoid the mistakes I'd made with Anna. Today's Ayesha was a different person from the girl who stepped off the plane at Kigali.

'No, "offensive" is you taking our principals on an excursion through my recent past,' I said.

Ryder and I walked in silence. He kept his thoughts to himself. I tried to have no thoughts at all and concentrated on projecting my senses beyond what I could see, which wasn't that far beyond my face. The rainforest was thick here – I'd be easy to cut our way into a clearing and find ourselves face to face with a hundred FARDC or CNDP troops or, worse, more shit-throwing chimps.

It took an hour of fending off vipers and spiders to reach the top of the hill, and still there were no sounds of battle. Something was up. We kept going west of south for another fifteen minutes. I hacked a hole into a screen of fronds and came out into a broad tunnel of broken vegetation; the trees, shrubs and bushes already cleared in front of us. I stood in the relatively open space as rain started to drip through the canopy. I took a closer look at the plant life. It had been cut, the still-green remnants lying trampled on the leaf litter. The tunnel had been cut recently. I crouched on my haunches. Some of the fronds had pressure marks on them that resembled the tread from boot soles. A lot of men had passed this way. Duke was about to say something; I put my finger to my lips and signaled him to follow. Creeping forward across the cleared area, I found that it was roughly twenty meters wide.

I cut my way into the untouched bush and waited for Duke to come up behind me.

'Could be FARDC, could be CNDP,' I said.

'Could be elephants,' he suggested.

'Wearing combat boots?'

'Right,' said Duke. 'Still no gunfire.'

'One of the parties has called it quits and pulled out. Be good to know which one.'

'Why?'

''Cause I don't like knowing that there's stuff I don't know,' I told him as I took my Ka-bar and cut a notch in a tree trunk. 'We're going to stay off the track.'

I could tell that he wanted to ask me why, to discuss it and then give me a bunch of good reasons why we should turn back. So I didn't give him the chance, moving off and staying low, heading roughly east according to my Seiko, tracking parallel to the pre-cut path. The rain was coming down heavily; it hadn't rained for a while, so maybe it was making up for lost time. The sound of it eliminated all others as the fat drops slammed into leaves and fronds and trunks and rattled on my K-pot. Around a hundred meters from the notched tree, the forest road hooked to the south. It was heading back to the ground occupied by the FARDC, which seemed to settle my earlier question.

Then I saw movement. I stopped, crouched. Two men coming along the road cut into the forest, taking it slow and careful, watching each step like they were walking among rat traps. They were hunched over their rifles, wary. There were no blue patches on their shoulders – CNDP rather than FARDC. I dropped on my belly, keeping the movement slow and fluid. Ryder did likewise beside me. We lay there for several minutes, motionless, and they stepped past us no more than six feet away. Killing them served no purpose. I signaled Ryder that we were staying put for a while. Thirty meters down the road behind us, the two men stopped under an umbrella palm and lit up smokes. They felt secure enough to take five while on patrol and telegraph to any enemy downwind that they were prepared to risk lung cancer and/or a bullet between the eyes. Did their presence mean that the CNDP had come down from the heights and now owned this patch of turf? The men quickly finished their cigarettes, threw the butts on the ground and retraced their steps, sauntering past us with the barrels of their rifles pointing down, their body language now completely relaxed, like they were heading to a bar. The two were out of sight within minutes. I left it a while before coming up on one knee. Something bit me on the neck. And bit again. And again. I slapped at the bites. Ants. Shit, the fuckers must have been all over the ground I'd been lying on, and the way they were chewing on me suggested they resented it. I brushed myself down collecting another half dozen bites along the way.

Beside me, Ryder slapped at his arms and then fumbled with his rifle, dropping it. He picked it up and we crept along in the same direction as the CNDP duo, keeping off the cleared area. The FARDC company had broken off the engagement with the CNDP, and the two men we'd just seen had drawn the short straw to reconnoiter the enemy's retreat. They hadn't bothered finishing the job, which would have been to give their commander an indication of the enemy's new position. Most probably they would find somewhere to lie low, waste another hour or so, then return to their unit with fabricated intel.

The men moved faster on the road than Ryder and I could maneuver in the bush, and we soon lost sight of them. That made me nervous, but there was no way around it. I stopped.

'What?' Ryder asked.

'Hear that?' I said.

He lifted his head and turned it from side to side, concentrating.

'Still can't hear any gunfire.'

'No, rushing water. We're close to a ravine.' Maybe it was the ravine that ran alongside the FARDC encampment, the one that West and I had used to carry away the HQ guards we'd killed. We were coming up on the general area.

Ryder and I waited, staying still and quiet for a further ten minutes, to give the two CNDP guys time to cross whatever lay forty meters ahead in the forest. I stood up, ready to move.

'What are we doing?' Ryder asked, his voice low and quiet. 'We know the FARDC has moved out. Shouldn't we get back to the others before it gets dark?'

'We don't know dick, not for sure,' I replied. 'And if the people holding our principals are no longer holding their ground, I want to go have a look at what they left behind.'

'Why?'

'Remind me – which side of the Puma were you sitting on before we crashed?'

'I was behind you, the right-hand side. Why?'

'Just before the engines lost power – before we crashed – did you say anything, or hear anyone else say anything?'

He looked down, concentrating. 'No. I was asleep. I guess I could have said something – I talk in my sleep.'

'Just before we went down, I heard someone say, "What was that?"'

'No, I don't remember hearing anything.' He raised an eyebrow. 'What's with the questions? Something going on I don't know about?'

I wanted to tell him that his ass could be on fire and he wouldn't know about it, but that sort of thing's not helpful in the modern workplace. 'I want to go back and have a look at the Puma,' I said. 'I don't think we came down by accident. There'll be an inquiry when we get back home and we'll need a sample of the residue in the fuel tanks.'

'Shit . . .' He plucked an ant off his forearm. 'Do you *know* this or is it just a theory?'

'At the moment it's just questions that don't have answers.'

Ryder broke off the engagement and we patrolled in silence, and he was satisfied to leave it at that. I'd just told him that I thought our aircraft might have been sabotaged, but all he seemed to care about was hightailing it back to his love interest.

'Can I ask you something?' he said eventually.

I didn't say yes, but that didn't stop him.

'Why don't we just take Leila and Ayesha to Rwanda, then come back for Twenny, Peanut and the Frenchman? That'd make more sense, wouldn't it?'

'No, it wouldn't.' I said. 'Aside from having no firm idea of how long it will actually take to walk back to Rwanda, I doubt that we'd be able to find the FARDC unit holding them again once we leave the area. And we can't split our forces – have some of us go one way while the rest of us go another. There aren't enough of us to provide effective security as it is.' Having to explain this to Ryder was another reminder, if I needed one, that the guy was out of his depth.

He hardened his tone. 'For when that board of inquiry is convened, I want it on the record that my recommendation was to return our remaining principals to Cyangugu, rather than risk more lives in what could be a reckless adventure.'

I stopped. There was something else going on here.

'How much did Leila offer you to get her out now? She offered *me* a million bucks.'

'I don't know what you're talking about.'

From the way he squirmed, I could see that he knew *exactly* what I was talking about. I could also see from the look on his face that he'd been offered nowhere near seven figures.

'We're not going anywhere till we know what the situation is with our captured principals,' I said. 'But I've noted your point of view. In the meantime, you can tell Leila, no deal.'

Ryder looked at his feet and started to move.

The forest took us right to the edge of the groove cut in the side of the hill by the surging water but the cutting was narrower in the daylight than I remembered, which made me think that perhaps this wasn't the watercourse I thought it was. We went downhill a little, using a natural bridge provided by logs and sticks caught up in a rock fall that had formed a natural dam, the rain coming down hard on our K-pots and shoulders, unimpeded by the canopy. No sign of the two soldiers up or downstream, so we crossed. Another half hour of slicing our way through the foliage and the sound of falling water again filtered through the greenery. We came out on the verge of a far more substantial ravine than the last one, spray from the raging water rising to meet the rain. We worked our way upstream, the incline steepening markedly, and eventually crossed over on another logjam. Once on the far side, we came back downstream, eventually finding what I was looking for.

'Why are we stopping here?' Ryder asked.

I pointed to several smaller trees on the edge of what appeared to be a large cleared patch of the bush. 'Twenny and Peanut were roped up to those trees. This was the FARDC HQ.'

I turned around and recalled to mind Ayesha's rescue, saw the trees West and I had hidden behind. I walked the area, much of which had been trampled; found the remainders of the fires and the tree stump used as a chopping block. There was no blood. Something metallic caught my eye. I bent down and picked up several brass 5.56mm casings. Had people been executed here? No blood on the ground, but with all the rain I didn't expect to see any. All I could do was speculate. I went over to the trees that had kept my principals company and examined the ground. It was trampled, covered in broken leaves, squashed bushes and thin vines going brown in places, but I couldn't find anything of interest.

'Where to now?' Ryder asked after he'd finished drinking straight from the sky.

'This way.'

The FARDC had gone, probably during the night, which explained the lack of morning gunfire. Following the road they'd cut would lead us to them, so I could set that aside and come back to it. More urgently, it wouldn't be long before Colonel Makenga and his golden cock came down off the hill to occupy the recently vacated ground. No doubt he'd be waiting on a report from his scouts. We knew that two of them were using their recon duties as an opportunity for some free time, but there might be other scouts around who were more committed.

I double-timed it across the clearing. Trampled ground lay everywhere. The going was easier here, but the lack of cover was dangerous. I had a reasonable fix on the whereabouts of the Puma's wreckage, but we'd be lucky to find it – from memory, the bush was thick in that area. As the angle of the ground beneath our feet began to steepen, Ryder and I passed in and out of cleared areas that had been occupied by the men, strewn with trash that ranged from tins to plastic bottles, to used bandages, and to sodden wads of newspaper and banana leaves covered in human shit, rolls of Charmin being in short supply hereabouts. We crept into a small clearing.

'What the hell is this?' asked Ryder.

Good question. The smell of rotting flesh was in the air. Several small animals had been slaughtered here, their guts strung up with liana. Half a dozen skulls were also bound to the tree trunk, a vertical column of them. The ants were having a ball. It was some kind of ritual altar or offering.

'Black magic, maybe,' I said.

We left it behind and continued traversing the hill, heading east.

'Look for holes torn in the canopy,' I said.

Soon after, we came on an area where trees had pieces blown out of their trunks. White sap leaked from the wounds and their limbs lay strewn across the forest floor.

'Hey,' said Ryder. 'Found this on the ground over there.' He showed me the back section of a mortar casing, a couple of the flight fins still attached to one end. It was part of an M4A2 high-explosive round, the flavor fired by the CNDP boys up on the hill. A cloud of flies buzzed at the base of a tree trunk blackened by a mortar blast. The noise distracted me. I stepped over to the area and the smell warned me what to expect. I lifted a branch and the face of a kid of no more than twelve years of age stared with milky, dirt-encrusted eyes. The flies went crazy with the fresh opportunity I'd just provided them and descended on his nostrils, mouth and, of course, those eyes. Ryder lifted another branch, saw what lay beneath it, and turned away. The kid's leg had been blown off at the groin. The body part shifted weirdly among the leaf litter as if it were somehow still alive. Driver ants, a hundred thousand of them, were attempting to drag it away. The look in the boy's eyes reminded me of the one I'd seen in Anna's, as if heavy doors had been welded shut behind them. A lump swelled in my throat. I broke off a nearby palm frond to sweep away the flies, then covered the kid's face with it and replaced the tree branch over his lower remains. I shook my head. Here, in a split second of completely useless violence, a short miserable life had ended.

I turned and saw Ryder thirty meters further up the hill, pulling on a liana vine, moving it left and right, trying to dislodge something caught up in a tree. I made my way up to him.

'What you got?' I asked.

'Don't know,' he said. 'Spotted it while I was looking for that hole.'

There was a partially obscured cream-colored object lodged in a fork in the tree maybe fifty feet above us. Whatever it was, the object was man-made and perched on the vine that Ryder was tugging. He gave it an especially hard pull and the object flew out and dropped, hit a branch and then tumbled into a nearby bush.

'Oh, man,' Ryder said, plucking it from a low branch. 'Am I gonna get lucky tonight.'

Well, maybe tomorrow night, and he was probably right. It was a case, either Leila's or Ayesha's. He turned it over. Settling the ownership question, a gold letter 'L' was embossed in the expensive tooled cream leather above the gold-plated lock. He pressed the mechanism and the latch flew open with an expensive *thunk*. Inside was a jumble of lipsticks, nail polishes, mascaras, eye shadows and various other bottles and tubes mostly all heavily branded with the double C of Chanel, tangled up in the leads of a curling wand and a hairdryer. He pulled out a lipstick.

'Your color?' I asked him.

I shifted my attention to the surrounding forest, searching it for movement other than that made by the rain smacking into the vegetation, which made it appear to shiver. A little like me. I saw nothing. Satisfied, I checked over the makeup case. It had come from the Puma – no doubt about that. The leather was uncharred and, except for a couple of scuff marks, in almost pristine condition. All of which suggested that it had fallen out of the chopper with the loadmaster before the aircraft hit the ground, and certainly before a few rockets were fired into it. I traversed the hillside, slicing through low bushes, and came out above a large old rotting log covered in moss. It looked familiar. I jumped behind it and leaned over the top, looking down the hill. Pulling the sniper scope from my pack, I rested it on the log and adjusted the focus, scanning the face of the forest. Yeah, this was the place – we took refuge behind this log while FARDC torched the chopper.

'I remember this. We've been here before, right?' Ryder asked, jumping in beside me.

I nodded, getting my bearings. The smell of burned kerosene was in the air.

'Down there, I think.' I lined up the sight on an area I thought might yield something, but saw nothing. I slid over the top of the log and cut my way down through elephant grass and scrub, the sweet smell of toasted aviation fuel growing stronger. A shard of Perspex from the aircraft's windshield dangling in a bush caught my eye. We were close. I saw the wreckage a few steps later, part of a main rotor blade draped with liana, pointing skywards like a broken finger. I peered into the twisted metal, then looked up into the canopy. The hole our descent had ripped through the treetops was clearly visible, drops of rain wobbling through the opening on their way down.

The aircraft wreckage itself was covered in leaves, fronds and branches. Almost the only indication that something lay buried beneath was the fact that the dead vegetation was starting to wilt like a salad left too long in the bowl.

Ryder and I climbed down to the Puma and hauled away a few of the branches. An attempt had been made to hide the wreckage. The remains were charred and blackened. I started poking around among them.

'What are you looking for?' asked Ryder.

'Not sure,' I said.

I gestured for the case and he handed it over.

'Find some high ground and keep watch,' I told him.

He turned away while I rummaged around among the cosmetics, looking for anything suitable for the purpose I had in mind. There were lipsticks, lots of them – pinks, reds and bronzes. They would have to do

I took several, fully extended the sticks and then broke them off. I could already hear Leila squealing.

I stuffed the tubes into a thigh pocket, left the case on the ground, pulled away another couple of branches and hoisted myself up onto the blackened, twisted fuselage. The port-side external fuel sponson was broken, the back half of it hanging down. I ran a gloved finger across an interior wall and transferred the oily, sooty residue to one of the lipstick tubes. I then went to the front of the wreckage and climbed in through the cockpit. Rocket explosions and fires had left the twisted interior charred and the paintwork black and blistered. Entering the main cargo area, which had been fitted with seats, I could see at a glance that there wasn't much left of the tanks. Internal explosions had ripped them up and there were gaping holes in the alloy floor. I crouched for a full minute in silence and took in the charred surroundings that included the remains of Travis and Shaquand. Sometimes a crime scene will speak to you. This one didn't. Maybe the exercise was a waste of time and effort. But I was here now, and I'd never get this chance again. The jet-fuelled furnace that engulfed the wreckage probably also consumed any chemical evidence of sabotage. Was that why the remains of this aircraft had been rocketed – to destroy evidence? And, if so, on whose orders? I reached down deep into the jagged black holes in the floor, which still smelled of jet fuel, and scraped some of the carbon deposits off the sides of the tanks and tapped them into the remaining gold Chanel tubes. Job done, I climbed back into the flight deck and out through the front of the chopper and sucked in some clean forest air. The whole operation took less than five minutes. My gloves were filthy and badly worn. I wiped them on the wet vegetation.

A rifle shot cracked the silence. I ducked and spun around.

Two more shots. Dammit! Ryder's M16.

A man screamed, a quick death scream, the type of scream that says a life has just been startled out of its body. My eyes went to the source of the noise. It was the two men we'd seen walking along the trail, reconnoitering. They'd wandered back across our path. However, one of them was now a lifeless body lying at the feet of the other. The man still standing had his hands in the air, and they were trembling like the leaves around him being slapped by the rain. He was starting to blubber. He was maybe sixteen, no older.

'No more shooting,' I calmly called out to Ryder, clamping down on the desire to yell it. 'There are gonna be more of these guys nearby, for sure.' And, as I said that, I knew there was only one possible outcome for this situation. 'Jesus,' I said to myself. And maybe the guy with his hands in the air came to the same conclusion, because he suddenly turned and ran.

'Shit,' I said, bolting after him.

He ran hard, thrashing through the bush. I followed, breathing hard, drawing the Ka-bar as I ran and hacking at the greenery, the machete left back at the crash site. Our presence in the area had to remain a secret. Nothing was more important. I thrashed at the leaves and the fronds, the palms and the lianas, leaped half-blind over logs, heading uphill, aware of the effort, the air starting to sear my lungs like flame. Fuck, he was getting away on those young legs. I heard a dull thud somewhere ahead and then – nothing. I came up on the guy a handful of seconds later. He was spreadeagled on the ground at the base of a tree trunk hidden by scrub, his eyes rolled back in his head and a concave depression in the skull over his left eye, a little moss and bark pressed into the grazed skin. Breathing hard, I put my fingers to his jugular and they confirmed that nothing warm was going to move through his veins ever again. I sucked in a few breaths and sheathed the Ka-bar. Hitting the tree at full throttle had done me a service; stopped me having to add another bad dream to my collection. I searched the kid's pockets and found some kind of a charm made up of bones, a little snakeskin and animal teeth. If it were supposed to be a protective charm, I'd be making a complaint to the witch doctor who gave it to him. I wondered if it was connected to the altar we'd seen. There was nothing else in his pockets. I stood and listened to the forest for a full minute but the loudest noises were my own breathing, the pumping of my heart, the ever-present impact of raindrops on leaves and the high-strung whine of over-excited mosquitoes. I cut some fronds, lay them over the body, then retraced my steps back to the Puma.

I found Ryder down on his haunches, his rifle across his chest, nervously glancing left and right. My arrival startled him.

'Where is he?' he asked, standing up.

'A tree jumped in front of him.'

'What?'

'Try not to shoot anything unless it shoots at you first.'

'I had no choice,' he said.

He was probably right about that.

'They were coming toward us . . . I've never killed anyone before. He was a kid.' Ryder's voice was cracking, the center of his chin trembling. 'No choice,' he said.

'You did your job, Duke,' I told him. 'If you hadn't, maybe it'd be you covered in palm fronds waiting for the ants.'

I walked past him. There was nothing I could say that would make him feel better about taking someone's life.

'C'mon,' I said. I was done with the Puma. I fastened the Velcro on my thigh pocket to make sure the lipsticks were secure and wrapped a hand around the rough wood grip of the machete propped against the twisted fuselage, and moved into the bush.

We were well into the hand-to-hand battle with palms, bushes, elephant grass and liana, approaching the first ravine before Ryder asked, 'We heading back?'

I'd been asking myself the same question. I gave it some more consideration as I chopped around the answer, clearing away the indecision. 'It's after three. We're at least couple of hours' walk away from the others, which means the last half hour or so we'll be walking in complete darkness.'

'So what are we gonna do?'

I considered whether the people holding Twenny Fo, Peanut and Fournier bugging out lessened the chances of our principals' survival, and came to the conclusion that the outcome could go either way. We hadn't found their bodies at the FARDC HQ's clearing, which was promising. I was leaning toward the conclusion – or maybe it was just the hope – that the officers holding our people captive were considering how to bargain with the US for their release in a way that wouldn't bring a unit of Navy Seals down on them in the dead of night.

'We still have to locate that FARDC company,' I said. 'We still don't know where they're holed up.'

Ryder took out his anxiety about this with his machete on the elephant grass.

Once across the second ravine, we picked up the road carved through the forest and found the passage we'd cut alongside it.

'You don't like me much, do you?' Ryder remarked out of the blue.

'What's *liking* you got to do with anything?'

'So I'm right.'

'Duke, all I care about is that you do your job. And if you can tell a joke or two to lighten the load while you're at it – and maybe even grumble with class – that's icing on the cake.'

'I talked my way onto this detail because I knew Ayesha. I know you know that. Maybe what you don't know is that I've been trying to get off that damn desk for two years. This came along, I saw my chance and took it.'

'And that desk is looking pretty good right about now, isn't it?' I said.

'I'm not trained for this and we both know that. Just help me out a little. Show me what I need to do and I'll get it done. Okay?'

A good speech. His hand was held out for us to shake on our newfound understanding. Duke was baggage. Frankly, I didn't think he had it in him to turn his shit around, but I shook anyway, if only to end this impromptu performance review.

We got going again and moved across through the pre-cut slip road. I stopped when I saw a bunch of rocks ahead. I didn't remember seeing them on the way out. And then the rocks did the strangest, most un-rock-like thing – they moved. A massive gray boulder lurched slowly from one side to the other, and then a tree trunk snapped with a crack like a grenade going off and it fell down with a crash, leaving a small hole ripped in the canopy. Another boulder moved and snorted and I realized what I was looking at – a couple of elephants enjoying the afternoon smorgasbord, grazing on the leaves higher in the trees. I was aware that Ryder and I were downwind of the beasts, because I smelled them and they smelled bad, like a platoon after a three-week bivouac in a dirty sock basket. Nevertheless, we took several slow steps backward and found some cover behind a tree too thick to be pushed aside, and stood there for twenty minutes, waiting for the animals to move off; not talking, not moving. They reminded me of Boink and of my childhood circus visit, and I had the fleeting, yet powerful, feeling that the threads of my life were coming together in a pattern that I should recognize but couldn't.

When we could no longer see, hear or smell the animals, we came out from behind the tree and moved quickly through the area. Ten minutes later, I found the notch made in the tree trunk on our outbound journey. I checked the Seiko. Taking a course eighty degrees to the north of the one we'd been on would bring us eventually and approximately back to the rocks where, right about now, Cassidy, West and Rutherford would be securing the area for the night ahead. Ryder ran his fingers across the notch.

'You make this?' he asked.

'Yep.'

The forest closed in solidly ahead, with no slashed fronds or bushes.

'This where we turned left, isn't it?' Ryder asked, reading the signs.

'Yep,' I repeated. 'Leave the makeup case here – hide it.'

He set it on the ground and covered it with foliage and liana. Satisfied that it couldn't be found without a concerted inspection, I stepped past him toward the forest flattened by the FARDC on the move. The track was clear as far as I could see. I considered taking the road more trampled but it wasn't worth the risk, so I turned back to the tree with the notch. We had two hours of daylight left in which to find the enemy's bivouac.

I SAW THE TRIPWIRE at knee height, just in time to avoid breaking through it. I thrust my palm back and stopped Ryder before he walked past me and set off whatever was attached to it. I hit him a little too hard and he was about to object, so I put my hand over his mouth to muffle any sounds that might attract attention, and set him down on the ground. Once he stopped struggling, I nodded at him and he nodded back, so I took my hand away and signed that danger lay just ahead.

'Jesus, Cooper!' he whispered before I could gag him again.

I grabbed a fist full of his webbing, pulled him up to my face and put my finger against my lips. He nodded again, finally getting the picture and shutting the fuck up. Okay, so he was pissed at me for pushing him around, but it was better than being dead. I let him go, got down on all fours and crawled forward till my eyes again picked up the thin line strung through the bush. It took me a while to find it a second time. Seeing it in the first place had been pure luck. I happened to focus on it rather than on a leaf or a frond or just the ground. It was a little after four pm, and the light was disappearing like someone was turning down a dimmer switch, the undergrowth starting to lose its colors to the monochrome of twilight.

I found the line again. It was fine and green, the pressure of it against my hand. I was familiar with this type of tripwire; had set a few of my own over the years. I ran the line lightly through my fingers till they found the business end, an M18A1, otherwise known as a Claymore; the raised words 'Front towards enemy' clearly visible on the anti-personnel mine's plastic, curved olive-drab face. Behind it was one and a half pounds of C4 embedded with the manufacturer's warranted seven hundred steel balls designed to explode outward in an arc of sixty degrees. In open terrain, the thing was a killer within a radius of fifty meters, potentially lethal out to a hundred meters, and just plain bad news to anything with a heartbeat out to two hundred and fifty meters. It would've detonated six meters from Ryder and me had we strolled through that tripwire, though we wouldn't have known about it till we were tuning our harps. I carefully felt around the mine, my fingertips finding some good news: a couple of cotter pins hanging from the corner of the mine on a piece of wire. Someone was going to come back and recover this device if it didn't detonate and he'd need those pins.

So, the mine looked brand new. Its presence told me we'd arrived at the FARDC's perimeter defenses. One hundred and eighty combat veterans were bivouacked somewhere close, probably scattered around the crown of the hill ahead. Convention said the company HQ would be sited on the highest ground. We had no choice but to infiltrate the enemy camp, only this time without West's skills up front. And the Claymore's message – the enemy was jumpy. Maybe the FARDC company leadership was aware that it had been infiltrated once before, or perhaps West, LeDuc and I just hadn't come across the mines when we'd rescued Ayesha.

First things first. I replaced those pins before releasing the tension on the tripwire. Then, approaching the mine from the rear, I disconnected the tripwire and removed the blasting cap from the detonator well. The device could now be handled without suddenly turning Ryder and me into mousse. A Claymore would come in handy, so I stuffed it into the backpack, together with the tripwire and blasting cap, got down on my belly among the damn ants and hoped they'd frightened off the scorpions.

'Stay close, move slow and, for Christ's sake, stop when I stop,' I told Ryder under my breath.

WE'D COLLECTED ANOTHER TWO Claymores with tripwires set up like the first before I smelled tobacco, indicating the presence of sentries ahead. We crawled forward and, in the last vestiges of light, watched a young guy in a poncho aimlessly throwing a knife into the ground at his feet, killing time, his rifle lying in the leaf litter behind him, the source of the second-hand smoke hanging from his lips. Ryder and I stayed put until darkness was complete. The rain started to fall again, heavy and determined, as we waited for the guard to light another cigarette. Eventually, a sudden flame flared in front of his face, destroying his night vision for a few minutes. Ryder and I used his temporary blindness to slide past.

The underbrush was thick and perfectly suited for our purposes, as was the fact that the army camped on the hill was far more focused on trying to stay dry and feed itself than it was on stopping unwelcome visitors at the door. Maybe it felt nice and safe behind its barricade of Claymores.

Ryder and I avoided any open ground and stayed low and slow. The vegetation around us was waterlogged, making it possible to move around without sounding like a couple of two-hundred-pound animals, there being no dry sticks to break underfoot and alert sentries to our presence. Occasionally, larger shadows hurried out of our way through the bush, and I chose not to think about what they might have been. As long as they weren't carrying guns, I was happy to leave them alone.

We broke cover as the angle of the climb lessened and discovered that the ground was miraculously open. The smell of sawdust and fire smoke was in the air. The hill – it was more of a plateau – had recently been logged. Tents were clustered on one side of the area, marking the area as the company HQ. Over on the opposite side, around two hundred meters away from both Ryder and me and the HQ, the bush was being cleared away.

'The scope,' I whispered to Ryder, who pulled it from the pack on my back and handed it to me. It wasn't of the light-enhancing type, but it had reasonable low light characteristics and there were several fires burning. I focused on all the activity. 'Shit,' I murmured.

'What?' Ryder asked.

'Civilians. And a chopper.'

Women dressed in brightly colored clothing that reminded me of the Rwandan prime minister's wife, were doing the clearing, overseen by soldiers. That meant there was some kind of settlement nearby. Parked in the middle of the cleared area the women were extending was an old Soviet Mi-8 of the sort I'd seen at the airport in Kigali and dismantled in the hangar at Cyangugu. I wondered who'd flown it here, and why. Its markings identified it as Rwandan. What was a Rwandan chopper doing over the border in the DRC, parked in the FARDC unit's bivouac?

I scanned the HQ, checking it over more closely. A couple of tents were still being pitched. Cooking fires were burning, providing helpful illumination. A slight wind shift brought the smells of meat sizzling on those fires, and glands pumped saliva into my mouth. I picked up our principals almost immediately.

'They're alive,' I said involuntarily.

Twenny and Peanut were strung up to trees, just as they'd been at the last encampment, their hands secured behind their backs, hoods over their heads. A third man was beside them, wearing a tattered flight suit. 'Fournier. He's there,' I said. I handed the scope to Ryder and showed him where to point it.

'I see 'em,' he whispered. 'It's Fournier, all right.' He turned his head slowly, taking in the rest of the camp. 'Did you see the helicopter there?'

'Uh-huh.'

Ryder took the scope on a quick reconnoiter. 'Hey, the Chinese guy, the one you told us about. That him? He just came out of one of the tents.' He passed me the scope.

It took a moment to locate him. 'Yeah,' I said. A tall, slender black man wearing a tailored combat uniform with a cream cravat tucked into the top of his shirt accompanied him. This had to be the FARDC commanding officer. They were both talking to a third man, though that person had his back to me and he was in shadow.

'I can't see his face,' I whispered, talking to myself. 'Wait – they're moving.'

The Chinese advisor put his hand on the unidentified man's shoulder and the three of them began to walk slowly over to Twenny Fo, Peanut and Fournier, collecting a couple of flunkies with machine guns along the way. Fu Manchu and his buddies were deep in conversation when they arrived in the area where their hooded prisoners were tied up. The captives didn't appear to react in any particular way to the arrival of the party within their midst. Fu Manchu stepped up to the guy in the flight suit and removed his hood. Damn – it was definitely Fournier. I noticed pretty much at this moment that the unidentified man was holding a pistol in his right hand, down by his leg, the muzzle pointed toward the ground. He raised it to the back of the Frenchman's head. I heard a muffled explosion and the front of Fournier's face blew out. He toppled forward, his arms dislocating from his shoulders as he slumped to the ground, dead.

'Shit, what just happened . . . what happened . . .?' Ryder said, way too loud.

'Shut up,' I hissed.

Twenny Fo and Peanut were now shouting at the man, who handed the pistol back to the Chinese guy, turning toward me as he did so.

'Christ,' I whispered.

'What?' Ryder demanded.

Fournier's killer. It was Beau Lockhart.

Discovery

I watched Lockhart and the Chinese guy stroll back to the tent, having a nice post-murder chat, and disappear inside it. Leaving aside the fact that Lockhart had just killed a man, why kill Fournier? That didn't make sense. Wasn't Fournier their guy? Perhaps it made perfect sense, only not to me. It didn't fit my theory and that meant I had to throw the damn thing out and start again from scratch.

I trained the scope back on Twenny and Peanut. The rapper was struggling and shouting something at the guards who'd moved in to recover the body, but I was too far away to hear what he might have been yelling.

So, our principals were alive and Lockhart was involved in a whole bunch of crap up to his eyeballs, murder topping the list. He was with Kornflak & Greene, a DoD contractor. His business began and ended at the Cyangugu base, yet here he was in the enemy's camp, capping a UN peacekeeper. His presence here, aiding and abetting the FARDC unit's capture of Twenny Fo and Peanut, heavily suggested that I was right about the ransom and kidnap angle. Maybe this had been the plan from the beginning, rather than it being an opportunistic grab. And now I had suspects. I handed the scope to Ryder, who returned it to my pack, and then we wriggled backward deeper into the bush as the rain started coming down with its usual biblical intensity. Turning one-eighty for the crawl out, we again took it slow and careful. All went reasonably smoothly until, around fifty meters later, we shinnied into several Africans who were rigging hammocks across our path. We had nowhere to go, which meant we had no choice but to share the shadows for a bunch of time with countless biting critters, waiting for the men to fall asleep.

The rainfall came to an abrupt end sometime after midnight. With water no longer finding its way through the folds of their ponchos, the men soon began snoring.

Ryder and I crawled through the mud beneath them, scarcely breathing, my Ka-bar in one hand, ready to fillet any light sleepers who chose the wrong moment to visit the john. We eventually found cover, crawling into another island of scrub forty meters away. Retracing our steps, there were no Claymores to worry about, as we'd disarmed and appropriated all the surprises on the way in.

It was a quarter past one in the morning before I felt confident enough to walk on my feet instead of my elbows. I stood and breathed the wet night air, my forearms swollen and throbbing with insect venom, a cloud of thirsty mosquitoes circling my head and humming for my blood. I went to the nearest anthill and reapplied the repellent.

By this time, I'd had plenty of time to think about Fournier and how he fitted into my theory. I realized that I'd been maneuvered to a particular point of view. I'd been told that it had been Fournier who'd switched the tanks; that it was Fournier who'd made the Mayday call. And Fournier had, for a time, disappeared, which cast these assurances in a certain light. But now I'd seen Fournier tied up and murdered by people I believed he might have been in league with, people who included a US military contractor. If Fournier wasn't Lockhart's inside man, it meant the real rat was still among us.

And his name was LeDuc.

Perhaps that had been part of the reason for the patrol sent out to check the Puma for survivors – to recover LeDuc. But there'd been a mix-up when we'd gotten the upper hand and the wrong Frenchman had been taken away.

LeDuc had accompanied West and me when we'd infiltrated the FARDC encampment and rescued Ayesha. There would have been moments when he could have escaped. Perhaps he hoped that we'd just conveniently get ourselves captured, allowing him to maintain his cover. When that didn't happen, why hadn't he just blown the whistle on us? Maybe he thought there'd be a lot of confusion and shooting, that it could potentially end up being bad for his health and therefore not worth the risk.

I thought back through all the conversations I'd had with LeDuc, sifting for clues about his true intentions, clues I'd overlooked. He'd been our translator on several occasions. Had he relayed information without putting a skew on things? Looking back on it, when Marcel was captured, there'd been recognition in his face when he laid eyes on LeDuc. *Looks like you remind him of someone.* That's what I'd told him. Perhaps LeDuc hadn't *reminded* Marcel of someone at all. Perhaps Marcel had actually *seen* LeDuc on a prior occasion. Perhaps at the FARDC camp, making a delivery of fresh-baked croissants. Marcel had jumped off the cliff behind the CNDP's position with the French pilot, but hadn't survived the fall. The African's skull was bashed in. LeDuc had suggested that Marcel had hit his head on a rock and drowned. Maybe LeDuc had been holding said rock at the time. Maybe he was worried that Rutherford, who spoke a little French, might find out something awkward from the African.

'Let me get this straight,' Ryder said, breathing heavily as we double-timed it down the wide cleared path. 'That was Lockhart you saw back there, the guy we met at Cyangugu – the DoD contractor?'

'Yep.'

'Jesus. You thought Fournier set us up, put us down in the jungle.'

'Yep.'

'But they killed him. They wouldn't have done that if he was working for them.'

'No, you wouldn't think so.'

'Then if Fournier didn't put us down here, it had to have been LeDuc. And if LeDuc is involved, then he's gonna be pretty nervous about what we might find out on this recon. Leaving him behind might have made him desperate.'

'Yeah, that's why we're running,' I puffed. Ryder had figured it out. Maybe there was more to the guy than I'd given him credit for.

The notch I'd made in the tree wasn't easy to find in the dark. I remembered that the cleared pathway cut to the south a hundred meters beyond my marker. We found the kink and worked backward, finally locating the tree with a handhold of wood hacked out of it at head height.

'Get the case,' I told Ryder.

He hunted around and eventually found its hiding place. I checked the Seiko for the time and made the eighty-degree change in direction, slinking off across the open trampled path through the forest.

We were soon heading down the valley, retracing our steps, taking us back to the rocks where Cassidy, West, Rutherford, Leila, Ayesha, Boink, and the rat, LeDuc, were waiting for our return. The canopy here was unbroken, and the darkness was complete. We soon found it impossible to move around without bumping into things. We had no choice but to find a little ground that was uncluttered by bushes, elephant grass, saplings, trees and undergrowth, and that was also clear of ants, on which to get some sleep. We couldn't find any.

RYDER AND I SLEPT back-to-back on a bed of tree roots and mud. We were both shivering with cold when I woke, my clothes and skin water-logged. It was maybe half an hour before dawn, the shapes of the world beneath the canopy barely discernible and still monochromatic. A large hairy caterpillar the size of my thumb hugged the stem of a plant inches from my face, probing carefully forward, trying to reach across the gap to my nose. I broke the stem and placed the bug on the ground beside me.

'Rise and shine, Duke,' I said, my throat thick with phlegm, giving him a nudge.

I felt his weight shift behind me.

'Fuck,' he said under his breath.

I stood up, using the M4 as a crutch, every joint in my body feeling cold and seized, and found a plant to water. Ryder did likewise. I was hungry, my stomach growling like there was a cat locked inside wanting out. I sucked the tube at my shoulder to settle it down a little.

I motioned at Ryder to follow. He nodded and dragged his feet behind me. I stopped and signaled him to look sharp. Most accidents happen close to home, and we were in the accident zone. No point tempting fate. It had been twelve hours since we'd patrolled through this patch of turf. Bad guys might have moved in behind us.

The forest dripped with water, only it wasn't raining. The morning slowly crept up on us as we made our way down the hill, the greens gradually taking over the palate as the day came out of hiding, birds waking with the sunlight and giving the world a good shriek. Frogs hopped out of the way of our feet and occasionally animals shot like runaway bowling balls through the undergrowth. A gentle mist floated around us, wrapping round tree trunks like gossamer web, and the air was thick, clean and as sweet as snowmelt.

'Take that step and you're dead, Cooper,' the tree beside me whispered.

Then the tree moved and I saw that it was Sergeant Cassidy, Ka-bar in hand, leaves and bits of shrub sprouting from webbing, his face streaked with camouflage paint. He came around beside me and scraped some leaf litter off the ground beneath my boot, revealing a hole. Pushing the butt of his M4 into the hole made a length of bamboo pole with bamboo spears embedded in the end rise out of the earth and swing in an arc toward me. Had I taken that step, I'd have collected a row of spikes from upper thigh to gut. Out here, that would have been a death sentence.

'Had some time on your hands?' I asked him.

He smiled. 'You just missed walking into another fun activity back up the hill a ways.'

We stepped around the trap and Cassidy fell in beside us. I took the pack off my shoulders and showed him the Claymores that Ryder and I had collected.

'Hoo-ah,' he beamed. 'Where'd you get them?'

'We took a stroll back to the Puma,' I said.

'What for?'

'I noticed Leila was all out of foundation,' I told him and Ryder held up Leila's makeup case.

'I was gonna ask you about that.'

'Next stop was the FARDC camp. They've moved.'

'Where to?'

'Well out of range of the CNDP's mortars.'

I reached down and felt my thigh pocket for the lipsticks containing what I hoped would be evidence of sabotage, and stopped in my tracks.

'What?' asked Cassidy.

The pocket was gone, torn clean away by all the crawling around. God only knew where those damn lipsticks were. 'Nothing,' I told him and consoled myself with the doubt I'd had that chemical analysis would've revealed anything significant. 'Anything happen while we've been gone?' I asked.

'We lost LeDuc.'

'You *lost* him?'

'He was with Rutherford. Went off to forage. Rutherford said he turned around and the Frenchman was gone. Could have been an animal. West found spoor from a big cat in the area. We searched, but found nothing. If a predator took him, West said his remains would be up some tree.'

'Law of the jungle,' Ryder said.

I didn't for a moment think that the Frenchman had been snatched by a cat. A more likely scenario was that he'd decided to rendezvous with his *real* friends, the ones we'd left up on the hill with our captive principals.

'We saw Twenny Fo and Peanut,' I said. 'They're alive.'

'All right!' Cassidy said, his mood-o-meter swinging to bright. 'Good news. Can we get to them?'

'There's been a development. You remember Beau Lockhart?'

'The Kornflak & Greene guy back at the camp?'

'Yeah. He's chummy with FARDC. We saw him in their HQ.'

'Hoo-ah!' Cassidy said, making a fist. 'So we just head on up there, collect our principals and Lockhart gets us flown out.'

'I witnessed Lockhart cap Fournier in cold blood.'

'What?'

'A nine to the back of the head.'

The face paint didn't camouflage the sergeant's anger and confusion. 'Jesus! What the hell's going on?'

'I'm not a hundred percent sure, but LeDuc and Lockhart are involved. The only thing that makes sense is that the French pilot put us down in the middle of it intentionally.'

'Aw, shit.'

WE ARRIVED BACK AT the rocks.

'Hey, look!' said Ayesha when she glanced up and saw us, giving Leila's shoulder a nudge.

Leila's eyes went straight to the makeup case in Ryder's hand and lit up.

'Oh, wow! You found it!' she squealed, jumped off the rock she was sitting on, and ran over and gave Duke a big kiss on the cheek.

'You'd think we'd found a case of Bud,' I said.

She wasted no time opening the catch and lifting the lid.

Cassidy and Rutherford wandered over with Boink, who, I noticed, had been reacquainted with a Nazarian, and they gave Ryder and me a bunch of assorted 'Hey's and 'Yo's.

A burst of automatic fire suddenly cut across the pleasantries. It was close; maybe five hundred meters up the hill. The unexpected sound was a jolt. I swung the M4 off my shoulder, pointed at Cassidy to lead off, and signaled at Ryder to organize the defense in our rear – leaving Ryder in charge worried me, but I wanted experience up front. Cassidy hopped forward into the bush; Rutherford, West and I close behind. Cassidy moved like he knew the terrain, running fast at a crouch, choosing a path higher up the side of the valley than the one we'd taken back to the rocks, then looped around, doubling back down the hill. We soon came upon a soldier lying beneath one of Cassidy's traps – a framework of stakes weighted with river stones that had dropped on top of him from the tree above. He'd walked through the tripwire – a length of plaited immature liana. One of the stakes had pierced his throat. The guy was as dead as yesterday. The lack of blue slashes on his battle uniform indicated that he was CNDP. Cassidy felt the barrel of the old AK-47 lying beside him.

'Cold,' he said.

West checked the ground for tracks. 'Looks like four, maybe five, others.' He motioned up the hill. 'They're running away.'

Cassidy immediately took off, jogging downhill back toward the rocks. We took off after him and, around fifty meters later, found a young boy of no more than fourteen who'd stepped on the trap that had almost claimed me. He was impaled on the row of spikes, one of which had torn through the femoral artery in his thigh. The kid was shaking with fear and cold as his blood drained away down his leg and into the hole in the ground. His eyes made contact with Cassidy before they went utterly blank, the lead doors welding shut behind them.

'Fuck,' said West, speaking for all of us.

I kneeled and picked up the kid's weapon, a new M16. Its barrel was warm, which suggested that the burst of fire we'd heard had come from this gun. Perhaps the boy had squeezed the trigger in shock when the stakes rose out of the earth and shanked him.

'I got a nephew that kid's age,' Cassidy said, hands on his hips, looking up at the canopy.

'THEY'RE GONNA MAKE A report,' said West.

I agreed. 'Time to change neighborhoods.'

'But we're safe here,' Leila protested, her hair brushed, her puckering lips now wearing a soft Chanel pink, and a long-legged spider crawling up onto her shoulder, which Ayesha flicked off before the singer became aware of it.

'Not for much longer,' I told her. 'Our best chance of survival lies out there.' I gave the forest a sweep of my hand.

'Cooper and Ryder found Twenny Fo, Peanut and Fournier,' said Cassidy. 'You want to fill everyone in?'

'You *saw* them?' Leila asked, her eyes open wide. 'Alive?'

'More or less,' I said a little cryptically. I passed on everything we saw, including the murder of Fournier, and concluded with my theory about Lockhart and LeDuc.

'Bullshiiiit,' said Boink, turning away.

'So the Frog crashed us into the forest on purpose?' Rutherford whistled softly, then added, 'Risky bloody strategy.'

'I don't believe it,' said Leila dismissively.

'Believe it,' I said.

The singer looked to Ryder for confirmation. He gave her a nod.

'Y'know, I saw something out the window,' said Ayesha, 'just before we went down. A bright green light, floating over the treetops.'

'A signal flare. Shit, that settles it,' said Cassidy. 'We were damn well set up.'

I shrugged. 'If it looks like LeDuc and walks like LeDuc . . .'

'It's a sodding fucking Frog bastard,' Rutherford chipped in.

'You didn't, by any chance, happen to mention seeing that light at the time?' I asked Ayesha.

'I did, but no one said anything. I thought everyone was asleep.'

Okay, so the mystery question that came through my headset before we went down – *What was that?* – hadn't come from Travis, but from Ayesha. Dammit, I might have gotten to LeDuc earlier if I'd quizzed everyone harder, done my job a little better. Ayesha was sitting on the right-hand side of the chopper, behind Travis and behind LeDuc. She saw the flare, and then the aircraft banked to the right, turning toward it. Seated on LeDuc's left, Fournier wouldn't have had the angle to spot the signal, which meant he was as much a passenger on the Puma as everyone else. It would have been LeDuc who'd then switched tanks, dumping contaminated fuel from the sponsons into the main tanks so that the engines flamed out. It was also, therefore, LeDuc and not

Fournier who faked the Mayday call that wasn't responded to. So, LeDuc, Lockhart and the FARDC commander, Colonel Cravat. Who else was hoping to get a cut of the ransom money?

'C'mon, people, clock's ticking,' said Cassidy. 'Shake it out.'

'Why? What are we doing?' Leila asked.

'We're gonna stick our hands in the fire,' I said.

IT WASN'T RAINING OR particularly hot, but the air was heavy with humidity. I glanced over my shoulder to check on Boink. His shirt was soaked with perspiration but he wasn't doing too badly, all things considered. The Congo Weightloss Program was agreeing with him, and his fitness was also improving.

'Making out okay?' I asked him.

'As good as you, soldier man,' he said.

'We need to rest,' said Leila, walking in front of me. 'Don't we, Ayesha?'

Her friend and makeup artist turned and gave me a look that told me she might as well hammer a nail into her own forehead if she disagreed.

'We took a break half an hour ago,' I reminded the celebrity. 'We've gotta keep going.'

'Then you can keep going without me.'

'I tell you what,' I said. 'You stay here and we'll come back for your corpse in a week or two.'

'I don't like you, Cooper.'

'I don't believe you.'

Leila tried to ignore me and kept walking, spritzing her face with a can of aerosolized water recovered from her makeup case.

'We'll take a break when we get to where we're going,' I said.

'And where's that?'

'I'm not sure. I'll know when I see it. And there's something I've been meaning to say to you.'

'Yes?'

'No one likes to think they can be bought cheap.'

'What?'

'Bribing my men could get you in a lot of trouble, especially if the person you're trying to bribe knows that someone else you waved your money at was offered a lot more.'

'I don't know what you're talking about.'

She glanced around to check on whether Ryder was within earshot – she knew all right, but I didn't push it.

'One thing I don't understand and I was thinking that maybe you could help me with it,' I said.

'No. Go make polite conversation with someone else,' she said.

'One minute you were desperate for us to head on in with guns blazing and rescue your ex,' I said, ignoring her request, 'the next, you're ready to cut and run. How come the turnaround?'

'I'm not cutting and running and I don't have to explain myself to you,' she said.

'C'mon. Help me out.'

'Go away.'

I wasn't going anywhere.

When Leila realized this, she sighed heavily. 'Look, Cooper, no one has ever tried to drag *you* away by the ankle to rape you, have they? Perhaps if they had, you might understand what I went through – what Ayesha and I are going through in this place.'

'We're all Twenny Fo and Peanut have got,' I reminded her.

'A ransom will get paid and they'll come home.'

'Not if Twenny knows his kidnapper's identity. If Lockhart thinks he's been made, Deryck's as good as dead whether he pays for his freedom or not.'

'But you keep saying there aren't enough of you to rescue him. So what are we doing? Where are we going? You're just tempting fate, keeping us all hanging around here. You have no right to put Ayesha and me at further risk.'

From a certain angle, she had a point, even if the angle was rooted in her own self-preservation. If we lost Twenny and Peanut's trail, I was as sure as I could be that we would not be able to find them again – not in this rainforest. I was also as sure as I could be that no matter what happened in terms of any ransom being paid, the hostages would be killed. 'We'll assess the situation when we get to the other side of the hill,' I said.

'What do you expect to see?'

'The other side of the hill.'

'Like I said, Cooper, I don't like you.'

'Stand in line.'

She pursed her lips into a seam. 'Look, I'm feeling faint. So can we stop for a little while? Will it help if I say please?'

I gave in and called a halt. If ten minutes of rest would buy some cooperation, it was worth it. Maybe Leila was just hungry. Our stores of python had run out and lack of food was now becoming a factor, though not a life-threatening one. My own survival training told me a person could go for a week on no food. It was a comfort issue more than anything – we were all conditioned to eating three meals a day and we'd barely snacked. My stomach was empty. Even the grumbling had echoes. Energy levels were low. Our principals leaned against trees, drank water and swatted mosquitoes while West, Rutherford, Cassidy, Ryder and I did our best to recall the lay of the land set out on LeDuc's map – which we no longer had – in particular, our intended destination, a ridge adjacent to the hill now occupied by the FARDC.

It was a steep two-hour climb through liana, elephant grass and stinging nettles to reach the ridge's spine. We came out from under the canopy a little after one o'clock in the afternoon, halfway up a gray basalt rock face that the forest hadn't managed to conquer. The break in the trees provided us with a much-hoped-for unobstructed view to the FARDC encampment half a mile across the valley. Hanging threateningly overhead, massive thunderheads jostled against a clear blue sky ruled by the afternoon sun, the warmth of which sliced through the chill clinging to my skin. Leila and Ayesha sank back against the rock face, closed their eyes and turned their faces toward it.

'Mmm, God, that's good,' Leila said with a moan. 'Ayesha, honey, go get me some sunscreen from my case, will you?'

We could plainly see individuals moving around across the valley at the company HQ. Smoke from several fires curled skywards and drifted toward a thicker haze out to the west. I was right about the hill having been logged. Compared with the virgin forest, the area the HQ occupied appeared to have been stripped bare.

Swinging the pack off my shoulder, I rummaged around and pulled out the scope. I braced it against a tree trunk and adjusted the focus. Ryder stood on one side of me, while Rutherford, West and Cassidy lined up off my other shoulder and shielded their eyes from the sun with their hands.

'Fuck me,' said Rutherford. 'Is that a truck down there?'

His eyes were good. I found it a second later, a deuce-and-a-half painted olive drab parked in the shadows at one end of the newly cleared scrub. The women were gone but the Mi-8 was still there.

'And where there's a truck, there's a road,' said West, the implication of the vehicle's presence occurring to everyone in the PSO team at the same instant.

I scoured the HQ for our principals.

'Found 'em,' I said. Twenny and Peanut were standing by themselves in the cleared area where I'd seen them last night, behind the blue tents. They were still hooded and their hands tied behind their backs. No Chinese guy in sight, no Lockhart and no Colonel Cravat, either, but there were plenty of folks in greens going about their business. I passed the scope to Rutherford.

'The high point of the hill. Look for the tents,' I said.

'Yep, there they are,' he said and then passed the scope on.

'What I wouldn't give for a radio and an Apache gunship on the other end of it,' muttered West as he adjusted the sight's focus a little.

After Cassidy and Ryder had scanned the hill, I took the scope back and went on a more extended tour with it, hoping to pick up that road and see where it led. I found it, a pale orange ribbon of mud that curled around the back of the hill, disappearing from view. I readjusted the instrument and came across something else I wasn't expecting to see.

'What?' Cassidy asked, sensing something.

'There's a village down there, to the west of the hill. You can just make out a couple of huts.'

Cassidy took the scope and trained it on the area. 'Got it,' he said. He was about to shift the view to another area when he took it back to the village. 'Shit,' he said. 'The fucks are setting fire to it . . .'

'Which fucks?' Ryder asked.

'The fuckin' FARDC,' said Rutherford.

'The fire explains the haze,' said West.

Now that I thought about it, the air smelt vaguely of burnt trash.

'Christ . . .' Cassidy muttered.

'What now?' said Rutherford.

Grim faced, the sergeant handed him the scope. 'Look.'

Rutherford trained it on the village. 'Jesus, they're hacking the poor sods to pieces.'

I took back the scope. I saw a man in civilian clothes run into view and then out of it, a soldier in pursuit with a raised machete poised for the strike. I saw another civilian – a woman – crawl out of the hut on her hands and knees. A soldier stood beside her and hit the back of her head with the flat of his blade, knocking her unconscious, or dead – I couldn't tell which.

'There's movement at the HQ,' said West.

I swung the scope back. The truck was rolling. It did a one-eighty, then stopped. A couple of men jogged toward it and one of them was Lockhart.

The passenger side door opened and Lockhart and his buddy jumped in beside the driver. The vehicle then accelerated off down the road toward the village.

I lowered the scope. 'I'm going down there.'

'Why?' It was Leila. She was behind me, standing with a hand on one hip in that determined, argumentative stance of hers I first saw in the departure lounge at Kigali airport.

'To see if what we find there provides us with any opportunities.'

'Then I'm going with you. And so is Ayesha; aren't we?' she continued.

Ayesha looked surprised.

'Nope,' I said. 'Too dangerous.'

'We all going, yo,' said Boink, jutting his chin forward. I pictured a porch coming away from the wall.

'Cooper, we're going with you or I scream.' The celebrity sucked in a breath, opened her mouth and closed her eyes.

What choice did I have?

I DROPPED BACK TO have a word with West.

'We need food,' I told him.

'Sure, it's all over the place here.' To prove the point he snatched a large cricket off the petals of a bright red wildflower and stuffed it in his mouth.

'I'd prefer a toasted sandwich,' I told him.

He shook his head. 'Fire's a no-no here.'

Further down the hill, the rainforest provided West with options more palatable for our principals. He took Cassidy and went off to gather it and they returned with a large bunch of wild bananas on Cassidy's shoulder.

'We also need protein,' said West. He dug into his pockets and produced handfuls of fat white grubs which he passed around. Leila and Ayesha screwed up their faces.

'You can't be serious?' the star said.

'No,' said Ayesha, waving her hand at the offer as if trying to push it away.

'It's just food . . . I'll admit they're better when they're fried but a fire's too risky,' West informed them.

Somehow I didn't think it would make a difference if they were lightly sautéed in a white wine sauce.

'What are they?' I asked.

'Mopane worms – off mopane trees. Critters are all over here.'

'How d'you eat 'em?' Rutherford inquired, sniffing the four large worms in the palm of his hand.

'Pinch their guts out, and pull out their backbone, which is prickly, so be careful.' He demonstrated. 'Then you do this with them.' He opened his mouth, popped one in and chewed slowly and deliberately.

'I'm going to throw up,' Leila muttered.

I followed West's demonstration – pinched out the guts, removed the spine and ate the thing. It tasted bitter, slimy and gritty. If I'd paid money, I'd be asking for a refund. But food was food, and we had to take what was on the menu to keep up our strength. I ate half a dozen.

'You can also do what I do and eat the grasshoppers. They're crunchy and taste of grass, and you have to eat a lot of them. The termites are also an option.'

Ayesha dry retched.

If it were possible for Leila to look gray, she did.

'Oh, and I also picked up some dessert,' said West, grabbing a long length of what at first glance appeared to be bamboo that he'd leaned against the rocks. He cut it into one-foot lengths. 'This here is sugar cane. You chew it, and suck it.'

Leila and Ayesha took the cane but examined it with suspicion.

'Tastes like sugar,' he assured them. 'Really . . .'

The banana was filling and the cane juice rich and sweet. Best of all it carried away the taste of Mopane grub. Cassidy took the lead heading down the hill. He moved fast and we all kept to his tracks. My intention had been to leave Rutherford, West and Ryder behind to provide the security for Boink, Ayesha, Leila, and Leila's makeup case, but that's not how it worked out.

I said to Leila, 'Stay, go, stay, go . . . You always so decisive?'

'I don't like you, Cooper, because you—'

'We've established that.'

'Because, for one thing, you butt in. Look, even though I don't like you, I do feel safe with you. And so does Ayesha.'

Ayesha glanced over her shoulder at me and produced a smile.

'When you go off somewhere,' Leila continued, 'it's like we're all just hanging around waiting for something to go wrong.'

'Stick with me and there's no waiting,' I told her.

'That's a reference to your former partner, isn't it, the one you think you killed?'

It was, but I wasn't going to give her the satisfaction of admitting it.

'Duke told me that she almost died when you first met her – in a car crash, right? Did you ever think that maybe she was *meant* to die in that crash, that her time was up? It could be that dying in that crash was her fate but, for some unnatural reason, she avoided it, cheated death. Perhaps she died in that room on your last case because fate had to settle the score.'

I was thinking that I still had a score to settle with Ryder and his blabbermouth. Aside from that, I also wondered which nutbag guru was doing the rounds of celebrity life counseling in LA at the moment. I dropped back a little to put some forest between the two of us, and fell in behind Boink.

THE SOUND OF WOMEN and children crying reached us long before we caught sight of the village. It was the same for the smell of blood, a metallic tang carried on the breeze that stuck to the roof of the mouth and triggered the gag reflex. It took *a lot* of blood to produce a smell like that out in the open. An hour and a half after leaving the ridge, we climbed a heavily wooded hill behind the village. It was spread out a hundred feet below us, laid out across an open cleared area, twenty-three grass and animal-skin huts arranged around a larger central hut. Half a dozen of these smaller huts – homes, I figured – were no more than smoking piles of gray and black ash.

We wrapped the shadows of the forest around us and watched, stunned. Ayesha and Leila covered their mouths with their hands as they did so.

The inhabitants of the village, around a hundred men and women, were sitting on the ground – women and children in one group, men in another. Most of the women carried babies. The men, all roughly between twenty and forty years of age, were sitting cross-legged with their hands on their heads. FARDC soldiers stood over both groups with machetes, the blades black and slick with coagulating blood. Some of the older members of the village had already been butchered, and flies clouded around crimson corpses tangled together in a separate group. People everywhere were yelling and screaming and begging for mercy, which seemed in real short supply.

The soldiers had separated a man from the group and were shouting at him. He wasn't doing what they wanted so they started beating him with the flats of their blades. He eventually got the message – to sit up on his knees with his fingers interlocked behind his neck – and the beating stopped. Two soldiers then pulled a woman from the female group and dragged her into the center with the man. She was carrying a newborn baby, which was screaming its lungs out. The two villagers risked touching each other's faces, both sobbing, the woman hysterically. One of the soldiers strode in and ripped the infant the woman was carrying from her arms, holding it upside down by one of its ankles. Unbelievably, he then swung it around his head twice and let go of it. The baby flew high and long, and landed with a crash in the bushes not fifteen meters down the hill from where we were hiding. Its crying ceased when it landed.

'Oh my lord,' Leila whispered, her hands shaking, pressed against her face to shut out the world.

The mother howled and the man tried to get up – I guessed, to run to the child – which was when the soldiers started chopping into him with their machetes. *Jesus Christ . . .* They kept chopping until his head rolled clear of his neck. The groups of women and men screamed and cried out, and beat the ground with their fists. The soldiers then dragged the mother away toward one of the huts, outside which several men and boys in uniform loitered, smoking and joking among themselves.

Then the man I assumed was the commanding officer, the man I dubbed Colonel Cravat, swaggered out of the hut, adjusting his fly. The other soldiers stood back, giving him room. He stood over the headless corpse and addressed the villagers. I couldn't hear specifics, but I guessed that he wanted them to do something in particular – cow them completely – or risk more bloodshed. No one moved, so he shouted an order at a couple of his men, who yanked another woman from the group. They pulled her infants away from her and hauled her across the ground by her hair as she kicked and shrieked and pleaded with them. My muscles twitched, wanting to get down there and *do* something – I wasn't sure what. The men took her to an old truck tire leaning against a hut, kicked it over, pulled her arms down onto it and hacked one of them off. Just like that. *Shit* . . .

The officer strolled across to a point directly beneath us, while taunting her, calling out so that everyone in the clearing could hear him.

'What'd he say?' I asked Rutherford.

'He said, "Now, woman, let us see how easy it is for you to hold your bastard children."'

It was settled. I wanted to go down there and rip the guy's heart, assuming he had one, out through his ribs. A second truck arrived and made a U-turn, mowing down the remains of a smoldering hut in a burst of cinders, its brakes squealing as it came to a stop in the open ground where atrocities were being inflicted on the locals by the army that was supposed to be their own. The older children of the village were marched to the truck from out of one of the huts and threatened with being shot unless they climbed up in back.

The men, who were seated on the ground, were pulled to their feet and pushed toward the vehicle. The front passenger window rolled down and revealed Beau Lockhart.

I heard him call something out to Cravat, add a friendly 'come here' wave and open the door beside him.

The colonel waved back, surveyed the devastation around him and, happy with what he saw, jogged over with a jaunty gait and climbed in beside his Kornflak & Greene buddy like they were off to play eighteen holes. The door pulled shut, hiding the men in the darkness of the enclosed cabin, and the truck started to roll.

'What the fuck is going on here?' I muttered to myself.

A baby crying in the bushes near our hiding place distracted me. Jesus, it was the kid that had been thrown. The soldiers didn't notice or care about one more infant exercising its lungs, so I got down on my belly and did the snake thing down and across to it. Minutes was all it took to reach the spot. I found the baby hanging upside down, its legs tangled up in the liana. A bush covered with vine had acted like a fireman's net, catching the kid, saving its life and holding its body secure. The baby – it was a girl – was crying because it had recovered from the shock of her first flight, and also because a driver ant had latched onto a toe. I killed the ant, untangled the baby girl's legs from the vines, and wriggled on my belly back to our position higher up the hill, resting the wailing child across my forearms.

Cassidy met me halfway. 'I count eight of them,' he said, the muscles in his jaw bunching like twisted steel cabling, motioning at the soldiers swaggering among the villagers. 'I can do five of these fuckers. Can you do three?'

'We're not doing anyone,' I said. 'Not now.'

I'd already weighed the odds. The suggestion was noble but dumb. Assuming that we managed to take these guys out, their hundred-and-seventy-or-so comrades would swoop in from their encampment, flood the area, hunt us down and capture us. My team and I would then be chopped up, or whatever these folks did to people they didn't like and couldn't ransom.

Another truck arrived and parked behind the one waiting, its engine idling with a steady diesel thrum.

Cassidy stroked the infant's head to calm it. 'The villagers are being taken somewhere close by,' he observed.

He was right. The trucks appeared to be making round trips. The baby had stopped crying and was starting to gurgle. 'I think she likes you. Go to Papa,' I said as I bundled the kid into his arms.

'Where you going?'

'Don't know, which is why I'm going there.'

'That's not a good enough reason.'

'Those trucks are headed someplace. I want to know where. It's worth the risk finding out. As you said, they're making round trips. Take our people further up the hill and if I don't make it back by morning—'

'I know, Lake Kivu.'

'Yeah.' I gave him a grin and slithered off down through the undergrowth toward the vehicle. Getting closer, I could read the label on its radiator grille. The manufacturer was Dongfeng – truck supplier to the PLA. This particular variant had off-road capability. Its bodywork sat high over the wheels with sheet steel flooring the load bed. A dull green canvas tarp over a high framework protected the load from the elements. My plan, insofar as I had one, was to stow away between the load bed and the chassis members. I sat at the edge of the bush, the truck parked only a couple of meters away, which was very considerate of the driver. The body of the vehicle obscured me from all but one set of unfriendly eyeballs up behind the steering wheel. I waited till they were preoccupied with something other than the vehicle's rear-view mirrors, snuck over to the wheels and climbed up into the truck's insides, between the tires and the bodywork. The chassis was crude but effective, no crumple zones here, only naked steel members, cross-braced – just what I'd been hoping for. I worked my way into the darker shadows at the rear of the vehicle, and waited. But not for long.

Within a few minutes, I heard the grief-stricken crying of the women being pushed up to the back of the truck, the soldiers snapping at them. The vehicle swayed as they climbed in and the metal tray above me began to sag under the weight, pressing me down into the chassis and onto the exhaust pipe. The loading complete, the driver revved the engine, then selected first, the gears in the transmission snarling at each other like old dogs. The brakes hissed as the truck lurched forward with a jerk, and the women above gave a collective wail. The exhaust pipe got hot very quickly and the heat radiated though my trouser leg.

The Dongfeng turned onto the road and gathered speed, the dust and grit picked up by the tires sandblasting my face. I couldn't see anything other than the road rolling by beneath, which it continued to do for twenty minutes. Two hills and a dozen tight, steep switchbacks later, my transport finally pulled off the main road and then bounced along a narrow track, the forest pressing in on both sides, branches and leaves slapping against the vehicle. Looking straight down, the track we were on seemed no more than a sodden strip of mud deeply scored with ruts, which shunted the truck violently sideways left and right.

Eventually the track widened and we came out of the gloom, but even before we stopped, men who were full of impatience were shouting and hammering on the vehicle with sticks. The women above me made noises of pure dread as they climbed off the tailgate onto the ground. I dropped my head so that I could see what was going on and saw a dozen soldiers milling about, waiting on the human cargo, smacking them with those sticks like they were cattle, herding them toward some kind of marshaling area. Another truck was parked beside my ride, pointing back the way we came in. I dropped onto the mud and scampered across beneath it. Beyond this second truck, on its far side, the forest beckoned with a thousand places to hide. I dived into a thick screen of elephant grass and worked my way clear of the parking lot.

The forest here was mostly banana tree, some other kind of palm with fleshy leaves that grew close to the ground, and the usual elephant grass. I figured that it was probably an abandoned plantation because I could move through it reasonably easily. I made a wide circle and, as I worked my way around to what must have been the downwind side of whatever was going on here, the air brought with it the smell of unwashed bodies, exhumed earth and the murmur of a crowd of voices. What the hell was this place?

I changed direction, got down on my stomach and wriggled forward through the scrub, taking it slowly, the smells and the sounds concentrating. And, suddenly, the earth fell away beneath my hands. I was on the edge of something. I separated the leaves in front of my face and dropping away more than a hundred feet was a pit of the damned. Several hundred souls caked in orange dust and mud, driven by soldiers with long sticks and rifles, passed buckets of the mud up a complex labyrinth of terraces, ramps and ladders, and they were then tipped onto bigger piles of mud being worked over by more human beings urged on by beatings. The captives here were slaves, no other word for it. As I watched the scene, which reminded me of one of those old church paintings depicting a vision of hell, a man slipped and dropped his bucket, and two of the guards thrashed him with their sticks while he cowered and eventually rolled himself into a ball. Unfortunately, he rolled a little too far and fell off the terrace, dropping ten feet to a lower level where he landed on his head. No one went to the man's aid, though several soldiers rushed at him with their sticks and the beating started over. They didn't seem to realize, much less care, that the guy wasn't moving, not even to protect his head.

I glanced over toward the area where the trucks were parked. Soldiers handed buckets to the women I had shared the truck with and then divided them into teams. Down in the pit, more women worked alongside the men. Some children were down there too, I noticed. The lethargy of the workforce was matched by most of the soldiers. But there were others in uniforms present who watched over the proceedings with more than a passing interest. These men occupied a couple of shanty-style buildings over by the parking lot that were set back from the edge of the pit. Unlike their uniformed counterparts down in the hole, these men were clean and dust-free. They loitered on the rickety, uneven verandas, waved away the flies and upended green beer bottles.

Bushes thrashed about nearby, distracting me. Jesus, there was something large and determined coming through, heading straight for me. Whatever it was came close, and then stopped. I pulled my Ka-bar and held my breath. I didn't want to think about what it might be, but thought sharp teeth and claws were probably in my immediate future. It moved again and suddenly a black face with wide yellow eyes burst through the foliage in front of me and stopped. We looked at each other, neither of us sure what to do. I saw his knife, an old rusty blade, and knew he'd figured it out. He stuck the thing into my ribs but the crude blade glanced off my body armor. The guy was small and determined and surprisingly strong. I grabbed his wrist, and managed to roll on top of him and pin his knife between our chests. He was a civilian, or maybe a soldier out of uniform. I held my Ka-bar across his throat and pushed the blade into his Adam's apple, his breathing coming out short and sharp.

'*Américain?*' he gasped, eyes widening with surprise. '*Vous-êtes Américain?*'

No point denying it, there being a low-viz brown and tan Stars and Stripes patch on my shoulder.

'*We*,' I told him, in the worst French accent I'd probably ever heard.

The guy stopped struggling.

'Then you help,' he said in broken English.

'Is that before or after you stick me?'

'Oh, *pardon, monsieur*.'

'You speak English.' I said.

'*Oui*, a little.'

'Then let's go with that.'

I happened to glance up just as the Chinese guy, the one from the FARDC encampment, emerged from one of the shanty hovels. Colonel Cravat was with him, following a few paces behind. Then Lockhart made an appearance, stepping from out of the hut and trotting up behind the two men. The three of them met out in the open with a man covered in orange dust accompanied by a couple of soldiers. The uniformed guys on the verandas were all turned toward them, their body language expectant. Something was going on.

One of the soldiers accompanying the man covered in orange dust held something toward Lockhart. He accepted it, examined it, and passed it on to Colonel Cravat, who then handed in to Fu Manchu. As all three examined the item, they became animated. Whatever it was obviously excited the crap out of them.

Lockhart and Colonel Cravat spoke with the orange man and he pointed down into the pit, showing where he found whatever it was that was getting them all in a lather.

Then Lockhart held the object up to the beer gallery and yelled, 'Door!' which was met by a rousing cheer, raised bottles and plenty of backslapping.

'Door? What door?' I muttered.

'*D'or*,' said the man lying beside me on the ground, also watching Lockhart and the others. 'Gold.'

Rendezvous

The soldiers and the man who made the strike each received a bottle of beer. A nugget of gold in exchange for a beer. I licked my lips and thought, yeah, fair trade. All three of them then shuffled off back down into the pit. Lockhart, Fu Manchu and Colonel Cravat headed for the shacks and the men on the verandas crowded around to inspect the find.

'Who is that man?' I asked the Congolese beside me. 'The officer – the one with the white scarf tucked into his shirt. You know his name?'

'He is Colonel Innocent Lissouba. A very bad man.'

I repeated the name to fix it in my memory.

'He came to my village. His soldiers took all the women and all the men. They killed many. I want to kill him.'

The man wriggled forward to get a better view of the pit.

'My wife, she is down there,' he said, trying to spot her.

'Where's your village?' I asked. He gestured off in a direction away from the village I'd just witnessed being plundered for the able-bodied. There were many more laborers down in the pit than I'd seen transported here, which meant there were other villages nearby. For all I knew, Lockhart, Lissouba and his cohorts were out scouring the countryside, press-ganging anyone strong enough to lift a shovel.

'You are American! You must help me free my wife, my people.'

'Do I look like Bruce Willis?' I said.

'Bruce Willis, yes!'

The guy was excited.

'I'm not Bruce Willis. I've got hair.'

He went back to scouring the pit.

'There,' the African said, pointing, suddenly agitated. 'Look, she is there!'

He indicated a group of women slopping around on the edge of a puddle in the bottom of the hole, digging at it with their hands and dropping whatever they could pull up into the steel buckets. I wasn't sure which of the women was his wife.

'She is alive,' he said, obviously relieved. 'I know these women. And there is my brother and my uncle,' he continued. He sat back on his haunches, his face split by a wide grin. He'd been expecting the worst, but this was obviously the best possible result.

A wall of rain, gray and leaning forward at an angle like it was in a hurry to get somewhere, thundered across the forest on the far side of the pit, coming our way. Its arrival didn't send anyone scurrying for cover. It seemed to arrive daily at this time in the afternoon. I knew of train services less reliable. Overhead, someone threw a blanket over the sun.

At that instant, Lockhart and his two buddies walked out of one of the shacks and started jogging toward the parking lot. I lost sight of them at that point, but a Dongfeng moved off soon after, probably heading back to the FARDC encampment or to the village to cause a bunch more misery. I'd seen enough and pushed back from the lip of the mine.

'Where are you going?' the African wanted to know, anxious, grabbing at my sleeve.

It was time to put him straight – that I was not some kind of advance guard for Tommy Franks. 'My unit and I made a forced landing in a helicopter and some of my people have been taken captive. We're all in the same boat with you and your wife, and it's got a big hole in the bottom.'

'Then *I* will help *you*,' he said.

'You're not Bruce Willis, either,' I replied, maybe a little too quickly. He was a local. He'd know the area, which put him way ahead of Bruce. I gave him a test. 'The road up there. It starts in the forest. Where does it go?'

'To Mukatano, a city twenty kilometer this way.' He gestured vaguely south. 'The men who took the trees make the road. They are gone now.'

Twenty kilometers – twelve miles – a lot more achievable than hiking out to Goma or Rwanda. I doubted the city bit. It had to be a small town, too small to be noted on LeDuc's map. 'Is there a sawmill at Mukatano?' I asked.

'*Non*.'

'Is Mukatano on a river?'

'The Zaire? *Non.*'

'Isn't that what this place used to be called?'

'It was named after the river.'

I scratched my cheek and an insect having a meal got caught under my fingernails. If the road ended at Mukatano and there were no sawmill there and no river, how'd those loggers get the logs processed? 'Where'd the loggers put the lumber – in the river?'

'There was a place for this, but it is gone. They had a dock, but even that is gone. People take it for cooking fires.'

'The road goes there too, yes?'

'*Oui*.'

'How'd you escape?' I asked. 'Why aren't you down in the pit with the people from your village?'

'I was at another village when the soldiers came. It is near the road also. *Médecins Sans Frontières* is there. They have medicines. I went to get them and when I come back, everyone in my village was gone . . . or dead.'

The memories of what he'd seen came back to him and large tears welled in his eyes. They ran down his face, mixing with the rainwater. The village I'd just come from gave me a fair idea of the scenes he was recalling.

'Where will these people sleep tonight?' I asked. 'What'll they eat?'

The man wiped his face with his hands. 'The soldiers will give them some food, but not much. Some will sleep in the mine; some are taken back to their villages. There is a camp nearby. My people will sleep there under plastic. There are some United Nations tents. But there is no clean water. Some have died from stomach sickness. It is bad.'

It didn't sound good. The scale of this cruelty was difficult for me to get my head around. 'So your people . . . they just work until they die?'

'No, they work until this army gets frightened away by a bigger army, and then we will go back to our village.'

'How many times has this happened?'

'They found gold here two years ago. Since then, many armies come through: CNDP, Mai-Mai, PARECO, FDLR, LRA, FARDC . . . Each one is worse than the last. Sometimes they punish us for helping their enemies, but we have no choice. They loot and steal, kill and rape and they pass on the sickness – the sickness I go to the MSF to get the medicine for. My village was once large and rich, but now it is small and we starve.'

'Where is the camp your people are taken to at night?'

'It is near. You wish to see it also.'

'Not now. What's your name?' I asked him.

'Francis.' He glanced at the nametag on my body armor. 'Your name is Cooper. I can read, also.'

'Francis. I'll be honest with you – I don't know what my men and I can do here. There are many more of them than there are of us.'

'You will do something, I know it.'

Yeah, and right there could be the problem. Who's to say that what we did wouldn't turn around and bite all of us in the ass right back, Francis and his people included? I parted the foliage, took another look at the mine and the shacks, but there was nothing of interest going on other than a lot of ice-cold beer being guzzled. A couple of soldiers were leering and calling out to a group of women working a section of mud nearby. Mud, beer, women. I could see where it was heading and this was one time I didn't want to be around when it arrived. I made a quick decision. 'Come with me,' I said to Francis, and backed away from the lip of the mine.

The Congolese hesitated a moment while he again located his wife down in the pit. Satisfied that she was in no immediate danger, he said, 'Yes, thank you. I come with you.' He turned for one last look over his shoulder before following me to where the trucks were parked. By the time we arrived there only three Dongfengs remained. At the edge of the cleared area, I gave Francis a quick briefing followed by a practical demonstration, scooting across open ground to the nearest truck and climbing up inside its wheel arches, and then waving him across.

We waited twenty minutes, squeezed into the truck's sub frame, before its diesel thrummed into life. Half a dozen soldiers piled in the back and the vehicle finally pulled out of the lot and onto the road, heading in the right direction at least – back to the village I'd come from.

The return ride was a different kind of uncomfortable from the trip out. Instead of dust and grit, the wheels flung water, mud and the occasional stone at us while steam boiled into clouds off the exhaust pipe. I counted down the hills – two of them – and waited for the truck to pull over into the village. But then we swept around a corner, the driver back-shifted into the lower gears, and we started up a third hill.

'Shit,' I muttered to myself. We weren't stopping in the village. The ride was taking us all the way into the FARDC camp. The truck came to a stop at a roadblock, a brief conversation ensued between the driver and the soldiers manning it, and then we were underway again. A few minutes later, the vehicle's brakes wheezed as we came to a stop, the engine died and the soldiers climbed down. I motioned to Francis to stay put and keep quiet. It was after five and the light was fading. We were stuck here until the night gave us some cover, shivering with cold, caked with mud – my teeth grinding with it – the rain causing small waterfalls to run off the sides of the truck and into the growing lake on the ground beneath us.

We came out of hiding an hour and a half later, when the darkness was complete and the smells of kerosene fires and cooking drifted across the encampment, the men preoccupied with food. I unfolded my cramped arms, legs and neck, and dropped with a splash into the puddles beneath us. Francis did likewise. There was another Dongfeng parked in front of our hiding place. Fifty meters ahead, I could make out the hazy shape of the Mi-8 chopper. I had no idea about the placement of sentries but I had to assume that they were around. I was thinking about all this as the rain softened into a fog-like mist and the air came alive with the sound of mating frogs.

I whispered to Francis, 'Follow me, stay close,' and then, doubled over, I headed for the uncleared scrub that marked the edge of the forest. We made it without incident and stopped roughly midway between the trucks and the chopper.

'Where are your men?' Francis asked.

Good question, and I wished I had an equally good answer to go with it. When I last saw them, they were babysitting. I wondered what they'd been up to while I'd taken the detour. 'Around,' I said, keeping it ambiguous, but the truth of it was that I had not the faintest idea where my unit might be – still back at the nearby village, or back on the hill that provided overwatch, or back at Cyangugu with drinks in hand . . . who knew?

As I sat in the scrub, dragging my hand across the back of my neck, smearing the mosquitoes that settled on my bare skin and watching several fires haloed by the mist, it seemed to me that the war effort around here had tapered off somewhat. If I weren't mistaken, the attitude of the men walking around was pretty relaxed; surprising, given that the CNDP force was somewhere nearby. I'd have thought that the proximity of its sworn enemy would have made these boys just a little nervous. I was considering all this, along with what my limited options might be, when I heard the familiar thump of a helicopter's main rotor blades away in the distance. The sound drifted in and out as the air currents shifted, silencing the frogs as it grew louder with each second. The aircraft was clearly inbound. A party of men arrived at the edge of the cleared area. Several of them waved flashlights blithely about for the benefit of enemy snipers, but no shots rang out.

The chopper arrived from the east. It wasn't a military aircraft. It was big and sleek and, as it flew overhead and pivoted almost a hundred and eighty degrees before settling on its retractable landing gear, its underbelly strobe light revealed a color scheme of gold with a white stripe running down the center. The pilots cut the engines and the whine of its turbines instantly dropped away. It looked like one of those big expensive choppers that ply between New York and Washington DC, carrying executive types overloaded with taxpayer-funded bail outs. A Sikorsky. I couldn't see what was going on once it had landed because, aside from being dark, whoever got out of it exited on the side of the aircraft facing the camp and the rest of the helicopter got in the way. I tapped my African friend on the shoulder and we crawled through the forest to get a better angle on the proceedings. The view quickly improved. Portable electric lanterns were turned on and flashlights waved about, illuminating a bunch of very interesting faces. Lockhart was part of the welcoming committee, as was Colonel Cravat – Colonel Lissouba – and the Chinese PLA guy. They were shaking hands with the guy from Swedish American Gold and his African American buddy. Both of their names escaped me for the moment, but I remembered them – the two ex-pat autograph hunters Lockhart declined to introduce me to back at Cyangugu on the night of the concert.

Their presence here was surprising and intriguing, equally as surprising and intriguing as the presence of the CNDP's Colonel Makenga, who'd probably been picked up from his ridgeline on the way through. And Makenga's presence was not nearly as surprising and intriguing as that of Colonel Biruta's, the CNDP officer commanding the brigade entertained by Twenny Fo and Leila at the Cyangugu training base; the officer with the nice symmetrical scar that divided his face into equal parts. Another guy stepped into the light. It was my ol' buddy, LeDuc – his presence here not in the least surprising or intriguing.

'Piers Pietersen and Charles White,' I whispered, the names of the two expats coming back to me.

'What?' said Francis.

I waved away the question, along with the mosquito cloud. Explanations would have to wait. Lockhart, Lissouba, Fu Manchu, Makenga,

Biruta, LeDuc, and a bigwig from a gold company. Or, another way to look at it – a US DoD contractor in cahoots with the PLA and FARDC, meeting the local CNDP commanding officer and his boss for a pow-wow with SAG. It read like a headline for a *60 Minutes* exposé. And all within spitting distance of a gold mine producing nuggets of the stuff. That was no coincidence either. More than likely it was the catalyst. And the presence of Makenga, the enemy – he of the golden chicken – accounted for the unnatural calm that seemed to have descended on the FARDC encampment. Obviously, a convenient truce had been called between the two warring companies. The only man I couldn't place in the get-together was Charles White, the African American accompanying Pietersen. I wondered how many of these people were involved in the scheme to abduct my principals.

The backslapping continued for a while as Francis and I watched on. Then half a dozen men from the camp came over and White accompanied them to the chopper. The fuselage of the aircraft obscured the proceedings for a few moments, but then I saw the men re-emerge, lugging heavy crates between them. They carried them to the back of the lead truck, placed them on the tailgate and went back to the chopper for more. Taking a flashlight, White led the group to the rear of the truck and opened one of the boxes with a jemmy that had been handed to him. He levered the lid off the crate, opened another box within it, took something out and held it up to show the party gathered nearby. He then strolled around the far side of the truck, the side nearest to Francis and me hiding in the scrub, placed the object on the ground and sauntered back to join the others. He held his right hand up high.

And, suddenly, a flash ripped through the darkness, accompanied by an ear-splitting explosion. Shrapnel raked the foliage inches above my head. Francis screamed, got up and ran.

I took off after him, expecting that, any second, gunfire would follow us. I tensed, waiting for the bark of M16s and the jacketed slugs that would drop us into the scrub, but they never came. I caught up with Francis eventually, after a sprint of two hundred meters through elephant grass that cut up my clothes, up toward the ridge that we'd used as an observation post earlier in the day. No one seemed to have followed us. I put that down to the explosion temporarily deafening White, Lockhart and the rest, and our moving shapes being black on black. Our enemies hadn't even known we were there, or that they'd almost killed us.

'Stop,' I hissed at Francis, but he kept running, bolting up the hill. As I watched, a tree appeared to snatch him clean off his feet. He shot skywards upside down, a gurgling scream choking from him. And then a length of warm black steel materialized from out of the night and jerked my head to one side and I felt the edge of a knife press across my throat, breaking the skin.

'Christ, Cooper,' said a familiar voice in my ear as the warm black steel, which I realized was a forearm, released me. Cassidy. 'How many fucking lives you got?' he said. 'Come three meters to the left and right about now you'd have a necklace of bamboo spears through your chest.'

My heart pounded like a tire with a bubble in the sidewall about to burst. I got down on a knee and sucked in some air to get the adrenalin under control.

'And who's that swinging by his ankles up there?' Cassidy asked.

'Name's Francis,' I puffed. 'He's friendly. Or was – wouldn't count on it now.'

'I'll get him down.'

'Good idea. What happened to the baby?'

'Leila wanted to keep it.'

'You talked her out of it, I hope.'

'No.'

I climbed to my feet. 'What? So we've still got it?'

'No, I didn't try and talk her out of anything. I just took it off her and put it on the edge of the forest and held my hand across her mouth until one of the women eventually came and took it away.'

'So now you and Leila have a very special relationship too,' I said.

'Not as special as yours,' he said, grinning. He found the liana taking Francis's weight and sawed through it with his Ka-bar.

'Where are the others?'

'Further up the hill. That explosion have anything to do with you?'

'No.' I gazed up at Francis, who was spinning slowly, hanging by an ankle. 'What's with all the bushcraft?'

'Didn't want anyone sneaking in through our back door.'

He grunted as he took the weight on the vine and lowered Francis into a bush.

A LOW WHISTLE FLOATED through the scrub.

Cassidy returned it.

A shadow stepped out from behind a tree ten feet further up the hill.

'Look what I found,' Cassidy told it.

'Hey, skipper, you're back,' said Rutherford's familiar voice. 'Duke was getting worried.'

'Fuck off,' said Ryder, suddenly appearing from his hiding place behind us, a 97 cradled in the crook of an arm. Ryder was grinning, his teeth glowing pale blue in the darkness as he walked toward us. This was a different Ryder to the one who'd joined the PSO team because he was hoping to rub pink bits with an old school flame. Crawling through the bush and the insects the other night had done him some good. Ryder 2.0 was an upgrade.

'Who's your friend?' he asked with a nod at Francis.

While Francis shook their hands with enthusiasm, I explained that he'd volunteered to be our guide. 'How're the principals?' I asked at the conclusion of the meet and greet.

'Bedded down for the night,' said Rutherford.

Ryder went to resume his watch.

'Duke,' I said, 'there are some things going on that we all need to talk about. The path's clear behind us.'

Rutherford led the way up the hill, stopping eventually at a stand of young saplings. There was a half moon blazing out from behind a roll of silvery cloud and, with little canopy to obscure the light, I could just make out Leila, Ayesha and Boink lying on woven liana hammocks strung between the young trees, which got our principals off the ground and out of reach of the ants. Boink was snoring loudly, Ayesha softly. Leila was dead to the world, the way I liked her best.

'West?' I asked.

'Keeping an eye on things across the ditch,' said Rutherford.

The Brit took us up to the rock face, our earlier observation post.

West lowered the sniper scope when he heard us coming up behind him.

'Hey, boss. I couldn't work out whether you were MIA or AWOL,' he said with a smile when he saw me. 'What happened?'

I provided a brief account of my last six hours – the trip to the mine, the folks being used as slaves, meeting Francis, seeing Lockhart.

Rutherford shook his head. 'Shite. So this is all about *gold?*'

'Gold doesn't explain why our principals were kidnapped,' said Cassidy.

No, it didn't. 'Which reminds me,' I said. 'Twenny and Peanut still in plain sight?'

'Nope,' said West. 'Either they've been moved into one of the tents – out of sight of the guests who arrived in the chopper. Or they've been whacked and their bodies disposed of.'

A positive thinker. 'What's your money on?' I asked him.

He shrugged.

'Cassidy?'

'They were there, and then they were gone,' he said.

'From what you've just told us, boss,' said Duke, 'I'd say everyone down there's a little too preoccupied with mining interests to send Twenny and Peanut down the road after Fournier.'

'Maybe,' West conceded.

'We have to work with the assumption that they're still alive,' said Cassidy.

There were murmurs of agreement.

'Sir, what promises have been made to Francis about his wife in return for his guide duties?' Cassidy asked.

'Only that Bruce Willis and Tommy Franks will ride on in and rescue her.'

'Yes, Bruce Willis,' said Francis, doing a little jig on the spot.

'I didn't want to over-promise,' I said.

'Jesus,' Cassidy muttered.

I asked West, 'What can you see down there at the moment?'

He handed me the scope. 'Take a look for yourself. There's not enough light to get a good resolution, especially once they turned off all their flashlights. Were you down there on the ground when the chopper arrived?'

'Yep.' I rested the scope against the tree trunk and brought the executive helicopter into focus. The image was heavily ghosted and dark blue on black. I scanned the area. From the little I could make out, Lockhart and his entourage appeared to have vacated the clearing. 'So you didn't see who came in on it?'

'No,' said West.

I kept talking while I scanned the HQ. 'It's a Swedish American Gold aircraft. The passenger list included Colonel Biruta, the CNDP commanding officer from Cyangugu; Colonel Makenga, the CNDP asshole who tried to do us up on the ridge. Piers Pietersen was on it – he's possibly the pilot – and so was Charles White. We met those last two back at Cyangugu after the concert.'

'I remember them,' said Ryder. 'The autograph hunters, right?'

'That's them,' said Rutherford, West nodding.

'Pietersen and White brought in a cargo of weapons,' I continued. 'Claymores, we know about. White set one off.'

'We heard,' said West.

'They put them all in that truck.' Thinking on the run, I added, 'Maybe they're going to pull the C4 out of 'em and use it to open up the mine.' The realization gave me an idea.

'Was that the explosion I heard? A Claymore?' West asked.

'Yeah,' I said. 'White giving a demonstration. Lockhart, the PLA guy and the FARDC commanding officer were the official welcoming party, by the way. And LeDuc was with them.'

'I'm going to adopt the local custom and throw a big handful of shit at LeDuc when I see him next,' said Rutherford.

'So FARDC and CNDP are now hopping into bed together only a couple of days after they were trying to kill each other?' Ryder asked. 'Is that likely?'

'Maybe – if there's a fortune in gold greasing the wheels,' Cassidy suggested.

'That's what they might have been fighting about – control of the mine,' I said. 'Could be that both parties decided the fight was a stalemate and a better course of action was to split the spoils instead and live to fight another day.'

'Rich and alive beats dead poor and proud any day,' observed Rutherford.

'I want to bring in Lockhart,' said Ryder.

I admired his ambition.

'You and whose army?' the Brit asked.

'We're still no closer to releasing our principals,' Cassidy reminded us.

'I think we're plenty closer,' I said.

West scratched his chin. 'How?'

'It's sitting in the back of that truck.'

IT WAS STILL DARK when Ayesha woke and wandered up to the rock face. 'Vin! My God, you're safe!' she said, surprised to see me back in the fold. 'We were so worried about you, weren't we?'

'I had kittens,' said Rutherford, grinning.

'Where'd you end up?' Ayesha continued.

I gave her a brief rundown.

'Oh, man, those poor people down there,' said Ayesha. 'I had no idea. This country – it's like totally—'

'Fucked in the head,' West said.

'So who's this?' Ayesha asked, nodding warily at Francis.

I went through a round of introductions.

'Yo, Cooper! That you?' Boink asked as he pulled himself up the last step onto the shelf. 'What up, dog?'

Twenny's head security guy walked over and held out his fist so that we could bump knuckles, the male air kiss.

'I never seen nothin' like what happen' down in that village, yo. When you stowed away on that truck after what we seen?' he shook his head. 'That was brave, fucked-up shit. I thought you was a goner.'

'Who's a goner?' It was Leila. She reached behind her head, wrangling her hair into a ponytail as she came up the step. 'Cooper . . . When did you get back?' She caught sight of Francis and said, 'What's going on?'

'Got movement down there,' said West, interrupting, holding up the scope for me to come take a look.

'Excuse me,' I said to Leila.

'No, you're not excused,' she replied.

'I'm sorry?'

'Cooper, you're not going nowhere till I know what's going on. We went with you yesterday. I hoped it might keep your eyes on the prize – getting us back to Cyangugu. But instead, off you went. You put us all at risk *again*. And we're still no closer to getting out of here.'

'I thought we were in agreement about rescuing Twenny,' I said, keeping the annoyance out of my face and tone.

'Which agreement was that?' she said.

'I've made it plain to you that it's our responsibility to protect *all* our principals, not just your Hollywood ass.'

A hand went to her hip. She didn't like that, a suggestion that the universe might not revolve around her ass.

'I'm sure if you asked Deryck, he'd want me to be safe.'

'As far as I can see, you are,' I said. 'You're not tied to a tree with a hood over your face, not knowing whether you're going to live or die from one moment to the next.'

'There mightn't be a hood on my head, Cooper, but what's the difference between Deryck's situation and ours? We don't know whether we're going to survive either.' She looked to Ayesha for backup. Her friend and makeup artist gave a reluctant nod. 'Y'know, I don't think this is about getting us out of here. It's not about getting us to safety,' Leila continued, stabbing a finger in my direction. 'Maybe that's where you started out, but it's not what's happening now. You think you've uncovered a crime. You're a cop, so you want to arrest someone. This has become *a case*, hasn't it? And you're going to solve it or die trying. Which is fine by me – go ahead and die, if that's what you're determined to do. Just don't take the rest of us with you.'

'Shut the fuck up, woman,' said Boink. 'Pulling Twenny out and getting your sorry ass back over the border – they're both the same deal. You still think we can just walk in an' ask for him and Peanut back? Damn you, woman. If we want them back, we have to go an' *convince* the motherfuckers that *we* want 'em more than *they* want 'em.'

Maybe I'd underestimated Boink. The guy summed up like a math professor.

Leila dismissed him with a flick of her hand. 'I don't care what you think, Phillip, 'cause you never do any damned thinking for yo'se'f.'

Phillip? I tried mentally to pin the name on Boink and had a lot of difficulty making it stick.

'This guy, Cooper?' she said, pointing at me. 'He's damaged goods. He killed his fiancée and now he wants to die to make amends for it. He doesn't care what happens to you, or me, or any of us.' She turned to me again, her face . . . ugly. 'That's what this is all about, right? You're in pain and you want out of your misery. You have a death wish.'

Maybe she was right. Maybe that's exactly what I had. And maybe she was right about Death having a score to settle with me, just like the one she figured it had settled with Anna.

'Well, Cooper?' The singer's arms were folded, her weight on one slender long leg, a study in self-righteous impatience.

'Lockhart and his friends cooked up a scheme to capture you and your ex and extort money for your release,' I said. 'And that's just part of what they're into. Your ex is still down there – the man you said you still loved – and we're hoping he's still alive. Also down there are trucks and a road going *somewhere*. You get that? So, the plan is simple – we snatch Deryck and Peanut and take the trucks. And we make a lot of noise doing it. The alternative is a fifteen-mile hike through the forest to the nearest town. In this terrain, the way we move, I figure that will take us three more days – three more days without enough food, three more days of battling the elements, three more days of mosquitoes and snakes, three more days of you and me rubbing up against each other like nitro and glycerin. Walk if you like, but I'd rather roll outta here.'

'So, what? Now we just hang around and wait to see what you do?'

'No. I'm hoping that you can make yourself useful and learn how to shoot one of these,' I said, lifting my M4.

She clenched her fists in frustration. Hmm . . . Leila somewhere behind me with loaded assault rifle. What was wrong with that picture?

'Sir . . .' West called out again, impatient.

'Can I go now, *ma'am*?' I asked the star.

She ignored me and turned on Cassidy as she stormed off. 'As for you, we could have rescued that baby girl and you know it.'

Boink sidled over like he had something illegal to sell. 'Cooper,' he said under his breath. 'That name you heard from her. It stays right here in the jungle, yo.'

'What name?' I said as I retreated in West's direction. The sergeant handed me the scope and I braced it against the tree. There was some movement on the hill. The camp was beginning to stir.

'We've got maybe an hour and a half of useful darkness before dawn,' I said to myself.

'Boss, if you're cooking up one of those half-plans of yours,' said West, 'right about now might be a good time to share.'

Ambush

We came down off the observation ridge, retracing our steps in the pre-dawn light, the ones that brought us up behind the looted village. As we picked our way across the higher ground, the broken sounds of women wailing for their lost children and husbands drifted up through the dense growth like the tendrils of mist curling through the trees.

'I have heard this many times,' Francis whispered. 'I do not need to go down there to know what has happened.'

No, I guess he didn't.

Leila appeared particularly anxious and, for once, not about herself. I overheard Ayesha whisper to her, 'I'm sure she's fine.' The 'she' referred to I presumed was the baby we'd rescued briefly from the brutality.

Above, the cloud cover thickened into a solid slab and the rain started to fall, not heavily, but constant, drenching and cold. I caught the sky in snatches through the canopy and saw that it was lightening to the color of wet concrete. There was not a lot of time to get into position. We came around behind the village, and started down the hill on its far side.

'We stop,' said Francis, around halfway down the slope. 'This is good place. Your people will be safe here.' He gestured at a stand of larger trees that would provide our principals with some cover should they need it.

'What now?' said Leila. 'Is this where you're going to desert us? Again.'

I signaled Cassidy and West and they handed out a couple of the spare Nazarians, giving one to her and the other to Ayesha. 'Try not to shoot the good guys,' I said to Leila as I double checked its safety and magazine and handed it back to her. 'Do I need to worry?'

She gave me a look that suggested that maybe I did, and then sighted down the weapon.

'Come back safe – both of you,' said Ayesha, giving Rutherford and me a quick peck on the cheek.

'See? Is that so hard?' I asked Leila.

My face sang with a slap that rattled my eyeballs. Leila was breathing heavily, angrily. I grabbed two handfuls of her jacket, pulled her to me and kissed her. My tongue found hers, took it prisoner. Her breath shortened and she resisted, but the resistance faded and she kissed back. And then we released each other and it was over. Rutherford cleared his throat and Boink looked the other way.

She raised her hand to slap me again.

'You want seconds?'

'What gives you the right, Cooper?'

'I usually get slapped *after* the kiss so I figured it'd already paid for it. Not as much of a gentleman as you thought, right?'

She flexed her hand, opening and closing it. She'd hurt herself, and my face didn't feel that great, either.

'Okay, I apologize,' I said. 'Now, can we be friends?'

'No.'

West cleared his throat, stepped in and gave both women a quick weapons refresher, reacquainting them with the Nazarian's safety, reminding them to leave the selector on three shot burst and demonstrating again how to aim. There'd been no target practice. For all I knew, both of them would have trouble hitting the sky.

'You're the man, Boink,' I heard Rutherford say.

'As it should be, yo,' he said with a grin.

The big man was enjoying himself.

Cassidy and Ryder were looking their weapons over. I joined them. 'Duke, I want you to stay here with the principals, set up a defensive position.'

Ryder hesitated before giving me a nod. The old Ryder would have been happy to stay back. The new model wanted to get involved. But someone had to stay behind and Ryder had no combat experience.

'Sorry, Duke,' I said.

'Just call me into the play when you need some real muscle, okay?'

'Will do. If this goes well, we'll be back in an hour,' I said with my back to the principals.

'And if it goes badly?' he asked.

'Then I'll give one to the Gipper for you.'

LEAVING CASSIDY AND RYDER to secure the principals further up the hill, West, Rutherford and I pushed down through the vines and bamboo, following Francis, hoping to get a glimpse of the road. I was thinking about that kiss. Leila had kissed back and that had been a real surprise. Was there something going on that I wasn't tuned into? Or was she just frightened? Maybe the kiss was a final plea not to go, or not to be left behind, which, I suddenly realized, was Leila's one consistency where I was concerned – having me right where she wanted me, a moth under a pin. It was a distraction I could do without so I put the soap opera out of my mind.

Francis crouched down. The rest of us did likewise abreast of him. 'This is good place for you,' he whispered, gesturing left and right with his hand through the trees. 'See here and here.'

We all took a good long look. He was right – this vantage point was perfect. He'd brought us to a place above the road that provided a clear view of the ribbon of mud as it swept out of the village and wound along the valley floor, flanked on one side by thick rainforest and on the other by a slow-moving water channel. The position also provided a good angle on the road from the direction that led eventually to the mine turnoff. At that moment, the road was clear in both directions but the dawn was behind us even if the sun had yet to crest the hills. That meant the traffic between the FARDC camp, the village and the mine would soon begin to shuttle back and forth. We didn't have a lot of time.

'I go back now,' said Francis. 'Good luck.' He shook all our hands, his grip firm, his skin warm and dry like the python's. He disappeared instantly into the foliage behind us, heading back up the hill to rejoin the others.

'Down there,' said Rutherford, motioning at a stand of banana trees a dozen feet below us. 'One of those will do the trick.'

The sergeant slid down to it on his butt, took hold of his machete and started chopping away at one of the thicker trunks. I joined him, gave the tree a couple of chops from the low side to finish the job.

'Mike,' I called up. 'Stay high. You've got overwatch. The road clear?'

'Clear,' said West as the light faded. 'Rain's coming in, though.'

Of course it was. 'Whistle when you see traffic.' The rainforest was coming alive with the shrieking calls from unseen birdlife, either welcoming the rain or complaining about it.

Rutherford and I dragged the fallen tree down through the scrub and onto the road, blocking most of it off. We then clambered back into the scrub, climbed up the hill twenty meters or so, and waited.

After half a dozen minutes, I heard a whistle climb over the top of the chorus coming from the treetops, silencing some of it. Company was coming.

I heard the truck's engine before I saw it, and that's because I was looking the wrong way.

'Oh, fuck,' said Rutherford, tapping me on the arm so that I checked over my shoulder. A Dongfeng was coming from the direction of the mine – the wrong direction. So my assumption that the first truck on the road would be the vehicle taking those Claymores to the mine was blown. How many more trucks were behind it?

The vehicle slowed as it approached the roadblock, then stopped.

The front passenger door opened, and a man jumped down and called to his buddies to lend a hand. A couple of men hopped out of the back of the vehicle and wandered around to the front. All three carried rifles slung over their shoulders, which told me that they weren't expecting any trouble. The two who came out of the back of the truck were having a friendly chat about something.

Pointing at the men in the cabin I said to Rutherford, 'They go first. The other two are yours.'

'You don't want to let this one pass, wait for the target?' Rutherford said.

The Africans were clearing the road. If our target truck came along within the next few minutes, we wouldn't be able to bring it to a stop before assaulting it. 'No. Two trucks are better than one anyway.'

Our original plan was a bust, but in my experience the operation that runs like clockwork is a myth. Special Ops are often just the best intentions stitched together with luck, and they come off when the fuck-ups favor you and not the enemy. We had no choice but to go with the flow. I moved down and across the hill, using the treeline for cover, until the angle brought the driver into view through the door window. He was listening to music, head bobbing from side to side, those familiar white buds in his ears. I swung the QCW submachine gun off my back, took the safety off, aimed through the open driver's window and waited. Meanwhile, the three men had dragged the tree from thc side of the road and were rolling it into the irrigation channel, sharing a laugh while they worked. I wondered what constituted a joke in these parts. One of the men, the front seat passenger, jogged back to the cabin and hopped up beside the driver. I waited till the other two walking down to the back of the truck came around the end of the vehicle, into Rutherford's fire zone.

I squeezed the trigger and the QCW jumped twice in my hands, making a sound like padded hammers hitting brick. Two streams of three spent cartridges arced from the right-hand side of the receiver and dropped beside my boot as the interior of the Dong's cabin became a collection of arms waving about in a red mist.

I got up and moved at a half crouch down the hill, the short stock of the submachine gun buried in my shoulder. I didn't see or hear Rutherford's shots, but there was no question in my mind that there would be two dead bodies lying in the mud behind the truck's tailgate. I came out of the bush on the side of the road a split second before Rutherford. Nothing moved in or around the vehicle. The road was clear in both directions. I ran to the back, grabbed one of the dead by an arm and dragged the body into the anonymity of the forest, the heavy rain immediately going to work on the blood trail left behind, eradicating it. Beside me, Rutherford pulled the other corpse along by its shirt collar. We raced back. I opened the driver's door and a man fell out backward onto the road with a wet thud, the dead air wheezing from his lungs. I heaved him across the road to the forest, while Rutherford sprang up into the cabin and hauled the deceased passenger out, throwing him over his shoulder and lugging him to the spot where his buddies were beginning their big sleep. The whole operation took less than three minutes, which was fortunate because we'd run out of time.

Over my panting breath, I heard West whistle again.

Rutherford glanced back over his shoulder toward the village as he changed mags.

Through the rain and the gloom I could see a truck coming down the road between the last of the huts. The odds were good that this was the vehicle we wanted. I climbed up into the truck's cab. The interior was like a slaughterhouse, with blood spatter everywhere, especially across the windshield. Trying to wipe it off would just create a big smear and reduce visibility further.

'I've got the cab. The passengers are yours again,' I called out to Rutherford, slamming a fresh mag in place.

The Brit darted into the forest, gone in an instant.

I picked up a beret left behind by its previous owner and put it on to improve my profile and confuse the issue. Something warm and wet slid out of it, ran down the side of my face and plopped into my lap. I didn't want to know what it was, instead keeping my eyes fixed on the approaching vehicle. Through the blood-speckled windscreen and the rain, I could see three men sitting abreast in the approaching cab. I had no idea how many were in back, under the tarpaulin cover stretched high over the load area. The Dongfeng came to a halt twenty meters away. The driver gave the horn some exercise, a lightweight *toot* better suited to a cheap Chinese motor scooter. I gave the driver a wave out the window and he waved back. The number of choices I had open to me had narrowed to one. The front passenger door opened and a man swung out of the cabin and impatiently motioned at me to get my vehicle off the road, out of the way.

I angled the barrel up and pulled the trigger and the windshield in front of me shattered into a screen reminiscent of crushed ice, before collapsing inwards. The next burst had the same effect on the windshield of the truck facing me. I sprayed the cabin as the glass exploded inwards, and made doubly sure with another burst that the occupants wouldn't cause any trouble. And suddenly men were everywhere, jumping out the back of the truck like folks escaping a burning building, running in random directions, looking for safety but not knowing where to find it. I dropped out the QCW's mag, jammed in a replacement, cocked the weapon and did what I had to do, hitting one guy on the run in the thorax. He fell down dead. Rutherford took down two men running around on the passenger side of the truck and they slammed into the road face first, the way the living never do. A man was creeping down the driver's side of the vehicle, hidden from Rutherford's view, his rifle up and looking for trouble. He found it. I took aim and fired and he slumped back on his ass in the mud like he'd decided to have a quick nap.

The remaining four soldiers running toward me figured pretty quickly that their present predicament had something to do with the truck stopped in front of theirs. They turned, the way schools of fish get the message all at once without any obvious communication, and started fleeing toward the village, shooting back over their shoulders. I raised my M4, aimed and fired. Their chances of making it to the village were zero.

Rutherford appeared from out of the bush, running onto the roadside as I changed mags and then jumped down out of the driver's seat and onto the mud. I felt something slide off my thigh and land on the toe of my boot. I glanced down and saw an eyeball attached to a length of optic nerve. I flicked it off my toe into the bushes.

Among the bodies sprawled on the road and its verge, nothing moved.

'We'll put 'em all back inside the truck,' I told him. 'Take that guy's hands. I've got his feet. Let's do this quick.'

We picked up the nearest corpse and walked it to the rear of the truck. I set my end down on the ground and lifted up the flap of the tarpaulin, and a shower of bullets blasted past my head as the bark of full automatic fire spat from the shadows within. Rutherford and I dropped to the mud beneath the tailgate with the body as the rounds clanged off the Dong's metalwork and my heart thundered in my chest. *Shit!* I swore at my own stupidity. I nearly walked straight into that. The stream of hot lead had been far too close.

On full automatic, the shooter's magazine emptied itself within a few seconds. I was tempted to jump up and send a few rounds back, but there was going to be cargo in there that I didn't want damaged. I heard the hollow clatter of a magazine being ejected, hitting the metal floor of the truck. My cue. I bobbed my head up, then ducked below the lip of the truck's cargo tray. Stacked Kevlar cases, just as I'd hoped. There was also the movement of a soldier fumbling with his weapon, anxious to get it reloaded. I came up for a longer, more confident peek, submachine gun shouldered, and Rutherford was beside me, his QCW likewise trained on the moving shadow which was trying to hide in the twilight, tucked into a corner behind the cabin.

'Jesus,' said Rutherford.

The shooter was a boy of around eleven or twelve years of age. I could see the large whites of his eyes darting between Rutherford and me.

'Drop it!' the sergeant yelled at him.

The kid stuttered something at us in a high-pitched, prepubescent voice, but held onto his rifle.

'Drop. Your. Weapon,' Rutherford repeated.

The kid got the message second time round and threw down his rifle, an old AK-47, which clattered against the containers.

I gestured at him to come forward.

He didn't move.

'Come!' I said, adding a little authority to the command.

He inched forward, frightened and confused, his eyes darting between us. We were obviously out-of-towners, but from which town? I could see that there was a lot going through the kid's mind, overloading it. When he was close enough for me to grab his shirt, I lifted him one handed out of the truck. He was a lightweight, all skin and bone, his nervous brown eyes the biggest part of him. His weapon was on the truck's metal floor, within reach. Rutherford leaned in and retrieved it. We glanced at each other, both knowing the score. There was a lot at stake and the boy was a problem.

The SAS sergeant checked that a round wasn't left in the AK's chamber. 'I'm not killing kids, skipper,' he said, in the event that his actions with the rifle appeared ambiguous.

'Then how do you feel about standing him in the naughty-boy corner for around twenty-four hours?' I asked.

The boy watched me carefully with a mixture of curiosity and fear, eyes shifting to the weapon in Rutherford's hands. 'How old are you, kid – twelve?' I asked him.

No answer.

'The only things you should be shooting live on XBox,' I said.

The urchin had no idea what I was saying.

I gave the road a visual check – clear as far as I could see. Nothing from West to indicate otherwise.

Rutherford leaped up into the cargo space and inspected the goods. I heard something rattle.

'Seven cases, a dirty great padlock on every one,' he called out.

'Officer?' I asked the boy. 'Officer. Which one? Him?' I pointed to one of the men lying on the road. The kid looked at me like I was from outer space.

'*Qui est l'officier?*' said Rutherford, jumping down. '*Qui est le boss?*' he asked, pointing to several of the dead in turn. '*Lui? Lui? Lui?*'

'*Lu . . . Lui,*' the Congolese stuttered, pointing to the nearest dead man, a cluster of nameless symbols on his epaulettes.

I went to the body and searched it, finding what I was looking for on a chain around his neck, along with a bag on a leather thong. I held up seven bloody bronze keys and rinsed them off in a puddle before tossing them up to Rutherford.

'Nice one,' he said. 'What's in the pouch?'

I'd noticed that most of the dead Africans had been wearing similar muslin or leather bags around their necks. The man who'd run into a tree back at the Puma also had one. I untied the leather fastener, opened the bag and found a collection of teeth, small bones, some seeds and feathers. 'Magic,' I said, returning it to the dead man's pocket.

'What about the kid?' Rutherford inquired. 'What are we gonna to do with him?'

'Speak English?' I asked the boy, standing up and walking over to him.

He looked up at me slack-jawed and shook his head.

Dumb question. I noticed a bag of spells around his neck also. I reached out to inspect it and the boy flinched and tried to draw back, terrified.

'Ask him why everyone's wearing these things. You know enough French for that?'

'Give it a go,' Rutherford said. '*Tu portez ce: pourquoi?*' he asked the kid.

There was a nervous reply.

'He says spirits have been coming into camp and stealing people's souls, leaving them dead.'

'*Vous êtes Américains, vous n'êtes pas fantômes,*' the boy said, his eyes on the flag on my shoulder.

My turn to translate. 'You're American, not spirits.'

'See, you do speak Frog,' said Rutherford.

Setting the boy free worried me but, as Rutherford and I saw it, there was no alternative. We couldn't keep him prisoner, carting him around with us. Pointing my finger at him and then down the road at the village, I said, 'Go.'

He didn't move.

'*Allez! Va t'er!*' said Rutherford. 'In other words, sunshine, fuck off. On yer bike.'

Realization dawned on the boy. He seemed unable to believe that he'd been spared and released. But then he got it, said '*merci*' a couple of times and broke into a sprint, running toward the village and taking our element of surprise with him.

Rutherford shook his head as he watched the boy getting smaller in the distance. 'I was stealing my first kiss at his age. You?'

'Cadillacs.'

'Tough neighborhood?'

I didn't answer. A New Jersey shithole rusting into its own gutters had been the backdrop to my upbringing, but compared with this place it was a country club.

'Back to work,' I said. There were the bodies sprawled around us on the ground, getting washed by the rain, and we had to do something about them. The intention had been to load them into the truck, crash the vehicle into a ravine after pilfering those cases, set fire to the lot and make the whole thing look like an accident. Only, the kid was going to give his superiors a report on what had happened to the truck, making that plan worthless.

'Hey,' said Rutherford. 'Look . . .' He motioned off in the direction of the village.

The boy had stopped running a hundred meters down the road. He was looking back at us, and then he started running again, making for the forest, heading west, *away* from the FARDC's encampment on the hill. The kid was either deserting or reclaiming his freedom, depending on how you looked at it.

'Run, Forrest, run,' I said, a stupid smile on my face.

Cassidy jogged out from the tree line.

'Came down to check on progress,' he said. 'Looked to me like you needed a hand.'

Good call. We decided to stick with plan B in case the kid changed his mind. After three trips each, the bodies were all out of sight in the bushes. Next, we collected the weapons strewn about – all old AK-47s – removed the bolts, and tossed the lot into the channel.

'We need to stow the cargo before the road turns into a highway,' I said.

No sign of movement from the village and no warning whistle from West.

A few moments later, Francis appeared at the edge of the road. He checked left and right before stepping out onto the mud strip. Then Leila, Ayesha, Boink and Ryder materialized behind him and they all ran through the rain toward us.

'Great,' I said under my breath.'What do you think you're doing down here?' I asked Leila when she was close enough to hear. I glanced at Ryder and he shook his head, frowning, not happy.

'I'm not staying up there with the ants and the mosquitoes any longer than I have to,' she informed me.

'Don't you ever do as you're told?' I asked her.

'No.'

Exposing our principals to direct danger down on the road was not part of the program, but then, not much that had happened so far this morning had been on the list worked out in the pre-dawn darkness. There was no time to argue.

'Follow me,' I said, and then ran to the back of the truck carrying the cargo and jumped up into it. Rutherford was already inside, untying the straps that stopped the olive drab-painted Kevlar containers from sliding around.

'We need to get these offloaded and taken up the hill,' I said. 'And it has to be done fast.'

'What's inside 'em?' asked Boink.

'Dunno,' said Rutherford impatiently. 'And right now, we don't bloody well care. We just need to do what the man said and pull our fingers out.'

'What language yo' speaking?' said Boink, grinning, taking no offense. 'I ain't never heard shit like that.'

'The Queen's English, mate.'

'No queens I've met speak like that, yo.'

Rutherford and I lifted the first container off the smaller of the two stacks and threw it, skidding, across the cargo deck toward the tailgate. Boink hoisted it off single-handedly and set it down on the mud.

'Next!' he called out.

We worked quickly. Once all seven containers were offloaded onto the road, Rutherford and I leaped down, grabbed one of the largest and heaviest, each taking an end, and started hobbling with it toward the edge of the forest. Cassidy was ahead of us, a container on his shoulder, pushing up into the undergrowth.

'Duke – head 'em up, move 'em out,' I called behind me.

The containers were all soon secured behind the tree line and we were still more or less on schedule. I checked my Seiko. Only eleven minutes had passed since the first truck had pulled up behind the banana tree laid across the road.

'The trucks – where can we hide them?' I asked Francis.

'I know good place,' he replied.

'Is it close?'

'*Oui*. One-or-two-minute drive from here.'

'Cooper, I saw what happened with that boy,' Leila said, seeking some attention. 'I think you did the right thing.'

'You might change your mind if he comes back with his babysitters,' I said.

Leila was standing above me on slightly higher ground, her weight on one leg, a 97 crossed under her breasts so that her cleavage was lifted up and out of her jacket. With her makeup oddly immaculate, she looked like some kind of hot action movie character. I shrugged off the thought and asked Francis, 'Which way are we going?'

He pointed in the direction of the mine, away from the village.

Two trucks rather than one. I needed a driver and someone to ride shotgun on the following truck.

'Francis, you and I have got the lead truck.' I glanced at the faces around me. 'Rutherford, Ryder. You're in the second truck. We don't stop for any reason. Understand?'

Both nodded.

Francis scratched his top lip with the back of a long, curved thumbnail.

'Cy – collect Mike and get everyone further up the hill with the gear, all right? As high as you can go.'

Cassidy nodded and lifted a container onto his shoulder.

'Leila. For your own safety do as you're told – for once,' I said. She lifted her chin and looked away. 'I mean it.'

Ryder, Rutherford, Francis, and I ran down through the forest, stopping to check that the road was still clear. It was. The engines of both vehicles continued to run, clouds of oily diesel smoke coughing from their exhaust pipes. Francis and I went for the first Dong – the one that had come up behind us, the one facing the wrong way.

The bench seat was covered in glass crystals clotted with blood and brain matter. I brushed them into the floorboards before climbing in. Francis removed a mound of bloody, glass-studded goop from the dashboard in front of him and nervously glanced sideways at me.

'I'm much nicer to my friends,' I reassured him.

A diagram of the gearbox was helpfully etched in the gearstick knob beside my hand. Depressing the clutch, I selected reverse and found the handbrake. With some gas, the Dong leaped off the mark, going backward. I spun the steering wheel and brought the ass end of the truck around. Now heading in the right direction, I selected second gear, stomped on the gas pedal, and we accelerated away, the wind and rain blast coming through the space formerly occupied by the windshield competing with the roar of the engine.

'How far?' I yelled

'Drive for one minute,' Francis shouted back.

I kept my foot on the gas, changing down for the corners but keeping our speed up in case we met another truck mid-corner. If that happened, I intended to run it off the road if I could, or crash into it if I couldn't. The sun was yet to rise over the hills and the road remained clear of traffic. Maybe folks were doing us a favor and having a sleep in. We took the corners on the limit, the trucks sliding around on the mud. The road started to climb, slowing us, the forest encroaching on all sides. A minute had passed. Where was that hiding place?

'We are here,' Francis yelled, squinting, wiping the rainwater off his face.

'And where's that?' I yelled back. At this point, the forest was overhanging the road. I couldn't see anywhere to go except straight ahead.

'Turn here.' He pointed at the greenery trying to push its way through my window.

'Here?'

'*Oui*. Turn! Turn now!'

I pulled the wheel hard over and flinched, but the wall of foliage wasn't as solid as it appeared to be and we barreled through elephant grass and immature palms. There were no seatbelts in this crate and I braced for the inevitable meeting with a tree that would pitch me through the open window.

'Too fast! Stop!' Francis yelled.

I slammed on the anchors, pushing the pedal almost to the firewall, and the vehicle skidded and slid sideways, coming to a stop, palm leaves crowding in through the hole in the door by my shoulder. I flinched as the vehicle Duke was driving bashed through the plant life beside us, several tons of Chinese steel hurtling past, its wheels locked up solid. It came to a stop a couple of meters in front on our right-side fender, festooned with broken fronds and branches.

I breathed deep. Jesus, that was too close.

Francis opened his door and jumped down.

Cutting the motor, I opened the door. This wasn't forest. The palms were adolescent and uniformly planted in lines. Francis appeared around the front of the truck, machete in hand.

'What is this place?' I asked him, climbing out of the cabin.

'Plantation.'

'Where's the owner?'

'Dead since many years, I think.'

'Our tracks will be seen leaving the road,' I said.

'The rain will hide them.'

I hoped he was right. Rutherford and Ryder joined us.

'Sorry about that, sir,' said Ryder.

'Yeah, we lost you in the bush, skipper,' Rutherford added. 'And then that big-ass truck of yours was stopped right in front of us. Gave me a bloody heart attack, that did.'

'I show you why it is good that you stop,' said Francis, walking away.

He cut a path through the dense but lightweight foliage, which suddenly gave way to a deep gorge and a fast-running watercourse at the bottom of it.

Rutherford peered over the edge. 'Shite!'

Reload

We double-timed it on foot through the old plantation and into the forest, heading for the lower ground of the valley and the irrigation channel, back to the scene of our earlier dirty work. Along the way, I caught glimpses of the road through the greenery. Two trucks coming from the direction of the mine drove past, and one came from the village. There didn't seem to be much urgency.

'Boss . . .' West waved to us, crouched behind a shrub a dozen meters up the hill.

I gave him a thumbs up and he led the way through a warren of bamboo stands to a hardwood tree high on the hill shrouded in liana. Leila, Ayesha and Boink appeared from around the tree and came to meet us.

Ayesha went straight to Ryder and embraced him.

'Any trouble?' Boink asked.

I shook my head. 'No. How about you?'

'We're good, yo.'

'Sir!'

It was Cassidy.

'Over here.' He held up his hand.

'Duke, Mike – take the watch,' I told them. The last thing we needed now was to be taken by surprise.

Cassidy was sitting on one of the larger trunk-sized containers. Rutherford produced the keys and handed them to me.

'It's like opening Christmas presents,' he said as I crouched in front of the other especially large case.

'Let's hope it's not socks,' I said.

I pulled up the padlock and examined it quickly. There were no numbers or markings on it that corresponded with any of the keys, so I just tried them one by one. The catch sprang open with key number three. I flipped back the lid and took a peek. Hmm . . . disappointing. No socks, but plenty of old forest-green uniforms and backpacks. I moved to one of the other cases and jiggled the keys in the lock.

'Now you're talking,' said Rutherford when I pulled the lock and lifted the lid.

Lying inside, barrel to stock between sheets of brown, grease paper, were M16A2s. The case smelled of clean oil and plastic, the way a new car smells under its hood. Rutherford and I pulled out a rifle each and checked them over.

The numbers were filed off the receiver. Rutherford showed me his; same deal. So White, the American, the guy whose presence I couldn't place here, was arms dealing and who knew what else. The numbers missing on these weapons meant that they were either stolen or purchased illegally. White was confident around things that killed people, and that suggested he'd seen combat. But with what service and which conflict? And of course there was Lockhart, formerly US Special Forces and now Kornflak & Greene in these parts, making him a local big wig. He was using that position and influence to line his own pockets in all kinds of ways. Facilitating the arms dealing and playing both sides of the field were only two of them. I couldn't immediately pull up all the statutes he was breaking from the Uniform Code of Military Justice, but they started with kidnap and extortion and moved on to slavery and murder. This guy was a peach.

And where did Fu Manchu and the Chinese-made weapons fit into the picture?

'Let's get to the other cases,' said Cassidy. 'The suspense is killing me.'

I set the rifle down, took hold of a handle on the end of the container while Rutherford took the other, and hoisted it off the stack. The first key I tried worked. I flipped back the lid.

'Nice,' said Cassidy over my shoulder. 'I can have some fun with those.'

Claymores. I picked out one of the devices. Unlike the mines we'd captured, these ones were equipped with clackers, electronic firing devices connected to the mine via a wire that allowed it to be fired remotely when the target was within range, rather than having to wait for a line to be tripped – although these could be rigged to fire that way, too. Handy. There were maybe thirty Claymores in the box. Rutherford and I set it beside the one containing the M16s.

Fumbling with the keys, I opened the fourth case.

'Now we're cookin' with gas,' Rutherford said, his eyes lighting up. Inside the container were two M2A1 ammo cans containing sixteen hundred and eighty rounds of ball ammo for the M16s, plus magazines. According to the stencils on the wooden crates packed within, there were also smoke grenades and M67 HE frag hand grenades, as used by the US Army. 'We've got enough ammo here to start a war.'

'And hopefully finish it,' I added.

Cassidy nodded. 'Amen.'

There was another container with the same dimensions. Opening it revealed more ammo, smoke and frag grenades, just in case we were in danger of running low.

We moved to the remaining cases, the ones Cassidy had been sitting on. I repeated the juggling act with the keys until the lock sprang open.

'Oh shite,' said Rutherford when I lifted the lid.

Oh shite, all right. Packed into the top of the case were six ammo cans, each holding six 60mm M49A4 HE rounds. I lifted one up. Below was the base plate for an M224, which gave a massive clue to what was in the last unopened container.

Sure enough, when I managed to find the right key, the box contained the tube and sight assembly as well as the bipod. We had us a brand-new, fully operational M224! This was the same light mortar system we'd seen Colonel Makenga's forces using to chew up Lissouba's men. Ol' Colonel Cravat had obviously put in his order, and Charles White and Lockhart had obliged so that the two Africans could go for each other's throats on a more even footing. Both men were currently in the FARDC's HQ. I wondered how they were getting along. I also wondered how Colonel Biruta was enjoying being in the company of Makenga. Maybe the gold being pulled out of the ground smoothed over any past differences; at least until they could all get back to their people. Perhaps none of these men had any intention of going back at all and were taking their gold and heading for retirement in the south of France.

'Man, we can get real fuckin' loud with this stuff,' said Cassidy gleefully.

'On me,' I signalled. Ryder and West both acknowledged and trotted up the hill.

'Christ,' said West, his eyes lighting up when he saw what we'd acquired.

'If we get isolated and things go from bad to beam-me-up-Scottie,' I said, 'this is where the trucks are stowed.' Using my Ka-bar, I drew a map in the leaf litter pinpointing the location of the vehicles in the abandoned plantation. 'According to Francis, the road between the encampment and the mine ends at a place called Mukatano, twenty klicks away. That's where you go.'

Rutherford clapped his hands and rubbed them together like he was about to tuck into a Thanksgiving turkey. 'So then, how're we going to use our little windfall, lads?'

I PLANTED AN EIGHTH Claymore in line with the others – back a meter from the edge of the road and well inside the foliage, which, along this section of the forest, had begun to grow up through the exposed mud. It was clear that the road here had been used very little, if at all, once the loggers left the area and so the plant life had been marshaling forces to reclaim it, inching forward with each new shoot. I looked up at the long straight incline that disappeared over a crest, the tunnel of overhanging leaves and fronds that lined the road here smeared with the orange mud thrown up in the trucks' wakes as they motored back and forth along it. Fifty meters downhill in the other direction, the road curved away out of sight on its way to the village.

I heard a truck approaching from the blind, village end of the road, engine revving in a low gear. It was going slower than the others that had passed regularly through the day, which suggested it had a different purpose to the trucks rumbling back and forth between the encampment, village and mine. I retreated into the forest, got down on my belly and waited for it to pass. That took some time. It eventually drove by, doing around five miles per hour, creeping along, armed men hanging out the back and a couple of others riding the running boards. They were all peering into the forest, probably hunting for a missing truck or two; one of which was full to the brim with expensive items purchased to kill people and vital to the FARDC if it were to continue its important work here on that score.

I pulled up the M4, just in case I was spotted, aware that there was a full mag in the slot and five others in my webbing along with four frag grenades. And, of course, in my hand was a clacker for the Claymore just set, with seven more within reach if I needed them. I could easily take care of this truck and the men it carried, but if it came to that and I was forced to go hard-core, things would get chaotic thereafter. A firefight right here and right now was not part of the plan, and the plan – what was left of it – called for stealth until we were ready to show our hand, which wouldn't be for several hours yet. But the truck roared by like I wasn't there and continued noisily up the incline. I crept forward to the road's edge and watched it rumble out of sight over the crest two hundred meters further up the hill.

Bushing the ants off my clothing as I stood, I wondered what theories about the disappearance of the two trucks were doing the rounds in the camp. Seemed that they'd quickly come to the conclusion something had gone wrong. The road to the mine was steep in several sections, with plenty of opportunities for a Dong to misjudge a hairpin corner and go crashing to the bottom of a ravine. The typical Hollywood depiction of an accident like that would have the truck bursting into flame, pinpointing its whereabouts. That was fiction. The Dong sucked diesel, which didn't catch fire easily, and the explosives on board were designed to withstand severe battle shocks without blowing up. So it was possible that an accident *could* happen, and the terrain made it possible that the location, cause and nature of the accident *could* remain a mystery. And maybe there was another theory doing the rounds – that the trucks had been taken by the spirits that cut people's throats.

'You done, sir?' Ryder asked, walking into sight,

'Yeah,' I said, hands on hips, surveying my handiwork. I could only make out two of the devices and that was only because I knew exactly where to look. 'Let's head back.'

Threading through the plantation, a familiar sound in the sky caused Ryder and me to stop and crouch. A helicopter, and it was getting closer. It wasn't the ancient Soviet Mi-8, which made a sound like an old washing machine with rusted bearings trying to grind out a spin cycle. This was the executive chopper, the aircraft from Swedish American Gold. I could almost hear the rocks clinking into glasses holding a couple of fingers of something aged. The bird turned and hummed away out of sight, which wasn't such bad news. Our hiding place was vulnerable from the air and if we could see the helo, the pilot could eyeball our trucks.

The departure of the Sikorsky did raise the question of who was on board: White and that Swedish slime-ball, Sven? Did they leave Makenga and Biruta behind, or were they also passengers? What about Lockhart? Had he also departed the scene of the crime, along with that fuck LeDuc? The Sikorsky was a large chopper. It could take all those cocksuckers and still have room to include a rap singer and his buddy on the manifest. And if that were the case and our principals were no longer in-country, then the escapades we had planned for the evening were about as useful as a chain of bikini wax clinics in the state of Utah.

'Shit,' I muttered.

'What?' asked Ryder.

'Ever been to Salt Lake City?'

Using the backpacks, Leila, Ayesha, Boink, Francis, Ryder and I had returned to the trucks with most of the Claymores, the spare uniforms and a large helping of ammo and grenades. There was almost eighty pounds of M16 ammo alone. Strung between us, we'd also brought five of the seven Kevlar containers, most of which fitted one inside the other like a Russian babushka doll. We'd kept the QCWs, but left almost all of the Nazarians behind on the hill, minus their bolts, swapping the Chinese rifles for the new US-made M16s and burying the ordnance we couldn't take. The loads we'd carried had been heavy, but featherweight compared to the one that Cassidy, West and Rutherford had had to lug between them back up onto the ridge overlooking the FARDC encampment.

I gave a soft whistle before approaching the trucks to avoid being shot at, not that I thought there was a snowball's chance in hell that I'd get hit, given who was on guard duty.

'Halt, who goes there?' hissed Leila.

'Duck Dodgers,' I replied, 'and his faithful sidekick, Porky Pig.'

'Thanks a bunch,' said Ryder.

'Is that you, Cooper?' she called out.

I could see Leila before she could see me, because she wasn't looking in my direction.

'Over here,' I said, shaking a branch to give her fair warning. She jumped, nervous as a chihuahua. Francis and Boink stopped what they were doing, our return being a good excuse to take a break. They'd been using the utility trenching tools hooked onto the Dong's chassis to fill the spare uniforms with mud, turning them into sandbags. The ammo cans, which were sitting up on the back of the truck's load trays, had also been filled with mud.

'How's it going?' I asked them as Ryder and I walked into view.

'We're done,' said Boink. 'Got me some motherfucker blisters, yo.'

He showed me his hands, the skin rubbed off the inside of his thumbs and his palms weeping blood.

Francis leaned on his shovel and smiled briefly. It wasn't raining yet but both men's clothes were soaked. The air steamed with the imminent afternoon downpour, the clouds in the sky piling up on top of each other like armfuls of cotton balls.

'Good,' I said, slapping the large can they'd been filling. The hollowness was gone, replaced by a gratifying bullet-stopping heaviness.

'We're calling it the Alamo, yo,' said Boink, nodding with satisfaction.

'We lost at the Alamo,' I reminded him.

'Whatever. We might just pull this shit off.'

We had a few surprises up our sleeves but we were still just five PSOs and a few civilians against a vastly superior force of combat-hardened killers. I wasn't prepared to high-five anyone. *The Alamo . . .*

'How we doing with those magazines?' I asked. 'Where's Ayesha?'

She heard me and leaned out the back of the second truck. 'Nearly done, five more to go. And I've got blisters, too,' and she held up a forefinger to show me whereabouts.

I climbed up to inspect her handiwork. There were fifty mags contained in the metal case, each holding thirty rounds. That meant a total of fifteen hundred bullets to be individually loaded into the spring-tensioned housings. It was tedious, repetitive work. Added to this store were another thirty magazines collected from our various interactions with the local population during our time on the ground, plus the mags we came in with. That gave a total of two thousand four hundred rounds that Ayesha had pushed into the magazines. The mags – eighty of them, if my calculations were accurate – were neatly stacked in five piles of sixteen, one stack each for Cassidy, Rutherford, West, Ryder and myself. The number seemed like overkill, but things were going to get ragged with the FARDC and we'd probably need every one of those mags and more.

'How many rounds we got in reserve?' I asked her.

'Twelve to fifteen hundred,' she replied.

Not much left to fight off a counterattack.

'I need to eat something,' said Leila, interrupting my thoughts. 'And I don't care what it is.'

The innuendo was too easy to hit out of the park so I left it alone. I swung the pack off my back. 'There are Mopane trees over there and the worms on it look mouthwatering.'

She chewed the inside of her bottom lip at me, a hand on her hip.

'Okay, okay,' I said in mock surrender, and pulled bananas out of my pack. 'If you're still hungry, Duke will show you where there are more.'

Francis said, 'There are fish in the water also. I can show you how to catch them.'

'I'll come back with my rod next time,' I told him.

I ate a couple of bananas for a quick energy burst. Before moving ahead with the next phase of the plan, we had to consolidate our position. A far-off peel of thunder sounded like a heavy load dropped down a distant elevator shaft and a fat droplet of water landed on my forehead. I checked my watch, though I don't know why I bothered. The rain was right on time: three-fifteen.

'Let's get these containers into position,' I said to Boink and then called Ryder over to lend a hand.

The three of us wrestled them into place inside the Dong so that they formed a box, stacked the uniforms filled with mud around and on top of them and then, with rope and liana, lashed it all to the floor.

I jumped down out of the truck, Ryder and Boink following, and said, 'We should test it.' I nominated the QCW for the job because it was silenced. Ryder handed me the weapon. Selecting three-shot burst, I disengaged the safety, aimed and fired into the sandbags. The weapon leapt in my hand. We climbed back into the truck for the inspection and quickly found the holes in one of the makeshift sandbags. On further inspection, the rounds hadn't penetrated to the Kevlar container behind it, the wet mud stopping them cold. But the defenses had a weakness. While we'd be covered by the cabin behind us and by the containers on three sides, one of those sides offered less protection than the other two, there being not enough of the larger Kevlar containers to complete the box. This side was of a lower height than the other two. I compensated for it with additional sandbags, stacking them higher on that side, but if massed incoming fire hit them, they'd get chewed up quickly, leaving those inside the box exposed. There was nothing I could do about it, except perhaps not to dampen the enthusiasm by drawing attention to the potential problem. So I left this flank untested and instead shifted everyone's attention to getting a decent night's sleep. This meant first transferring the ammo-filled magazines and the grenades to the assault truck, and then collecting palm fronds to use as bedding, laying them down inside the load area of our spare truck.

These jobs took some time and were completed while the thunderstorm was in full swing, the massive cloudbanks pelting us briefly with marble-sized balls of hail mixed into the rain. When we were done, Duke handed out dry uniforms. Leila and Ayesha slipped into them, using the assault truck as a changing room. With the fronds, dry clothes and weatherproof tarpaulin covering the Dong's load's space, it would be our driest, most comfortable sleeping quarters since departing Cyangugu.

'Get your weapons load-out organized,' I said to Ryder, making a final inspection of our mobile barricade in the last of the ambient light, rearranging a heavy pair of green pants filled with mud, the bottom of the legs tied in knots and the waist secured with loops of liana. 'I'll take the first watch.'

'What time do we rock and roll?' he asked.

'Oh-four-thirty.'

'I've been thinking . . . what if Twenny and Peanut aren't there in the FARDC camp? I mean, they could have been taken out on that chopper. We might be risking our lives for nothing.'

Okay, so Ryder again proved that he could think tactically. I gave him the answer I'd given myself. 'And what if they *are* still there?'

'From up on the hill, Cassidy, West and Rutherford might have been able to see who got on board. We should wait and get some confirmation one way or the other.'

'Rutherford will be here soon,' I said.

'What if something happens to him and he doesn't make it back here?'

'Duke, we're never going to have enough intel to plug the holes. A FARDC patrol might stumble into us. Lissouba might wise up to who stole his toys and wait for us to make a move, or ambush us as we come in. And we've also got our own problems with hunger and morale. Every extra hour we spend hanging around here works against success. We have to go at the earliest opportunity. That's in around eleven hours from now.'

Ryder nodded thoughtfully. 'I had to ask.' He absently tapped a full magazine on the side of one of the sandbags. There was something else on his mind.

'I've never been in combat. I . . . I don't want to fuck up,' he said.

I didn't want him to fuck up either. 'I had you lined up to stay with Leila and Ayesha. Or had you forgotten that at least one of us has to accompany our principals at all times?'

'What about Boink? Can't he be the sitter tonight? And he can have Francis for company. You're going to need all the firepower you can get when you hit that camp.'

'Rutherford and I will handle it.'

'Look, I want to come, sir. I'm not going chickenshit on you. I'm just scared, is all.'

I wanted to tell Ryder that the only people who weren't scared in combat were already dead, but I didn't think that would cheer him up at all, so I said, 'I'm scared. Scared is natural.'

I'd seen far too many people die in battle and every single one of those deaths reminded me that bullets don't have brains. That can work in your favor and against it. You can feel lucky and take a bullet. And you can feel with naked certainty that you're not going to live to see the following day, and write letters for your buddy to send home on your behalf, convinced that you won't be far behind them only zipped into a body bag. And then, before you know it, within a few hours of the last shot being fired, you can be drunk in the arms of a girl who has your money in her pocket, while the guy you gave those letters to is lying in the morgue. But one thing is a constant: once those lead doors were welded closed behind your eyes, you knew nothing, saw nothing and felt nothing. About anything. I pushed the image of Anna lying on the carpet, her eyelids heavy with death, out of my mind.

'Do you know what it was like before you were born?' I asked him.

'No,' he said. 'Of course not.'

'Me either . . . But I think that's probably what it's like to be dead. You don't even know that you know less than nothing.'

Ryder stared at me, head at an angle, thinking about it. 'Hey, that's kinda comforting.'

'Yeah.' I turned and saw Leila standing behind the truck.

'You always sneak up on people?' I asked her.

'I don't sneak – I glide. Anyway, Ayesha and I, we've been listening to your conversation,' she said, using a banana leaf as an umbrella substitute. Ayesha drifted in beside her, also holding a leaf over her head. 'We're not staying here. We're coming with you.'

'Oh, c'mon! No!' I said, folding my arms tightly across my body armor. 'It's just too damn dangerous.'

'Cooper, I'm not asking, I'm *telling*,' Leila said. 'You're leaving us with no protection and you're not supposed to do that. We know the rules.'

'What rules?'

'Your own stupid PSO rules. Duke told us.'

Jesus! I glanced at Ryder and he looked away. 'I've got a pretty uneasy relationship with rules, Leila, or hadn't you noticed?'

'You're going off again and leaving Ayesha and me with Phillip, aren't you?'

My eyes flicked to Boink, who was nearby, keeping watch. He turned his head at the sound of his name, not real happy to hear it, and glared at Leila.

'You stand a much better chance of seeing tomorrow if you stay here with Boink,' I said, massaging Phil's ego.

'But we trust *you*,' said Ayesha. '*You* do this for a living.'

'No, actually I'm a cop,' I said. 'I sit on the phone all day, asking people questions. Occasionally, I might have an argument over who gets the last donut.'

'You came with a reputation, Cooper,' said Leila. 'Twenny talked about you. I read the newspaper stories about you, and we've all seen first hand what you're capable of doing. It's dangerous being around you, but we think it would be more dangerous *not* being around you. We're going to take our chances with you – and with Duke and the Englishman.'

'Rutherford's a Scot,' I said. 'On his father's side.'

'Whatever,' she said, brushing the correction aside with a wave of her hand.

I glanced at Duke. He gave me a what-choice-do-we-really-have shrug, reminding me that Leila was an immovable object. And maybe he was right. I couldn't think of a single instance where I'd succeeded in talking her out of something she intended doing. But what she was demanding this time was seriously nuts. A lot of hot metal would be flying around where we were going. By coming along, they posed a risk not just to themselves, but to Twenny, Peanut and everyone else in our merry band – me included.

Leila was giving me that stance, the weight-on-one-leg-and-a-hand-on-one-hip stance that announced she was going to have her way on this, no matter what. I hoped I had more success with the FARDC than I had with her.

'You will do everything I tell you, when I tell you,' I said.

'Waitresses take orders,' said Leila.

I didn't respond, so she sighed dramatically and said, 'Okay, I'll do my best.'

Ayesha didn't look nearly as sure as her boss did about what they were letting themselves in for. Smart girl.

'Let's give the doing-as-your-told concept a test, shall we?' I said. 'Go get some sleep.'

'I'm not tired.'

'I don't call that doing your best.'

Leila shook her head, took Ayesha by the arm, and they disappeared from view, heading for the sleeper.

I heard a faint whistle.

'Who's that, yo?' Boink whispered, talking into the plant life.

'Rutherford,' came the reply. The SAS sergeant materialized out of the shadows behind the big man, who jumped about a foot when he sensed the presence behind him and glanced over his shoulder.

'You nearly give me a heart attack, man,' he said, a hand to his chest.

'Sorry, sunshine,' Rutherford said. 'Where's the skipper?'

'Over here,' I whispered, standing on the back of the truck.

He trotted over and bounded up beside me.

'Any problems?' I asked him.

'FARDC's sticking to the roads, acting spooked, like the kid told us. They know something's up. How're we doing here?'

'Ready as we'll ever be.' I didn't give him the news about Leila and Ayesha.

Rutherford went to the fortifications and looked them over. 'Good job. You test it?'

'It'll work. We're calling it the Alamo.'

'You lost that one, didn't you?'

'Keep that to yourself,' I said.

Rutherford noted the magazines stacked high on the floor. 'Someone's nervous?'

'I've had four craps in the last half hour,' I said, 'but I put that down to a bad banana.'

'How about you, Duke?' Rutherford asked.

'I'll be okay.'

'Shitting bricks too, then, eh?'

A brief, tight smile animated Duke's lips.

'How's Cassidy and West. They all set?' I asked Rutherford.

'Bit of a climb carrying that kit between the three of us but, other than that, no probs.'

'You see that chopper lift off?'

'Yeah.'

'Don't suppose you saw who was on it?'

'I was already on the move by then. Why?'

Ryder laid it out for him.

'I get the picture,' Rutherford said, chewing the side of his cheek. 'Doesn't change much for us, though, does it? There's no time to go get a roll call on who's still in camp.'

'We read it the same way,' I told him.

'So what's the timetable this end?'

I briefed him on the plan for the coming morning. It was straightforward and only took a couple of minutes. 'Questions?' I asked. There weren't any, not even about the news that Leila and Ayesha would be hunkered down in the Alamo. 'So that leaves two things left to do – say our prayers and get some sack time. I want the last watch; do a last-minute walk around before we hit it.'

I got down out of the truck to look for Francis – I hadn't seen him for a while – and found him curled up under the front wheels of the second Dong. I woke him and outlined the morning's activities and told him to go sleep in the truck with everyone else.

Ryder relieved Boink, who urinated long and loud in the bush before heaving himself up into our sleeping quarters. With all the palm fronds laid down on the load tray as bedding, the interior smelled like the Puma after it came through the tree canopy like a five-ton food processor. That smell of chopped foliage conjured in my mind pictures of Shaquand and Lieutenant Colonel Blair Travis, who were now sleeping like they were before they were born.

I climbed up behind Boink. Leila and Ayesha were spooning, the rain hitting the tarpaulin covering, and the frogs around us getting horny in the rain, their personal lubricant. Francis had laid himself out directly behind the cab, flat on his back, with his hands behind his head. Boink settled in beside Ayesha, which left the space behind Leila for me. I wasn't sure I wanted to take it but didn't have a lot of alternatives. I lay down on my side on the bed of fronds and turned away from the women. I had been lying like that for about a minute when an arm draped itself over my body armor and Leila pulled herself toward me, her body curling into mine.

'I hate you, Cooper,' she whispered, her voice dreamy with sleep.

Attack

A familiar *beep* from my Seiko woke me at one-thirty am.

'Vin?'

It was Ryder.

'I'm awake,' I said, searching my surroundings with my senses. Leila was no longer spooning. I propped myself up on one hand for a few seconds to get my bearings, then moved down on my butt bones to the back of the truck, where I could see Ryder's shape illuminated by moonlight. The rain had stopped. The air was cool and smelled of banana. Even the ever-present mosquitoes appeared to be on a break. I felt refreshed after the best sleep I'd had in a week.

'All quiet?' I asked him.

'Nothing's stirring, not even a frog.'

He was right. 'When did they knock it off?'

'Just before the rain stopped. I thought it was significant, like an early warning sign of visitors approaching, but . . .'

'Maybe the orgy just ran its course,' I suggested as I hopped down beside him.

Behind us, Boink stopped snoring momentarily to call out some gibberish in his sleep.

I looked over the sleeping bodies and conducted a subconscious body count. We were one short.

'Where's Rutherford?' I asked.

'In the cab, stretched out on the full-width seat.'

I wished I'd thought of that.

'How much time have I got for a little shut-eye?' Ryder asked.

'Around two and a half hours.'

'Well then,' he said, laying his rifle on the floor of the truck and then hauling himself up with a grunt, 'nighty-night.'

I strolled away from the trucks to take in the evening and realized that I was casting a shadow. The moon was full, almost directly overhead, and it blazed away like an LED, the effect quite eerie. Just our luck. A clear night sky and a goddamn searchlight hanging right in the middle of it. I prayed for rain. I wondered how West and Cassidy were doing, whether they had been able to sleep.

The one hundred and eighty minutes of my watch dragged by. The night was still and breathless with just the occasional distant clucking of some unknown animal to punctuate it. I went into the Alamo, counted and recounted the magazines; fiddled with the barricade and watched the minutes tick past, one by one. I went for a stroll and collected bananas for breakfast and also came across a stand of sugar cane and cut a couple of lengths. That job done, I nosed around till I found an ant nest and reapplied the mosquito repellent, as the insects had finished their break.

With nothing else to do, I walked in slow circles around the trucks and wondered about Lockhart and his treachery, and about LeDuc and his perfidy. I wondered whether Twenny and Peanut were still alive in the FARDC's camp, and made a deal with the universe that if they were still there when we arrived, I'd eat less meat and more vegetables. I wondered whether Lockhart intended cutting the PLA guy in on any ransom monies that might come his way. I wondered whether Biruta, Makenga and Lissouba might enjoy being tied into a sack with a couple of those cat-sized scorpions. I wondered whether my team would make it back to Rwanda in one piece, complete with the same number of principals we'd departed Cyangugu with. I wondered whether Masters, wherever she was, blamed me as much as I blamed myself for her death. In fact, I was surprised at just how much wondering could be achieved in a hundred and eighty minutes. And then, with the familiar note sounding from my Seiko, time was up. I woke Rutherford, Ryder and Francis at exactly 0401.

Handing out bananas and cane, I suggested that they gear up while they ate. Ten minutes later, they returned, webbing stuffed with spare mags and grenades. They took over the watch while I went into the Alamo and likewise raided the stores. When we were all set, I had Ryder wake our principals.

A couple of minutes later, they wearily vacated their sleeping quarters. I handed Boink a backpack full of our staple diet.

'Breakfast,' I whispered. 'Eat more than you need and see if you can't get the girls to do the same. This might be the only food you'll get for the rest of the day.'

'Yo,' he replied.

I could've also said that this might be the last meal they had period, given that they were so all-fired keen to ride with us into the valley of death.

Boink hesitated, then said, 'What's my job today, soldier man?'

Francis interrupted. 'We must go. It will soon be light.'

I looked at my Seiko and pinched the illumination function. Just past 0432. The schedule wasn't running away from us quite yet.

'Two minutes,' I told him, then said to Boink, 'Walk with me.' I led him away from the trucks. 'Today, for one day only, consider yourself a personal security officer.'

'What I have t' do?'

'Follow a bunch of rules.'

'And?'

'Chew on a bullet for Leila and Ayesha if you have to.'

'Oh . . .' He had to think about it.

'You have to stay with them at all times. On no account let them leave the truck. Use force if you have to, but set your phaser to stun.'

'What's that?'

'Never mind.'

I handed him two spare mags for his Nazarian. 'Use single shot only. Conserve your ammo – no full auto. Fire when you have a target, and don't hesitate to pull the trigger.'

'I got it, yo.'

We found ourselves back at the trucks.

At 0442, Leila and Ayesha climbed up into the back of the Alamo. They turned to give Boink a hand but the big man waved them away and climbed up under his own steam, his weight rocking the truck from side to side.

'Couldn't'a done that a week ago,' he said, pleased with himself as he raised himself to his full height and looked down at Rutherford and me.

'You'll be swinging from the trees next,' said Rutherford.

'Throwing shit,' I added.

Ryder climbed up into the truck and joined Ayesha, Leila and Boink. I locked eyes with the star. 'Now, if you don't mind, you could get behind those containers with Duke and stay there.'

'I don't do orders, remember?'

'Then consider it a request. You're a singer. You do those, right?'

I earned a frown but she did as I asked, Ryder appearing and directing them back behind the defenses. Then I gave them all just one simple life-preserving rule to follow: 'Keep your heads down.'

I jumped out of the truck and trotted to the driver's side door. Rutherford was sitting behind the steering wheel. I sprang up onto the running board, the adrenalin starting to do the rounds; my skin was cold and hot at the same time, and I had a constriction in my throat that made swallowing difficult. It was the feeling I always got before combat. It was like an old friend, one I wished would go find someone else to play with.

'Been a pleasure working with you, guv'nor,' said Rutherford, holding his hand out through the window opening. He wanted to shake. It looked suspiciously to me like the Brit expected this to be *it*. I hoped he wasn't going to hand me a letter.

'Likewise,' I said, shaking. 'Let's move. Take it slow. There are Claymores out there and we don't want to run them down. If I tell you to stop, hit the brakes.'

He punched the starter button, the diesel instantly coming to life and settling into a noisy thrum.

'You ready for this?' I asked Francis, who was sitting on the passenger side.

He nodded, but didn't look too sure about it.

'Okay,' I told Rutherford. 'Do a one-eighty. No headlights. I've done a recce – there's nothing to hit.'

The Dong lurched forward, Rutherford winding on the steering wheel – that gorge was not too far in front of us. Palms and small trees went down under the Dong's front grille as we left the support truck behind.

'Okay, straighten her out,' I told him.

Rutherford let the wheel slip through his hands. A palm tree slapped against me, nearly swatting me off the running board.

'Stop in another dozen meters or so and kill the motor.'

After a few seconds, Rutherford gently applied the brakes and turned off the ignition.

I leaped down off the running board and probed forward on foot. After a few paces, the plantation came to an end and I crept out onto the road lit by the moonlight. There was no traffic. Holding my breath, I listened to the night, scanning it for engine noise and human voices, but nothing disturbed the silence except for a little tinnitus inside my head. I ran back through the palms to the truck but went to the passenger side this time. The door swung open and I jumped in beside Francis.

'Hit it,' I said to Rutherford.

The Brit fired up the Dong, ground the gears, and we moved off the mark with wheel spin, the tires fighting for traction in the mud. The truck's nose pushed the fronds aside as we entered the road, and Rutherford hauled on the steering wheel, turning left so we faced downhill, and stamped on the accelerator pedal.

'How are we doing for time?' he asked over the gathering roar of the wind through the non-existent windshield.

'Two minutes ahead of schedule,' I told him.

He backed the speed off a little as the road flattened out and swept onto the flat plain of the valley shimmering in the moonlight; a silver-painted version of the scene I remembered from the day before. We motored past the area where we'd hijacked the trucks and hidden the bodies. With no rain, they'd quickly start to reek. Small carrion-eating animals would be turning up to contest the spoils with the columns of driver ants that were, no doubt, already on the scene. A sudden flurry of movement in the bushes caused my heart rate to spike. Rutherford and I both went for our guns.

'*Vantour*,' Francis shouted over the wind noise. 'Vulture!'

Large black shapes separated from the forest, flapped into the air and then settled again, marking the spot just inside the tree line where we'd stacked the dead. Come morning, the FARDC patrols would see the birds, investigate what the buzzards were feasting on, find the bullet-riddled corpses and know that its weapons had fallen into enemy hands rather than disappearing into a ravine hidden by the forest. Only, by that time, of course, the point of this discovery would be moot because we were about to inform the FARDC exactly who it was who had stolen those weapons, by turning the cache on them. I glanced at Rutherford and he returned the look as he shifted into a lower gear, the road climbing gently to the village.

'Time?' he asked.

'We're on it,' I told him after checking the Seiko's countdown function.

I pulled up the QCW, took it off safety as we passed the village, and made sure the selector was on three-shot burst. There was no motion in or around the huts. Nothing was moving that I could see. So far so good.

The road swept around the base of the hill on which the FARDC camp was situated.

'What the fuck?' said Rutherford.

He took the words right out of my mouth. Up ahead, instead of the makeshift bamboo pole boom operated by a couple of sleepy guards that we expected to see, there was a Dong parked across the road, completely blocking it. A dozen men milled around the vehicle and one of them waved a flashlight in our direction. We had no choice but to slow down and stop, at which point the light went out. We were prepared to fight, but this wasn't part of the plan. This was about to get ugly, the enemy making moves we weren't prepared for.

Rutherford had time to reach for his M4 before the shooting started.

'Down!' I yelled at Francis, pushing him hard into the floor as the Africans opened fire on us. We were hemmed in. No choice but to slug it out or die here and now.

I shot over the front of the hood. Lead traveling supersonic crackled past my left ear, giving that tinnitus of mine some competition. I leveled the QCW at a knot of FARDC soldiers standing too close together, who obliged me further by getting down on one knee to steady their aim. They all died right there before firing off a shot. Rutherford looked at me and shook his head. This was not how it was supposed to go. Having just learned a very quick and bloody lesson, the balance of the Africans rushed for cover behind their truck.

I had a moment to consider how to handle this when our cabin suddenly filled with light reflecting off the rear-view-door mirrors. Spotlights had been turned on us from behind. I cracked open the door, and banged off a couple of shots at the source of the beams before popping my head out to see what the hell was going on. A Dong had come up behind us. Shit – it might well have been parked in the village, hidden. Another four-letter word sprang to mind: trap.

I heard single shots being fired behind me from an M16. That had to be Ryder – Boink favored the Nazarian 97. I hoped that Leila and Ayesha were doing as I asked and keeping their heads down behind the barricade. One of those spotlights went out, followed by its partner. Then two explosions erupted behind the truck. Grenades. I heard a man scream an instant before the first explosion, the percussion wave ringing through my head. Men were running around, appearing from the shadows, shouting and firing at us. I fired back, around one out of three shots finding a moving target. Average shooting on my part. Rutherford was doing better.

A red tracer spat from my QCW and flew into a man's chest, where it was extinguished. I fired twice at people shooting at me, ejected the magazine and jammed in a fresh one.

'Out, out!' Rutherford yelled as he flung open his door and jumped down into the night. He was right. Only ducks sat around waiting to be shot. Actually, not even ducks did that.

I hit the door with my shoulder and rolled out, landing on an African waiting there below the door with his rifle raised and ready to shoot. Unfortunately for him, he was not prepared for two-hundred-and-forty-odd pounds of falling ammunition and special agent. The combined weight knocked him to the ground, a cry strangling in his throat. When I got up on a knee, the guy was raising his weapon in my direction, so I tapped him on the head with the QCW's stock a couple of times and his lights went out. Scooting under the Dong, I started shooting at feet, then at the screaming shapes that dropped to the ground on top of them.

I worked my way to the truck's rear axle. The volley of gunfire spitting from the back of our Dong was now a serious horizontal rain of lead. The truck that had come up behind us was beginning to roll back down the hill, steam hissing from its smashed radiator and shattered engine, bullet holes punched all over the fenders. The truck slowly gathered speed, freewheeling backward. It quickly departed from the road, mowing down the forest. Several Africans ran with it, followed by a swarm of tracer; lethal fireflies zipping from the black hole under our tarpaulin chasing them.

The incoming fire that began as a fusillade was reduced to ragged individual shots, the enemy having lost its resolve in the face of the concentrated firepower unleashed on it. And, of course, it had also lost numbers. I rolled out from under the Dong and kept the roll going off the road and into the forest. I came up to a crouch and worked my way forward to flank the truck blocking our way into camp. Coming around from the side, I could see that two men were kneeling behind it, using the wheels as cover, hiding their ankles from me. I put the QCW down and swung the M4 – a more reliable weapon at this extended range, of around fifty meters – from my shoulder and took aim. But then Rutherford appeared from the forest shadows and shot the man nearest him from the side, so that the soldier's pal kneeling beside him died a spit second later, his brainpan stopping the round that had killed the first man an instant before. Economical shooting. 'Waste not, want not,' I muttered.

Rutherford stepped fully into the moonlight and raised his fist in the sudden shocking silence, letting me know that the area was clear. I made my way down toward him warily, just in case there were any FARDC lying in wait among the elephant grass and shrubs, but there didn't appear to be. I gave a low whistle as I approached, to avoid friendly fire.

'It's all right, mate,' Rutherford called out, breathing heavily. 'I gotcha.'

I ran the last twenty meters. Jesus, there were bodies everywhere, black shadowy lumps on the ground. No one wanted this. 'Move that vehicle,' I told him as I went to the back of ours. I couldn't hear any sound coming from inside. 'Everyone okay?' I asked before arriving at the tailgate. Ryder stepped forward out of the darkness under the tarp.

'The damn truck came outta nowhere,' he said. 'Drove up fast behind us, then hit the high beams. Freaked the shit out of us.'

'I think you freaked 'em back.'

'Yeah, Boink threw a couple of grenades straight through their windshield.'

'I got a mean fast ball, yo,' came his voice from the shadows. He stepped into the moonlight and looked down at me, grinning broadly.

'Are we nearly done yet?' Leila called out.

'No, not nearly. Stay there and stay *down*.' I asked Ryder, 'How're the defenses holding up?'

'We took a lot of heat, but they look okay,' said Ryder.

I heard the truck blocking our way fire up, followed by roaring engine noise and the crash of snapping trees and palms as it headed off the road, a weight on its accelerator pedal.

'Top off your mags and get ready for round two,' I said and headed back to the front cabin. Rutherford was already back behind the wheel. Blood was all over the seat. Francis was leaning forward, holding his forearm.

'I think he took a round,' said Rutherford, punching the starter button.

'It is nothing,' said Francis. '*Allez!* Go . . . let's go!'

Rutherford didn't need to be told a fourth time and the Dong leaped forward up the hill. I ripped part of my sleeve off and used it as a pressure bandage, wrapping it around Francis's upper arm, staunching the blood flow. He'd taken a bullet splinter, which had peeled his forearm like a banana, a loose flap of skin revealing the muscle beneath. I ripped off another bit off my sleeve, tied it around the wound and told him to keep pressure on it. It was going to sting like fuck, but he'd live.

A flash of light burst on the ground somewhere ahead, just as we came up into the outer reaches of the area cleared by the logging company. The boom of the percussion wave reached us through the windowless cab a few seconds later and made my cheeks wobble.

'It's started,' yelled Rutherford, the rough ground and the increasing speed of the vehicle causing us to bounce up and down on the seat like we were on a trampoline.

Francis threw up onto the floorboards.

The skirmish at the barrier had delayed us an extra two and a half minutes but Cassidy and West, up on the observation ridge with the mortar, couldn't know that. This first round was the ranging shot. West would be spotting, rushing forward, once the mortar had been fired, to check the shell's detonation point in the encampment, and relaying elevation and azimuth corrections to Cassidy. A second shell would verify these adjustments and, assuming the round was on the money, the barrage would start in earnest, another eighteen 60mm HE rounds in the first stick.

'Get us the hell up there!' I yelled.

'Pedal's pressed to the floor here, skip!' Rutherford shouted back.

A couple of FARDC men scattered out of our way.

The second mortar round fell fifty meters away on our right, an orange and yellow flash swallowed quickly by its own smoke mixed with the earth blown into the air.

'We're on the wrong side of the encampment,' I said.

'That's because we're late,' Rutherford shouted.

I knew that.

Cassidy and West would be dropping rounds on the FARDC HQ, using the blue UN tents as the bull's eye. The plan was that they'd then march the bombardment back toward the clearing closest to the ridge where the Mi-8 was parked. All of which meant that if we didn't get our asses out of this general area, pronto, a round could land close enough to kill our vehicle, and us.

A round hit a tree not far in front, exploded somewhere high, and snapped off a branch that came crashing to the ground. Rutherford couldn't avoid it. The truck hit the obstacle hard, bounced up over it and launched the three of us at the ceiling.

I smacked my head hard and, an instant later, the truck's rear wheels hopped over the tree, throwing me against the dash. I wondered how Ryder and our principals in back had fared. Francis was back in the foot well, heaving.

'Count 'em off,' Rutherford yelled.

'Count what off?' I asked him.

'The mortars. Count 'em off so we know where we stand.'

Another mortar landed close – too close – exploding less than fifty meters away, and shrapnel rattled off the Dong's metalwork. A tight ball of orange fury burst among five men running for cover and when the earth cleared, none of them was there.

'That's six!' I yelled over the noise of the motor, the explosions and shouting men.

Soldiers were running everywhere. Some were shooting their rifles from the hip as they ran, but I had no idea at what; the dark, maybe, or their own shadows. Just as long as it wasn't us they were shooting at. I glanced through the window opening by my shoulder and clearly saw Lissouba, alias Colonel Cravat, yelling at Colonel Makenga, both men waving their arms around like a couple of Frenchmen, Makenga brandishing that cane of his. Makenga was accompanied by two men – his PSOs. Lissouba had a much larger entourage, outnumbering Makenga's three to one, and the two groups were separated by twenty meters of moonlit open ground. I could feel the tension from where I was. And then both groups charged at each other, grappling, wrestling. I saw a muzzle flash and one of the men fell to the ground – I couldn't see who. Lissouba ran in and kicked the fallen man in the head like he wanted to boot it clean off his neck. Jesus, that was Makenga lying in the mud. He was dead for sure; if not from the bullet, then from the punt.

The two groups of soldiers, Makenga's PSOs and Lissouba's FARDC posse, started exchanging wild shots before closing with each other again for some serious hand-to-hand machete action. Makenga's bodyguards were overwhelmed and cut down in seconds.

Perhaps Lissouba saw an opportunity to get rid of his enemy and took it. Or maybe he thought that, once again, Makenga's men were shelling his troops. But that didn't make sense. Why would Makenga have shells sent down on his own head? Whatever the reason, the CNDP colonel was now a long way from caring.

'How many is that?' Rutherford asked as he flicked the wheel from left to right to avoid hitting a man who had tripped and fallen in our path.

'Fourteen. Six to go,' I shouted.

Francis had pulled himself up off the floor and a string of puke hung from the corner of his mouth. He pointed at a gap between the trees.

'There!' I yelled at Rutherford. 'Turn there.'

He reefed the wheel hard over. The tires bit into a rut and the Dong came up on two wheels, almost on the verge of tipping on its side. We came down again with a crash but Rutherford kept the gas pedal welded to the floor.

With the direction change, the mortars were now falling on our left side; the safe side. We'd somehow managed to come through the shower of high-explosive anti-personnel ordnance unscathed. The FARDC still registered the Dong as friendly, even though we were driving at speed through their midst. Our luck on that score had to end sooner or later.

The twentieth mortar round – the last – hit the upper branches of a tree and showered the area below it with splinters of wood and steel.

The plan said we now had two minutes and counting to get the job done and clear out before the second barrage began. I could see where we had to go. 'Over there.' I pointed out the area where a couple of the blue UN tents in the target zone had been wiped out. Around thirty meters beyond them, where the bush hadn't been cleared to any great extent, I could make out half a dozen men dangling from trees.

'Shit,' I muttered. Maybe we'd found Twenny and Peanut. The men were hanging by their broken necks, hands tied behind their backs, just like the men strung up in the CNDP camp. The more I saw, the less difference there was between FARDC and their enemy. As we came closer, I could see that there *was* a difference – three of the corpses swinging from the trees were women. Human life was worth a buck fifty, maybe less, in this place. Twenny Fo and Peanut were nowhere to be seen, no longer tied up in the area we'd noted from the ridge. 'Where the fuck are they?' I said aloud. Rutherford didn't have to ask who I meant.

The camp HQ appeared almost deserted.

'Stop!' I shouted. 'We need to check those tents.' Rutherford stood on the brakes and we slid to a halt as I opened the door, the Brit busting his open a split second later. 'Stay in the truck!' I yelled at our principals through the tarpaulin as I ran past. I could see several holes and tears made by flying lead and steel in the green fabric. I could also see that the sky was lightening and the silvers of moonlight had given way to murky grays and greens. In the harsh light of day, the cat would well and truly be out of the bag and we'd be seen for what we were – enemies to be cut off, surrounded and killed.

'Time!' I shouted over my shoulder at Rutherford.

'Sixty-five seconds.'

I reached the first of the tents that hadn't been destroyed and ripped open the front. Empty. Rutherford continued past, heading for the next tent five meters further on, a big luxury four-manner, and pulled aside the flap. I saw him back up as a man came out into the open, holding a pistol leveled at Rutherford. I recognized him: Fu Manchu.

'Stop!' I yelled, the M4's stock buried in my shoulder and the sight bobbing between the Chinaman's eyeballs.

He saw me out of the corner of his eye and glanced around to see if assistance was handy. He was shit out of luck on that score. Rutherford's M4 was on his hip, the muzzle less than six inches from his belly button, nice and discreet. Fu Manchu appeared to make some mental calculations and not like the number he came up with: his. He shrugged and lowered his gun. Rutherford snatched it from his hand.

'Americans!' the Chinaman demanded. 'You are not welcome here.'

'We're not all Americans,' said Rutherford. 'One of us is Scottish and we're welcome *everywhere*.'

'You speak English,' I said.

'I speak many uncivilized languages,' Fu Manchu replied, his face devoid of emotion. I was itching to have a go at changing that.

Rutherford frisked him one-handed, resting his M4's muzzle on top of the man's belt buckle. 'He's clean,' he announced.

Realization dawned on the Chinaman. 'It was you. *You* stole the weapons.'

'Bad upbringing,' I said. I wondered who they thought had hijacked them if it wasn't us; at the same time, the obvious alternative dawned on me: Makenga. They believed the CNDP had pulled a double-cross. And maybe it was a CNDP posse that they were expecting to turn up at the roadblock. If so, that would explain the fight that ended in the death of the man with the golden chicken.

A voice in my head interrupted this thought and screamed, 'Sixty seconds!' I had half a dozen questions for this jerk, starting with where Lockhart and LeDuc had disappeared to. I wasted a few seconds considering whether the Chinaman was worth capturing and taking with us, but decided against it, the words *International Incident* flashing incandescent in my mind. Even as it stood, if we managed to get out of this alive I was sure that there'd be bullshit complaints from this guy, and that rounds of claims and counterclaims would ensue, concluding in some kind of official apology that I would somehow have to pay for down the line. But that didn't mean I was going to give this fuck a free pass. I pictured Ayesha being dragged from his tent, naked and trussed, fruit stuffed in her open mouth, and I felt that she deserved compensation for what he'd done to her, and that it was the least I could do to collect some of it on her behalf.

'You've got five seconds to tell us where our people are,' I informed him. 'And don't say you don't know who I mean – the people you and your friends took prisoner. If you don't, my usually friendly Scottish buddy here shoots your nuts off.'

Rutherford gave the Chinaman a grin, took the M4 off safety, and lowered the angle on the weapon's barrel. A vertical crease appeared between Fu Manchu's eyes, and he was suddenly not so inscrutable.

'Four,' I said.

The encampment had begun to calm down. Folks had stopped running around.

'Three.'

Rutherford poked the weapon an inch into the Chinaman's pants and lifted his man-sack so that his balls straddled the flash suppressor.

'Hey, I think he's going commando here,' Rutherford observed as the crease between the man's eyes deepened and lengthened.

'Two,' I said.

'They took them to the mine,' the Chinaman blurted, sweat beaded across his forehead, a stain spreading down his left leg.

'Who took them there?' I asked.

'Your countryman – Rockhart.'

Lockhart. 'Was the Frenchman, LeDuc, with him?'

'No. He go with other men in the chopper.'

My inner revenge said 'Fuck' and smashed a fist into the palm of its hand. I wanted that asshole's head on a plate – with freedom fries.

'With Pietersen and White?' I asked.

'Yes, them.'

'What about Biruta?'

'He go too.'

I wanted to ask him what the PLA was doing here, and whether his people knew about his involvement in rape, kidnap and extortion, or if he knew how the folks back home in the Forbidden City would react if they knew that he was lining his pockets with gold mined by slaves his buddies were torturing and killing. I also wanted to know about the American-made guns, the M16s, but the answer to that I could get from Lockhart and his buddy Charles White, if and when I caught up with them. Somewhere in the background, the sound of men shouting something penetrated my thoughts.

'We got company,' said Rutherford.

I glanced to the side and saw maybe a dozen men tentatively approaching us fifty meters away through an early morning haze of smoke, steam and airborne mud particles. They were pointing at us, gesturing. Colonel Cravat, easily identified by the cream scarf tucked into the neck of his jungle-pattern shirt, was out front. As I thought, the arrival of daylight wasn't doing us any favors.

Rutherford and I had to finish up with the Chinaman, but not before I delivered a small parting gift from Ayesha. I balled a fist and drove it into the side of his face. His lips went in the opposite direction to the rotation of his head, kissing my thumb, and a tooth shot out of his mouth. The force of the blow spun him around unconscious and he fell face first into the side of his tent, collapsing it.

A rifle cracked and I felt the shock wave from a round rip past the tip of my nose, close enough to ruffle my nostril hairs. Our guests had tired of our company. By my calculations, we had maybe thirty seconds up our sleeves before Cassidy and West went to work again on our hosts with the mortar. I ran to the truck, Rutherford half a step behind.

Diesel smoke coming from the end of the Dong's exhaust pipe told me the motor was still running. I went for the passenger door and opened it as Rutherford leaped onto the running board I was standing on, dived in and crawled over Francis to get behind the wheel. I threw myself in after him and we were moving before I could close the door.

I glanced back at Lissouba, who was being passed a rocket-propelled grenade launcher, which he wasted no time hoisting onto his shoulder.

'Oh fuck,' I said. The tube jumped as he fired the weapon, and the warhead streaked toward us, ahead of a vapor trail scribed on the dense morning air.

'Oh fuck,' I said again, or maybe I just thought it, as I closed my eyes and waited for the explosion that would rip us all apart and incinerate the pieces. But the detonation came a second later than anticipated; the warhead blasting unexpectedly against a tree twenty meters on the other side of the truck. Not that I was complaining, but how the hell had Lissouba missed from point-blank range?

There was no time to launch an investigation. I heard a vague whooshing sound and the air was suddenly full of fire and noise and the rattle of shrapnel on the truck's metalwork, as the first of more mortar rounds fell from the sky and slammed into the HQ, turning the area around us into a boiling sea of bursting orange high-explosive blisters that raised storms of flying earth and pebbles. Lissouba and his men were blotted from view. Cassidy and West had the range and were firing off the remaining forty rounds they'd carried to the top of the ridge, and this time their rate of fire was nudging the M224's limit – a round every couple of seconds. A ball of orange hell swallowed Fu Manchu's tent less than forty meters away, and clots of mud rained down on the Dong's hood and showered us through the windshield opening, along with a man's bloody forearm, hand attached, that landed in my lap. I threw it out the hole it came through and noticed blood on my shoulder, the fabric around my upper arm shredded. I couldn't feel anything. I gave the wound a closer look. The blood seeped rather than squirted. Not serious, but nothing to laugh about either.

Francis's mouth was open and he looked to be screaming through the deafening roar and the falling earth and the clatter of whirling metal fragments, but I couldn't hear him. Rutherford's jaws were clenched, his teeth streaked with the orange mud. I watched him wrestle with the steering wheel, trying to carve a path like a slalom skier between the explosions that filled our world and blotted everything out with a storm of fire and shrapnel and mud.

He changed direction and drove a route that took us around the circumference of the encampment, away from the deadly blasts. Cassidy and West were concentrating on the camp's HQ, hoping to cut off the serpent's head. I knew that's what they were doing, because that was the plan we'd laid down. And this part was pretty much running like clockwork except for one pretty important fact – the folks we were risking life and limb to rescue weren't here. The only good news was that it appeared I didn't have to eat less meat and more veggies. Leila, of course, would give me hell about the fact that Twenny and Peanut weren't in the camp, that I'd put her life at risk for nothing, and I felt sure there was a big I-told-you-so moment in my immediate future.

A different kind of fireball erupted on the far side of the clearing and boiled into the sky, snapping me back to the reality of the moment. A deep *boom* rolled through the hills. The Mi-8 had taken a direct hit.

The continuing destruction caused by falling mortars was now pretty much confined to the area framed by the glassless opening beside me in the door. I could still see men running around screaming and diving for holes in the mud. We bounced over mud and bulldozed our way through the brush with no opposition, heading back to the scene of our first encounter of the morning, where the Dong had been parked across the road.

Silence arrived with the same suddenness as the explosions. It lengthened from a couple of seconds to a dozen of them. The last echoes of the exploding HE returned from the surrounding hills. The attack was over. Right about now, Cassidy and West would be spiking the mortar so that it couldn't be used again.

Lissouba and his men had known that an attack was coming, even if they weren't fully prepared for it. Why else have that welcoming committee waiting at the boom gate? And why move their hostages to another venue otherwise? One thing was certain, though: Lockhart would be waiting for Act II at the mine.

'Can you hear that?' Rutherford asked.

Now that he mentioned it, I could hear something. I could hear women screaming. And one of them, I was sure, was Leila.

Rescue

Rutherford pulled up at the bottom of the hill, before the road swept past the village, the forest pressing in on the truck. Rutherford, Francis and I got out as a soft rain began to fall, the sky clouded over and leaden. Leila was making enough noise for two, giving her lungs a serious workout. Something was obviously troubling her. I examined the canvas tarpaulin as I jogged down the side of the truck, and saw more rents, tears, bullet and shrapnel holes. We'd attracted our fair share of attention – more than I realized.

'Everything okay?' I asked as I came around the back. Leila, her arms outstretched, was pushing Boink away, Ayesha leaned over Ryder, who was motionless on the floor.

'I killed him,' Leila screamed. 'Get away from me. I killed him!' If there were neighbors, they'd have been out on the street.

Ryder groaned and moved a leg.

'Killed who?' I asked.

Leila shrieked when she saw that Ryder was still with us and fell to her knees beside him.

'Can someone tell me what the problem is?' I asked, hoisting myself up into the load area. 'Boink . . .?'

'When the mortars fall,' he began, 'Leila started to panic, man. I kept telling her to stay down, but she was fighting me. When the explosions stopped and you got out of the truck, she wanted to go with you and Rutherford. I tol' her she couldn't and we struggled around some. But then she said she was okay and I let her go. Soon as I did, she jumped to her feet and Ryder tried to stop her. That's when it came through. I don't know what it was, but something going fast came in one side and went out the other. It nearly took Duke's head off, man. He lost his balance and fell, hit the side of the case and knocked hisse'f out cold. I pulled Leila down and kept her quiet for a time but she bit me. We was out of the danger zone, so I let her go, and she started screaming and carrying on like you just saw. You want my opinion, I think she lost it. It's rubber room time for her, yo.'

He took his hat off, smoothed the rim between thumb and forefinger, then resettled it on his head, over the bandage that was now dirt and blood-stained.

I glanced at Leila, who was hovering over Ryder. She appeared a little disconnected from reality, but that did seem to be her natural state.

'How's Duke?' I asked Ayesha.

'He'll be all right, but he's got a bump.'

Yes, he did, and I didn't need to go in for a close-up to see it. It was like the side of his head was pregnant. This was his second concussion. He'd have to be watched.

'I'm fine,' Ryder told me, voice cracking, moving his head from side to side.

Ayesha gave him some water.

'Make sure he doesn't fall asleep,' I told her, though with all the noise Leila was making, I didn't think there was much chance of that.

'I'm sorry, I'm sorry,' Leila cried, fussing over him.

So now I had an account for the RPG Lissouba had fired. I thought he'd hit us and he had, but the round had passed clean through the truck's load area without detonating. Looking up, I saw that there were matching tears on both sides of the tarpaulin at around head height. RPG grenades traveled fast, a little under three hundred meters a second, and pushed a lot of air around because of it. That grenade, big enough and powerful enough to stop a Bradley, would have come through this enclosed space like a bullet train.

Leila was blubbering. I crouched beside her in the puddle of water that had drained out of our sandbags. She was scared and in a mild state of shock. Although I wanted to tell her that she should have listened to me and stayed with the other truck, this wasn't the time, though at least I now had an I-told-you-so moment to counter the one she had on me. Boink looked down at her, shaking his head, unimpressed by the star's latest performance. 'How are the defenses holding up?' I asked him.

'We're all still here, yo,' he said.

'C'mon, Leila,' I told her. 'Let's get you back behind these barricades.'

'You're wounded,' she said. 'Looks like something chewed on your shoulder.'

Yeah – a cheese grater maybe. The wound looked worse than it was.

'I want to ride up the front with you and Lex and the African.'

Here we go again . . . 'No,' I said. 'There's no protection there. The safest place to be is right here.'

I knew this wasn't going to fly. Leila was going to bitch and moan until she got her way. This time, though, I was prepared to hog-tie her for her own good, if I had to.

'Okay, if you say so,' she murmured.

What? I didn't think Leila had compliance in her. Maybe she finally realized, after her scene nearly resulted in Ryder having an RPG round parked in his earhole, that her bullshit had consequences. 'That's the spirit.' I said, patting her shoulder while I threw Boink a shrug of 'go figure.' 'Now I want you to do what Boink tells you.'

She nodded.

'Can you move?' I asked Ryder.

'Think so,' he replied, and Ayesha helped him up to a seating position.

I stood. 'How about shoot? Can you do that too?'

'Can't guarantee I'll hit anything.'

Then you're in good company, I was tempted to say.

'Skipper,' said Rutherford, some urgency in his voice. 'You might want to move it along here.'

I glanced over my shoulder and saw Francis pointing back up the road to where Dongs were cresting the rise and bearing down on us at an alarming rate.

'Get back behind those barricades,' I said. Ryder was struggling to move and Leila just sat beside him, staring up the road at the oncoming trucks, a deer in the headlights. Rutherford and Francis had already disappeared. I shouted through the tarpaulin. 'Rutherford, get it going! I'm staying here. Stick with the plan.'

'Got it!' I heard him yell as I dragged Ryder back and pulled him over the sandbags.

'Sorry, Vin,' he said. I propped him up and put an M16 in his hands.

'Just squeeze off a few rounds every now and then,' I told him.

Leila, Boink and Ayesha joined us behind cover just as our truck sprang forward, causing everyone to lose their balance and fall over each other. The first enemy shots drilled into the sandbags as we untangled ourselves.

I swung the M4 off my wounded shoulder and winced at the movement. Nothing was broken, just a little ragged skin. I took aim at the truck jumping around in my sights and got off a few rounds, probably none of which found their mark.

The Dong in pursuit was gaining on us, but the rate at which it closed the distance slowed as Rutherford wrung what he could out of our engine and gearbox. The road was narrow. A man kept popping his head out the passenger window when the overhanging foliage allowed it, firing off a mag at us on full auto. Tracer indicated the volley flying high and wide. The road curved onto the valley floor near the village, onto land cleared of forest for agricultural purposes, and the one truck behind us became three, all bristling with soldiers hanging off them, bright points of light twinkling from their weapons as they fired into us. The air inside the truck began to fill with flying lead and tracer and particles of mud and water vapor, the incoming fury chewing up our sandbags.

I heard Leila and Ayesha screaming and tried to ignore it. I unhooked a couple of frag grenades from my webbing, removed the safety clips, pulled one pin and then the other, keeping a tight grip on the spoons. The first truck was maybe fifty meters behind us. I threw one grenade and the second a moment later – not hard, just with enough force that they cleared the back of our truck.

'Frag out!' I yelled, and counted five. The vehicles immediately behind rolled in front of the grenades at the instant they exploded, kicking up a pall of mud and water that was sucked into the Dong's radiator grille. The front vehicle peeled off the road almost instantly, both front tires shredded, soldiers jumping from it as it began to roll onto its side. It toppled over completely and slid for a distance down a slight incline before coming to a steaming halt. The truck behind it kept more of a distance and men with machine guns hung out the front passenger door, lined us up and began emptying their hoppers into us. Our own back tires were shot out pretty much right away and Rutherford struggled to keep the Dong running true, the vehicle swaying precariously from side to side. But this was a double axle truck, which meant we had another set of wheels protected from the sharp shooters by the ragged remains of the rear-most set.

We roared past the village, though I couldn't see it through the tarpaulin. I fired back at the remaining vehicles in pursuit and yelled myself hoarse while I did it. Boink joined in, along with Ayesha and Ryder. I glanced at Leila and induced her to pick up her weapon and bang off a shot or two. I popped the mag when I saw the tracer round, put in a new one and kept firing, Boink and Ayesha reaching for fresh mags straight after me. Five assault rifles could bring plenty of heat to bear. The Dong dropped back further. Maybe the driver realized that we couldn't actually go anywhere and that there were a lot of FARDC forces between us and that nowhere destination. The windshield of the Dong behind us, white and opaque and full of holes, shattered completely and fell back inside the cab over the men crowded along the front seat. The driver slowed a little more and the vehicle fell back well beyond a hundred meters, but that barely had an impact on the volume of lead finding its way into our sandbags, the shooters having sorted out their aiming issues. Rounds were now starting to strike the Kevlar cans directly, which meant that the sandbags were shredded. We rumbled on past the spot where we'd ambushed the weapons truck the day before, but no vultures flew into the air this time.

Our vehicle took the corner at the bottom of the hill and the inbound gunfire stopped instantly. We were getting close . . .

I got up on one knee and banged the metal stock of my M4, against the cabin. The brakes were slammed on. The force of the emergency stop threw me back against the truck's cab but I was prepared for it. Fighting the deceleration, I got up and ran, launching myself out the back of the vehicle and landing on the road. The brakes groaned and the vehicle rolled backward a couple of meters, and I found myself beneath the truck, between the shredded rear tires where the air smelled of burning rubber, diesel smoke, fried grease and wet mud.

'Go!' I yelled to Rutherford, his head out of the window. I waved at him as I picked myself up, and ran into the forest through a stand of banana trees.

The Dong's engine roared as Rutherford floored the gas pedal and pulled his foot off the clutch. The vehicle jerked forward, diesel exhaust spewing from its pipe. Barely half a second later, the trucks loaded up with FARDC troops in hot pursuit came into view, swerving around the corner, and copper-jacketed rounds from assorted Nazarians, M16s and AK-47s once again resumed their assault on our vehicle's metalwork. I ran for a spot I'd marked with a length of sugarcane hung with banana leaves. Where was the damn thing? It took me a long couple of seconds to find it. Timing, always tight, was getting critical. *There!* I dove for the small green-colored clackers at the base of the cane marker and started squeezing whatever came to hand, and the forest facing the road immediately burst apart as a gauntlet of Claymores detonated and a dozen pounds of C4 sent thousands of steel pellets ripping into metal, rubber, flesh and bone.

Smoke from the explosions curled lazily through leaves, elephant grass and palm fronds. I got up, somewhat dazed, the taste of oxidized explosives in my mouth, and went over to the road to investigate. A couple of blood-spattered men were lying in the mud, barely moving, torn apart, likely unaware of how they came to be that way. Both enemy trucks were wrecked, their tires no more than loose flaps of rubber hanging from the wheel rims, their chassis slightly warped by the force of the explosions that lifted them sideways off the road. Clouds of steam boiled from under their hoods. The back wheels on one of the twisted Dongs were off the ground, revolving slowly. Jesus, so many men – all dead.

As planned, Rutherford had brought the Alamo to a stop a hundred and fifty meters up the road. I started running toward it as it began to move forward slowly, turning off the road into the old plantation. I caught up with it just as Rutherford parked beside the second truck and killed the motor.

After a few long seconds, Boink walked out from under the tarpaulin like a man who'd had too much to drink, his balance a little off, Leila sobbing in the crook of one of his massive arms.

'Man,' he said, 'that shit's gonna give me nightmares for the rest of my damn life.'

Perceptive.

Rutherford appeared from around the far side of the truck.

'Nerves aside, everyone okay?' I asked Boink.

He shook his head to himself like he couldn't believe what he'd just experienced, and then looked at me open-mouthed and nodded.

I checked Rutherford next.

'Milk run,' he said.

I forced a smile. 'You been talking to my buddy Arlen?'

'Who's he?'

'Someone I'm going to have a few words with when we get back home.' For Leila's benefit, I didn't say *if* we get home. 'How's Francis?'

'Rattled.'

'Go get him. We need to talk.'

Boink got down from the truck, then gave Leila a hand. She looked utterly beaten, her eyes on the ground. The mindless bludgeoning violence of combat had given her an insight into her own insignificance. I imagined that might be a terrifying experience for someone who believed they were special.

Ryder and Ayesha appeared from under the tarpaulin and hopped down from the truck.

'How's the head?' I asked Ryder.

'Not sure. You tell me?' he said.

'Still where it should be,' I muscled up a grin and passed it along to Ayesha, who returned a blank stare.

'The poor bastards wouldn't have known what hit them,' said Ryder.

'Spirits, maybe,' I replied.

Rutherford and Francis walked into view. Francis looked haggard, the dressing on his arm soaked with blood.

'Anyone happen to see if Colonel Cravat was killed back there?' I asked.

'Colonel who?' Rutherford asked.

'Lissouba.'

'I am sure he is alive,' Francis ventured. 'He will come for us. He is a proud man.'

'Stylish, too,' I said.

'So what's next?' Rutherford asked.

As I saw it, we had little choice. 'We're going to have to take the mine. And we have to do it now, while we've still got surprise on our side.' Our principals would be there, and so would Lockhart.

'I can't do it again,' said Leila, looking up from the ground, her eyes vacant and yet intense, zombie-like. I'd seen that look often enough in the eyes of people who've spent too long in combat or who have just experienced it for the first time.

'Me, neither,' said Ayesha.

Best news I'd heard all day. For their own safety I didn't want them or Boink anywhere near my immediate future. 'Okay, you and Leila can stay behind and debrief Cassidy and West when they arrive. Boink, I need you here too.' He opened his mouth to argue the call. At that instant, I noticed that the big man's trademark bowler was sitting a little askew on his head. I reached for it, but he took it off before my fingers got to the brim. 'Do you mind . . .?' I asked and he handed it over. I turned it around. There was a hole – no, two holes, one on each side. I held it up and looked at him through the ventilation. Bullet holes – entry and exit. I gave it back to him and he wiggled a pinky through one of them.

'Shee-it,' he said.

'I need the security here locked down by someone I can trust,' I told him. 'That's you.'

The close call he'd had without even realizing it nudged him in the right direction.

'Okay, soldier man,' he said. 'Can do that, yo.'

'What about Duke?' Ayesha asked. 'He has to stay with us. He's injured.'

Injured or not, I needed Ryder. 'Can you fire a weapon, Duke?' I asked him.

He glanced at Ayesha and then detached himself from her a little. 'I guess so.'

'Duke . . .' Ayesha said, holding onto his arm.

'This is why they pay me.'

Okay, okay – so I'd *really* misjudged him. 'Can you drive?' I asked.

'I think so. What do you need?'

I wasn't a hundred percent sure. We had a loaves and fishes situation: too many tasks and not enough people to tackle them. But at least as far as my principals were concerned, their immediate safety was not something I had to worry about, even though I was breaking the number one rule in the book, which was to never, under *any* circumstance, leave your principals without PSO protection. So, in a nutshell, if this leg of our little adventure turned into a cluster fuck, I'd be court-martialed. There'd be a guilty verdict and a dishonorable discharge would follow. Assuming, of course, that I managed to survive said cluster fuck. A cold uncertainty about what lay ahead in the next hour blossomed in the pit of my stomach and the roots grew into my scrotum. 'Francis, can you shoot a rifle?'

'*Oui*,' he said. 'We go now to free my wife, my people, yes?'

No, we weren't, not in as many words, but it would most likely happen by default if we also managed to bust out our principals.

'Can you drive?' I asked him.

'*Oui*, but not so well. I have shot more than I have driven.'

'Can you shoot *and* drive at the same time?' I asked, pushing my luck.

Francis was looking increasingly uncertain. '*Oui.*'

'But you can drive one of those?' I gestured over my shoulder at the Dongs.

'*Oui.*'

I told Rutherford to take the watch. Then, with my boot, I scraped away the leaf litter on the ground until I had a square of earth to work with. 'Gather 'round. Francis, if I get the layout wrong, let me know. Boink, Leila, Ayesha – when Cassidy and West get here, you'll need to debrief them.'

'What should we tell them?' Leila asked.

Using my Ka-bar, I drew a map of the mine and described the approaches as I remembered them. Francis pulled me up twice. The distances from the wooden beer huts, the mine's administrative center, to the open pit were underestimated; the distance to the camp, where Francis's people and many others spent the night under patches of plastic sheeting, was overestimated.

'The only buildings at the mine are two huts made of wood,' I said, scratching a cross in the mud with the point of my knife. 'I'd say that's where Twenny and Peanut are being held – somewhere close to these.'

'Busting them out,' said Rutherford, glancing back over his shoulder at the map. 'How we gonna do that?'

I wish I knew. I was still trying to figure out what we'd be facing when we got there. It was around five miles from the encampment to the mine, or a little over four miles from our current position. Unless the FARDC used radio, which I hadn't seen, my guess was that the left hand still didn't know the right hand had been smacked. If the soldiers at the mine had heard anything – the mortar bombardment – they might have put it down to a localized thunderstorm, something that happened often enough around here.

I turned to Francis, hoping for a little information on the communications front. 'Do the government troops use radio?'

He shook his head. 'I have not seen this. When they can, they use the cell phone, but they do not work here.'

'How many men usually guard the mine?'

'Not many. Perhaps ten.'

'What about the trucks? How many do they have?'

'I do not know,' he said.

Hmm . . . Lockhart and Lissouba had moved their hostages because they suspected an attack was looming, which meant there was a better-than-even chance that the mine was garrisoned to protect their hostages. And there seemed to be significantly fewer than a hundred and something armed men at the main encampment on the hill.

'Leila and Ayesha, I need you to refill our magazines,' I said. 'We're heading out in ten minutes.' I handed over my empties. Rutherford came over and added his to the stack. I expected a complaint from Leila, but didn't get one. Still in zombie mode, I figured. Boink tag-teamed with Rutherford, taking over the watch.

'If you see any traffic,' I told Boink, 'let us know. Stay out of sight, okay?'

'Yo,' he said simply, and went off.

I watched him go and decided that a fart in a crowded elevator had more chance of hiding than a human being the size of Boink. But there were deep shadows in the forest and, after more than a week on the run, he knew the drill.

'On the trucks front, we've accounted for four of them,' said Rutherford. 'And one was destroyed at the checkpoint. That's a total of five.'

I counted six at the mine when I arrived there yesterday. Including the one I stowed away on and the one back at the village, that made eight trucks that we knew of.

'There are at least four more trucks running around,' I said. 'What are you thinking?'

'You can carry around a lot of men in four trucks.'

A picture was being painted that I didn't like the look of.

'Vin,' said Ayesha, interrupting my thoughts. 'What do you want us to do with these?'

She was holding up a couple of Claymores, one in each hand.

'How many we got?'

'These two and six more.'

The Claymore. It was both a defensive and offensive weapon, or so we were told in basic, the operation of which was only limited by the user's imagination. Mine kicked into overdrive.

'I've seen that look before,' said Rutherford. 'What are you thinking?'

'You sure you're okay?' I asked Ryder. One of his eyes was blood red.

'Lemme at 'em,' he said.

Duke Ryder – a real surprise package. 'Follow me. Got a job for you.'

Release

We rolled out five minutes behind schedule, maneuvering toward the road at a crawl. Boink stepped out from behind a bamboo stand and approached the passenger-side front door. I leaned out the opening in the door.

'Anything?' I asked him.

'You're good to go, man.'

'See you in around half an hour,' I said. At least, we would if we weren't all full of holes. I gestured at Francis. He rolled us forward at a creep, then left the cover of the forest and turned onto the road, heading up the incline. Around a hundred and fifty meters downhill, the trucks blasted by the Claymores were still nosed into the greenery. A trail of black smoke rose from the vehicles and climbed toward the lowering cloud base. Someone would turn up to investigate that.

Francis accelerated up the hill, grinding through the gears, the wind roar as it blasted through the non-existent windshield building steadily. We drove through a swarm of unidentified bugs that burst wetly against us like we were being spat on. The morning was steamy and my clothes were sticking to my skin, especially where the blood from my shoulder wound had dried. Clouds were building up for something extra-specially impressive. A heavy rumbling echo of thunder rolled down through overhanging trees, confirming that a big one was on the way.

I started listing the variables in our immediate future, but soon ran out of fingers and toes. There were way too many and most of them were armed to the teeth. If there was the glimmer of a bright side, it was that the enemy's intelligence was even thinner than ours. Obviously, FARDC knew something was up, but didn't know where, when, how or who. Rolling up to the mine, we'd appear innocent, just another truck like any of the others, at least until the absent windshield was noticed, along with the bodywork shot up like an Alabama road sign.

There was the stained FARDC beret on the seat. I passed it across to Francis. It was sticky with blood and smelled of iron. 'Put it on,' I told him.

He looked at the thing with distaste for a moment before placing it on his head. We were by now about a mile and a half from the mine. There were no signs of danger. The thunderstorm was moving in, lightning forking the clouds, flicking on and off like an old fluorescent light on its last legs. Thunder rumbled distantly. It was time for Rutherford and me to make ourselves scarce. I slid down off the seat and onto the floorboards, Rutherford doing likewise. Francis glanced at us briefly but said nothing. I watched Rutherford go through his umpteenth weapons check, which prompted me to do the same.

'Checkpoint ahead,' said Francis. 'Many men. Two are coming forward. They are waving at me to stop.'

'Do *not* stop,' I told him. 'How many men?'

'Perhaps eight or ten.'

Shit – that was a lot of guns. And this was just a roadblock.

'Can you drive through? Anything across the road? Like a truck?'

'No – just armed men!' he said through gritted teeth and took his foot off the gas.

'Don't slow down!' Rutherford snapped at him, then reached over and pushed the gas pedal to the floor with the stock of his rifle. The Dong bucked forward and Francis panicked a little, swerving off the road briefly.

'Take it easy,' I told Francis. 'And for Christ's sake don't use the horn – not yet!'

'They are pointing their guns at me,' said Francis.

'Tell them something!' I yelled at him. 'Tell them the mine is being attacked.'

Just for Christ's sake don't tell them it's being attacked by us, I thought.

Francis stuck his head out the window and shouted, '*Gare! Gare! Regardez en arriere! Ils arrivent! Les fantômes! Les fantômes!*'

I heard random terrified shouting coming from the men at the roadblock.

Rutherford's face widened into a grin.

'What'd he say?' I asked.

'"Look out, the ghosts are coming! They're right behind us." Sounds like they're all shitting themselves out there.' He pulled his rifle off the pedal.

The men's shouts faded behind us. No gunfire, suggesting that we'd managed to pierce the outer defenses without alerting the main body of troops within.

'Francis – how much further to the mine?' I asked him.

'Not far. Soon.'

'You can slow down now. Tell me what you see.'

The Dong freewheeled, slowing gradually. Francis gave the steering wheel more than half a turn. From memory, this almost-ninety-degree right-hander was the last corner before a hundred-meter straight section of road that ended in the parking lot.

'I see many men,' Francis said, his voice agitated.

'How many?' I asked.

'Too many to count. More than sixty.'

Sixty! 'Are they looking at us?'

'*Non.*'

'What are they doing?'

'They are making walls with sandbags.'

Fortifications. 'Can you see our hostages?'

'*Non*.'

'Shit,' said Rutherford, beating me to it.

'Wait . . . *Oui*, I see them,' he said a few seconds later. 'They are chained to old machinery away from the huts. There are guards with them – ten or twelve.'

'Are there any civilians in the area?'

'*Non*.'

'Can you see a black male with shiny hair that looks like it's come straight from the seventies?' I asked.

'I do not understand.'

What I meant was, could he see Lockhart. 'Can you see any foreigners?'

'*Non*,' he said.

'Drive toward the main body of men,' I said. 'Head to a spot where you can't see the hostages. Drive slow.'

Francis waved out the window a couple of times and said, '*Bonjour, bonjour.*'

'That means "good *jour*", right?' I whispered to Rutherford.

The Brit grinned. It was a tight grin, and was mostly for my benefit. He had things on his mind, and so did I. I didn't like what we were about to do but, as I saw it, we didn't have a lot of choice. I heard a barrage of French directed at Francis from someone close by. Francis answered, then told us, 'They want to know why we are so damaged. We have been told that we cannot go further.'

'Just tell him you need to turn around,' I said. 'Make sure you smile when you tell him.'

Francis told him, and told him nice. He then pulled the wheel a couple of turns before straightening out.

'Can you see our people?'

'No, they are behind the two buildings.'

If he couldn't see them, they weren't going to get hurt. 'Stop here,' I said.

The brakes bit with a squeal and we stopped. Francis pulled the handbrake, the ratchet sounding like a burst of machine-gun fire.

Outside, I could hear men shouting at us. Wherever it was that we'd stopped, we weren't supposed to. Any moment, people were going to get pushy.

'Do it,' said Rutherford.

'On the count of three,' I said, eyeballing Francis, who he gave me a nod. 'Three, two, one . . .'

I reached up past him, found the horn on the steering wheel, pressed it, and the Dong's pathetic horn blew its motor scooter *meeeep.* According to the plan, I had five seconds. I pulled Francis from behind the wheel and dragged him down into the footwell, over Rutherford. As I threw myself over both of them, the entire world suddenly came apart in a burst of heat, light and noise that lifted the truck off the ground and filled the cabin with a swirling metal storm of hot steel pellets. Needlepoints of pain flared across the exposed skin of my face, neck and free arm. Jesus, I was burning. I lifted my head and slapped my face and neck, and small, hot steel balls dropped into the footwell, rattling as they fell. I wiped my arm next and saw that it was now pocked with small burns no bigger than nail heads, and more steel pellets dropped and bounced around the truck's metal flooring. The smell of burned truck and scorched human caused me to gag. I pushed myself up to the seating position, and pulled Francis and Rutherford up after me.

'Come on,' I said, half-dazed, to Rutherford, opened the door and kicked it wide. We had to hit the enemy while *they* were dazed, before they had a chance to regroup and realize that their attackers were just a few half-starved stragglers and not an invading company.

Men lay dying and wounded all around the truck. I took a few uneasy steps, my balance affected by the shock wave of the multiple explosions, willing myself not to stumble. It wasn't easy. I steadied myself against the side of the truck and saw that our khaki-green tarpaulin had been reduced to remnants while the metal frame that held it in place was twisted like liquorice. The rest of the Dong hadn't come off much better, now just scrap metal on torn tires.

'Ryder!' I shouted.

Nothing.

'Ryder!'

A hand came up and waved above the mud-filled steel cans. Ryder's head followed it.

'You all right?' I called out.

He nodded and pointed to his ears and gave a thumbs up sign. We'd used plugs of mud to save his eardrums. He threw across to me the two sets of body armor Rutherford and I had given him for added protection. I put mine on and passed the other set to Rutherford. The defenses had worked. And so had the Claymores we'd placed around the edge of the Dong's load tray, three on each side and two at the back – eight in all. The firing clackers had been taped together in a row and set up inside one of the smaller containers so that all Ryder had to do to fire off all eight in unison was close the lid on the box. The signal to fire was a long blast on the horn.

Rutherford jogged twenty meters to take up a firing position around the front of the two huts, both of which had been severely damaged by the multiple Claymore blast. I looked around, but tried to be selective about what I saw. The scene in the immediate area of the truck was just plain frightful; bodies everywhere – more than ten – many limbless and headless. Some sick puppy had put a lot of careful thought into the Claymore's physics. The sudden shocking assault had driven the FARDC soldiers to dive for cover and wait to see where all this was going. Their reluctance to engage wouldn't last long. I figured we had a two-minute window, maybe less. Once the enemy figured we'd blown our load, the tables would turn.

Rutherford signaled that he had visual contact. Weapon up, I went over to where he was kneeling, behind a stack of rusted oil drums and pipes.

Holes punched the drums beside me – gunfire. Christ, that window was less than I'd thought, down to a minute. A round smacked into the ceramic plate in the back of my body armor and the force of the hit pushed me face first into the drums.

I groaned as Rutherford turned and fired. A number of men were sniping at us from behind another pile of rusting pipes and old gas cylinders fifty meters away and they were getting bolder by the second. Rutherford ran twenty meters to his left into open space to get a better angle on the Congolese pinning us down. I watched him fire three bursts on the run, taking down two men. The rest of them stood up and sprinted in the opposite direction.

The sergeant returned as I struggled to my feet.

'Twenny and Peanut,' he said, breathing hard. 'Over there, eighty meters.' He gave me the direction with his hand.

I had to take his word for it – I couldn't see past the metal scrap. Rounds were pinging off the junk all around us, their passage marked by small puffs of rust. A round nicked my left upper arm – it felt like I'd been whacked there with a tire iron. Rutherford and I were pretty much outflanked. Time to move. We both changed mags as a rain squall marched in a straight line across the open mine, nice and orderly. A burst of thunder arrived simultaneously with a blinding flash of lightning.

I slapped Rutherford on the shoulder, got up and started walking at a fast crouch, hunched over, the metal butt of the M4 reassuringly hard against my cheek. I came around the trash heap looking for targets, and saw Twenny and Peanut. They were hooded and chained to what looked like an old boiler, their chains hooked through a bend in a pipe. At least a dozen men were arrayed around them. Four guards were in the firing position, standing side on, feet apart, lining us up. Two others thought better of it and, as Rutherford and I approached, got up and ran into the forest. Rutherford fired and one of the shooters took a bullet in the cheek. His buddies started firing on full auto and I heard the rounds pass overhead. I dropped a second guy, who spun like a revolving door before landing face down in a puddle, his arm at a crazy angle. And, like that, the resistance melted. The remainder of the guards dropped their weapons and fled helter-skelter. Maybe they thought Bruce Willis was in the house. *Yippee ki-yay, motherfuckers* . . .

Rutherford and I kept moving in the crouch position toward our captured principals, sweeping left and right, looking for threats but not finding any – not in front of us, anyway.

'Twenny! Peanut!' I called out.

I got no reaction from either of them. I grabbed Twenny by the shoulder.

'What's going on?' he yelled, spinning right and then left, unaware of my presence until there was physical contact.

I pulled the black hood off his head. He squinted and blinked at the light like some kind of night creature, even though the heavy cloud cover and the rain made it seem like early evening.

'Who is it?' he said. 'Get away from me . . . Who is it?'

He clearly didn't recognize me.

'It's Cooper and Rutherford. We're getting you out of here.'

'Cooper's a cracker. You're black. Who the fuck are you?'

'It's Cooper, your bodyguard. You wanna hear a bad joke?'

'Oh, shit. It *is* Cooper. Oh, man. Oh, shit. It's you. Oh my god. Fuck. Fuck! How's Peanut? Oh, Jesus, Cooper. It *is* you, right?'

I steadied his face and looked into his eyes. The guy was on the edge. 'Yes, it's Cooper,' I said. 'We're getting you out.'

'That's not the joke, right?' he asked me, suddenly worried.

'No, no . . .' I cupped the back of his neck in my hand and squeezed it.

Rutherford was taking care of Peanut and dealing with their chains. It turned out that they weren't locked – merely looped through the pipe and secured by a simple U-bolt.

The FARDC hadn't taken particularly good care of their hostages. It looked like both men had been forced to defecate where they stood. It didn't appear that they'd had much in the way of nourishment, either, and the cuts and bruises on their faces suggested a little recreational beating.

The chains removed, Twenny started cleaning his ears, reaming them with his index finger.

'Fucking candle wax,' he said. 'I wanna shoot these fuckers.'

With the hood over his head and his ears plugged, Twenny Fo had been in a kind of solitary confinement for a week and the guy was understandably pissed. But there was no time to talk about it. We had to get out of here. Our spectacular entrance had caught the enemy with his pants down, but they weren't going to stay around his ankles much longer.

I felt arms around me, hugging me. It was Peanut.

'Thank you thank you thank you thank you thank you,' he said over and over.

'Cooper . . .'

Rutherford's voice. There was urgency in it.

I turned around. *Oh, shit* . . . Around forty armed Congolese men and boys were arrayed in a loose semicircle fifty meters behind us. In the centre of the formation was Ryder and Francis, and both had pistols jammed against their heads.

One of the Africans stepped forward and called out, 'Your weapons. Throw them down or we will kill your people.'

Would giving up our weapons save Francis and Ryder? I doubted it. There'd be no prisoners taken here today.

'I will not ask again,' he said, flicking the rain off his forehead with a finger.

'Where's Lockhart?' I called out.

'You have no bargaining power.'

'I can take his head off from this distance,' Rutherford said out of the corner of his mouth, sighting down the barrel.

And afterwards? We'd been dealt our hand and the guy across the table – which, in this instance, was fifty meters of mud and weed – thought we had a pair of twos.

'My friend here says he can shoot you in the head from this distance,' I said loud enough to be heard by everyone. 'He's good. He can do it. You don't want to die. Release those two men and send them over. Then we'll leave and you can go back to your gold.'

The African grinned. His teeth reminded me of piano keys – white and black where a couple were missing. 'I do not need one lucky shot,' he called back. 'Drop your weapons now or you will die in a storm of lead. Your bodies will not be recognized by your mothers.'

I was trying to come up with something to say that would make the guy eat his words when I heard a boom of thunder. Deep in a place where I was in tune to these things, I wondered why it wasn't accompanied by lightning. And, suddenly, the wood huts barely ten meters from where the FARDC men were holding Ryder and Francis blew apart in a huge explosion, and splinters the size of spears fired in all directions as if a giant porcupine had stepped on a land mine. I had just enough time to turn away and drop to the ground as these spears came down with the rain all around us. When I looked back, at least a dozen Congolese had fallen where they stood. Others were staggering away, leaning on each other. One man limped off with a piece of wood the size of a fence paling sticking up out of his back like some kind of weather vane.

I wondered what in Christ's name had just happened. That was one hell of a powerful, timely lightning strike. Without lightning. 'Stay with them,' I shouted at Rutherford, and got up and ran to the spot where I'd seen Ryder and Francis. I found Ryder immediately. He was laid out flat on his back. His eyes were open and he was dazed but otherwise unhurt.

'You okay?' I asked him.

He nodded. I looked around but couldn't see Francis. There was a lot of blood on the ground. Most of the men I'd thought were dead were just wounded. They started to groan. One with a chunk of wood protruding from an eye socket began to howl. I watched as a dead man missing an arm and a large piece out of his torso impossibly raised himself up and fell to the side, and Francis was revealed as the person beneath him doing the pushing. I pulled Ryder to his feet, then went to Francis and did the same. The African's eyes were wide and he was shaking violently.

The sound of a racing engine caused me to look up. A Dong was barreling toward us in a hurry. It clipped the back of our old wrecked truck and bunted it to one side. *What the fuck now?* I took aim at the driver, just as the vehicle's horn started *meep-meeping* like an anxious moped in a Beijing traffic jam. A man popped out through the space where the windshield had been, and waved at us with both arms as though he were having a seizure. It took me a moment to recognize him. Jesus, I knew that guy. It was Mike, Mike West! There was a short barrel protruding from the cabin, lying flat along the vehicle's hood. The damn truck – they'd turned it into a tank using the tube of the M224 as a cannon. The boom I'd heard had been the mortar round being fired, and it wasn't lightning but a round of 60mm HE that had blown the huts to kindling.

The Dong drove over the remains of the wooden huts. As it turned toward us, I signaled West to keep going and pick up Twenny, Peanut and Rutherford first.

I yelled at Ryder. 'Can you walk?'

He signaled that he was okay.

'I have a problem,' said Francis, looking down.

Yeah, he did – a leg wound to add to the damage to his forearm, his thigh slick with blood; the rain sluicing through it, washing it off his boot into a pale pink puddle on the ground. Using the Ka-bar, I cut his pants away from the damaged area and found a piece of wood twice the length of a pack of cigarettes embedded in the muscle. From the way his leg hung and moved around as if disconnected, his femur was fractured. Soon, once the shock wore off, Francis was going to need more help than we could give him.

'I'm going to carry you,' I told him and didn't wait for permission. I took his wrist, bent down a little and hoisted him across my shoulders. He grunted as I stood up and the air was forced out of his lungs. The guy was a lightweight, maybe a couple of sacks of cement worth, but no more than that. I jogged the fifty meters to the truck, Francis grunting with every step, and arrived as West and Rutherford were helping Twenny and Peanut up into the load area. Leila, Boink and Ayesha swooped on them, and hugged it out and had a good cry and said 'Oh my God,' between them a dozen times or so. Meanwhile, with Rutherford's assistance, I laid Francis out on the metal floor. The guy was in a bad way.

'My people. My wife . . .' he said, his eyes rolling around in his head. 'You must get them. You must help, you must . . .'

From the tone of his voice I figured he thought I was going to welsh on my part of the deal – just another broken promise from a white guy with a First World passport.

Ryder climbed into the truck, straight into Ayesha's arms.

Leila hugged Twenny, but then she pushed him away and smacked him hard across the face, and then pulled him close and kissed him equally hard on the lips before slapping him again.

Showbiz people.

Just for an instant I forgot where we were, but a couple of helpful supersonic cracks close enough to pull the air out of my eardrums reminded me that folks were shooting at us.

Ryder dragged Francis further into the back of the truck, and the African cried out in pain as the agent propped him up against a stack of shot-up sandbag uniforms.

'Boink, Duke,' I called out. 'Lock and load! Get everyone organized.' I turned to West. 'I'm riding up front.' We jumped down and ran to the front cabin. 'Drive!' I yelled at Cassidy as I wrestled open the door.

'Where to?' he replied.

'The fuck outta here!'

Cassidy jammed the stick into gear, gave it a boot full of gas, and West and I were thrown back in the seat. The sergeant raced quickly through the gears, careless of what was going on behind us in the load area. People were going to be tossed around back there.

'Take it easy,' I told him. 'We've got a casualty.'

'Who?' he yelled over the engine roar.

'Francis. What took you so long?'

'Those booby traps at the base of the hill?' said Cassidy. 'Had to detour and dismantle them. Couldn't leave 'em lying around.'

He was right. That village was too close. I didn't want innocent people being turned into human kebabs on my conscience.

'What did you do back there?' Cassidy asked. 'A lot of dead and wounded.'

'Shock and awe,' I said, preferring to skip the details. We'd left a lot of widows and weeping mothers in our wake. And none of it would have happened if Lockhart hadn't made a deal with LeDuc to make some extra cash out of our principals. I was going to make that Kornflak & Greene asshole pay. To my surprise, the asshole himself suddenly appeared behind a group of men armed with rifles and machetes surging up out of the mine ahead of us. Cassidy had three choices to avoid hitting the human roadblock: swerve into trees, drive off the road and take a lethal drop into the mine pit of around a hundred feet, or hope the men waving their blades around got the hell out of the way. He chose option three, and two men who moved too slow wore the radiator grille before sliding off and disappearing under the front axle and briefly making the road extra bumpy.

As we drove by, Lockhart and I stared at each other for what seemed an age. He was either smiling or snarling, I couldn't tell which. I thought of all the misery he'd brought to this place with his double-dealing, weapons trading, slavery, murder, extortion and hair gel. A lot of people were dead because of this guy. I pulled up my M4 with the intention of shooting him dead right there, but before I could act on the impulse the DoD contractor was gone, slipping behind us as we sped along the road. The fuckhead would have to wait. I just hoped I'd get to him before karma beat me to it because, no doubt, there was a steaming pile of it headed his way.

The road curved around to the left and then forked.

'Go right,' I yelled, pointing.

Cassidy braked hard to make the two hundred and seventy degree turn, wound the steering to the stops and then let it unwind as the Dong swung around.

'Why?' he yelled.

Because I had a deal with Francis. We'd been lucky so far. Could we push that luck just a little further? We'd have been dead in the water without him. Say I welshed on the deal . . . Could I do that and ever get dreamless sleep again? 'We have to make a pickup – civilians,' I added before he could ask me what kind.

Occupying the front seat between Cassidy and West was the mortar tube.

'Whose handiwork is this?' I asked, tapping it.

Cassidy turned to me with that gummy, milk-tooth grin of his, taking ownership.

I wasn't that familiar with the 224. It had a trigger mechanism, which was unusual on a mortar barrel. With mortars it was conventionally the weight of the round dropping onto the firing pin that ignited the propellant and sent the package on its way.

'Works well,' West shouted. 'You just set the trigger, which pulls the firing pin back, fuse the round to detonate on impact, drop it down the barrel and squeeze the trigger . . . The round has a pretty flat trajectory over a hundred meters but then it drops away quite fast. Targeting's a bit random and you probably won't hit the bullseye, but with this baby you don't have to.'

'How many rounds you bring with you?'

'Got two left,' he said, patting the rucksack on the seat beside him.

'Up ahead,' said Cassidy, ending the chitchat. He gestured at a roughly cleared area on the side of a gently sloping hill that was dotted with a hundred or so blue UN tents. 'That where we're going?'

Through the rain I could see maybe forty people in the camp gathered in a circle, preoccupied by what was going on in the center. Many of the folks gathered around were dancing and cheering – celebrating. It seemed an odd thing to be doing, given the circumstances we'd just come from. A number of people saw us approaching and word of our arrival spread quickly through the group. The dancers on the periphery stopped performing a jig, and ran away from the party like they'd been caught doing something they oughtn't.

'Do they think we're FARDC?' Cassidy wondered aloud.

Maybe. We were in a FARDC truck – stood to reason.

The crowd melted away but for several individuals at the core. It was hard to see through the rain exactly what was going on. A man kicked something on the ground and slipped over with the follow-through. His buddies, who'd seen us by now, hurriedly picked him up and half dragged him away as they all ran off like muggers caught mid-assault, checking behind them to see if we were giving chase.

'Where to now?' Cassidy yelled through the wind and the rain, and

I gestured straight ahead. We came to a stop another thirty meters further on. I opened the door, climbed down onto the mud and jogged over to the area where the crowd had gathered. There was something on the ground and it wasn't a soccer ball. In fact, there were quite a few objects and a lot of blood. It looked like a big patch of roadkill.

'Jesus Christ,' West muttered, standing beside me and looking down at the human remains scattered around. The crowd had literally torn some guards – three, from the leg count – limb from limb. The pieces, except for an arm here and a leg there, were still wearing most of their uniforms. A white-hot anger had been vented on these men. The people here had endured first-hand the cruelty of the FARDC and this was a little payback. Looking down at the mess on the ground, I felt nothing for the victims and realized that probably wasn't a good sign. And right about then, I realized how much the Congo was getting under my skin.

I turned and scanned the blue tents. Some people here and there were staring at us. They knew we were different from their captors, but past experience informed them that we were more than likely not going to be any better than the devil they knew, which, understandably, made them wary.

'We can't take all these people with us,' said Cassidy, walking over to me. 'There's well over a hundred.'

'We made a promise to Francis. We're taking the people from his village.'

'And how many is that?'

'Don't know,' I said. 'Give me a moment.'

I ran to the truck, where Rutherford was leaning way out the back to see what was going on, holding onto the tarpaulin framework for support.

'How's Francis?' I said as I approached.

'Hanging in there.'

'And everyone else?'

The Brit jumped down to meet me and, from the way he glanced back over his shoulder, he was doing so to put a little discreet space between himself and our principals.

'You're going to have problems with Leila down the track,' he said.

'Tell me something I don't know.'

'She's telling Twenny that we could have gotten him out a week ago, but that you wouldn't agree to it.'

I took my own advice and breathed deep. Then I jogged the few steps to the rear of the truck and pulled myself up into the back of the vehicle. I was immediately struck by the stink of human sweat and a funk I've always associated with fear. Peanut rushed toward me and again threw his arms around my waist. I gave him a reassuring pat on the shoulder and sat him back down next to Twenny, who refused eye contact and stared at the floor, his dirt-ingrained face lined with tear tracks.

'You see what you've done to him?' Leila hissed, her eyes narrow and fierce, back to her old self. She was seated beside Twenny, perched on top of a couple of sandbags, one arm over his shoulder. She glared up at me like any moment she was going to spit venom at my face.

I looked at Ryder, who was sitting with Ayesha, his head back against the tarpaulin, legs drawn up and an M16 between them. The guy was clearly exhausted.

Boink stood in Twenny's corner. No eye contact from him, either.

I didn't respond to Leila. The fact that Twenny Fo was alive and no longer chained to a boiler with a hood over his head was all the defense I needed. Some people reacted irrationally to the stress of combat and maybe that was Leila's excuse. Or maybe conflict was the way she exercised control. Or maybe she was just a bitch.

Twenny and I needed to talk, but it would have to wait. I was hoping he'd be my star witness in the trial that'd put Lockhart in Leavenworth for the rest of his life.

Francis groaned. I thrust Leila and her bullshit out of my mind for the time being. The African's eyes were shut and his head, soaked with rain and sweat, lolled from side to side. He was fighting a losing battle against the pain. I felt his forehead, his temperature soaring.

'Where's the morphine?' I asked Rutherford.

He shook his head. 'Got none.'

'Antibiotics?'

'The kit's empty,' he said. 'Blame LeDuc.'

In other words, the deadbeat had ransacked it before he split. I checked Francis's wound. It had stopped bleeding but the skin surrounding the length of wood embedded in the muscle was already livid with infection. We had to get this guy to a hospital. And if we hurried, maybe all he'd lose was his leg. I'd been hoping that we could move him to the open end of the truck, stand him up and have him call his people over. But that wasn't going to happen. And I realized I didn't even know the name of his damn village.

'Francis,' I asked him. 'Your village – what's it called?'

He rolled his eyes around and sweated at me.

'Francis, can you hear me? What's the name of your village?'

There was a moment of lucidity and he mumbled something. I took fistfuls of his shirt and lifted him a little off the truck floor to bring him closer. The guy screamed and the wound in his leg leaked some blood. *Not smart, Cooper.* I lowered him gently back onto the floor and he started babbling.

Rutherford came in closer. After a few seconds he said, 'I think he's saying he lives in a place called Bayutu.'

'Try and confirm it.'

'Bayutu? *Habitez-vous là?*' Rutherford asked him and Francis gave a good impression of a nod.

'See if you can get his full name,' I said, checking the view outside beyond the truck. I was getting edgy. Even taking their losses into account, there had to be more than a hundred FARDC troops in the area and most of them would be looking to even the score.

'*Francis, quel est ton nom de famille?*' said Rutherford.

'Nbekee . . . Nbekee . . .'

'Francis Nbekee?' Rutherford asked.

'*Oui, oui, oui, oui . . .*'

'Okay,' I said, standing up. We had something we could work with.

'Where you going now?' Leila demanded to know.

I ignored her and as I jumped down I heard her say, 'Come back here!'

'We still clear?' I called out to West, leaving Leila and her inner cow behind.

He motioned toward the camp. More people had wandered to the edge of the settlement closest to the truck. Several men waved machetes at us in warning.

'Call it out,' I said to Rutherford, who jogged up beside me.

He made a funnel with his hands, yelled the name of Francis's village across to the gathering and asked in French if anyone else lived there.

Nothing. No reaction.

'Tell them we're here with Francis Nbekee.'

Rutherford called this out to the crowd.

A woman suddenly began howling above the sound of the rain and the noise of the growing, restless gathering. It was a large woman in colorfully printed cotton clothes and she was bustling her way to the front of the crowd. She belted out something in French at us.

'*Oui,*' Rutherford replied. To me, he said, 'I think that's his old lady.'

'Tell her that her husband's wounded and he's in the truck. Tell her we're American and that we'll take home everyone who lives in Bayutu.'

'That's getting beyond my command of French, but I'll give it a go.' He took a moment to work it out in his head and then called, '*Il est blessé! Il est dans camion! Nous sommes Écossais! Chacun qui habite à Bayutu; nous vous guiderons chez-vous!*'

'*Écossais*. Did you just tell her we're Scottish?'

Rutherford grinned.

The woman burst through the crowd and started running across the open ground toward us. Several of the men tried to stop her, but she palmed them off into the mud with the ease of a linebacker. The woman met us, blubbering a bunch of stuff that I had no chance of understanding, though the gist of it was probably that some days it just didn't pay to get out of bed. We hustled the woman to the truck, while behind us, no doubt fearing a trick, several of the men with machetes waved them and advanced threateningly.

'Boink,' I called out into the truck. 'Need some help here . . .'

The big man came out of the gloom, took the African woman's hands and hauled her up into the truck without too much effort. She saw her husband an instant later, shrieked, then ran to him crying and babbling, kneeling beside him and smothering his face with kisses. I waited for her to hit him around the head a couple of times but it never happened. Leila's behavior was altering my reality.

I heard a couple shots fired. Rutherford and I both went to investigate.

'Company's on the way,' Cassidy called out, the stock of his M4 pressed against his cheek. I peered in the direction he was aiming, the general area of the mine, and saw a man in baggy green camos scuttling behind a mound of scrub-covered earth. I hurried back into the truck. Reinforcements would be on the scene in no time.

'What's happening?' Leila wanted to know.

I ignored her, which I was starting to enjoy doing.

'Tell Francis's wife to call her people over,' I said to Rutherford.

He passed this on to the woman and the brief conversation was punctuated by gunfire, which seemed to work as effectively as anything the Scot said. She motioned at Rutherford and me impatiently to help her get to her feet, which we did, and then brought her to the back of the truck. She started frantically waving at the Africans, most of whom were now hiding from the gunfire behind their plastic shelters, and called out to them in a shrill voice. The call was answered by cheering and waving, and around thirty people, mostly women and children, broke cover and began running for the truck, their meager possessions and crying infants under their arms. Jesus, we were going to get swamped. The horde ran through and around West and Cassidy, who were standing a little away from the truck, keeping their eyes on the scrubby patch of forest that separated the camp from the mine.

'Jesus, Cooper – that's too damn many,' Cassidy yelled at me.

Who were we going to turn away?

The truck rocked and swayed as the human wave engulfed it. People threw themselves inside and then helped others aboard.

'Let's go!' I yelled at Cassidy and West, as I jumped into the rear of the truck. 'Move it!'

The two soldiers backed away from their positions, then lowered their rifles and ran for the front cabin.

At least forty people were squashed into the back of the truck, compressed like a month of fruit in the bottom of a school kid's bag. There was almost no room to breathe and so much chatter that I couldn't even hear Leila complaining. I felt the Dong's engine rumble into life through the soles of my feet and everyone screamed as we lurched forward in first gear, and screamed again – though not so loudly – when second gear was selected. We went round a gentle bend in the road and the truck leaned at a frightening angle, lifting the outside rear wheels.

'Sit, sit, everyone sit,' I yelled, miming with my arms and hands as I spoke.

No one sat.

'Rutherford. Get 'em all the fuck down on the floor before we tip over.'

He shouted instructions and people began to sit. The lack of space meant that they mostly did so on top of each other. The truck went round another corner a little less precariously and the camp disappeared behind a screen of forest.

'Where are we taking them?' Rutherford asked. 'We don't know where this Bayutu place is.'

'See if you can't get some idea from Francis's wife. And maybe get her name while you're at it.' I wondered whether Bayutu was the best place to go. There was always Mukatano. At least we knew where that was – at the end of the road.

The forest appeared to close in tightly around the truck, cutting the road's width in half. That figured. Beyond the mine, the road got almost no use at all. It was also getting bumpier, with deeper ruts, which pulled the truck left and right viciously as the tires tracked through them. I sensed Cassidy backing off the gas and felt the downshift, the conditions forcing him to take it slower. I scanned the human cargo crammed into this confined space. Mothers nursed young children, old men sat impassively when they weren't attending to the women and kids, and none of the eyes that met mine gave away anything. All except Leila's, who looked up at me crying with joy, a baby in her arms.

I turned back to watch the road unraveling behind us, just in time to see a rocket-propelled grenade streak toward us from the far end of the tunnel.

Flee

The RPG round skipped off the road into the forest, angled away slightly by a rut, and detonated against a tree close by. Shrapnel tore through our tarpaulin at about head height and I heard a couple of pieces ping against our metalwork. That was too close. Women screamed and one of them started picking feverishly at her leg. I crawled back to her on my hands and knees, across the human carpet, but she managed to get hold of whatever the problem was before I reached her, and flicked it off her skin. It looked to have been a twisted chunk of the warhead's green casing, and it smoked as it arced through the air and got caught with a metallic *clink* between the tarpaulin and the side of the truck.

A second warhead flew overhead and exploded harmlessly out of sight deep in the forest far ahead. It was Marcus who'd warned us that this Lissouba asshole was a persistent fuck. The fact that he wasn't letting us leave without a fight was going to make things difficult. The truck in pursuit showed itself two hundred meters behind us and it was slowly gaining ground. Soon enough the range would become point blank. I was out of grenades. The M4 slung over my good shoulder was all I had. Rutherford was armed, as were Ryder and Boink. We could maybe pick off the driver, but we couldn't afford an exchange of small arms fire with the enemy, especially when they had RPGs.

'We need that mortar,' Rutherford yelled. Good thinking, only there was a slight problem – the barrel was pointed the wrong way and doing a U-turn wasn't possible. The long tunnel had come to an end and our truck began laboring up a steep incline, which included some tight corners.

'Find out where the turnoff to the river is,' I shouted back. 'Get what you can out of Francis and his wife about Bayutu and any other settlements nearby. Francis mentioned something about *Médecins Sans Frontières*. They're operating in the area. And while you're at it, see if someone else here can drive this rig.'

Rutherford signed WILCO as I reached across to get a hand on the tarpaulin framework.

'And when we stop,' I told him, looking back, 'jump off. We've got a job to do.'

Using the framework to keep my balance, I walked down toward the front cabin along the top of the metal sides of the load tray, the only space not taken by Francis's people. Glancing over my shoulder, I saw Leila still with the baby in her arms and she was rocking it back and forth, totally engrossed, having finally met her match in the needy department. Peanut was teaching a girl of around six to play scissors paper rock, and losing, apparently unperturbed by our current situation – maybe he was completely unaware of it. Twenny was also engaged with Francis's people, re-tying a bandage around a man's head, assisted by Boink. I couldn't see Ryder or Ayesha tucked away in the opposite corner behind the cabin, as the press of bodies obscured them. I suspected the crack Ryder had received on the head was worse than he let on, but there was not a lot anyone could do about it except provide some comfort, and Ayesha had put her hand up for that.

When I got to a point behind the cabin, I reached for my Ka-bar and made a long vertical slit in the tarpaulin. A moment later I was through it, out in the open air and being swatted by the trees and bushes trying to reclaim the road. We crested the hill and the Dong quickly picked up speed heading down the other side. I ducked under a loop of liana that would have taken my head off if I hadn't seen it at the last second, pulled open the passenger door and leaped inside.

'Fuck, boss!' yelled West, taken by surprise, his M9 pointed at my ribs. 'You scared the living crap out of me.' He lowered it. 'What's up?'

'Stopped by to borrow a cup of sugar, but I'll settle for the mortar if you don't have any.'

'What's happening back there?'

'The folks on our tail are two hundred meters behind and closing. We need to give them something to think about. What have we got left?'

West tapped the container on the floorboards and said, 'Two frag grenades, lots of smoke. Eleven mags for the M4s between us. And the two M49s.'

In other words, we were down to the dregs.

'Let me off then give me another hundred meters of clearance and pull over. Show me how to fuse the 49s.'

West hesitated. 'If you miss, you risk getting isolated and cut off. I'm the one who knows how to use it. You should stay on the truck.'

I didn't see it the same way. I'd made the deal with Francis for his assistance, which included the burden of getting his people to safety. If any dick was going to get hung out in this shooting gallery, it was going to be mine. 'We can draw straws to see who'll be stupid next time,' I told him.

West was set to continue the discussion, but the urgency he saw in my face changed his mind. So he hurriedly produced the remaining two rounds of HE from a pouch on the floorboards and fused one of them while I looked on.

'Make sure the base plate has a secure bed,' he said. 'And keep the barrel as steady as you can. The further the distance to target, the more chance you have of missing it. This round has a lethal radius of around twenty-five meters. So, while close is easier to hit, too close and it'll be raining Vin Cooper.'

An RPG round streaked through the bush and boomed against a tree trunk fifty meters ahead and well wide – another random shot.

Smoking shards of hot metal clipped off several branches that crashed into the scrub below.

Cassidy brought the truck to a sliding halt and screams of fright could be heard behind us.

West looped the pack strap containing the spare round over my head and neck, and held the mortar barrel toward me.

'Fuck them up the ass, Major,' Cassidy said.

'You Army guys . . .' I said as I opened the door and dropped onto the ground through the leaves of something fleshy and wet. Spines jagged into my skin the length of my arm and broke off.

'Son of a bitch,' I cursed as the passenger door slammed shut. There were pinpricks of blood up and down my arm. West threw me a wave as the Dong accelerated down the hill, the African faces floating in the darkness under the tarpaulin. Rutherford was standing on the opposite side of the road. Scoping the area, I found what I was looking for almost instantly – a large tree with a broad root system close to the road, with plenty of leafy cover to keep us well hidden. The crest was maybe seventy-five meters back up the hill to my left. Our DF had already disappeared around a slight bend fifty meters to my right.

'They're close,' said Rutherford, the enemy vehicle's engine laboring noisily just behind the crest.

I ran five meters to the tree and jammed the mortar's base plate against a smooth buttress of roots.

'Hold the barrel up,' I told the Scot.

'Got it,' he said.

I took the round from the pouch, checked that it was the correct one, and double-checked that it was fused for an impact strike. Satisfied, I cocked the trigger then loaded the round, fins first, down the business end of the barrel and let it drop, turning my face away at the last instant just in case the round decided to launch anyway. It didn't.

'Aim at the road around ten meters beneath the crest of the hill,' I told Rutherford. 'If we screw it up and they stay nice and still for us, we've got a second chance,' I added, patting the backup round in the pouch as the truck lurched over the crest, blowing clouds of smoke. A man hung out the passenger door with an RPG. Several more soldiers rested their RPGs and assault rifles on the roof of the cab, the tarpaulin having been removed from the framework over the load area. They had a lot of firepower and were obviously keen to use it.

'On a count of three,' I said, grasping the mortar's trigger close to the bottom end of the barrel. 'Three, two, one . . .'

I squeezed the trigger and flinched involuntarily as the barrel jumped with a loud bang. Shards of hot material blew back on us as the shell flew from the muzzle. I glanced up in time to see the round skip off the road just under the vehicle's front axle. A massive *boom* followed and the back of the truck lifted high off the road as if held there by a giant hand. The radiator dug into the road and the vehicle teetered there almost vertical as it slid forward, carried by its own momentum, pushing a wave of mud. The men standing in the bed area were catapulted over the front cabin. They landed on the road and were almost instantly run over by the truck sliding along on its nose. And all of it was heading straight for Rutherford and me. We dived for cover as the Dong ploughed off the road and smashed against the tree shielding us with a sickening crunch of metal against unyielding hardwood. Rifles, grenade launchers, ammunition and men were thrown high into the air and came down all around us, crashing through the bush. A man who landed quite close screamed as he came down. An emphatic meeting with the earth silenced him briefly before he started groaning.

I looked at Rutherford. Both of us had come through okay but the mortar barrel wasn't so lucky, having been crushed beneath a couple of tons of wrecked Dong on the other side of the tree.

A few feet away from Rutherford, one of Lissouba's men reached slowly, painfully, for the rifle beside him. Rutherford stood, kicked it beyond his reach, turned the man over and saw that the left side of his face was completely crushed inward from eyebrow to chin.

'Persistent fucking sods,' he observed, kneeling over the man.

I made my way to the road and waited for Rutherford. The forest was silent but for one horribly familiar sound.

'Do you hear that?' I asked him.

'Hear what?' He shook his head. 'Wait . . .' he said, changing his mind.

The sound was drifting in and out.

'Jesus – more fucking trucks,' Rutherford muttered.

They were a little way off, maybe just starting to climb the hill on the far side of the crest. I turned and ran down the road, the Brit beside me. Life was starting to get complicated. FARDC was chasing *us*, not Francis's people. But they were going to become collateral damage in the crossfire. We were going to have to part company with them for their own safety.

'We have to ditch the vehicle,' I said as I ran. 'They're going to keep following it. Can Francis be moved?'

'If we make him a stretcher.'

'Where's the turnoff to the river?'

'Patrice said there was a fork in the road near the bottom of this hill.'

'Who's Patrice?'

'Francis's old lady.'

We ran through the bend and saw our truck stopped, West and Cassidy standing beside it, keeping watch.

'Get our principals ready to leave,' I told Rutherford. 'We're going our separate ways at that fork in the road.'

I ran to Cassidy and West, signaling frantically at them to get back in the truck, but they weren't urgent enough about it so I ran past them to the driver's side and jumped in behind the wheel. I had the thing in gear and rolling before Cassidy and West had both feet on the running board.

'What's going on?' Cassidy demanded as he climbed in through the passenger door, West behind him.

'There's more company on the way – change of plan,' I said.

The truck was heavy with all the people on board, the acceleration sluggish and the engine more reluctant than I remembered.

'Watch for a fork in the road,' I said.

We rounded a corner and the strip of mud beneath our wheels divided in two, just like Patrice said it would, the fork heading off to the right disappearing almost completely into thick bush. I stamped on the brakes and heard muffled screams coming from the cargo area behind us.

'C'mon,' I said to Cassidy and West, the brakes protesting with a loud moan. 'We're outta here.'

I grabbed the ammo container on the floorboards by its handle, hauled it out and jogged with it across my chest to the back of the truck. I arrived at the tailgate in time to hear Leila say, 'I'm not going anywhere.' The infant in her lap began screaming. 'Now see what you've done? I just got her off to sleep.'

We had no time for this. 'You want the kid to live, right?' I called out to her.

She stared at me, her eyes hot and defiant but her body language nervous.

'Boink, pick her up and carry her,' I told him.

The big man looked at me and then at Twenny.

'Yo!' I yelled at him. 'Now!'

He took a step toward her

'There's no need for that,' she said, handing the baby to its mother and getting to her feet.

The truck was full of uncertain people.

'Rutherford, explain to Francis's old lady that everyone has to get off the truck immediately. Tell them to stick to the forest and stay away from the road. See if you can find out where that *Médecins Sans Frontières* outfit is.'

'Patrice told me that already: it's an hour's walk from here.'

'And the river?'

'About an hour and a half in the opposite direction. You still want that driver?'

'No,' I said.

I watched Ayesha help Ryder to his feet. He nearly passed out and slumped heavily against her before pulling himself up. Twenny came up to me as our Congolese passengers began to get the idea that this bus was going on without them.

'I've heard both sides of the story, Cooper – Leila's and Boink's,' he said. 'I think I had things round the wrong way, you feel me? Anyway, Boink set me straight. Anythin' choo need, choo lemme know . . .'

'Then help me get everyone off this truck, and manage Leila,' I told him. A little cooperation from the stars of the show would make a nice change.

Patrice and Rutherford began calling out in French. I caught the gist and started repeating it, saying, '*Allez! Allez!*' and sweeping my arms toward the tailgate to emphasize the point.

The message sank in. People were starting to move. I went over to Rutherford and helped him lift Francis to the back of the truck.

'Cassidy!' I called out, seeing him standing watch with West. The sergeant trotted over.

'Give Rutherford a hand getting Francis into the trees. Keep everyone off the road. Patrice – that's Francis's wife – she knows what's going on. They're going to need a field stretcher.'

'Roger that. What are *you* gonna do?'

'Ditch the truck. You take the right-hand trail – that'll get you to the river. I'll rendezvous with you there. Our African friends are headed elsewhere. We need to move it.'

'Roger that, boss,' he said and went off to hustle while I kneeled beside Francis.

'Mercy bowcoop, Francis,' I said, his face sweating beads of pain.

'You have the worst accent in the whole of the Congo,' he croaked. 'It is I who thanks you. My people owe you their lives.'

'I was going to say the same thing to you. Good luck.'

'And to you,' he said, finding my hand and squeezing it weakly. 'Get to the Zaire.'

I gave Cassidy and Rutherford a nod and they lifted him off the back of the truck as Patrice rushed in, threw her arms around me and squeezed until I coughed. The woman was a cage fighter in drag.

'*Merci, merci,*' she said and kissed me wetly on the cheek before hurrying off to tend to her husband while he was being carried behind the tree line.

The rainforest quickly swallowed everyone and I found myself alone on the road, the Dong idling noisily behind me and the sound of approaching vehicles getting louder by the second. I ran to the driver's door, jumped in and selected first from the snarling gearbox. The vehicle charged forward, far more willing in the acceleration department without all the weight on board. The road was almost completely overgrown. I was considering slowing down but changed my mind about that when a bullet shattered the rear-view mirror on my door and slivers of glass speared into my neck and cheek. The Dong burst through a wreath of liana obscuring the view forward. I had no idea where the road was going, so I took a guess and kept the wheels pointing straight ahead. I could hear small arms fire being shot off behind me. I was thinking how not much of it was finding its target when a single round punched through the passenger seat beside me and buried itself in the dashboard.

I was driving way too fast for the conditions. An RPG round exploded somewhere unseen but close and I swerved and cut a path through the trees. The road found me before I located it, and the tires slithered around on the muddy strip, hunting for traction. And then, suddenly, there was a log lying diagonally across my path, big and immovable. Swinging the wheel violently, I still struck the massive obstacle a glancing blow that smashed my face down into the steering wheel. The log bounced the truck into the forest and it began to crash through the scrub again, but beyond my control this time, rumbling down a steep hill with increasing speed. And then the world tilted on its side as the earth fell away and the truck tipped and I hung onto the steering wheel with plants and liana and mud swelling into the cabin, coming through the windshield area and welling up through the passenger window below my feet.

And then everything stopped moving.

I wasn't unconscious – just stunned. The crash and the resulting detour had happened so fast, I needed a moment to catch up with it. Jesus, my face hurt, my eyes watering with the pain.

Get out, Cooper, said the voice in my head but I couldn't recall why.

And then I remembered about the people with guns not far behind and that they would be coming for me. I found my M4, hitched it over my shoulders and pulled myself out onto the canted hood and slid into a thicket of elephant grass, bamboo and liana. The forest was so dense it was almost impossible to move through it. That was good. If it delayed me, it would have the same effect on the folks who would be coming to investigate the wreckage.

'JESUS, BOSS, YOU'RE A mess,' said West, examining my face after he gave me a pat on the shoulder.

'It's my party lifestyle,' I said. I'd tried to clear my blocked nose earlier, snorting out a couple of plugs of coagulated blood. The pain I felt when I pinched it told me it was broken. It had happened when I'd tried to turn the steering wheel with my face after hitting the roadblock.

The hike back to rejoin my merry band of travelers took two hours, a little longer than I expected. It was mid afternoon before I came across the road, followed it back to the fork, then doubled back to find everyone. Boink had the watch while West and Rutherford were building beds for everyone up off the ground, away from the ants and other biters.

'How are our principals?' I asked West when I found him binding saplings together with liana.

'Subdued. I think they're finally getting the message.'

'Which message is that?'

'To shut the fuck up and let us do our job.'

I doubted it. 'Where are they?'

By way of an answer, he pointed into the bush. Leila and Twenny were silhouetted sitting on a rotten log. They appeared to have reached some kind of amnesty, each sitting with an arm around the other. A couple of orange butterflies danced in the air above their heads. I could almost hear the violins. West having relieved him of the watch, Boink came and stood a few meters behind his employer and, bearlike, scratched his back against a tree.

'How's Ryder?' I asked.

'Milking it for all it's worth . . . not that I blame him,' said West. 'Anyway, I think he's on the mend.'

He indicated Ryder's whereabouts with a thumb over his shoulder. The captain was lying on one of the cots, Ayesha in attendance.

'Francis, Patrice and the rest – they get off okay?' I asked.

'Yeah. Patrice assured Rutherford that they knew where they were going. How about you? How'd you make out?'

'I died,' I said.

'No, really, what happened?'

I gave him a quick rundown.

'By the way,' he said when I'd finished, 'there were two trucks in pursuit of you. And both of them had a lot of men on board.'

I wondered how much time my little decoy run had bought us. Eventually those truckloads of armed men would backtrack and investigate this road. It started raining. 'Must be three-fifteen,' I said.

West checked his wristwatch and nodded.

'Where's Cassidy?'

'Setting up a perimeter defense. Ryder was sitting on two Claymores we forgot about, the last of the ones with the trip wires you guys found in the FARDC camp.'

That was the best news I'd heard in a while.

'What's down at the river?' I asked him, fanning uselessly at a cloud of mosquitoes attacking my face.

'Mud, insects – not a lot else. Come take a look for yourself.'

West sheathed his Ka-bar and we headed for the river, detouring via an ant mound. We exited the forest into a semi-cleared patch of wet earth that, here and there, had sections of steel matting laid over it. Strangely, the mud here wasn't orange, but white. The river itself was fifty or sixty meters wide, a tea-brown slick dented with raindrops that slid by at a fast walking pace between banks of mostly unbroken forest. A fish broke the water, no doubt chased by something hungry. Half a dozen heavy hardwood posts were driven vertically into the water just off the riverbank I was standing on, which was low and marshy. I could easily imagine that at one time there'd been a reasonable amount of infrastructure here to offload the sawn logs that would get floated down the river to the mill, wherever that was. But now almost nothing remained aside from those pilings, a little rusting steel scrap and few old oil drums half submerged in the mud. There was one small troubling detail – as Francis said, the Zaire flowed the wrong way for our purposes, heading west *away* from Lake Kivu and Cyangugu.

'Seen anything useful – like a riverboat with slots and a bar?' I asked.

'What do you think?'

I took a deep breath. When Lissouba's men came down that road, we'd be trapped with our backs against the river. We could swim for it, but I didn't like our chances against what the fuck else that might be lurking in that murky water chasing the fish.

'They got crocs here?' I asked.

'Nope. Tigerfish.'

'Great.' I had no idea what they were, but they sounded unfriendly.

I scoped the area a second time and the shred of an option formed.

'You guys make pretty good cots.'

'It ain't hard.'

'Can you make me a cot around a few of those oil drums?'

'So you want a raft?'

'It'd make me sleep a whole lot better.'

ALL THE DRUMS WERE recovered from the mud, lined up and inspected. I stomped on the side of one of them and put my boot clean through it. Similar tests on the remaining five showed only one to be sound, with just a little superficial rust. A second drum was also free of holes and corrosion, but had no lid. We could use it as long as we kept its brim above the waterline.

There were ten of us – a combined weight of around two thousand pounds. Buoyancy was critical. Six types of sapling were tested. West placed them all in the water and a clear winner emerged, floating higher than the others. It completed one spin in the eddy by the bank before the Zaire carried it away.

'Okay, that's settled,' he said. 'These are the guys we want.' He held a second length of the winning sapling, about two inches in diameter and trimmed to a length of about twelve feet.

'We'll need six bundles of these, about the same length as this,' he said. 'And each bundle should be about two foot in diameter. That's around thirteen saplings per bundle times six bundles. So seventy-eight saplings in total. We'll use vine to lash the bundles together, with a drum fore and aft. Keep it nice and simple.'

'Paddles?' Rutherford asked.

'No paddles. We'll use the main current, pole off the banks.'

'How long will this raft take to build?' asked Leila.

West smiled. 'As long as it takes you to cut the wood, then a bit longer after that.'

I could tell the answer didn't please her, but, as West said, she was apparently learning to shut the fuck up.

'We'll assemble it in the marsh so we can just float it out.'

'How much liana will you need?' Ryder asked.

'Fifty meters ought to do it. Make sure it's green and young.'

'And when it's built?' Leila wanted to know. 'Then what?'

'We float down river to a settlement with boats for hire, or a road out,' I said. 'With a little luck, we'll reach Cyangugu by early afternoon tomorrow.' Invoking luck probably wasn't smart, but I was all out of smarts. 'Work in pairs,' I continued. 'Stay within sight of your partner and at least one other pair. Boink, you work with Rutherford.'

Rutherford walked over to Twenny's security chief and presented him with a machete.

'Everyone know what to do?' I asked.

'Leila and me, we'll take Peanut wit us,' said Twenny and gestured at his friend, who was nearby, throwing sticks into the river.

West took me aside. 'That river's not going our way. It'll take us to Kinshasa.'

'Does it matter?'

'I suppose not. Where there's a river, there are towns.'

'That's what I was thinking.'

‘Till we get the raw materials, I’m going to help Cassidy out with the defenses, and maybe rustle us up some food.’

‘Toasted ham and cheese on rye, thanks,’ I said.

‘See what we can do,’ he said, and trotted out of the cleared area and disappeared into the bush in the direction of the road.

Ayesha and Ryder walked past.

‘You feeling all right?’ I asked him.

‘Hooah,’ he said under his breath without lifting his head.

We were all running on empty.

THE CHOSEN SAPLING DIDN’T grow in stands, but it was here and there and all over. I worked on my own, scouting for the right materials, cutting the saplings and liana where and when the opportunity presented. Apart from the odd fright from spiders and small vipers, and an occasional deep cough from what Rutherford believed was a big cat somewhere in the forest, there were no incidents. All up, we managed to collect fifty-eight saplings before the light failed completely. Not ideal, but as there was no moonrise for quite a few hours, we had to go with what we had.

Cassidy and West appeared from the shadows just as the last of the saplings and liana lengths were delivered to the riverbank, Cassidy carrying in front of him what appeared to be two large basketballs.

‘Chow time,’ West called out. ‘We got avocado, palm oil fruit, watermelon, sugarcane, and grasshoppers for protein.’ He opened his pack, found a patch of ground where the steel matting was a little above the mud, and emptied the contents onto it. Cassidy also placed those basketballs of his on the matting, two almost perfectly round watermelons, and pulled his Ka-bar. He sliced one of them up and handed around the wedges. Peanut was first in line; he took a piece, buried his face in it and seemed pretty happy about what was in his mouth.

‘This stuff is all over,’ said West. ‘You want some more, we’ll go get it.’

Ayesha and Leila were next in line, followed by Twenny and Boink, the hired help bringing up the rear.

'After you,' Rutherford said to Ryder.

'Just leave me some of them grasshoppers,' I said.

'You may laugh, boss, but those little critters are awesome,' said West.

'So you keep telling us.'

'That's 'cause they are – crunchy on the outside, kinda gooey when you bite into 'em, and the taste is nutty. They're good clean food. Try one.' West picked a medium-sized insect from the mound, the head already pinched off, and presented it to me in the palm of his hand.

'Reminds me of that dumb-ass reality show, you feel me?' said Twenny.

I took the insect, put it between my teeth without thinking too hard about it and bit down. Like West said, crunchy, gooey and nutty. 'Not bad,' I said when I'd finished. 'But I like my nuts without legs.' And, in truth, the goo wasn't much of a hit, either. But if I had to eat them to stay alive . . .

The fruit disappeared quickly, so Cassidy went out to get another couple of watermelons and was back within five minutes with two more, bigger than the last. West, meanwhile, went to work on the raft, with Rutherford and Ayesha and Ryder resting nearby.

'We need the perimeter secured. What's your thinking?' I asked Cassidy through a mouthful of melon, the sugar from the fruit running through my system like a mild electric current.

'The forest's pretty thick hereabouts. There are two ways in. One's easy, one's not so easy. West and I figure the folks we're up against will take the path of least resistance. If they do, Mr Claymore will keep us informed. If it detonates, everyone should assemble at the raft on the double – I'll give the word. We planted a few other surprises out there that'll slow down any assault. I think you can afford to chill for a while, Major Cooper. You've earned it.'

I wasn't sure I'd earned anything, but it was nice of him to say. I found a spare oil drum and sat down on it, but was sitting for less than thirty seconds before I heard my name called.

'Vin.'

Enjoying the feeling of having a full belly, I blocked out the sound of my name and listened instead to the two-hundred-part acapella mosquito choir humming around my head.

'Vin . . .'

It was Leila. I braced for the latest complaint/threat/abuse.

'I warn you . . .' she said.

Here it comes, I thought, tensing.

'I've come armed with a pair of tweezers and I intend to use them.'

Tweezers? She'd brought her cosmetics bag. 'Thanks, but I think I like my eyebrows the way they are.'

She took my hand in hers and I smelled perfume, moisturizer and branded insect repellent; the combination conjured up the cosmetics counter at Macy's, Arlington, an altogether other world to the one we were in. I resisted the desire to rub mud over her – that smell was a potential beacon to any would-be attackers.

'Eyebrows? You got points of dried blood up and down your arm, like you've landed in a cactus. I know what that's like. Happened to me when I was a little girl. My mother threw me into one of those big ones you see out in the desert, on a trip to California. Stopped the car, dragged me out the door and just threw me.'

'How many times did you ask, "Are we there yet?" '

'My momma didn't need a reason to do bad things to me. Just the way she was.'

'She still around?'

'Can't get rid of her, her hand out all the time. I give her money and she drinks it all up. Giving her money is like giving her a loaded gun. Sometimes when I remember all the things she did before I got big enough to stop her, I think that's exactly what I should do – give her that loaded gun she wants so bad. She's young – only fifteen years older than I am. And beautiful – or was.'

Leila's fingertips were cool and gentle on my skin, seeing in the darkness, probing for the barbs that stuck out like pins hidden in a new shirt. I felt a little disoriented, but now that she mentioned it, my skin was throbbing at various spots all over: on my cheek, from tiny shards of glass; the small burns from the hot Claymore pellets; the torn flesh on the point of my shoulder; the nick on the back of my upper arm; and, of course, the spines along my arm that it collected when I exited the truck with the mortar. Actually, now that I stopped to think about it, I was sore all over. I closed my eyes.

'They're big suckers,' she whispered. 'I'm going to pull one out. This might hurt. If you need to cry, don't you feel embarrassed.'

'Do you have a hanky, just in case?'

She extracted a spine and I felt a small stab of pain that almost immediately began to itch. Sweetness and light from Leila? The universe was tilting.

'You like kids,' I said. That much was obvious. She had instantly been smitten with the baby rescued from the bushes behind the village, and with the child she had nursed in the truck. Dangerous ground, perhaps, if she blamed me for having to give them back.

'Yes, I love them. I'm going to have children one day. Lots of them. And I'm going to be the momma I wanted, not the one I had.' She yanked out another quill, this time with feeling. 'What are your parents like?'

'They're dead,' I said, hoping to bring that line of questioning to a stop.

'Then, what *were* they like?' Leila persisted.

'I didn't get to know them; neither lived long enough.'

'Who brought you up?'

'An uncle – my father's brother.'

'What was *he* like?'

'Okay, mostly.'

'Getting anything out of you is like pulling teeth.'

'Let's see how you do with those spines first,' I said.

'Well . . . your uncle?'

I gave in. 'He was a good parent, but three tours in 'nam had rewired his sense of normal and occasionally the craziness came to the surface.' I remembered one night in particular. I woke up to find his face three inches from mine, his eyes wide and bloodshot, sweat dripping from the tip of his nose onto my pajamas, a knife half the length of a baseball bat in his hand and, according to him, the house full of Charlie. I was ten years old.

Leila's fingers worked their way up my arm.

'We're gonna make it, aren't we,' she said after a pause.

There was no hint of a question in her tone. This was a done deal.

'Yes,' I said, mustering the necessary conviction, but the truth was that we were still some way from cracking open the champagne. With my white hat on, the raft was going to get us quickly downstream to safety. But with my black hat on, the raft was going to sink shortly after launch, just before we were sucked over a two hundred foot waterfall around the next bend in the river. I had to take some of the blame for this outbreak of certainty with my earlier pep talk about arriving back at Cyangugu in time for afternoon tea. I was as eager as anyone to get back to Rwanda, if only to wipe the smug superiority off Lockhart's face when I snapped a pair of bracelets on his wrists.

'. . . I hope you're not jealous,' she said.

'I'm sorry?' I replied. 'I missed that. What were you were saying?'

'I was saying that Deryck and I have reconciled. We're going to give it another try. I hope you're not jealous about that.' She smiled, and there was mischief in it.

I smiled back. Leila couldn't conceive of a dimension where every male of the species wasn't wrapped around her pinkie. 'I'll just have to get over it,' I said. 'Another time, another place . . .'

'And, anyway, you got your own issues with your dead girlfriend and I don't want anyone else's baggage right at the moment.'

Okay, by invoking Anna, Leila was pushing the delusion boundaries way out of shape. My arm felt hot with an itch that flared its entire length. I wanted to get up and leave, but there was nowhere to go.

'I have some antiseptic cream,' she continued. 'Probably should have washed it first, but this will have to do.'

She reached into her cosmetics bag of tricks, pulled out a tube, squeezed some of what was in it on my arm and rubbed it in. It felt like it was going on someone else's arm but I told her thanks.

'Go see a doctor at Cyangugu tomorrow. There'll be one there for sure.'

There was something totally unreal about this conversation.

Sensing this, she said, 'Are you okay, Vin?'

Fucked up, insecure, neurotic and emotional. 'I'm fine.'

'Good. I know we got off to a bad start, you and I. It has been a journey, hasn't it?'

'You still gonna to sue me?'

'Yes of course, but it's nothing personal. The military will pay.'

All of a sudden the feeling of having a full belly soured and the watermelon, palm oil fruit and grasshopper caught the freight train leaving my stomach and roared out of my mouth and onto the ground at her feet. Leila screamed, said fuck half a dozen times and danced on the spot briefly before running off into Twenny's arms. I sat on the barrel, bile burning my throat, gave them both an apologetic shrug and felt a whole lot better. Twenny Fo left his girlfriend and came on over.

'Tell me that wasn't intentional?'

'I got a few talents, but throwing up on cue ain't one of them.'

'I just thought I'd check. I know you and Leila haven't hit it off.'

Interesting choice of words. 'I think we hit it off just fine. And I think I still got the handprint on my face to prove it.'

'With Leila, you gotta learn when to duck.'

'Uh-huh,' was all I said.

'I haven't got 'round to thanking you properly for what you done. You could have left me behind, man.'

'A few things went our way.' A beetle landed on my head. I swatted it away. 'We need to have a talk about what you saw and heard in that camp.'

'Leila told me you think an American we met at the concert in Rwanda planned all this with our pilot, the short French guy. The idea from the beginning was to drop us into the jungle and hold us to ransom, right?'

'That's what it looks like. The dickfuck's name is Lockhart. He was in the camp where you were being held prisoner. I saw him murder Fournier, the French co-pilot, not five feet from where you were standing.'

'I heard the gunshot, but that's all. They put a hood over my head and beeswax went in my ears almost from the moment I was captured. I saw nothing, heard nothing, man.'

Wonderful.

'. . . But I smelled him.'

'You smelled him?'

'I have my own cologne. It's called "Guilty". Maybe you heard of it?'

Now that I thought about it, I had seen the advertising poster: two women, naked and embracing, shadows hiding the interesting bits, Twenny lying in a nearby bed, a white satin sheet strategically placed.

'How many people you think wear cologne in these parts? Anyway,' he continued, 'that's what your man wears, you feel me? Splashes on a little Guilty after trimming his man hair. I know that smell anywhere. I couldn't believe it – thought I was dreaming.'

I wasn't sure that a court would send Lockhart away for life on a little olfactory evidence, but it was *something*.

'Like I tol' you already, anything I can do to help, just ask,' he said, standing. 'You got a friend for life, you feel me?'

I thought about asking him to tell his girlfriend not to sue the Air Force on my account, but my service could take care of itself.

Trapped

It rained most of the night. Used to this by now, I scarcely noticed and shivered my way through it without too much swearing. I grabbed what sleep I could on one of West's cots, out of reach of the driver ants, under the shelter of several broad umbrella palm fronds. I liked that arrangement better than sharing a poncho, which just caused me to sweat. I took the second-to-last watch, relieving Rutherford, who had nothing to report other than that there were plenty of frogs.

I checked on the raft's progress at the start of my watch at three-thirty. The job was done and West was snoring under a poncho on the raft, which was long and narrow. Only one of the fifty-five-gallon drums had been used in its construction, up at what would have been the bow. The SS *Sapling* was ready to go, sitting in a pool of shallow brackish water among the reeds.

My watch was uneventful. When it was over, I passed it to Ryder, who said he was feeling human again, which probably had a lot to do with him feeling Ayesha. Boink had been given the night off. He'd done his fair share. Peanut snored the night away, oblivious to everything except the mosquitoes, which he slapped and waved at as much as anyone. Twenny and Leila shared a cot and covered themselves with a poncho. Twenny talked in his sleep, yelled occasionally, dreams beginning to stalk him too.

I went back to the cot and before I knew it, I was asleep, having a nightmare about eating a steak that tasted of grasshopper. But this was cut short by the distinctive and unpleasant crash of an exploding Claymore, which sounded like a thousand ball bearings hurled explosively against a glass floor. I sat up instantly.

In the moonlight, a shadow ran past that I recognized as Ryder. He stopped at Ayesha's cot. 'Get up!' he shouted.

'What's goin' on?' Twenny asked no one in particular, bewildered, half asleep.

'Get to the raft,' I hissed. 'Look after Peanut. Go now.'

I raced to Boink's cot and shook him.

'What!' he said, snapping awake.

'Get up,' I said and spun around and woke Leila.

'Don't,' she said, still asleep.

'Hey!' I kept shaking her until her eyes popped open.

Cassidy arrived and, with a hand under her armpit, roughly lifted the celebrity to her feet and then started dragging her toward the raft.

'Stop!' she yelled.

Cassidy let her go and she turned and stumbled back to snatch the makeup case hanging off one of the saplings supporting her cot.

'Leave it,' I told her, but she reached it and clutched it closer to her chest.

A moment later, we were all on the move and splashing through the reeds, sprinting toward the raft.

'Push,' West yelled when we arrived. He was trying to heave it out of the shallows and into the river single-handedly, his feet slipping in the mud.

The first gunshots from the FARDC were unaimed and inaccurate, but the bright moonlight wasn't doing us any favors. A Dong burst through the bushes into the area at the rear of the cleared land and the first RPG of the day streaked through the air, over our heads and lit up the trees on the opposite bank with an almighty clap of percussion.

West and Boink got the fuel drum at the bow of the raft into the river.

'Push!' yelled Cassidy.

Twenny, Leila, Ayesha, Ryder, Rutherford, Cassidy and I heaved and grunted and slipped around and the heavy main body of the raft began to slide over the reeds. A burst of automatic fire chewed into the bundle of saplings between Cassidy and me, sending blinding clouds of powdered wood into my eyes.

'Get on!' Cassidy and I shouted at our principals.

Searchlights on the truck suddenly blazed and lit up the reed beds and the air was alive with tracer, deadly supersonic red fireflies.

Ryder and Ayesha leaped onto the bundled saplings. I lifted Leila and threw her onto the raft after them. Twenny jumped on, followed by Boink. The tail of the raft slipped off the reeds into the deeper water and started to drift away with the current, leaving Cassidy and me behind in the reeds.

Cassidy jumped off the bank and got his hand on one of the saplings. I sprang after him, managed to grab a handful of his webbing and trailed behind him underwater. I coughed and gagged when I pulled myself above the water, but the weight of my gear dragged me under again. I felt myself hauled to the surface. I looked up and saw Rutherford, his hand clenched around my collar. Boink was pulling Cassidy onto the saplings. West came to Rutherford's aid, grabbed my hand and pulled me up onto the raft as I hacked up a cupful of river slime.

Ayesha and Ryder were poling us along, glancing behind them as they dug into the mud. I looked back toward the clearing. The beams from the FARDC searchlights were dancing around, illuminating the spot in the otherwise unbroken darkness of the riverbank, and I saw that we were already a hundred meters down river. I caught a muzzle flash from an RPG and the grenade streaked toward us. It rocketed just over our heads and into the darkness of the forest and exploded in a bright orange display a hundred and fifty meters away, the delayed boom reaching us over a second later.

'We got a problem here,' said West over his shoulder.

'Oh, really?' I said under my breath. I moved unsteadily toward him and saw that the raft had split in two. The long burst of automatic fire had torn through the liana that held the front and back of our craft together.

'There are a dozen big holes in that drum up front, too,' he said. 'It's filling fast and it's going to sink.'

The raft spun lazily around its bow where the drum was located, our makeshift vessel coming apart, turning into driftwood.

Me and my black hat.

'Everyone move to the rear section,' West yelled as he cut through the last of the liana with his Ka-bar.

All of us were now sitting on just two of the bundles of saplings, which, carrying all our weight, were barely above the level of the water. As the wood became waterlogged, the raft would sink.

'Are we gonna to be okay?' I heard Leila ask.

'We're gonna be just fine,' I heard Twenny say.

Fine. Yeah, that about summed it up.

Rutherford poled us around a couple of bends as the dawn turned into a dull morning, the sky low and heavy with rain clouds that looked like they'd gotten out of bed on the wrong side. Mist clung to the trees and hung over the water. Occasional howls and screeches from the rainforest knifed through the early morning quiet.

'We got maybe another hour before we go under,' West told me quietly.

'We go as far as we can,' I said. 'Start looking for a place to step off. Let Rutherford know. I'll tell Cassidy and Ryder to keep their eyes open.'

There was three inches of water lapping over the raft before, an hour and ten minutes later, we found another break in the heavy dark green greenery crowding the riverbank. The landing was well hidden by overhanging branches, but rows of thin poles were sunk into the mud a dozen meters into the main current, giving away its presence.

'There's going to be a village nearby,' said West, gesturing at the poles. 'They string nets to catch fish between them. And where there are nets, there are pirogues.'

I must have given him a look.

'Pirogues – boats, dugouts,' he said.

There was no sign of any village – just a solid wall of green that rose quickly to the base of a near-vertical wall of limestone around three hundred feet high, hung with ferns and vines.

Rutherford and Ryder took us over to the riverbank and we clambered onto white mud and then the raised ground behind it. All around was evidence of human activity hidden from the water: a table made from hardwood; and trash, lots of trash – old tins, plastic bags and drink containers, old lengths of rotted bamboo, tangled fishnet, plastic water bottles used as floats and watermelon rinds. A quick search of the surrounding brush didn't turn up any boats, but there were steps cut into the damp earth in the hill behind the clearing, reinforced with worn hardwood logs.

West returned to the raft. Carrying no weight, it was floating a couple of inches above the surface of the water. He pushed it off the bank and using a pole shoved it out toward the main current. He was thinking the same thing I was: Lissouba wouldn't stop. He'd come looking for us. Best not to hang out a sign that said 'look here'.

'If there *is* a village nearby, you'd think they'd come and see who just turned up on their front doorstep, wouldn't you?' Cassidy whispered to me out of our principals' earshot.

Strangers in this place seemed to want to cut things, like appendages, off folks. Perhaps they were just plain wary. Whatever the reason, Cassidy was right. This place was quiet – like they say in the classics, too quiet.

'I'm going to take Rutherford and scout around,' I said. 'What have we got left in the way of discouragement?'

'A little frag, one Claymore, lots of smoke and whatever mags we're carrying.'

In short, throwing spitballs was becoming an option. Also, the river continuing its course west rather than east, we were further away from Goma, Cyangugu and Mukatano. But, at least for now, no one was shooting at us, which made a pleasant change.

'Keep a watch on the river,' I said.

If there was one person I didn't have to remind to stay sharp, it was Cassidy, but he nodded anyway.

Rutherford glanced in my direction. I sucked some water from my camelback to get the taste of the river out of my mouth and gestured at him to come over.

'We're going to have a snoop around,' I told him. 'Find out where everyone's hiding.' Prior experience told me that I had to hold a conference and announce my intentions so that they could be approved. I went over to Leila and Twenny.

'Where are we?' Leila asked.

'As a matter of fact,' I said, 'Rutherford and I are just going to take a quick walk up the hill and ask someone that very question. We'll be back soon.'

'What do you want Leila and me to do?' Twenny asked.

I could think of a few things where Leila was concerned.

'Stay out of sight until we return.'

'We can do that, right?' Twenny said to Leila. She gave him a hesitant nod.

Good luck with that, I thought. I repeated our intentions to Boink, Ayesha and Ryder and then asked the captain if he was up to taking the watch with Cassidy. He said he was. I didn't want to disturb Peanut with details. He was making like a frog, hopping around, chasing a couple of them across the ground and into the trash heap.

'Take the scope,' said West, handing it over. 'You might be able to see something useful when you get to higher ground.'

Rutherford and I went to the steps behind the hardwood table and started climbing through thick, wet palm fronds and elephant grass. Ten minutes later we were still climbing and the earth became a chalky limestone wall. Still no sign of human life. The wall had steps cut into it, which zigzagged ever higher. After a climb of over a hundred meters, we came to the lip, and a knoll covered in a close-cropped variety of grass opened out, surrounded by scrub. The presence of a manicured area the size of a couple of basketball courts somehow made the stillness all the more eerie. Folks had to manage this patch of turf – a kind of assembly area, I figured – keep it maintained. I looked back down at the river below, our landing hidden by the tree canopy. It was possible that no one saw us arrive, but I doubted that. The river, a dark brown snake coiling through the green of the rainforest, could be seen for some distance in both directions and I was relieved to find that it was clear of boats filled with soldiers, a point I further confirmed with the scope.

I heard an animal sound – a grunt. It came from the rainforest, which began where the grass ended. An adolescent pig appeared out of the darkness beneath the canopy, at the boundary line with the grass. Its arrival was a surprise, at least to us. The pig, however, looked our way as if we were expected. It then turned and waddled back in the direction it had come from, stopped, glanced back over its shoulder and eyeballed us as if to say, 'You coming, or what?' and moved off at a canter.

'Hmm, ham,' I said. 'With luck, we'll find cheese.'

We followed the pig. The path split into quite a few tributaries that threaded the rainforest dripping with rainwater, the dense canopy snuffing out much of the ambient light. Eventually, the trail thickened up, the tributaries rejoining, and exited the forest at the edge of a large banana plantation that opened out on either side of what was now a small road. The trees were hung with drooping purple sacks pregnant with flowers. More pigs wandered among the ordered rows and our guide trotted off to join them. I counted a dozen chickens scratching at the earth here and there. Rutherford and I stuck to the road and pushed on. Next came two large fields where rows of vegetables grew, bisected by the road. I could identify immature tomatoes, but the other plants were a mystery. Pigs were here too, digging up and eating whatever was interesting them. They were like kids causing mischief while the grown-ups were out. This was obviously a well-organized village with a sizeable population doing a good job of feeding itself. But where was this sizeable population? If an armed force had come through here and taken the villagers, they'd have pilfered the animals. I was mentally basting a couple of those chickens myself. No, something else was going on around here and I didn't like whatever it was.

Rutherford nudged me in the arm and gestured ahead. A roof thatched with dry grass beckoned through a gap in the trees. We headed for it along the path, looking for people but seeing no one. A monkey of some variety sat on a low bough and ate a snack between its hands, took a few fidgeting steps in our direction, stopped, nibbled some more, squealed and scampered up into the higher boughs. The thatched roof belonged to a large single hut. I heard flies buzzing and birds calling but still no human sounds.

The hut was open, the door wide. The M4 in my arms was on safety with a full mag loaded. I put my head around the corner. There was no porridge on the table, but I went in anyway. Rows of well-used shovels, rakes and other implements were neatly stacked against one wall. It was some kind of work barn. Most of the space was given over to furniture making. Half a dozen chairs were under construction, along with a few tables and beds. Benches were equipped with various woodworking tools, all of them manually rather than electrically powered – saws, drills, chisels and so forth. Checking down the far end of the barn, we found a potter's wheel, a lump of white clay sitting on the wheel, too dry to be made into anything. On the wall behind the wheel were tiers of shelves lined with jugs, cups and bowls, all made from the white clay. There was a regular industry going on here. The village probably traded furniture and pots with other villages on the river. Interesting, but not as interesting as knowing where the hell everyone had gone off to.

Rutherford waited for me at the doorway. 'This place is creeping me out.'

'Keep an eye peeled for bears, Goldilocks,' I said.

I took a couple of steps and stopped. I'd just caught a whiff of something familiar and unpleasant. Another few paces and I became enveloped by it: the smell of blood and feces and death. It hung between the bushes as if from a rope. My palms started sweating. The road curved around behind a small stand of banana trees and I saw a couple of dark brown feet lying on the trail. Opening out the angle, I saw that they were attached to a body curled in the fetal position, turned away from me.

I signaled Rutherford that I was going in for a closer look. He nodded, rubbing the stock on his M4 like he was hoping a genie might spring forth.

The body was that of an African male somewhere in his twenties. He was wearing dark green shorts and a loose dark blue shirt. Blood had seeped from his nostrils, eyes and ear holes. His shorts were also stiff with dried black blood. The man had bled out. His palms and kneecaps were white, the color of the mud in the area, which suggested that he'd probably crawled here to die.

'Could that be Ebola?' Rutherford asked, taking several steps backward just in case. I did likewise for the same reason.

This should have been a bustling village, but the place was a ghost town and the animals were running amok. All the buildings that we could see were intact. Something like Ebola, the hemorrhagic fever found in these parts, could explain what we'd found. If it was the virus, and depending on how long ago the first villager started displaying symptoms, it might already have killed almost everyone here, burned through the place the way fire moves through dry grass. Ebola was extremely contagious and had a mortality rate that made bubonic plague look like a head cold. It was so lethal that some countries had considered using it as a weapon of mass destruction, which was why I knew a little about it. There would be a radio somewhere in the village, but wc wouldn't be able to get to it. Shit. It might as well have been on the moon.

I wondered if the guy on the ground was still hot with virus, and whether any of the flies that had landed on me when I was in the vicinity of the body had virus on its fly feet. I sneezed involuntarily.

'Christ, skipper,' said Rutherford, taking a step away from me. 'You got pretty close to that poor sod.'

'I don't think the bug works that fast.' *I hope.*

'You sure?'

'Yep.' *Nope.*

He relaxed a little and we retraced our steps ten meters or so. I scoped the village with the sight and counted four more bodies lying out in the open. One of them moved an arm. Ebola turned internal organs to rotting mush. If that's what we had here, I pitied the survivors still in that village. Depending on a range of factors, including the size of the village's population, there'd probably be several, but going in to help was way too risky. And there wasn't much we could do anyway, unless the cure involved a makeover, courtesy of Leila's little white case.

'There's gotta to be a road out,' said Rutherford.

I wasn't so sure. The village appeared to be nestled within the crook of three imposing mountain-like hills behind it. Perhaps the only way in and out was by boat. Could be those survivors I wondered about had taken the village's boats and headed downstream, which would explain why there weren't any craft pulled up on the riverbank.

We cut through the banana plantation to where the rainforest began. After two hours of battling through a virtually impassable blockade of bamboo, liana, elephant grass and a variety of difficult prickly bush with red and orange berries on it that seemed to be everywhere and left us no room to swing a machete, we admitted defeat. We tried to cut a path through on the other side of the village, but we ended up in the same place – nowhere.

'We're just going to have to wait for a boat to come along,' Rutherford said as the sun appeared overhead and the bush came alive with the sound of happy insects.

I sweated and sucked some water from the camelback as we walked up onto the grassy knoll. A vicious cramp clenched my stomach. A bout of diarrhea was coming down the pipe, thanks to all the river water I'd taken in. Rutherford brushed something off my back, an action I no longer gave any thought to. Looking down at the river, I stopped and dropped to a knee. Half a mile away, a boat, a type of ferry, was heading down the brown water, another small open boat in its wake. I took the scope and trained it on the vessels.

'Fuck,' I said under my voice. Armed soldiers were bursting from the ferry's seams, like stuffing from an old cushion. The craft under tow behind it was a lighter. Crammed onto it were maybe fifteen men bristling with RPGs. I went down on my belly. I kept the scope on the boats and willed them past our landing point as they came nearer. I imagined that Cassidy would have posted a lookout, seen the convoy before it was upon them, and had everyone squirreled away out of sight. I could make out that there was a man on the forward deck of the ferry. Jesus Christ – it was Lissouba! This bastard put the asshole in persistent, that was for damn sure. He had binoculars, which he was training on the rainforest either side of the boat, looking left and right. The boat drew abreast of our landing point. I held my breath. Foliage overhanging the river obscured the boat from view. We waited for it to reappear in the gaps between the greenery, the tension growing with every second.

'I've lost it,' said Rutherford.

'Wait,' I whispered. 'There . . .'

The boat's dirty white bow appeared in one of the gaps and its exhaust pipe chugged a perfect smoke ring into the air, which rolled out over the water. The two boats slid past the landing without altering course or engine speed. They hadn't seen us.

'Shit,' I said, turning onto my back, breathing again, closing my eyes, the powerful but rare sunshine like needles on my face. I suddenly felt exhausted. The thought of keeping my eyes closed and drifting off to sleep was incredibly seductive, but not possible. I got to my feet and gave Rutherford a hand up.

'IT'S COOPER, YO,' I heard Boink say as Rutherford and I came down the back stairs. Twenny's head of security was standing guard, a Nazarian looking like a half-size toy in his arms. Everyone stopped what they were doing and gathered round. There was no opportunity to give Cassidy, West and Ryder a separate briefing.

'We can't go that way,' I said with a lift of my head, meaning the rock wall.

'Why not?' Leila asked immediately.

'There's a village up there, but they've had a few problems. An epidemic of some kind. Almost the whole place has been wiped out.'

'We think it could be Ebola,' said Rutherford, jumping right in.

'What's that?' Twenny asked.

'It's like the worst flu you ever had,' said Ryder.

'Doesn't sound too bad.'

'It's a flu that makes yo' insides melt and run out your asshole, yo,' said Boink. Twenny, surprised and disbelieving, looked at him. 'Discovery Channel,' the big man said with a shrug.

Cassidy took half a step back from Rutherford.

'If could be any number of things,' I said. 'But it's not worth taking the risk walking through it. If it is Ebola, I'd rather take my chances with the FARDC.'

'You were up there. If it's as contagious as you say, how do you know you ain't caught it already?' asked Twenny.

'Because I didn't get near enough anyone to catch it,' I said, though I was wondering about those flies and their dirty feet. 'But best not to swap bodily fluids with me for a while.'

'So what do we do?' asked Ayesha.

'You saw the boats?' West inquired.

'It's Lissouba,' I said.

The SOCOM boys all nodded.

'We can't stay here,' I continued. 'If they come back to take a closer look, we can't defend the riverbank and we'll be trapped against the hill. We have to move up there.' I gestured with my thumb over my shoulder. 'Hold the high ground.'

'But you just said we couldn't,' Leila pointed out.

'I said we couldn't get through the village. But it's set back more than half a mile from the top of the hill. There's plenty of room to retreat.' I could tell from Cassidy and West's body language that they agreed with me, if reluctantly.

'And now for the good news: there's food up there,' Rutherford added.

'What kind of food?' asked Leila, unimpressed. 'More worms and bananas?'

'Sure, but if you'd rather, there's also roast pork with crackling,' I said. I explained about the pigs. The prospect of meat that didn't slither or crawl was as good a bribe as any, and ten minutes later Rutherford was leading the way up through the lower bush to the steps cut into the limestone face.

The climb was no easier the second time around and soon my shirt and the V at the back of my pants were black with sweat, the increasing mid-afternoon cloud cover raising the humidity to the point where the air was thick enough to swim in. All of us except Cassidy and West collapsed when we arrived at the grassy knoll on top of the ledge, and so Rutherford called a rest.

'This a good vantage point,' said Cassidy, taking in the view. 'We got the box seat up here.'

'Shit,' West muttered under his breath as both men sank into a crouch. 'Look at this . . .'

There was a problem. I opened my eyes and rolled over. Oh, fuck . . . Lissouba and his men were coming back up the river. This time there was a third boat in tow, if our raft could be called a boat. The throb from the ferry's engines died as its bow turned toward the riverbank and the craft disappeared under the canopy almost directly beneath us, the towed litter and our raft following.

'Brilliant,' said Rutherford, though I knew he meant 'fucking shit fuck'.

Evade

'We have to give ourselves up,' Leila insisted. 'We all know that. They're going to follow us until we do, right? They're not going to give up.'

'And then what?' Cassidy asked.

Twenny put his arm around Leila, the ex who was now his present. 'We can't. That ain't no option, you feel me? They're killers.'

'They held you and *you're* still alive.'

'They killers – trus' me.'

'Well, they've got theirs and we got ours,' she said, glaring at me accusingly. 'He's just killing us all slowly. Death by incompetence.'

Go right ahead, I wanted to say. Be my guest and head on back down.

She pointed at me. 'Our killer just leads us from one impossible situation to another.' She looked angrily at Cassidy, then at West and Ryder. 'Can't someone else take charge here? Is no one man enough to take responsibility? He ain't never gonna to get us home. Am I the only one who can see that?' She went to Boink. 'What about choo, Phillip?'

Phil found something interesting to stare at on the ground.

'Duke? Got nothing to say?'

Ryder moved toward her to put a hand on her shoulder. 'Leila, I think you should calm dow—'

Realizing that no one was going to join the mutiny, she parried his arm, turned away, sank to her knees and sobbed, beaten. Or acting, I couldn't tell which. Twenny and Ayesha, like air filling a vacuum, rushed in to comfort her.

I turned away and tried to think the situation through. There was no dealing with Lissouba and his partner, Beau Lockhart – not now. We'd come too far and seen too much. Lockhart would have to believe I had enough evidence, even if it were just eyewitness accounts, to build a case against him. The fact that I didn't; well, he wouldn't know that, would he? He'd consider that his interests were best served if we never made it back. All of which meant that if we were captured, then, no question about it, we'd all end up in the FARDC's downsizing program administered by machetes.

'Forget that crap, boss,' said West. 'You got my vote.'

'Who said it was a democracy,' I answered.

'The enemy force is between thirty and forty,' Cassidy said, the sideshow over. The pressing business of what the hell we were going to do had to be dealt with and the PSOs, me included, were feeling the weight of it.

'They picked up our raft downstream and this is probably the closest hamlet to where they found it,' I surmised. 'They'll go over the area down there with a fine tooth comb.'

'We cleaned up our landing pretty good, but you can bet your ass there'll be a boot print in the mud that we missed, or something like that,' said Cassidy. 'We all bagged our shit but our principals weren't so diligent. They'll know we're up here.'

'We've given them a good mauling already. They'll be cautious,' said West. 'They'll send out a recon patrol first and get the lay of the land. They'll find the village and come to the same conclusion you did about the risks, sir. They'll figure they've got us bottled up.'

There was a murmur of general agreement.

The time was approaching four pm. We had an hour and a half of useful light left; less, if the cloud build-up continued.

'That recon patrol should never get to make its report,' Rutherford suggested.

He was right. It didn't help us any for Lissouba to know that we couldn't retreat. We had to fight our way out. 'I've got two mags left, and only one of them is full,' I said. 'What's everyone else got?'

Only Ryder had two full mags. Like me, the rest of us were down to the dregs: Rutherford had just two rounds; West one full mag; Cassidy half a mag. We also had that one frag grenade, one Claymore and twelve smoke canisters. Assuming one bullet, one kill, we had enough ammunition to get the job done, but we were kidding ourselves if we thought we could pull that off. These guys would come at us hard and they knew how to fight. We'd taken them on several occasions already, but we'd had the advantage of surprise, along with a hell of a lot of anti-personnel iron to throw around. Those days were now well and truly over. Rutherford chewed something off the inside of his cheek.

'So how're we going to pull this off?' I asked. 'Any thoughts?'

'Use the night,' Cassidy said.

WEST AND I KEPT watch, hunkered down in a patch of the elephant grass bordering the grassy knoll. There was only one way up that we knew of, and that was via the steps cut into the limestone wall. First port of call for Lissouba's scouts would be this relatively open ground, same as it was for Rutherford and me when we first arrived. Meanwhile, the rest of our band was heading to the thick rainforest bordering the plantation, where there was also plenty of bamboo for Cassidy's purposes. Leila, I knew, would take one look at the berry-laden thorn bush coiled up there like razor wire that we wanted her and our other principals to hide in and refuse to take another step. But that was Rutherford's problem, or Cassidy's, or Ryder's, or maybe even Twenny's, if the guy were prepared to step up. I was happy to leave them to it. Hanging out in the long wet grass with insects, snakes and frogs, waiting for Lissouba and his killers, was a far more appealing option.

It had been dusk for a while when West, whose angle on things encompassed a view of the limestone wall and was thus better than mine, raised a finger to inform me that the recon party had arrived.

A dozen seconds later he displayed two fingers – two scouts. The first guy, skinny and crouched over almost double, came into my view; he was carrying an M16 but not a lot else. Traveling light. His slightly taller, but equally flyweight, buddy walked into my line of sight a few moments later. Though obviously on edge, given the way they gripped their guns – tightly, like they were handrails in a fast-moving train – both men moved well, their heads achieving an owl-like range of movement. They spent some minutes surveying the knoll, though they avoided coming into the elephant grass. Satisfied that the area was clear of threat, they found the trail into the rainforest and slunk into the darkness collected under the canopy. I shifted an arm, getting ready to stand, and West urgently held up a finger, followed thirty seconds later by a second. Two more men had arrived, uniformed twins of the first pair, and crouched in the middle of the knoll for several minutes before skulking off on the double along the path that led to the village of the damned.

We had no choice but to stay put and wait, just in case a third pair of scouts might pop up. This is, in fact, what happened, but with a variation. This time it was one guy on his own and he didn't waste time checking out the knoll, probably figuring that the scouts preceding him had done it, but immediately made a beeline for the rainforest. Jesus, crafty bastards. The first pair of scouts was a decoy for the second pair, and all were decoys for Tailend Charlie here. This was a bad situation. The more recent arrivals meant that we would lose touch with the first pair of scouts, and the second pair would likewise get a good head start.

There was sudden movement beside me – West. He jumped up and threw his Ka-bar at Tailend. The blade shimmered through the twilight like a steel bird, impaled the guy's left arm against his chest with a solid thud before he had time to react. West followed the knife, running at the man and hitting him with a flying tackle a split second later, taking him to ground. I ran at a crouch toward them from the elephant grass, grabbed the scout's shirt collar and helped West drag him to the opposite side of the knoll and into the bush. West dropped the mag from the man's rifle and stuffed it into his webbing.

'And then there were four,' he whispered, feeling for a pulse in the African's neck and not finding one. He extracted his knife and wiped the blade on the man's shirt. We wasted no time and ran to the section of rainforest that separated the knoll from the banana trees, where the other scouts had gone. We caught up with the second pair by the time they were a third of the way through the forest. The light was fading fast, like it does at the movies before the picture starts. The trees were alive with small monkeys, and the noise they made masked the fact that West and I were moving at a trot to get ahead of the second FARDC recon party.

We took a position either side of a bend in the path as it bisected a thicket of umbrella palms, and waited. The two Congolese crept by, so close I could see the sweat glistening on their skin and smell their body odor, a powerful unwashed smell that was sour and distinctly human, spiced with stale smoke from cheap tobacco. The men were moving slow, not talking, making a judgment call on each step, carefully placing their boots on the ground, expecting something was going to happen. They were right. One of the men was shaking, either from fever or nerves, I couldn't tell. Maybe he was clairvoyant and could see his life coming to an end within the next few seconds.

And suddenly something moved in the bush close to where West was crouched and the men began firing into the shadows wrapped around the sergeant's position. Their rifles spat death in the darkness, the Africans shouting over the rapid sound of their own gunfire cracking away on full auto. They sprayed away till their chambers came up empty. And then a pig broke cover and squealed in agony and fright as it ran down the path on its two front legs, its back bloody and broken, dragging its limp body behind. West leaped from a different set of shadows and jumped on the first shooter, taking him down like he was prey. My target stood his ground but shook like he'd spent the night in the freezer. I rushed him and kicked his legs out from under him so that he fell heavily onto his back, where he lay still with his eyes closed but mouth open.

'Yours is still breathing,' said West panting, standing over the African at his feet. The man's neck had an odd kink in it.

I checked the pulse on my guy. He had one. I felt the back of his head. His hair was soaked with sweat and gritty with dirt and leaves, but there was no blood, no broken skin, no depression in the back of his skull. He'd hit his head on a gnarled tree root growing up through the compacted mud. 'Out cold,' I concluded. I checked him for ammo. Again, just the one mag. I knew what West would want me to do with him. 'He's going to be out for a while. We can do everything we need to do before he comes back.'

'You the man, sir.'

I could tell he didn't agree with the man's decision.

We dragged both men off the path deep into the rainforest and covered them with palm leaves.

'Look,' said West, holding a bag made from recycled plastic sheeting tied around the African's neck with a shoelace.

Mine had one too, though his was made of cotton cloth tied with sinew.

'Superstitious bastards,' West observed.

'Yeah,' I said, sucking in air, the adrenalin only just starting to ebb away.

'Two to go.'

'Where'd the pig come from?' I asked.

'Dunno. It was just there – turned up out of nowhere. I moved my foot and gave it a scare. Our shooters here were jumpy as hell.'

West was damn lucky and we both knew it. The broken back could just as easily have been his.

A familiar low whistle came from the direction of the path.

'You expecting company?' I asked West.

'Nope.'

I looked hard but couldn't see anyone. Then a familiar shape bobbed up and signaled, 'on me.' I couldn't see a face in the dark but knew it was Cassidy. West and I, staying low and quiet, made our way over to him.

'How many you accounted for?' Cassidy asked, keeping his voice low.

'Three,' West replied.

'I found two in the banana trees.'

'Where are they now?' I whispered.

'Meeting their maker, whoever that is around here.'

'Then that's everyone accounted for,' said West.

'Five scouts?'

I nodded. 'This Lissouba guy has been around. He staggered them. We didn't expect to see you.'

'The forest is the place to ambush the main force, where the trail splits. We hit them, fall back, hit them again. We can't let them advance to the plantation. Once they reach those trees and the more open ground, with their numbers they'll spread out and flank us. Boss, how much time we got, you reckon?'

'It took us three hours to recon the area, travel time included,' I said.

'Then let's give them the same amount of time,' said Cassidy. 'We can do a lot in three hours, especially with the stuff you told us about in the barn.'

'Getting nervous doesn't mean they'll come out and fight,' observed West. 'Going on past experience, they seem to wait till dawn before they work up to it.'

'I hope you're wrong,' said Cassidy, ''cause if you're right, we might as well show those motherfuckers our jug'lars. We can only handle their numbers on our terms.'

That gave me a thought. 'Come and get me two hours and forty-five minutes from now – I don't want to be walking into any of your handiwork.'

'Where you headed?' West asked me.

'Back to the knoll.'

'Mind telling me what you're going to do?' Cassidy asked, checking his watch.

'Poke Lissouba in the eye,' I said. 'See if I can't provoke a reaction.'

EXACTLY TWO HOURS AND forty-four minutes later – three hours after the first of the scouts appeared – I was looking over the edge of the wall toward the riverbank below. All was quiet, except for my constant companions, the mosquitoes. There were fires down there. A temporary shift in the air brought the smells of cooking up to my swollen nose and saliva filled my mouth the way seawater floods a torpedo tube. I spat onto the ground. I had company with me on the ledge: namely, the last scout Lissouba had sent up, the man West had killed with a knife throw. I had him standing on the edge of the limestone wall, balanced on a single leg. Rigor mortis had set in. I had him on one leg because its partner was bent out at an odd angle and locked in place by the rigor.

I took another look over the edge. A shift in the air took away the cooking smells and replaced them with the aroma of Tailend beside me. I switched to breathing through my mouth. The guy stank. Not his fault – death doesn't wash – and at least the smell made him easy to find in the almost complete darkness. Once I found him, I brushed the ants off him, dragged him from the elephant grass to this spot and hoisted him to his feet. Correction, foot. The corpse's arms were locked straight out some distance from the side of his torso. Come to think of it, given his body position, there was a pretty fair swan dive coming up. With a bit of luck, the body would land on someone important, maybe even Lissouba himself, and then the heart would go out of the Africans and everyone would just go on home. Wishful thinking.

'Sorry for what I'm about to do, pal,' I whispered. 'But thanks for helping us out.'

I gave the corpse a shove in the back and over the edge he went, disappearing quickly into the void below. A moment later I heard Cassidy's familiar dry whistle. He came and stood beside me and looked down.

'That your poke in the eye?' he asked. 'Doing something like that – I wouldn't have thought a guy like you would have it in you.'

'What's a guy like me?'

'The righteous kind.'

Technically speaking, what I'd just done – desecrating the dead – would have had consequences if witnessed by unsympathetic eyes. The book said it was okay to maim and kill, but once dead, we were expected to leave the corpse in peace and not disturb the flies. But the Congo was like an acid bath that burned through civility. The only rule that seemed to count here was kill or be killed, the original law of the jungle.

'Don't worry me none, Cooper.' Cassidy sucked something from between his teeth. 'When in Rome, right?'

'They do this kind of thing there too?'

I heard him grunt.

'Where are our principals?' I asked.

'Where you left them. Nice and cozy, surrounded by bamboo, thorn bush and elephant grass. Boink has overwatch and we've armed Twenny for backup to release our guys.'

That meant we had a strike force of five: Cassidy, Rutherford, West, Ryder and me. The thick night air suddenly came alive with shouts and cries carried up to us from the darkness below. Gunshots barked among them. The rainfall was heavy in these parts, but a body coming down through the trees was just a touch heavier than usual. The folks below were mad. We needed them mad enough to make a very bad mistake.

'We ready?' I asked Cassidy.

'I'll let you know in the morning, if we're still alive.'

Not the confident reply I'd hoped for, but we had little choice other than to force a showdown. Lissouba's men could bottle us up, wear us down and sooner or later overwhelm us. Right now, we were as strong as we were going to be. We held the high ground, and we'd also reconnoitered it reasonably thoroughly. We didn't have numbers but, for a short period of time, we held all the other cards worth holding. The only exit strategy left to us was to maul Lissouba so bad that leaving us alone was his best option. I again mentally went through the odds as we jogged back to the rainforest. Five against fifty, give or take. Only a lunatic would bet on us.

WHEN THEY CAME WITHIN throwing distance, Lissouba's men tossed grenades up and over the wall and onto the knoll, presumably to clear it. But there was nothing to clear, except maybe a path through the mosquitoes. The knoll was some way from our positions, lying in the mud, curled around tree roots in the rainforest, but we heard the explosions as dull thuds that punctured the night. And we waited.

Maybe it was the lack of resistance that emboldened them, but their first charge through the rainforest was all war cries and wild-ass shooting from the hip. A force of around twenty men swept along the trails, yelling and hooting across a front fifteen to twenty meters wide, straight through the area where Cassidy and West had hung clay pots in the trees over the trails. These pots had around three quarters of a pound of C4 and 350 steel balls distributed between them – about half the business end of our remaining Claymore – and were positioned to provide a short, violent interlocking field of fire. Detonators from the smoke grenades rigged to liana trip wires set them off. They exploded above the FARDC's heads almost in unison and the hail of steel that beat down on them wounded more than half their number; a couple of them fatally, as far as I could see, from the way they fell.

Five men made it through and kept coming. I shot one, Rutherford got the other and I figured a third passed a little too close to Cassidy for his own good. Far over on my left, the remaining two tripped one of Cassidy's surprises, a sapling onto which had been lashed some stools taken from the village workshop, their legs sharpened to points. The trap was positioned so that the sapling would swing through an arc of around ten feet and catch the unwary in the chest.

The Congolese were unwary.

The survivors from Cassidy's hotpots retreated, dragging off their dead, but leaving behind the two men impaled on the stools. I crept left toward them, around and behind Cassidy, moving fast and, to avoid friendly fire, giving a cautionary whistle as I went. When I got close enough, I could see that one of the men was moving, his chin on his chest, three legs of a stool buried in his ribcage. His head moved languidly around in a circle. He hummed as if he had a gut ache and doing this somehow took away some of the pain. He died before he could get to the chorus. A grenade hung from his webbing. Both men had a spare mag tucked into the tops of their trousers. Their rifles were nowhere to be seen. I quickly hunted around for them but couldn't find them. I figured they'd probably dropped them when the forest came to life and took theirs.

I fell back fifty meters, as we planned to do after the first attack. Rutherford, Cassidy, West and Ryder had already done so. I found Cassidy and handed over one of the spare mags. Neither of us said a word. I headed for a hole in our line that I thought needed to be plugged and took up a position against an old hardwood whose roots came down from above. I could see Rutherford, but only because I knew where to look. I couldn't see Cassidy even though I knew where he was. I crept across to Rutherford, gave him the captured mag and then returned to my tree.

An hour and a half passed. I urinated where I stood. The liquid running down my leg was warm and comforting but then the cold quickly seeped in to take its place in my bladder and I began to shiver. It started to rain at around the same time, making a noise that sounded like a stampede of small animals as the squall line passed over the canopy. We'd been in this part of the world long enough now to know that sound would be used as cover.

Frag grenades suddenly detonated in and around our previous positions, the noise of the explosions booming around us, close and personal this time. I could hear fragmented metal tinkling like wind chimes in a hurricane as the metal storm lanced through the foliage, became embedded in tree trunks or fell steaming onto the soaked ground. The attacking force gave its whereabouts away moments later, charging along the forest trails once more, certain that we were half dead, or worse, shooting randomly, throwing ammunition around like rice at a wedding. Tracer, supersonic pencil lengths of red light, lanced through the trees all round us, but it was mostly high and all of it was wild. I guessed that the enemy was less than thirty feet from Ryder and West before they returned fire. The Congolese's cries turned into screams, but still they kept coming. The shooting became point blank, desperate and anonymous, a rush of death in the darkness. And then silence. It hung between the trees, heavy and dark like blood-soaked cloth pegged out by the Reaper.

I looked toward the epicenter of the fight, over in Rutherford and Ryder's direction, but couldn't see anything, my night vision wrecked by the bright flashes of exploding ordnance. I turned back to scan the bush in front of me, just as the machete swung at my head out of nowhere. I lifted the M4, an instinctive reaction. The blade sparked as it glanced off the barrel and buried itself in the trunk of the hardwood. The man holding it wasted a precious second trying to work it free, during which time I swung the M4's butt in an arc that caught the bottom of his chin. I heard his teeth splintering, a sound that reminded me of crunching ice. The force of the blow pushed his head up. He staggered back and I shot him through the hip, which was like hitting him with a five-pound sledgehammer. It blew him clean off his feet and landed him on his back. It was only when he fell that I saw that there was a boy accompanying him, and that he was close. The kid, shaking violently, was also pointing a large black rifle at me. The rifle discharged but the slug missed. The boy fidgeted with the selector mechanism, going for full auto I guessed, moving back and looking at the mechanism while he did so. I darted forward while he was preoccupied and kicked the gun out of his hands. He stood there, a small black shadow, slightly pigeon-toed, looking like any moment he was going to start bawling. I went to grab him but he shouted something, dropped to the ground and was gone, snatched by the shadows.

A short, sharp rustle in the bush to my left informed me that Cassidy had had his own visitors, but I couldn't go to his aid without leaving a hole the enemy might penetrate and get in behind us. I had to leave him to it. Two gunshots and the situation there was resolved. Cassidy whistled a low note to let me know that it was resolved in his favor. I answered with a whistle. Time to fall back again.

We withdrew our line a hundred meters or so, mixing up the distance of each withdrawal as planned. When we were set, Rutherford whistled and approached.

'Any more mags, Cooper?' he asked, waving at his own personal cloud of bloodsuckers. 'Duke and Mike are almost dry.'

'No,' I said. I did a mental count. 'I got two rounds left in my Sig – nine, maybe ten in the M4.'

I popped the carbine's mag and racked out the rounds with my thumb, counting ten as the spring released them into the palm of my hand. Ten rounds – better than nothing, but only by ten. I handed over six and fed four back into the slot. I also had the grenade the enemy had donated to our cause, which I kept. Rutherford said thanks and disappeared.

How many more people was Lissouba intending to sacrifice? How many men and boys did he have left at his disposal? He'd tried the full frontal assault and then the decoy run. What next? My PSOs and I all sat in the darkness, listening to the night, and faced our own terrors. Mine was that, no matter how hard I tried, I couldn't remember Anna's face. But, for some reason, I had no trouble remembering the hole in her chest and the way her heart rolled around beneath her shattered ribs, the way a fish founders when it's dumped on the pier with a hook in its mouth. Maybe this faceless dying person without an identity was my subconscious providing me with a representation of everyone I'd been close to in recent times, almost all of whom were dead. Maybe Leila's comment about me being a killer was right on the money. I kept sticking my hand in the fire until someone tried to pull it out and it always seemed to be that someone else who got burned instead of me. Like Anna.

'Mr Cooper, are you there?' called a voice through the night.

I snapped out of it. The accent was thick, with African and French overtones, 'Cooper' pronounced 'Coopah'.

'Mr Cooper. I am Colonel Lissouba. We can work something out, you and I, yes? We can make a deal.'

Colonel Lissouba. How about that? I was disinclined to give away my position by opening my mouth. And, of course, any deal from this shitbird wouldn't be worth the blood it was written in. Folks would die – my folks.

'You and I need to talk, Mr Cooper. You do not like to fight my boys, I know this, but the boys are all I have left. You will be killing children. Are you a child killer?'

There was a sudden burst of automatic fire and the screams of two men dying, way out past Cassidy on our far flank. The sergeant signaled that he would go check and that I should cover his position, which was reasonably close to mine. He also put his finger against his lips to let me know that talking wouldn't be smart. He didn't need to remind me.

'You try my patience, Mr Cooper,' Lissouba called out, angered when he realized that more of his people had just died anonymously, hung up on another of Cassidy's tricks. They were the screams of men, not boys, but the fact that they'd at least made it past puberty didn't make me feel any better. All of us had had more than enough of killing. I heard a choking, gurgling noise on the night air – Cassidy making sure of death with his Ka-bar.

'You must have very little ammunition left,' Lissouba continued after a lengthy pause. 'When was the last time you ate real food? You have civilians with you. They need to be cared for. Come out now. End this.'

I returned the offer with a loud silence.

'I know that you cannot retreat. I have heard on the radio that there is the blood fever in the village. Your only way out is to negotiate with me. I have food. I can get you back to your friends across the border. I would like to help you.'

No doubt about it, this sorry puke could play the game.

The luminescent hands on my watch told me that it was around an hour before sunrise. I couldn't make up my mind whether the night had flown past or crept by. My stomach was cramping, I ached in every joint and muscle, and the skin on several parts of my body was rasped away by the mud and the grit embedded in the fabric of my clothes. Keeping my eyes open required force of will. Even allowing myself to blink slowly wasn't worth the risk – the urge to leave them shut was almost overwhelming.

'You must come out and talk. If you make me come and get you, you will all die.'

So much for Mr Helpful.

'I will give you one hour to discuss this with your people, enough time to agree that this is your only option, but not enough time to set more traps for us. One hour.'

We had a truce till dawn, but then Lissouba's troops would be more able to avoid the booby traps with a little light on the situation. I waited for the colonel to continue but he'd stopped yapping. The rain continued its rant, however, coming down heavy and unrelenting, the drops from the canopy overhead obese, Boink-sized. I ran my left hand, still sheathed in the remains of a shooter's glove, down my face and dragged anthill grit over my skin. The rainforest around me appeared as a series of black shadows edged with silver lines and the air smelled heavy and loamy, with a hint of rotting leaves and gunpowder.

I looked between the lines of Lissouba's offer. He wouldn't be trying to make a deal unless he, too, was down to his last reserves. Most probably he had one final charge left in his people. We, on the other hand, had less than the resources required to stop it. But whichever way it went, we were going to be killing young boys, kids who'd been press-ganged into fighting, abducted from their villages. These kids, however, could shoot and the reality was that their bullets killed and maimed just as effectively as the rounds fired by grownups. Jesus, this was even more fucked up than usual. I heard a soft whistle and, a moment later, Cassidy materialized out of the shadows beside me.

'What you got left, boss?' he asked, nodding at my M4.

'Four rounds, one grenade and real bad breath.'

A row of his small teeth flashed in the darkness. 'Yeah, where's a mint when you need one? I got five rounds. And there's half a Claymore deployed in our rear, out on the left flank where the rainforest thins out a little. What about West and the others? What stores they got?'

'A few rounds apiece.'

Neither of us said anything for a few seconds. We both had the same question and answer running through our minds.

'We can't surrender,' said Cassidy. 'We know what they're gonna do.'

I nodded. We did.

'We could pull back through the village,' he suggested. 'They won't go through there.'

'We could, but we won't,' I said. 'You don't want Ebola – trust me.' It had been almost twelve hours since my brief exposure to the flies that might also have buzzed around the body Rutherford and I found in the village, and I still had no cold or flu symptoms. I had no control over my bowels though, which, when I thought about it, was probably every bit as unpleasant for anyone walking behind me as it was for me. Worse, maybe.

'We got no choice then, have we?' Cassidy dropped the mag from his M4 and checked its load. 'Yeah, five rounds.' He gazed up at the canopy. When his eyes came back down from the unbroken blackness, they were glistening. I noticed that around his neck hung a ju-ju bag of the type worn by nearly all of the Congolese we'd come across. 'Jesus, Major. I don't know . . . They're just fucking kids, goddamn it,' he said. 'We got seven smoke canisters left. Maybe we could pop them, cause a diversion. We could slip through their line while it's still dark, steal their boat.'

'With our principals?' I reminded him. Something like that might have been an option if it had just been us – the PSOs – on our own, but I couldn't see Leila and her makeup case pulling it off . . . 'But maybe . . . maybe we can bluff our way out,' I said. And that was quite an interesting thing to say, especially as I had absolutely no idea what I meant by it. Bluff our way out? The statement had come from the part of my brain that was gathering threads, tying and retying them in different ways till it came up with an answer, only I couldn't see it, not consciously. The threads seemed to be these: smoke canisters, ju-ju bag, Leila's makeup case, kids. *Bluff our way out?* Then it suddenly crystallized into an image. And, damn, it was one helluva long shot.

Cassidy scratched a sore on his scalp. 'What sort of bluff?'

'We need to get West and the others and go ask Leila a question.'

'And what are we gonna ask her?'

'Whether we can borrow her lipstick.'

Escape

The hour flew like minutes. Five forty-five am, but still not a glimmer of the morning light that was due to sneak up behind the mountains sitting black on black against the Congo sky. The heavy cloud saw to that. The rain had turned to drizzle, light and annoying like the insects, and I shivered with cold as I walked slowly through the banana trees toward the rainforest and the last of Lissouba's force. The mud in my clothing was removing whole swathes of skin from my thighs, crotch and under my arms, darkening those areas with my blood.

We came line-abreast through the last row of banana trees, out into the clear, ten meters between each of us. Cassidy was to my left, Ryder on my right, Rutherford and West out on the right flank. We knew we could be walking toward our deaths. I spat on the ground. Bring it fucking on. I was tired of this shit. So fucking tired. We all were. Time to roll the dice and put an end to it now, one way or another. My own anger surprised me. Two weeks ago in Afghanistan, I'd have cared about my own death about as much as I cared about slapping the life out of a mosquito. Something had moved on. Maybe it was just time. Perhaps if I ever managed to get comfortable again, I would go back to flipping off the Reaper.

Leila had been cooperative – more than I'd expected her to be. She'd not only given us everything we needed, but actually *helped*, rolling up her raggedy designer sleeves and taking direction from Ayesha. I finally put my finger on it. It wasn't enough for Leila to be wanted – she had that from millions of fans and a legion of staff, business managers, attorneys and accountants. What she required was to feel *needed*. So, Leila had personal worth issues. I shouldn't have been surprised. Maybe if I'd handled her differently – treated her as a person rather than as an object to protect – we'd have gotten on better. Or maybe not.

I glanced over my shoulder again to check the dawn. It had arrived, three minutes behind schedule, or maybe it was my Seiko that was behind the times. Cassidy had four smoke canisters and I had three. There was no breeze to speak of, but if the air was moving at all, it was coming from behind our left shoulders and drifting to the right. As the night slipped into its morning grays, around fifty meters from the edge of the plantation, I gave the signal to halt. I hoped this dumb-ass idea worked. If not, we were dead.

The stillness of the morning was breached by a high-pitched war cry coming from within the rainforest's throat, a black open hole wrapped around the access road in the tangle of liana, palms and hardwoods directly ahead that as yet remained untouched by the dawn. I gave Cassidy the agreed signal. He cracked the first of the smoke canisters and tossed it half a dozen meters to his left, and pitched another one twenty meters further out in the same direction as the first. The cans hissed and green smoke poured out of them. I broke the seal on one of mine and dropped it behind me. Orange smoke swept between my legs, merged with the green and began to form a wall that climbed and spread out across our line. I popped the other cans and scattered them behind us. Cassidy did the same and then gave the signal to advance. We walked forward into the smoke, taking long strides, our rifles brandished one-handed and held high over our heads.

A scream of many voices rose from the rainforest ahead, a scream of boys – some high and squeaky, some breaking with adolescence. They were beginning their charge. It stopped at the edge of the rainforest and so did the noise, suddenly and eerily, echoes bouncing around the hills. And then the shooting started. Red tracer rounds whizzed around and above me, the air alive with them. I couldn't see Cassidy and the others, but I guessed they were getting the same deal. The opposing force was firing blind into the smoke, unsure of what to make of it. I felt a round pass close to my wrist, dragging the smoke behind it. I kept walking. And then the swirling green and orange wall was behind me and I was striding toward the rainforest and the line of children armed with assault weapons, out in the open ground with no cover, through the light drizzle.

I glanced to my right and saw that Ryder, Rutherford and West had come through the smoke, their rifles held high. On my left, Cassidy waved his M4 and made a sound that was almost a snarl. I saw three boys charging toward me, firing from the hip, and when they saw me, they came to a sudden stop. Fear swept across their faces like a Congo storm front. I heard the words '*Les fantômes! Les fantômes!*' They threw their guns down into the mud and ran back into the rainforest, a scream coming from their throats that was different from the one they charged forward with – terror in it. I saw movement out in front of West – four boys who wouldn't have been more than ten or eleven, young even by the standards here – fleeing back into the trees, their hands up in the air, all desire to fight replaced by a panic to get away from the white zombie soldiers with heads that looked like living skulls, striding toward them out of their worst nightmare, coming to take them to hell.

'The horror,' I murmured.

The soft patter of rain was the only sound they left behind.

'Shit, skipper,' Rutherford called out, 'you're a fucking miracle worker, you are.'

West and Ryder began hooting.

There was a tingle between my shoulder blades that ran up to my mud-caked scalp and down the back of my legs. Had we really pulled this off?

'Cooper!'

I knew that voice, and it wasn't friendly. *Coopah.* It was Lissouba. I saw him, eighty meters or so away, over on our far left. Something was struggling in his grasp. It was one of his boy soldiers, the kid running in midair like a cartoon character, his feet off the ground.

'You think you have won with this trick of yours, but you have not. I will regather my men and assure them that they have more to fear from me than from men painted to look like devil soldiers.'

He then raised his free hand, shot the boy in the head with a handgun, killing him instantly, and threw the body to the ground.

'No!' Cassidy yelled.

'I will be back for you soon and you will all die!'

He turned, took two and a half steps into the rainforest and an explosion tore him into sausage filling.

A Claymore will do that – even half of one.

CASSIDY AND I SCOUTED the trail and surrounding areas to the grassy knoll while Rutherford, Ryder and West went back to the razor wire to give our principals the news, and bring them forward to meet us.

The sergeant and I found nearly a dozen rifles, a mixture of Nazarians, Kalashnikovs and 'scrubbed' M16s. We took their bolts, without which they were useless. We also took the mags that had any ammunition compatible with our M4s. We saw no one along the way. At least, no one with a pulse. We found no dead child soldiers, aside from the boy Lissouba had murdered in front of us. We buried the kid, with a toy monkey made from clay that Leila found in the village workshop. Dreams with dead kids joining the scorpions I could do without. Lissouba must have been holding his kindergarten back for some reason that we'll never know. Cassidy said not a single word the entire time we were scouting and I just knew that the image of Lissouba blowing the boy's brains out was on his mind. It was on mine. We came across the pig that had lost the use of its legs. It had bled to death, and was giving its ham to the flies and maggots, one tiny piece at a time.

When we got to the knoll, we found evidence of a hasty evacuation –

lots of discarded army greens, rifles and so forth. Maybe the boys had got word that their guardian was gone for good and that they could now go and do whatever. I hoped that meant they were heading back to their villages. We didn't need to climb down the wall and scout the landing to know that the boat would be gone.

It wasn't long before our principals arrived in company with the PSOs. Cassidy and I stood up for the reunion. Leila, Ayesha and Peanut ran forward and I soon found myself in a group hug with them, all crying. I wondered why Peanut was all tears. Did he know what had been going on? Maybe he was just channeling the vibe.

'Vin, I . . .' Leila stuttered, 'I want to say sorry for everything.'

'But let me guess – you can't,' I said.

She glared at me in that ferocious way of hers, then let it go.

'Can't you ever be serious?'

'You wouldn't like me nearly as much.'

'Thank you, Vin. I mean that. I . . . I . . .'

I wondered what it was that she couldn't get out. I've been a pain in the ass? I'd settle for that.

Ayesha and Peanut stayed for a one on one.

'I'll never forget this, Vin. Never,' Ayesha said. 'You and your men – thank you.' She kissed me on the cheek and then moved on to Cassidy. I figured West, Rutherford and Ryder had already received a little sugar from our principals.

'You did it, ghost man . . . you motherfucking did it!' said Twenny, slapping my wounded shoulder. 'You need anything, you feel me, *anything . . .!*'

'I had help,' I reminded him.

Boink pointed at me and said, simply, 'Yo.'

It was great that we were suddenly just one big happy family, but there was still one minor problem to contend with – namely, how the hell were we going to get out of here? I was setting up the watch, considering the wisdom of a signal fire or building another raft, when Ayesha, looking skywards, said, 'You hear that?'

'Hear what?' I asked her.

I caught it a couple of seconds later – a chopper. The sound of its main rotor blades grew louder, thudding up and down the river valley.

'There,' said Ayesha, pointing.

It was no bigger than a bottle fly when it flew out of the distant low cloud at about five hundred feet, following the river bends, but it grew quickly in size and was headed our way. We hurriedly led our principals back into the rainforest. We had no idea whose chopper this was, but experience told us that it was likely to be someone unfriendly. And all I wanted to do was go to sleep. Hiding in the rainforest, we loaded fresh mags into our rifles. And, of course, I still had a grenade.

The chopper settled onto our knoll, nose toward the rainforest. It was a civilian job, a Bell Jet Ranger. The doors opened and three men and one woman jumped out, all wearing navy rain jackets and US Army BDU pants, the older-style jungle-pattern battle dress uniform. A couple of the guys were older, in their fifties, and chubby. The woman was somewhere in her forties, with a butt that reminded me of a couple of hot air balloons bumped together, and scraps of red hair escaping from beneath a navy ball cap with the initials CDC embroidered on its peak. She was the boss, pointing at this and that, setting the pace. There was nothing in the least military about any of them, aside from their jackets and pants. The two men got their act together and pulled a brown plastic trunk with the initials CDC stenciled in black on its side from the aircraft. The pilot kept the motors running – he wasn't going to hang around. I went to stand up, but Cassidy held my arm.

'It's okay,' I told him. 'Take a look at those buns. They gotta be American.'

I grabbed a nearby palm frond spotted with water droplets and used it to rub the mud off my shoulder and reveal the Stars and Stripes. Looking at Cassidy, West, Ryder and Rutherford covered in white mud from head to toe, their eye sockets blacked out and vertical red stripes of Chanel Rouge Allure lipstick drawn down across their mouths, it was clear that we were going to make an interesting first impression. Maybe if they saw the flag they wouldn't instantly jump into their chopper and fly away. I moved across to Leila to have a word with her.

'I need you,' I said, appealing to her inner demons.

'You do?' she answered.

'I need you to come with me and talk to these people. You're the only person among us who looks halfway presentable. Can you do that?'

'Yes, I can do that.'

'If anything goes off the rails, I've got you covered.'

'Okay. I trust you,' she said.

It's about time, I nearly replied.

'When I give the signal, bring everyone up,' I told Cassidy.

I stood and moved to the trail, breaking cover, Leila behind me. We walked through the rainforest and into the open area of the knoll, now occupied by a small chunk of Western civilization.

The woman and her team had their backs to us, and the pilot, moments from departure, was involved with his instruments.

'Morning, ma'am,' I called out.

The woman turned and saw me and took a step back, her hand going to her chest in shock. The guys all dove in behind her, taking cover.

'Who . . . who are you!?'

'Major Cooper, United States Air Force. And this is Leila,' I said, bringing the star forward. 'Our chopper went down.'

The woman's hand moved from her chest to her mouth when recognition dawned on her. 'Oh my God. It's you . . . You're alive. They've been searching the lake for the wreckage – Lake Kivu.'

'The Center for Disease Control,' I said. 'So you know about the village?' I gestured behind me.

'Yes, we've got a whole team about to arrive and . . .' Her look of surprise and wonder shifted into the fear zone. 'Wait, you haven't been *into* that village, have you?'

'No, ma'am,' I said, telling a half-truth. 'We surveyed the area from a distance. There were bodies out in the open. One of my men thought it might be Ebola.'

'Several people fled the village, went down river. They became sick and we were called in. It's not Ebola, not as contagious, but it's still a level four biohazard – Crimean-Congo hemorrhagic fever. A tick that lives on infected animals carries it. Probably bush meat in this instance. You sure you went nowhere near any infected persons?'

'I'm sure, ma'am.'

I gave the signal to rejoin and the balance of Team Ghost Watch accompanied our principals out of the shadows.

'Oh my God . . .' the woman said when she saw the parade.

'You mind giving us a ride?' I asked her.

THE JET RANGER DEPARTED and a MONUC Puma, identical to the one LeDuc and Fournier piloted, arrived half an hour later, stuffed with the equipment and personnel required to set up a makeshift hospital, lab and decontamination facilities. People stared at us, even though the woman, whose name was Andrea, gave us what we needed to clean up a little. We rode the chopper to a place called Dutu, a small town on the shores of Lake Kivu. From there, we hired a boat and motored fifty miles south to Bukavu, on the DRC side of the border, directly opposite Cyangugu. I'd told Andrea to stay off the radio and keep our status of being among the living to herself for twelve hours at least. She didn't ask me why, which was fortunate because I was sure she wouldn't take the answer in her stride – that I didn't want a certain Kornflak & Greene contractor knowing that I was on my way to kill him.

We crossed the DRC/Rwandan border in a bus full of chickens, paying the guards with various trinkets, and did the last two miles on foot, arriving at Camp Fuck You, Cyangugu, eight days after our departure, at three-fifteen. I'm certain of the time because it started raining.

Verdict

It was six-fifteen am before I jogged past the main gate, having run five miles by then, my head no clearer than it was when I climbed out of bed, a headache throbbing in my left temple and keeping time with every footfall. I had a late night with Macri and Cheung to thank for that, though maybe it was the midnight visit from my old buddy Jack that did the real damage. Out beyond the gate, the daily demonstration in support of *moi* was ramping up. I went in for a closer look and caught sight of a few of the placards. 'Free Cooper!' said one. Another said, 'America needs heroes!' Yet another proclaimed, '#12? Cooper deserves better!' That last one threw me – what was that all about? The rest, and there were quite a few, were variations on those themes, except for the 'We love Leila!' placards and one that said, 'Twenny – feel *me*!'

Today's circus would be bigger and better than usual and, indeed, there were more than a dozen trailers out there, parked among network vans, all of which were present for the biggest show in town. This was the day when witnesses would be called, and that meant Twenny Fo and Leila, now officially his fiancée, would be making an appearance. The networks were salivating.

Outside the wire there was plenty of support. Inside, where it counted, it was a different story. All the legal maneuvering and wrangling was done and dusted and none of it favored me. Cheung and Macri had tried to convince the court that my assault on Lockhart was provoked, and that I therefore acted in self-defense. After hearing counter mumbo jumbo from the USAF prosecutors, Major Vaughan Latham and his hot captain assistant, Colonel Fink ruled that, as Lockhart was unaware that I was in the camp, it was ridiculous to claim provocation on his part and that therefore the charges stood. In short, only the circumstances around the assault were admissible. Every thing that transpired over the previous eight days, including my testimony that I'd observed Lockhart shoot French *Armée de l'Air* Lieutenant Henri Fournier dead in cold blood – among many other crimes including rape, kidnapping, extortion, and slavery – were deemed to be outside the court martial's purview. My problem was that we had no evidence, hard or otherwise, produced in disclosure to support my counter claims.

Though Ryder had been with me at the time of Fournier's murder, he hadn't actually *seen* Lockhart at all, let alone witness the shooting – the murderer having disappeared into one of the tents by the time I'd handed the scope over to the captain. At the village, when the baby had been thrown into the bushes and Lockhart had pulled up in a Dong, it was a similar story. I saw him, but no one else could corroborate. Same again at the mine, when we were escaping in the truck with Francis and his people and Lockhart had tried to stop us with some FARDC troops. I'd seen him, but it seemed that everyone else had had their heads up their asses at the time. Francis had noted Lockhart at the mine when the gold nugget had been found, but Francis was lost somewhere deep in the Congo rainforests, if, indeed, he were still alive. And even if he were breathing and could be contacted and his video testimony delivered to the court, Cheung believed that Fink and his co-judges would not have accepted Francis's word over Lockhart's.

Of course, there was Twenny Fo's belief that he smelled Lockhart in the FARDC camp. When they heard about it, Cheung and Macri laughed.

So, basically, I was screwed.

I ran back to my rooms, trying to work out what *#12. Cooper deserves better!* might mean. When I got there, a man was waiting in ambush for me by the front entranceway to my accommodation: fortyish, balding, tall in a flaccid way that suggested no exercise and too much booze, and jowls that reminded me of a bloodhound's. His name was Rentworthy, the *New York Times* reporter. I slowed to a walk to throw off his targeting. It didn't work.

'Vin. Can I call you that?'

'What else you got in mind?'

'You're a hard man to catch.'

I remembered Cheung's advice: play nice with this guy. 'You've written some interesting stories about what happened out there.'

'Thanks,' he said.

'Mind telling me who your source was?'

'Sorry, can't reveal that.'

'Then how about narrowing it down a little – one of my principals, or one of the PSOs?'

'Does it matter?'

It only mattered because whoever the source was had selectively edited the facts to make me out to be some kind of hero, which I wasn't. 'No, I guess not.'

'Our readers don't want you to go to prison, Vin.'

'I'm not so keen on it either.'

'You mind if I ask you some questions?'

'You've got me cornered. Shoot.'

The guy took out a tape recorder and showed me the red light.

'I got a bad memory,' he said, a half smile compressing one of his jowls. 'I want to know whether you had sex with Leila. There are allegations . . .'

'No.'

'The first night you were down on the ground, when it was your watch. Leila didn't pay you a visit? Make an offer that was too good to refuse? Was it true she wanted to cut and run, leave her fiancé behind?'

I remembered the night and I remembered Leila down on her knees in front of me and I remembered that nothing happened. Where was this coming from? 'This doesn't sound like a story the *New York Times* would be interested in,' I said.

'Till an earthquake bumps you off, you're the big news at the moment, Vin; do you realize that? The media is chewing on the same information, presenting it different ways, digging up people who know you; people who know your principals. You could make a lot of money. Our readers just want the full story.'

'And sex sells.'

'Indeed it does.'

'Can't help you, I'm afraid. Nothing happened.'

'Not according to *People*.'

He handed me a rolled-up magazine. Leila was on the cover, dressed in an Army battle uniform, her shirt undone and her breasts looking like they were trying to punch their way out. She was in a jungle setting and a large snake was coiled around a nearby branch. Plenty of symbolism. The cover announced that it was the 'Sexiest People On The Planet' issue. Another headline read, 'Sex on the run. What *really* happened in the Congo – an insider tells.'

'This your source?' I asked.

He shrugged. 'I've been the go-to-guy on your story, but not on this chapter.' He held up the magazine. 'I wanted to see if someone else got the drop on me. And I figured only you'd know.'

'Nothing happened.'

'Shame. She's hot.'

And loopy.

'There's a story in the paper tomorrow. It's not mine either. Twenny Fo and Leila want to adopt two orphans from the DRC – girls; twins. They're also hoping to build a school in some village you passed through. Maybe you know which one.'

I thought of a baby girl caught upside down in the bushes, a driver ant biting her toe. I shrugged.

Rentworthy clicked off his tape recorder, handed me his card. 'I can write your story, Vin. It's a good one. There's a book in it somewhere and it'll sell. Think about it. You'll need the money when you get out.'

'Nice to hear you're thinking positive on my account. Okay, I'll think about it,' I told him, pocketing the card, but I already knew what my answer would be.

'Oh, I see you made number twelve. Congrats. And today in court – break a leg, eh?'

I said thanks and see you later and jogged up the stairs with the magazine. *Number twelve?* I had a shower and shave, dressed, ate breakfast and flicked through the magazine while I waited for Cheung and Macri, who were escorting me to court. I opened the mag at its halfway point, found the story pertaining to the coverline and read it. The inside source wasn't named. The story insinuated that Leila and I were eating each other's forbidden fruit in the Congo's primordial Garden of Eden while everyone else slept. I could see a lawsuit heading *People* magazine's way from Leila's team. That aside, the story would be good for my bar cred, if I ever managed to get to a bar while this edition was still on the newsstands, which didn't seem likely. I skimmed the rest of the rag and stopped at a page showing the photo Fallon had taken of me on his iPhone that day back in Afghanistan. My jaw went slack. The headline on the photo said, '#12. Special Agent Vin Cooper, OSI'.

'Shit,' I muttered. I flicked forward and back. There I was, number twelve in *People* magazine's list of the World's Sexiest People. Leila was number one and Twenny was number seven.

A knock on the door. It was Cheung and Macri.

'You've read it, I see,' said Macri as he walked in, nodding at the magazine dangling from my hand.

'Congratulations,' Cheung added.

'The poster was right – number twelve is an insult,' I said.

'What poster?' asked Macri.

I let the question hang, exchanging it for my blouse dangling from a hook on the back of the door. 'What can I expect today?'

'You're gonna see your friend,' Macri told me.

'Lockhart?' I asked, though I knew who he meant.

'Word just came from Latham's office. He's going to testify in person,' said Cheung.

'He knows we've got nothing on him,' I said. 'That's why he's here. He knows we can't touch him.'

'He's come to gloat,' Macri concluded.

I closed the door and we walked in silence down the stairs to the blue Ford Explorer parked out front.

'This is how it will go today,' said Cheung, opening the front passenger door for me. He drove and Marci took the back seat.

'I know how it will go,' I said before he could get started. 'I'm in the same game, remember? Who's our first witness?'

'Duke Ryder.'

'Why Ryder?' I asked.

'He's an OSI agent and his eyewitness testimony differs from the prosecution's eyewitness testimony in a key area. We can amplify the difference and perhaps throw some doubt on the flames.'

'What key area?'

'Leave it for the courtroom,' said Macri.

'What about Cassidy, Rutherford and West?'

'They'll also be called.'

THE COURTROOM WAS INSIDE 1535 Command Drive, a red-brick rectangle façade with a rotunda built off the back, like the architect couldn't quite make up his mind. The eighties were a confusing time. Milling in front of the building were at least a couple hundred folks hoping to get a seat in a courtroom that could seat less than a quarter that number. Several reporters were doing live feeds, the network trucks I'd seen out beyond the main gate now parked along Command Drive. There were no placards.

'We'll go round the back,' said Cheung, taking a detour.

The back turned out to be every bit as crowded as the front. Reporters swarmed over the Explorer once we'd stopped. A couple of security police managed to get themselves between the reporters shouting questions at me, and hustled Macri and me up the stairs and into the building, leaving Cheung to field the questions. He threw them a few bones and then came up the stairs that were blocked by more security forces. We made our way to the courtroom, which had yet to be opened to the public, and took our seats at the desk reserved for the defense, facing the members of the board.

Major Latham and Captain Pencilskirt, whose name I'd since discovered was Polly Blinkenspiel, took their places at the desk opposite the military judge.

Latham caught me looking in his direction or, rather, in Blinkenspiel's, and gave me a shrug that said, 'No hard feelings, hey.'

He was just doing his job. If it wasn't him it'd be some other trial counsel and it was unlikely his or her assistant would be nearly as hot as Latham's. While I was considering all this, allowing my thoughts to wander to the aforementioned assistant, the doors at the back of the room opened and people poured in. I saw a few familiar faces – Arlen's, for example. We acknowledged each other and he gave me an it's-gonna-be-okay nod, the kind of nod I imagine they give you when you go into surgery with a minor leg wound and come out an amputee. A familiar face was beside him – Summer from *Summer Love*, the vegetarian restaurant on the ground floor of my apartment. She wore a yellow hat and a long lemon dress pulled in tight under her smallish breasts, accentuating them. She looked good. I was surprised to see her, vegetarian food not being high on my favourites list. She waved and I gave her what I hoped was a smile. There were a few other people I knew, agents I'd worked with and so forth. Lockhart was somewhere close by. I was sure I could smell him.

The bailiff, in this instance an Air Force lieutenant colonel, closed the doors and walked to the front of the room, and everyone settled down, the talk dying to a low murmur and then ceasing altogether. 'All rise,' he said and everyone stood.

The side door opened and Colonel Fink came in, still short and bath plug-like, and climbed up on his stage to take his seat in front of the Air Force seal hanging on the paneled wall behind him. One colonel, one lite colonel and seven majors – more males than females – came in. They all took the seats behind the mahogany desk panels, each wearing a stern Mount Rushmore-like face.

Fink cleared his throat, shuffled a stack of loose papers in front of him and held a black fountain pen poised above them. Without looking up, he read through the usual script, outlining the defendant's rights to counsel, followed by a series of oaths that counsels had to take, followed by the charges I was facing, followed by my plea – which was not guilty – followed by instructions to the court outlining, for example, what reasonable doubt meant. Then followed challenges – whether either my counsels or the trial counsel believed there might be any bias or competing interests amongst the members of the court that could leave justice short changed. The script Fink went through was forty pages or more in length. There were no challenges, the right people said 'yes, sir,' and 'no, sir,' when they were supposed to, including me. Eventually, Colonel Fink gave the stack of papers in front of him a big tick, shuffled them into order, then called on Latham to outline the United States' case against me.

'Yes, your Honor,' said Latham. He got up, buttoned his coat, and walked to the dais in the center of the room with his cheat notes. He then read through the charges, repeating much of what Fink had already said, the court reporter putting it all down again. There was fidgeting from the bleachers. This was a long way from a Grisham novel.

'Excellent,' said Fink when Latham had concluded, adding another flamboyant tick. I wondered if maybe the guy was going to introduce himself to the audience and take a bow. The courts martial I'd attended in the past hadn't been in the least theatrical. Fink was enjoying himself.

'I note that several members of the media have taken up the commander's offer to attend this trial and are in the room today, this case having attracted more than its fair share of public attention,' he said. 'But I would remind you that you are here at the pleasure of the United States Air Force. This is a military court martial, and you are on a military base and you must conduct yourselves accordingly or your privileges here will be withdrawn.' Fink took his stare around the courtroom. 'While we're on the subject, if I see tomorrow the scenes I witnessed out front of this building this morning, I will end public access to these proceedings and you will have to satisfy the cravings of your listeners, readers, watchers and bloggers with an Air Force-approved press release the morning after the previous day's hearings. Do I make myself clear?'

I heard a pin drop.

'Then, without further ado, gentlemen,' he continued, turning his gaze on Latham. 'If you please, Counselor . . .'

Latham stood, buttoned his coat, went to the dias and recalled the scene at Camp Come Together, Cyangugu. As far as I could tell, he had it pretty much squared away with the facts. From the way it was recounted, I'd have found me guilty.

Then it was Cheung's turn. He expanded on my not-guilty plea, told the court that I was innocent of the main assault charge, that I was just going my duty, and that there were witness who would back me up.

Not even I was convinced.

Fink then invited Latham to call his first witness. A procession of US personnel who had been present at Cyangugu took the stand and recounted the events of the afternoon that had led to me sitting in this courtroom. The two MPs who had pulled me off Lockhart began the parade, starting with the big redheaded Army sergeant with the badly busted-up nose. They all told identical stories, well drilled. Cheung had no questions for any of them and neither did the court board members, who were within their right to ask them if testimony had been unclear.

After the seventh witness went over exactly the same ground as the six before him, Fink interrupted the show. 'Counselor,' he asked Latham. 'How many more broken records do you intend playing the court?'

'If it pleases the court, sir, thirteen more,' said Latham, buttoning his coat as he stood.

'Any of them have anything fresh to add?'

'Only one, sir. The prosecution's case rests on consistency. I have twenty witnesses who can swear that the events that took place at Cyangugu happened as we say it happened, and not the way the accused and his witnesses will claim.'

'Is it necessary to get every one of those witnesses in the box, Major?'

'What does the court president say?' Fink said, motioning at the colonel, who then conferred with his board members.

'We don't think there's a need, your Honor,' said the colonel.

'And the defense sees no need to cross-examine?'

Cheung stood, buttoning his coat. 'No, your Honor, not at this time.' He then unbuttoned it, and sat.

'Very well, then, Counselor,' he said, waving at Latham. 'I think we get the picture. No need to gild the lily.'

'Sir,' said Latham.

'Then call the witness who can add to our understanding rather than our desire to take a nap.'

Arlen caught my eye and signed 'okay' at me.

'I call Mr Beauford Lockhart to the stand,' the prosecutor announced.

'Now it starts,' Cheung whispered under his breath.

'Yeah, this is when I jump over the table and finish what I should have finished back in Rwanda.'

'Sit still, don't say a word,' Cheung said in a voice so low I could barely hear him.

Lockhart entered, wearing an expensive navy blue suit and red silk tie, the black locks of his hair glistening with product. I could smell his cologne, the same smell I remembered from Cyangugu, Twenny's 'Guilty'. I could have smirked at the irony, only I was all smirked out. The bailiff accompanied him to the stand. He looked at me and smiled, enjoying the moment. The muscle fibers in my legs twitched. I felt Cheung's hand on my forearm.

'So, Mr Lockhart, would you tell the court what you do?' said Latham.

What followed was five minutes of gratuitous turd polishing – about how, through Kornflak & Greene, he'd helped deliver peace to a troubled region, working with indigenous populations to bring about a brighter future for communities that had been ravaged by war and so forth. Latham then asked whether we'd had any contact prior to the incident between us, and Lockhart told the court that we had met during Twenny Fo and Leila's concert. Latham then guided the witness to the events being examined. The guy had a perfectly reasonable account of my unreasonable – as he saw them – actions. At the end of this, Latham turned to Cheung and said, 'Your witness.'

Cheung buttoned his coat, stood, said, 'No questions,' unbuttoned his coat and sat.

'What?' I whispered.

Both Macri and Cheung shot me a look that said, 'Quiet!'

'The prosecution rests, your Honor,' said Latham.

Fink glanced at his watch. 'Is it that time already? We'll recess for an hour for lunch. See you all back here at one. Perhaps we can get all this wrapped up in the afternoon session.' He directed this comment at Cheung, raising a bushy eyebrow at him.

I wasn't sure I appreciated the bench's keenness to get this over and done with.

Over a toasted ham and cheese sandwich, I asked Cheung what he was doing. I'd been in enough trials to know that I was sunk.

'Laying the foundation,' he said.

I asked what foundation. He told me to have another sandwich, but I'd lost my appetite.

Back in the courtroom, Fink asked Cheung to call his first witness.

'Yes, sir,' said Cheung as he stood, buttoning his coat. 'I call Captain Duke Ryder to the stand.'

The word went out and Ryder was brought forth. He satisfied the usual requirements oathwise and Cheung asked him to remember the day we arrived back at the camp.

And then a ruckus outside the court halted proceedings. The doors swung open and in walked Twenny, Leila, Ayesha, and Boink, towering over them, a bowler hat in his hand, gold bling in those giant earlobes of his. The public twittered and hushed, and looked around and craned their necks to get a better look at the celebrities. Twenny wore a purple suit. Leila wore a snakeskin dress cut high above the knee and as tight as a . . . well, as a snakeskin. I took an educated guess about where she'd acquired it. Ayesha wore a purple stretch cotton dress and was obviously pregnant. She looked good. All four of them did. Ayesha urged everyone to squeeze up and room was made for them at the end of the row.

Fink tapped his benchtop a couple of times with the point of his pen – something I'd never seen a military judge do. The guy was pissed. 'Order!' he shouted. '*No one* arrives fashionably late to my courtroom. I don't care how famous you are. Are we clear?'

I saw Twenny raise his hand, fingers spread wide in a gesture of apology, and this appeared to appease the judge.

With an imperious wave, Fink said to Cheung, 'Continue.'

'Your own words, Captain,' Cheung reminded Ryder.

'We'd been eight days in the rainforest. We were all a little sick – not enough food, some bad water. Some of the PSOs had minor wounds caused by engagements with elements from the—'

'Objection,' said Latham. 'What happened before the incident at Cyangugu has been deemed beyond the court's purview.'

'Sustained,' said Fink. He turned to the witness. 'This court martial is solely interested in the charges and specifications established, Captain Ryder. And I remind you about this too, Counselor. I don't want to hear about what you may consider to be justification. The court wants to know this: did Major Cooper assault a Department of Defense contractor or not? Simple. Establish that one way or the other and we can all go home.'

Or straight to Leavenworth, if you happened to be me.

'Yes, sir,' said Ryder.

Cheung changed tack and took the straight-in approach. 'Did Agent Cooper assault the defense contractor named Beau Lockhart?'

'No, sir.'

'And what makes you say that, when the prosecution has paraded a large number of witnesses in front of the court who've assured us that he did?'

'Because Agent Cooper was merely trying to arrest the contractor and he was resisting.'

'And why was he trying to arrest the contractor?'

'Objection! Irrelevant and immaterial,' Latham said, standing and buttoning his coat. He unbuttoned his coat and sat.

'Sustained,' said Fink.

'Judge, I am attempting to establish that an assault never took place. Cooper merely used justifiable force in the pursuit of his duty. I understand that the court has no desire to know *why* Cooper was trying to arrest the contractor, but the fact remains that that's what he was trying to do, and is therefore innocent of the charges against him.'

'As Major Latham correctly states, there were no charges against the assaulted party. I don't believe any *facts* – facts supportive of your point of view, at least – have been established. The objection remains sustained. Try a different way.'

Cheung looked up from his notes. 'Captain Ryder, you're with OSI. You're a special agent – police.'

'Yes, sir,' he said.

'As a policeman, you keep a notebook?'

'Yes, sir.'

'Do you have here the notebook you used on that day?'

'Yes, sir.'

'Please go to the notes you made on the incident over which the accused stands charged.'

Ryder flipped through the book.

'Please read your notes to the court.'

'Arrived Camp. Cooper sees Lockhart. Goes to him, draws gun. Cooper says, "You're under arrest." Lockhart moves. Cooper restricts further movement, hits Lockhart with gun. Lockhart says, "Damn, Cooper. You still alive, motherfucker?" Sergeant Cassidy says, "Cooper! C'mon!" Lockhart attempts to evade capture and Lockhart reaches for his side-arm.'

'Objection,' said Latham, leaping to his feet, forgetting about buttoning his coat. 'I have twenty witnesses who can testify that the victim of Cooper's senseless attack *never* reached for his side-arm.'

'Your Honor,' said Cheung. 'I have a number of witness who will state otherwise. We're going to end up in one of those "he says she says" dead ends.'

'Your Honor,' Latham countered, 'the testimony from his witnesses is surely cancelled out by the prosecution's witnesses on this point.'

'But, sir,' said Cheung, 'the issue of Lockhart reaching for his weapon underpins the accused's innocence.'

'The objection is sustained,' said Fink. 'Can't help you on this point, Counselor. Got anything else?'

I hoped like hell that we did but from the looks of Cheung – frowning, hands on hips, glaring at the floor – probably not.

My attorney looked up. 'Continue from your notes, please, Captain,' he told Ryder.

Ryder read from his notebook. 'Cooper strikes him again. Lockhart further resists arrest. Rwandan and American security forces arrive, detain Cooper.'

'Thank you, Captain,' said Cheung. 'So, Cooper was merely trying to detain the contractor; that is, perform his duty.'

'Yes.'

'Do you know why he was attempting to do that?'

'He thought Lockhart was dangerous.'

'Did you agree with that judgment, Captain?'

'Yes, sir, I did.'

'Did the words, "Damn, Cooper. You still alive, expletive deleted?" have something to do with that belief?'

I glanced over at Latham. He was itching to jump to his feet.

'Yes, sir. I believe so.'

'Is that notebook dated and signed by you?'

'Yes, it is.'

'Do you need it?'

'No, sir, I have no further use for it.'

'If it please the court,' said Cheung, 'I'd like to enter the captain's notebook as defense exhibit A.'

The bailiff stepped forward, took the notebook from Ryder and delivered it to the bench. Fink opened it, checked the entries, then handed it back to the sergeant, who took it to the colonel to flip through and pass on to the other board members.

'Your witness,' Cheung said to Latham and Blinkenspiel before he sat down.

Latham buttoned his coat. 'Did you keep this diary the entire time you were in-country, Captain?' he asked, standing up behind his bench.

'No, sir.'

'When did you acquire it?'

'Around an hour after we arrived back at the camp.'

'Where did you get it?'

'From the infirmary.'

'Someone in the hospital gave it to you to record your recollection of the, er, incident?'

'Yes, sir.'

'So the notes you just read out to the court were made at least an hour after the fact?'

'Yes, sir.'

'I also have some notes,' Latham said, holding up a couple of loose sheets of paper. 'This is the medical record of your treatment at the Camp Come Together medical center.' He waved the sheets in the air above his head. 'They treated you for cuts, abrasions, mild exposure, mild dehydration . . . and concussion.'

'I was over the concussion by then,' said Ryder.

'Not according to this report. It says here that your brain was significantly bruised. It's a wonder that you could remember anything, given your state, let alone details of events and conversations that occurred more than *an hour* before you were able to write them down, don't you think?'

Ryder looked like someone was about to step forward and offer him a blindfold and a cigarette.

'Well, Captain?' said Latham.

Ryder glanced at the judge. There was no refuge there.

'Answer the question, Captain,' Fink directed him.

'What was the question, sir?' Ryder asked.

A ripple of laughter filled the spectator benches.

Latham unbuttoned his coat. 'I think he just has, your Honor. Your witness.' He sat and gave Captain Pencilskirt a winning grin, which she returned. Someone was going to get lucky tonight; maybe someone in the Leavenworth shower block.

'Any further questions?' Fink asked the court, addressing the court president.

No one had any, except me. 'That the best we got?' I whispered to Macri as Ryder left the stand.

Macri *shushed* me, annoyed by my lack of confidence, as Cheung stood and called Sergeant Cassidy to the stand. Cassidy, followed by Rutherford, backed Ryder's account, including the fact that Lockhart went for his gun. This horse was well and truly flogged, but then he called West and extracted yet another laboriously detailed account of the same few minutes in the mud of Cyangugu that had everyone, including Fink, yawning. Latham declined to cross any of these witnesses, clearly believing that he'd discredited our account at its heart with the cross-examination of Ryder, the only person who had kept a record of the incident. I found myself wishing that I were Latham's client rather than Cheung's.

'It's four pm,' said Fink. 'Before I decide whether to break for a short recess, any more witnesses, Counselor?' he asked Cheung.

'Just one, sir,' said Cheung.

Fink sat back and gestured with his hand for Cheung to get on with it.

'I recall Beau Lockhart to the stand.'

The bailiff went off to fetch him. The asshole swaggered in a dozen seconds later, and made his way to the witness box. He took his seat and turned to face the gallery and, suddenly, Leila screamed. Or maybe it was a shriek. Whatever, it was loud and piercing and it belonged in the front seat of a rollercoaster. The courtroom went nuts. My former principal stood and pointed at Lockhart in the witness chair, her voice breaking in her throat. 'It's him, *him . . .!*'

'Silence,' Fink boomed. 'Remove this woman from the court,' he demanded, galvanizing the bailiff into action.

'It's him. I can show you,' said Leila, holding a gold iPhone high above her head. 'I have photos. It's *him.*'

I recognized that phone.

Fink hammered his pen on the edge of his bench like he was doing a drum solo. 'Get that phone!' he commanded, pointing at the bailiff. 'And *both* counselors – in my chambers. Now!'

'What's going on?' I asked Macri.

'I don't know,' he said, but the curl of his lips told me something different.

I glanced over in Arlen's direction. A couple of security police were on the doors. Lockhart was looking increasingly like a trapped animal, unsure whether he should, or even could, get up from the chair. He made the decision to stay put. Everyone in the courtroom was standing, talking, yelling.

The bailiff reappeared and took the members of the board and the court's president to the judge's chambers.

A couple of minutes later, Fink, purple-faced, returned with Cheung and Latham and the members of the board. He took his pen and attempted to tap some silence into the gallery. It wasn't working. 'Bailiff and security forces! Detain this man.' He pointed to Beau Lockhart.

Bedlam reigned. People stood and shouted at each other while Lockhart was surrounded. The court had no jurisdiction over the DoD contractor, but the judge could detain him for the folks at the Federal Bureau of Investigation. I wondered what had happened behind closed doors.

Fink roared, '*Silence!*' When he got some, he pointed at me and said, 'You! Were you aware of the existence of this phone?'

'Yes, sir,' I said. I had seen Leila trying to raise a signal on it when we first came down in the jungle.

'Were you aware that she was using it to keep a photographic diary while in the Congo?'

'No, sir, though I was aware that the phone's owner held the Air Force responsible for the situation we found ourselves in.'

'I see,' said Fink, his nostrils flaring. He glared at Cheung. 'You and I know what happened here today, Counselor. Pull a stunt like this in my courtroom again and I will personally see to it that you're discharged and disbarred.'

Cheung took the blast without acknowledgment, which was wise, and said, 'Your Honor, the defense moves for the dismissal of all charges.'

Fink's nostrils flared grandly. He went into a huddle with the board members as the bailiff and security police hustled Lockhart from the room. After two solid minutes of discussion with his fellow officers. Fink and the members of the court resumed their seats. Fink then did that thing with his pen on the edge of his bench until everyone stopped talking.

When he could make himself heard, he said, 'Court President, how do you find the defendant?'

The colonel stood. 'We find the defendant not guilty of offenses punishable by court-martial, but recommend that he be remanded to his commanding officer for Article 15 non-judicial proceedings.'

'Thank you, Colonel,' said Fink. The judge turned to me and said, 'Will the defendant rise?'

I stood and buttoned my coat.

'Major Vincent Cooper. The charges are dismissed.' Fink then threw his pen into an empty trash bin at his feet, slipped off his seat and stomped out.

Epilogue

'What was on the iPhone?' I asked Cheung as he and Macri drove me back to my box.

'Bad shit that'll give me nightmares,' he said.

'Take a number. What was on it?'

'There were photos of you standing over a man lying on the ground with your service pistol. It looks as if you've just shot him. The French pilot you believe was part of the ransom attempt is with you.'

I remembered the moment. Now that I thought about it, I also recalled glancing up and seeing Leila with her cell phone in her hand. At the time, I had thought she'd turned it on to see if she could raise a signal.

'There is another photo of Boink shooting the man in the head.'

I remembered that, too.

'They weren't the photos shown to Colonel Fink, by the way. What he saw was a woman having her arms hacked off in a village occupied by soldiers. There's also a picture of a truck rolling up, the window's down and Lockhart can clearly be seen leaning out the window. Colonel Lissouba – I assume it's him – is coming over to meet him. Her phone ran out of battery power at that point in your journey.'

Why didn't I think of using a damn cell phone to capture

evidence – especially after the business with Fallon and the photo he took of me in Afghanistan and posted on his blog? Maybe because my cell was a base model – no extras, no camera.

'The phone was your strategy all along,' I said.

'What do you want us to say?' said Cheung. 'There were *twenty* – count 'em – witnesses to your assault on Lockhart. I told you that we would have to use every trick in the book.'

'When did you find out about the pictures?'

'You really didn't know she'd taken them?' Macri asked.

'No. I'd have had Lockhart behind bars the moment we'd arrived back at Cyangugu had I known about them.'

'I interviewed everyone who was with you in the DRC,' said Cheung. 'Leila and Ayesha came forward and told me about the phone a week ago. I think you owe her.'

Or maybe now we were about even.

'Thank you,' I said.

'You've already thanked us,' said Macri.

'You played it a certain way to make sure Lockhart got nailed. Trotting out all those witnesses that were getting us nowhere . . . It was all just a diversion.'

'It's called a tactic where we come from,' said Macri.

'We had to make some kind of show of putting up a defense. If we hadn't, Fink wouldn't have been prepared to believe we knew nothing about those photos. We just had to stage Leila and company's late arrival to give us time to set it all up. Luckily, Fink *wanted* to believe it after he saw that photo.'

'And if the phone had come up in discovery,' I said, 'the case against me would've been dismissed and Lockhart wouldn't have stepped foot in the US ever again. You kept the cell a secret so that the trial would go ahead, and Lockhart would make an appearance and you could put a noose around his neck.'

'We figured you'd think it was worth it,' said Cheung.

I grinned. 'You guys are the most unlawyer-like lawyers I've ever met. And I mean that in the nicest possible way. While I think of it,

Leila insisted that she was going to sue the Air Force. That still going to happen?'

Cheung shook his head. 'Before anything else, the Air Force had her sign a waiver the thickness of a telephone book. And you brought her back without a scratch. What's she got to litigate about?'

Macri turned into my street and parked out front of my accommodation block, behind my old Pontiac.

'We'll pick you up in an hour and a half,' said Cheung.

'We're drinking. You're buying,' Macri informed me.

Seemed fair to me.

Ten minutes later I was sitting on the end of my bed with a single malt, feeling it evaporate up the back of my nose, and the relief I felt that I was free gave me a shiver. There was a knock on the door. 'Don't want any,' I called out.

'It's Arlen,' came the reply. 'Open up.'

I let him in.

'Hey, I missed you over at the courthouse,' he said, his spirits brimming. 'Congratulations, buddy.' He shook my hand warmly, a smile full of genuine pleasure on his face.

'You were in on it,' I said.

'What are friends for?'

'Did you put the idea in Cheung's head?'

'I don't think he'd recall it quite like that. Justice has a blindfold. Sometimes she needs a little help pinning the tail on the donkey's ass.'

'The investigation turn up anything useful yet?'

Arlen's smile flickered. 'Charles White. Former Marine Recon, honorably discharged three years ago, rank of sergeant. Went to work for FN Herstal. Lasted six months and then fell off the radar. Interpol believes he has connections with Somali pirates. He's a weapons trader, with plenty of connections to the military and military industry here in the US. He lives in Rio de Janeiro and is believed to be moving around on false passports. As for André LeDuc? No idea where he is. Interpol has a brief. Piers Pietersen is greedy and rich but clean, as far as we can tell.'

'I want in.'

'We've got people on it.'

'But they're just people,' I said.

He snorted. 'You've reminded me. The Article 15 non-judicial punishment. The CO has come to a decision.'

'And?'

'He told me to tell you that for pistol whipping Lockhart with your government-issue Sig, you're going to forfeit one week's pay.'

I'd gotten off lightly.

'He also told me to tell you that if you'd clubbed Lockhart with the butt of your M4, he'd have bought you a beer. '

'He said that?'

'Word for word.'

Maybe the old man wasn't such a bad guy after all.

'Oh, by the way, apparently you missed out on the Air Force Cross – though you don't know that. For what it's worth, I think you deserved to get it and so does Central Command. It's pissed at the Secretary of the Air Force for turning you down.'

There wasn't much to regret here. I wasn't even supposed to know that I *could* have won it.

'So instead, you're getting the Silver Star – next one down. CENTCOM was persistent and the SECAF caved, probably because of all the publicity.'

'Okay.' There wasn't much else to say. The action in Afghanistan was a distant memory. I couldn't remember most of the details, other than some of the people in my section lost their lives.

'More importantly, I also heard that you're now officially one of the world's sexiest people,' he said, grinning, the magazine open on the floor in the corner of the room. 'Don't they know they're only encouraging you?'

And I was going to get to a bar while the magazine was still on the newsstands after all. 'Call me Number Twelve from now on.'

'Think I'll stick with Vin.'

'You wanna drink?' I asked him as I moved to the kitchenette.

'No, I'm still on the treadmill.'

'Tell me about the ransom.'

'What's there to tell?'

'I heard you received a demand three days after we went missing – for Twenny and Leila and no one else.'

'You heard right. We think they were never going to let anyone get out alive – just take the money and run. At the time the ransom demand came through, Lockhart and Lissouba probably believed everyone not held hostage was already dead.'

'What about Boink?' I asked.

'What about him?'

I took a mouthful of scotch.

'Oh . . . right. Well, unfortunately, the only evidence we had for that incident was lost. Damn iPhone.'

I heard movement outside the front door, followed by a knock. 'Yo, Cooper. You in there, dog?'

Speak of the devil. It was Boink. I opened the door. Leila and Ayesha swept in, followed by Twenny and Boink, who took his bowler hat off but still had to duck to enter.

'Dere he is!' said Twenny. We shook, a weird combination of moves that I followed as best I could.

'Vin!' said Leila, embracing me, her French perfume doing likewise. 'We just wanted to come and congratulate you, you know.'

'Yes, congratulations on the win!' said Ayesha, pecking me on the cheek.

'Hey, soldier man,' said Boink. We bumped knuckles. 'Congrats, yo.'

I introduced Arlen. When we were done, he excused himself and I saw him to the door. He took a brown envelope from his blouse inside pocket. 'Have a look when you get a quiet moment.'

'What is it?' I asked.

'Just have a look. I don't want to spoil the news,' he said.

I shrugged, folded the envelope, put it on the kitchenette bench.

My rich and influential friends didn't stay long but long enough to tell me that they'd spent a considerable amount of money trying to locate Francis. While not confirmed, they'd only just now received word that he'd been found alive and still had both legs.

'So you've heard that Deryck and I are going to adopt a child from the Congo?' Leila asked me. Deryck's diamond flashed on her engagement finger.

'It's on the news,' I said.

'But what they don't know yet is that Deryck and I . . . we're having a baby.'

'The ol' fashioned way, you feel me?' said Twenny, grinning.

'We wanted you to be among the first to know,' she said. 'It's a boy. We're gonna name him after . . . can you guess?'

'You're not going to name him . . . Cooper,' I said.

Leila cleared her throat and looked at Twenny, a little embarrassed. 'Well, no, sorry. I . . . we . . . We're going to name him . . . Zaire.'

'After the river,' I said. *The river?*

'Duke and I are also having a baby,' said Ayesha. 'Did he tell you?'

'No, he didn't,' I said. 'It's congratulations all round!' The bump told me she had to be three months gone, which put her in the Congo at the time. In fact, Ryder had told me that Ayesha had fallen pregnant because of the rape, but they'd decided to keep it and bring it into the world together. 'Ayesha wants to break the cycle of violence,' he told me.

I went into the kitchenette and fixed drinks for those of us who weren't pregnant. While doing this, I thanked Leila for saving my ass, and she apologized for being a complete psycho bitch. Actually, she didn't. But, whatever, we buried the machete.

Twenny took me aside. 'The stories in the media, 'bout you and Leila. They true?'

I raised an eyebrow at him.

'Yeah, thought they was bullshit.'

He punched me in the arm.

'How's Peanut?' I asked.

'The same as he always was, but he does drawings. You should see them – frightening, man. He says they're his dreams. I get them too. I spoke with a doctor. He says the dreams will fade.'

I wished him luck with that.

We rejoined the others. All four said that if there were ever anything they could do for me that I should call. I wondered how long they'd remember my name. We said goodbye, they left and I cleaned up a little. It was time for me to leave too, go back to my apartment in the 'burbs of DC. I threw my things in a bag and walked to the front door before turning for a last look around. Arlen's envelope caught my eye – I'd forgotten to collect it. I picked it up off the bench and lifted the flap. There were a couple of sheets of official-looking paper inside, a report from Oak Ridge Police Forensics. Oak Ridge, Tennessee – that was where Anna had been shot, at the Department of Energy's Oak Ridge depleted uranium storage facility. I skimmed the sheets, then went over them a second time, and had to take a seat on the edge of the bed when the impact of the news hit me.

After completing laser analyses on the trajectories of all the bullets fired in Anna's last fateful moments, Oak Ridge forensics had *found the missing slug*. They discovered it buried in a tree trunk half a mile from the room in which she was killed. This was the bullet, the one forensics believed had blown a hole in Anna's chest. The gun I fired was a Colt. 45. The newly recovered bullet was a 9mm round *fired by a Glock*. Forensics had matched it to the gun used by the nutbag who was wrestling Anna when she was fatally wounded.

Jesus . . . I lay back on the bed, closed my eyes and breathed.

Author's note

While *Ghost Watch* is a work of fiction, there's plenty of fact woven into the narrative. The Democratic Republic of Congo is a mess and has been for a very long time. Since 1994, when the genocide going on in Rwanda officially ended there and moved across the border, it's estimated more than four million people, mostly innocent citizens and bystanders, have been slaughtered in the Democratic Republic of Congo.

There's a recently expanded UN force (MONUC) of twenty thousand operating in the North Kivu area of the DRC, where much of *Ghost Watch* takes place, but reports suggest that it is largely ineffective at curbing the violence between the warring Tutsi and Hutus and other factions and interests. And sometimes actually exacerbates it.

The situation has been made worse in recent years with the realization by First World nations the United States, China and Russia that there's significant and diverse mineral wealth in the area, and each promotes its interests by supporting a local army (there are at least six fighting in the DRC) with money, logistical support, training and arms.

You wouldn't want to live there.

I've been aware of the misery going on in the Congo since 1987, when a buddy of mine decided that he was going to Zaire (as the DRC was then called) to check out the gorillas made famous by the late Dian Fossey.

Vaguely interested in perhaps making this trek myself, I started to poke around through various news sources. They painted a pretty horrendous picture. My pal changed his mind and went to South America instead. I went to Amsterdam.

All these years later, I can't say definitively why I decided to send Cooper to Africa. It might have been the rumour I'd heard that the US had a secret training base in Rwanda, on the border with the DRC. But the discovery of a new US military command being formed to oversee America's national interests on the African continent (AFRICOM) sealed it.

I have to say that I found researching the recent history of the DRC, and the eyewitness reports of massacres happening there, harrowing to say the least.

Ghost Watch contains some pretty grizzly scenes based on that research, but they don't compare to the gruesome reality. Frankly, had I not pulled my punches a little, I fear I might have taken this story somewhere else.

A couple of months into the writing of *Ghost Watch*, Laurant Nkunda, the former DRC general who went on to form and lead the National Congress for the Defense of the People (CNDP), a Tutsi militia supported by Rwanda, was arrested in Rwanda. Nkunda's arrest came at the insistence of his former employer, the government of the DRC. The charges against him relate to various human rights violations and war crimes including rape, murder, the use of child soldiers and so on. He's being held under house arrest somewhere in Rwanda.

As one of my characters says in the story's narrative, I don't think he will ever come to trial, or be handed over to the DRC. I'll be surprised if this monster doesn't simply disappear. If ever there was a war criminal that deserved justice, it's Laurant Nkunda.

Acknowledgments

I'd like to thank Lieutenant Colonel Mike 'Panda' Pandolfo (USAF, ret.) for his tireless support, wealth of knowledge and unerring eye while I was writing *Ghost Watch*. Panda has helped me considerably for the past couple of years. In fact, he has almost moved from 'tech support' to 'co-collaborator', and now I've said that, the guy will probably ask me for a raise. Panda recently retired from the Air Force. After so many years in uniform, that's a big life change. I'd to take this opportunity to thank him publicly for the lifetime of service he has selflessly given (the guy flew in the Vietnam War, for chrissakes!).

Thanks also to Special Agent Elizabeth Richards, AFOSI, for assistance with OSI procedures, documentation and photo reference.

Thanks to Michael Jordan, USMC, ret., for technical support on weapons, ammunition, legal issues, and editorial assistance.

Thanks to Patrick Le Barbenchon from Eurocopter, and also Robert Holtsbaum and Loic Porcheron at Australian Aerospace, for help and technical support on the Puma SA360.

Thanks to Patricia Rollins for French lessons and editorial assistance.

Thanks to my attorney, Eric Feig, for keeping the dogs at bay.

Thanks to Emma Rafferty and Sarina Rowell, my editors at Pan Macmillan.

And thanks to Rod Morrison, my publisher at Pan Mac. It'd be amateur hour at snake gully without you all.

Keep reading for an extract from the next
Vin Cooper thriller from David Rollins, available
in all good bookshops from June 2012

The lavender sea rolled slow and languid beneath the white hull of the *Medusa*, the über-luxurious Mangusta 130 that was Benicio von Weiss's toy du jour. Diogo 'Fruit Fly' Jaguaribe's battered head rolled from side to side with the motion of the boat, unaware of himself or his surroundings, the naked overhead sun boring through the pure clean air and burning the skin beneath the dyed black grizzle on the crown of his scalp. A sound escaped his throat but nothing else had a chance of freedom. Not out here. Not now.

Von Weiss upended the chilled bottle of Evian, took a long drink, wiped his mouth with the back of his hand. He caught sight of himself in one of the smoked gray glass panels and liked what he saw: tall muscular build, thick blond hair and a new nose that combined with a laser peel to make him look closer to thirty than forty. His eyes moved on to survey the horizon: nothing but the crisp blue line where sea met sky, *Medusa*'s tender, and the small solitary green island of *Queimada Grande*. Brazil lay twenty kilometres behind the eastern horizon. Out to the west, four thousand miles of empty Atlantic Ocean stretched all the way to Africa.

'Maybe this will teach you a valuable lesson to take into your next life, eh Mr Fruit Fly?' von Weiss said in Portuguese to his unconscious captive. 'Having fingers that stick to other people's money can get you into trouble.' He lifted one of the man's hands to give the destroyed hand a final inspection and squeezed the thumb and forefinger together, producing from his captive a gratifying flinch accompanied by another groan as the knuckles parted once more.

Medusa's tender maneuvred closer, a white jet boat, its exhaust pipes gargling seawater. It gently nudged the mother ship's transom and von Weiss gave his men the nod. They hauled their captive across the gap between the two craft, timing the transfer between the peaks of the swell, and threw him into the vessel's spotless teak floorboards.

'Julio!' von Weiss called out after taking a mouthful of Evian. Julio Salvadore, a heavyset young man with a mean streak and a bright future looked up from the tender. Von Weiss twisted the top onto the plastic bottle and then tossed it underarm towards the smaller craft, making it an easy catch for Julio. 'We don't want our friend to die... of thirst.'

Salvadore gave O Magnifico a grin. He had a good feeling in his balls – other people's pain always did. 'Go!' he instructed the man behind the wheel.

The jet boat leapt high out of the water as it accelerated towards the island 200 feet away.

'Wake him!' Salvadore shouted over the roar of the wind and the engines.

A man using Jaguaribe as a footstool pulled the captive to his knees, slapped him several times and then threw a cup of seawater from a bucket into his face.

The shock of it brought Jaguaribe back to consciousness and he blubbered several times, blowing water from his swollen blood-encrusted lips. The jet boat slowed as it closed with the rock shelf protruding from the island.

Satisfied that the man was in control of his wits, Salvadore gave the signal and Jaguaribe was thrown overboard into the deep blue water. 'Swim, Fruit Fly!' he shouted as the man bobbed to the surface in a plume of silver bubbles, floundering and choking as he struggled to keep his head above water. 'Go! Swim!' he repeated and pointed in the direction of the island. Jaguaribe swam towards the boat, but when the craft reversed a few meters the man seemed to understand the implication of this and began struggling to the shore, the remains of his torn clothing and his injuries hampering his movements.

Salvadore watched patiently. Eventually, a wave lifted the man and pushed him up onto the black and gray rock shelf where he rolled and tumbled and got dragged back into the ocean by the backwash. A following wave deposited him higher, but not before pushing him through a patch of barnacles that tore the skin off his chin, stomach and legs. But then somehow the man managed to get his limbs going and drag himself higher before collapsing.

'Closer,' Salvadore said to the pilot and the boat surged forward. When it was just off the shelf, Salvadore took the half bottle of Evian and tossed it high and far so that it landed amongst the smooth rounded rocks above Jaguaribe's head, frightening half a dozen birds into the air. Salvadore spat into the ocean as the jet boat reversed.

JAGUARIBE'S EYES WERE GUMMED together with mucous and salt. He tried to move, but even the smallest movement sent bolts of pain shooting through his body. His hands, in particular, were spheres of agony. Blood and salt glued his clothing to the flayed skin on his belly and legs. He shifted a foot and his clothing tore away from his raw wounds and the pain made him cry out above the sound of the waves and the birds. Tears welled in his eyes, dissolving the mucous and allowing him to open them.

Birds were everywhere; screeching, darting through the air, rummaging through the bushes. He could see several on the ground in the dry scrub behind him, nesting. It was the noise of birds, he realised, that had finally penetrated his senses and woken him. His head dropped and he saw a plastic bottle nearby that was half full. Why had they left him with that? *Water*. He was suddenly aware of his thirst. He licked his dry cracked lips and tasted salt and copper. Managing to get to his knees, Jaguaribe cried out with the messages of pain his raw nerve endings sent to his brain with every movement. His wrecked fingers had swollen to the size of the Cuban cigars he liked to smoke. He reached for the Evian bottle and, with great difficulty, held it between his palms and used his teeth to remove the top. He tilted his head back and drank but the bottle slipped from his mangled hands and rolled down the rock shelf and into the sea. Jaguaribe swore, unable to move fast enough to it.

Jaguaribe told himself that he had to move. He knew he had been lying here for hours, and now the sun was heading towards the western horizon. They had taken his watch. He believed that it was perhaps after three o'clock. His pants were wet. He had urinated where he lay, beyond the waves.

They had brought him aboard *Medusa* in the early hours of the morning, but this nightmare had begun much earlier than that. It started when they dragged him from the bed of his favorite whore, his exhausted member still clasped within the warmth of her hand. The beating started out in the street and continued in the back of the truck as it sped through the streets of Rio. The serious abuse had begun somewhere in von Weiss's mansion, in the cellar where the walls were lined with bottles of wine, the atmosphere unnaturally controlled, and where it was cool and dry and sound-proofed. Jaguaribe had watched in horror as they had placed pencils between his fingers, which they then squeezed together until the joints separated one at a time. When they were done with his fingers, they worked on his knuckles. And when they were finished with those, they went back to his fingers, this time with a hammer, smashing them one by one.

Some time later, they had thrown him in the trunk of a car and driven for over an hour. The fact that they had not asked him any questions – that frightened him. It was as if they were sure of his guilt. But he had done nothing – nothing he could think of that deserved this treatment. At dawn they had pulled him from the darkness of the trunk. They stood him in the forecourt of a house Jaguaribe recognized. This was von Weiss's house on the beach at *Angra dos Reis*, a holiday town south of Rio. Jaguaribe had seen pictures of this house, sleek and modern and worth millions. Dragging him inside, they had then beaten him unconscious, and that's all he remembered.

Jaguaribe raised his head and saw that von Weiss's boat was close by, barely 150 feet away. Von Weiss himself was standing on the front deck, watching him with binoculars. *Where am I?* Jaguaribe asked himself.

O Magnifico had the wrong man. He was being blamed for something done by someone else. Jaguaribe had not double-crossed him. The risks were too great, as his current situation proved.

A man appeared beside Benicio on the bow. It was that dangerous pig, Salvadore. There was a rifle cradled in his arms. Yes, he recognized it – how could he not? It was a British RPA 7.62mm sniper rifle – the urban model. Jaguaribe had bought it himself and had it dipped in 18-carat gold and presented to O Magnifico as a present on the occasion of his birthday. The rifle flashed yellow in the afternoon sunlight.

VON WEISS HELD OUT his hand and Salvador passed him the weapon. Von Weiss dropped the magazine out and checked that it was full, and then pulled the bolt back to confirm that a round was in the breech. Satisfied, he slid the bolt forward, knelt on one knee and rested the long golden barrel against a polished chrome cleat.

'Can you see any of your little friends, O Magnifico?' Salvadore asked.

Von Weiss scanned the bushes behind Jaguaribe. 'Ah, yes,' he said. 'There's one. It's time to get our little fly's feet moving.' Von Weiss took the rifle off safety, and brought the telescopic sight's crosshairs onto the bridge of Jaguaribe's nose for a moment before shifting the fine black cross down and to the left. He breathed out and squeezed the trigger. There was a deafening crack as the rifle stock punched into his shoulder and, almost simultaneously, an eruption of blood blossomed on Jaguaribe's upper arm as a puff of powdered rock appeared behind him.

Salvadore complimented him. 'Excellent shot, O Magnifico.'

THE FORCE OF THE BLOW twisted Jaguaribe violently around. At the same instant a small bomb appeared to have gone off inside his arm, resulting in an explosion of flesh and blood. Shock paralysed Jaguaribe for a handful of seconds, but then he clambered to his feet and staggered up the rock shelf, towards the low bushes where the birds were nesting, where there was cover. There he sat for a full minute, behind the tree line, breathing heavily, his heart pounding, thorns in the soles of his bare feet. He tied to pluck them out, but his fingers were useless. Von Weiss was an excellent marksman. If Benicio wanted him dead, then why was he still breathing? Wounding him *had* to have been the intention, Jaguaribe told himself. Which meant that perhaps he had not been brought here to die after all. Perhaps O Magnifico would send the boat for him and toast his bravery with a bottle of *cachaça*. Jaguaribe lifted his head above the bush to see what was going on out on the water, hoping to find the tender coming for him, his crimes, whatever they were, forgiven. But the small bay was empty, the tender still tethered behind the *Medusa*.

Jaguaribe saw von Weiss hand the rifle back to Salvadore, exchanging it for binoculars. The flash of relief he'd felt only moments ago was gone, the dread rushing back. Von Weiss was watching him, waiting for *something*. But what? The pain in Jaguaribe's arm was beginning to bite. It mingled with the jagged signals from the wreckage of his hands, clouding his judgement. *What should I do?* Jaguaribe's eye caught sight of a blood trail across the rocks. It led to him, he realised. The length of his arm was now bright red and slick, blood oozing from the torn flesh of his arm, dripping from his fingers. Two birds began pecking at his naked ankles and bare toes, squawking and flapping their wings. Jaguaribe had to move again, get away from the birds and the shore, away from von Weiss's golden rifle, away from whatever it was that von Weiss was waiting and watching for. Jaguaribe had no idea what that might be, but he feared it. He got up and stumbled back through the bushes, which were low near the shoreline but thicker and taller as he penetrated them, climbing away from the shore.

Jaguaribe trampled half a dozen birds' nests before he found a trail and then he stopped, panting. A *trail*. It had to lead somewhere? He turned to look behind him. Through the leaves were now only glimpses of the sea sparkling through the gloom. He saw *Medusa* in one of those glimpses, von Weiss still standing there, watching.

Movement above distracted him. Jaguaribe glanced up. There, a small brown bird. It hopped along the branch and then flew away. Jaguaribe turned and took a step and froze. Something moved under the sole of his foot. It writhed and jerked its small but powerful body. He lifted his leg and brought his foot up. He jumped as it coiled and struck and its fangs punched into the fabric of his pants. Jaguaribe kicked out his foot in mid-air and the snake flew spinning into the bushes. Jaguaribe's heart pounded rapidly. Was it venomous? He closed his eyes and swallowed and wondered again, *Where am I?* Suddenly – he knew. Benicio's love of snakes, the barren island in the middle of the ocean, the birds. Oh, god, this was *Queimada Grande*. And Jaguaribe screamed.